Time

Ship

Time

Ship

By

GARY COTTRELL

MDC Press
Lexington, SC

ISBN 13: 978-0-615-58849-0
ISBN 10: 0615588492

Cover design by Derek Chiodo
http://www.ecovermakers.com/

For my wife, Jeannie. Whenever I am with her, time is my friend.

"Time is the ship that propels our lives"

Prologue
1970 — 1908

David did not in reality "experience" time travel, because there was no actual transition, nothing that could appropriately be referred to as "travel" at all. Not one second, not the swiftest blink of an eye, even the beginnings of thought itself, hardly registered the process before it was completed. David had not traveled though time; he had been hurled outside of it altogether. He had stepped out of the inexorable flow of time, allowed it to stream past him, and abruptly reentered along another — older — point along that mysterious continuum that allows us to measure, and therefore perceive, our own existence.

The images of the laboratory outside London and the enclosure from which the experiment began, bristling with countless gauges and myriads of flashing lights, did not simply dissolve. Rather in one chaotic mixture of contrasting realities, they were merged with other images of a different landscape, one of trees and earth, intersected by a narrow, winding gravel road. Before the eye could short-circuit itself in a vain attempt to record two simultaneous visions of existence, mercifully only the second remained. The experiment had succeeded.

David's only task on this first attempt by a human being to travel to another time was to verify the year to which he had been transported and return with proof that he had actually visited the past. Had he been content to confine himself to that assignment, his future could conceivably have taken one of two directions. He might have returned to the present to enjoy a long life, crowned by the accolades of his scientific colleagues. Just as plausibly, the journey itself could have altered his own existence so radically that he might find that the experiment had never been made at all.

However, David would not return to what was for him the present, on that day or any other. He had hoped that this trip to the past held the key to a successful future, and in one sense it did; for he would confront his destiny in the past. He would also discover that no matter how much we may expand our knowledge, we can never fully comprehend the universe we inhabit. He would also learn that fate was waiting for him in that earlier time to which he was transported, determined to reassert its mastery over his existence.

Chapter 1
1948

It was the kind of day that only a little boy, reveling in the last week of summer vacation could appreciate. The blistering Florida sun perched high overhead cast stark shadows across the sand, as it beat down on the palm trees lining the beach where little David Evans had gone to seek relief from the heat in the cooling ocean waves. David and his parents had spent the past two weeks vacationing on the Gulf Coast, and by now all of them were tanned enough to pass for natives. It was late August and felt every bit of it. But the oppressive heat, which kept the adults indoors seeking relief with their fans and cold drinks, was not enough to deter David. He was determined to extract every bit of play out of this day, oblivious to the disaster that was imminent.

During the past week the Evans family had been joined by Margaret Stetson, a longtime friend of the Evans family. Mrs. Stetson had come to the United States from England as a young woman, but even now in her late 50s, she still presented a striking appearance. Her hair was deep ebony, laced with a few strands of gray, which only served to emphasize her regal appearance, which was accented by her slightly elongated facial structure. Her stately mannerisms, combined with her English dialect, inevitably gave the impression of nobility, whatever her actual background may have been.

Although Margaret Stetson was not really a member of the Evans family, she might as well have been. David could not remember a time when she had not been a part of his life. Whenever he thought of her, the one characteristic which came to his childish mind was her rich British accent, which thirty-six years in the United States had not altered. To his parents her speech suggested culture and refinement. To David she just sounded funny. Not that he normally thought much about it. Rather he simply delighted in the attention she paid him. While the affection Margaret felt for the entire family was easily apparent (she was constantly babysitting with David and was routinely included in many of the family's social outings and virtually all holidays), she maintained an air of rigid formality, especially where David was concerned, insisting that he address her as "Mrs. Stetson." David's parents attributed Margaret's strictness to her British upbringing, but still thought her behavior somewhat odd. For his part, David's affection for Mrs. Stetson possessed all the fuzzy values of childhood, often linked to nickels at the soda fountain and dimes for a movie, without being any the less real for that.

Margaret had been acting strangely this week. David's parents had talked about her curious behavior at length when they thought he couldn't hear them. Although he seldom concerned himself with the moods of grownups, especially on the last week of vacation, David too had noticed that Mrs. Stetson seemed — the word he was searching for had he been old enough to have understood its meaning, was "preoccupied." He had heard them again last night, Margaret protesting that nothing was wrong, while even then displaying a nervousness that was highly uncharacteristic of her normally serene temperament.

This morning shortly after breakfast Margaret had attempted to coax David into taking a walk along the beach, even though the forecast warned of near record temperatures with few clouds to offer even temporary relief. He was reluctant at first, because his parents had talked about going sailing if the ocean breezes picked up enough to make the attempt worthwhile, and that sounded like terrific fun. In a desperate maneuver to entice David to come with her instead, Mrs. Stetson had gone so far as to violate one of her ironclad principles (another thing he had seldom known her to do) and resort to bribery. When entreaties failed to sway David from sailing with his parents, a three-flavor banana split was promised to convince him. Margaret Stetson understood David well enough to know that was one offer he would not be likely to refuse.

After Mrs. Stetson had granted David his promised reward, she had reluctantly allowed him to go off to play by himself, but only after extracting his solemn promise not to return to the beach house without first coming to get her. She had urgent plans of her own and gambled that David's normally cooperative nature justified the risk.

David roamed further along the beach than he had ventured before, and by the time he got back to the area where Margaret had left him, his stomach was insistently protesting his inattention to its demands. The single-mindedness of childhood had taken over, and at that moment, the only thought process going on in David's mind was a mental appraisal of the relative merits of grilled cheese or peanut butter and jelly. His earlier promise to Mrs. Stetson forgotten, he had unconsciously retraced his steps and was now within sight of the beach house.

As he approached the house, David sensed that something was not quite right, although he could not at first identify the source of his feeling. As he stepped on the front porch, he realized what had alerted him. It was the presence of an odor, at once disagreeable, as well as one he could not identify. The scent was in fact the smell of fresh human blood, and even though he was too young to appreciate fully the concept of danger, nevertheless the strangeness of the situation did prompt him instinctively to hesitate and then proceed more slowly.

David stepped inside the front door, which had literally been pried from its hinges. Suddenly he paused as he heard his name called from behind by a strange voice, strange not only because he did not recognize it, but also because of its disconcertingly menacing tone. Turning in response, David froze at the sight of a fearsome individual just outside the house, glaring intently out of eyes that, even to a child, indicated madness. In one split second his frightened mind instantly registered two aspects about this terrifying human being. One was his frightening physical appearance, a combination of the man's immense size and a full beard that served to magnify the animal like glare in the eyes. Then there was the curious shiny object David noticed strapped awkwardly around the man's waist, although there was no opportunity to hazard even a guess as to its purpose.

In one moment of terror David vaguely perceived that this stranger, for some reason that he could not fathom, was intent on killing him. He knew his only hope, meager though it might be, lay in running; however, paralyzed by fear, he found himself completely unable to move his body. Cowering helplessly, his lips emitting a small pathetic whine, David watched in horror as this massive human being deliberately lifted his right arm, the one carrying a thirty-eight revolver, which he pointed directly at David's excitedly heaving chest. To the extent that an eight-year-old is able to comprehend ultimates, David understood that he was going to die at the hands of this stranger whose existence he had not even suspected only one minute before. Still unable to move, he stared blankly at the now level weapon, powerless to do anything but watch the man begin to pull back on the trigger.

Just at that moment, something shiny flew over David's right shoulder and buried itself deep in the man's chest, causing him to emit an agonizing scream, both of pain and bitter disappointment at being thwarted just as success appeared to be within his grasp. Even so, in his last seconds of life the stranger attempted vainly to raise his weapon once more, but the hunting knife protruding from his chest had penetrated deeply, virtually cutting the heart in two. In another instant the maniacal light in his eyes was extinguished, and the limp body dropped to the ground, as the revolver discharged one stray bullet that landed harmlessly in the earth.

Off to his left David could hear his name being screamed frantically. It was the last conscious thought he had as his little body, having experienced more stress than it was designed to endure, caused David to lapse into unconsciousness.

Within moments Margaret Stetson was at his side. She had been feverishly searching for him, hoping desperately that she would not be too late to prevent the tragedy that only she had known would be stalking the Evans family this day. Taking in the terrible scene in a moment, Margaret ran to David and gathered him into her arms, pausing momentarily as she saw the now still body of his father lying across the doorway, his right hand still extended after summoning the last of his waning strength to hurl the knife that had saved David's life. She would discover his mother lying face down in a pool of blood on the kitchen floor, a shattered jar of peanut butter intended for David's lunch on the floor beside her.

Knowing she might have little time, Margaret had

anticipated and prepared for just such an eventuality as this and began hurriedly to implement her plan. She was faced with two difficulties. Her first instinct was to protect David from as much trauma as possible; however, her more immediate problem was to arrange the evidence so that her account of the events of this day would seem plausible to the authorities who might be arriving at any moment.

Racing against an uncertain deadline, Margaret carried David's limp body to a hammock that had been set up at the side of the house where, if he regained consciousness, he would not be in a position to observe her actions. Fearing the danger of shock, she hurriedly covered him with a blanket. She would have to tend to him later. Other matters were, at this moment, more urgent.

She knew that it would not do to allow the police to find the body of the man responsible for the murders. She did not even know his identity herself, but she had anticipated his arrival, and she knew from where he had come.

Recognizing she could not confide in David's parents, Mrs. Stetson had determined on the second-best option, keeping David away from the house when the murders occurred. She had almost succeeded, and yet David had still come perilously close to being killed. She was not surprised, but had to make the attempt. Today had turned out just as she had known it would. Because of that, she was able to take some small comfort in her belief that what she had planned in response to the tragedy would also be likely to succeed. She was already no stranger to grief, but now for the first time she also experienced a strong sense of guilt as she contemplated the future and the acceptance of her own role in manipulating it. She was also to discover that although grief is usually overcome, guilt can remain a lifetime. But just now she could not allow herself to think of that. Instead she hurried, driven by the fear of being discovered before she was ready.

* * * *

The first object David saw when he regained consciousness was a policeman's badge reflecting the afternoon sunlight. That frightened him, but almost immediately he heard Mrs. Stetson's cry of relief at his return to consciousness. Two police cars and an ambulance had been driven into the area around the short driveway of the cottage. Another ambulance was pulling slowly away, but its lights were not on, nor did it sound its siren. Even though David appeared to be unhurt physically, after a hurried consultation, it was decided that he should spend the night in the local hospital for observation. At first he was afraid to get into the ambulance and could only call out in desperate repetition for his mother, but finally, after Margaret assured him she would ride with him, the attendant was able to coax him into the ambulance.

The police would uncover no sign of the body of the man who had attempted to kill David and was responsible for his parents' deaths. By the following afternoon Margaret Stetson had been discounted as a suspect in the bizarre killings, and from a source even she had not anticipated. By some unaccountable coincidence, the sleepy little vacation community had experienced another seemingly unmotivated killing the previous day, the second occurring not more than a mile away and two hours later in time from the slaughter of the Evans family. Even though this killer used a different gun than was used to murder David's parents, the police naturally assumed that one maniac had been responsible for both killings, and their theory could never be challenged, since that murderer had died in a police shootout. In all other respects the circumstances fit the evidence neatly, and once the police discovered just how influential Margaret Stetson was, they were not anxious to pursue the matter further.

David's fainting spell had been no more than a normal and relatively minor result of shock. A night's rest in the hospital, and he was well enough to be released. Only one effect of the tragedy would remain with David, and that was his complete loss of memory of the terrible events of that fateful afternoon. He would know about them, but only from what Mrs. Stetson would tell him. Even as an adult, that one day in David Evans' life would remain a void. Otherwise, the resiliency of childhood allowed him to grieve openly for the loss of his parents, and in that grieving process, experience the healing that would allow him to continue on with his life.

David's future, however, was to be vastly different from his life before, both materially and emotionally. Since David had no other family, his parents had made provision in their wills that Margaret was to be his guardian in the event of their deaths. While she accepted responsibility for David, she never attempted to take the place of his parents, maintaining a distance that appeared to more than one person to be cold, if not actually cruel. For his part, David had always loved Mrs. Stetson with the unquestioning devotion of a child, and he seldom perceived the conflict that her behavior sometimes precipitated.

Not that her manner failed to have its effect on David. He never quite thought of Margaret Stetson as a foster parent. While he was a child, she became the basis for his security, the one who provided for his physical needs, a relationship which he accepted as a matter of course. When

David became an adult, the relationship deepened, and he came to think of Margaret as a dear friend for whom he felt genuine affection and gratitude for caring for him as a child. Perhaps because of the distance she chose to keep between herself and David, his memories of his parents remained strong (except for that one day), and those disposed to look kindly on Margaret Stetson's actions assumed that this had been her motive all along. In reality no one, not even Margaret's own son, would ever know that she had been faced with an excruciatingly painful conflict and that she had dealt with it in the only manner she knew how.

Margaret recognized that David possessed a quick mind, that he was in fact a highly intelligent boy. Determined to make the most of his abilities, she almost immediately enrolled him in one of the finest boarding schools in New England, where he found an outlet for his developing curiosity in a love of science. Margaret encouraged David's scientific bent, and as an adult, he came to feel she had even guided him in that direction.

When he was old enough to understand or care about such things, David discovered that Margaret Stetson was extremely wealthy, and so he grew up possessing everything he needed and most of what he wanted. While he missed the special relationship that a child normally enjoys with his parents, David's life was, for the most part, happy and content.

But David could not know that his future was not simply the result of a cruel fate. It had been planned for many years, and the results of that one tragic day set in motion events which he would not understand until the end of his life.

Chapter 2
Florida
1966

"What I don't understand, David, is this obsession with light and just how you think it can be used to help astronauts survive in space. That is still the objective of our research, isn't it?"

"Henry," David answered, his exasperation only thinly disguised, "you simply cannot evaluate every element of research solely in terms of its immediate application. It's essential to understand the broader implications of your investigation before you can implement your research properly, or even safely for that matter."

An outsider observing this dispute might never have concluded that Henry Lindstrom and David Evans were actually good friends. Conflict seemed to be built into the fabric of their relationship and tended to resurface from time to time.

Coworkers frequently tended to focus on the differences between the two men, or so at least it had seemed ever since David, fresh with a new PhD from MIT, had begun working at Norlander Technical Research, commonly referred to as NORTECH, an aerospace firm, engaged almost exclusively in contract work for NASA.

The very nature of the work sometimes tended to pit these two men against one another when they did interact, if only because they worked in different disciplines and usually pursued separate lines of research. In 1966 NORTECH was driven by one overriding objective, to support NASA in the race to beat the Soviets to the moon, and the time and performance pressures which accompanied that kind of urgency were certain to generate stress, which frequently manifested itself in conflict. The temperamental natures of brilliant scientists only served to increase the antagonism. Often the work required that men and women with a variety of specialized backgrounds cooperate to achieve a common goal, and sometimes the different disciplines didn't mesh as well as NORTECH officials would have preferred. In that respect the research of Henry Lindstrom and David Evans was typical of several conflicts within the organization. Henry's field was Nuclear Medicine, whereas David was a physicist, one a pragmatic discipline, the other more theoretical in its application. It was no wonder they often collided. With David and Henry conflict was even more frequent because of their differing personalities.

Henry could almost be said to fit the stereotype of the research scientist. If it is ever proper to say of anyone, "his work is his life," that description was true of Henry Lindstrom. He had never married, and as far as anyone could discover had never even been involved in a serious romance. Of course the twelve-hour days required of almost everyone at NORTECH made socializing of any sort difficult. But Henry's decision to carry his solitary lifestyle to an extreme could not really be blamed on the demands of his work. He was to a large degree single-minded (some people said "obsessed") in his dedication to science. In most instances he evaluated virtually any issue or situation by only one criterion, whether or not it would advance scientific knowledge. Not many women were willing to compete with such a jealous mistress.

Besides his dedication to science, Henry simply wasn't considered an especially desirable catch. Almost five years older than David and a lanky Texan with a drawl every bit as deep as LBJ's, Henry seemed to have inherited none of the expected physical characteristics from the Viking ancestors his name suggested were lurking somewhere in the murky roots of his family tree. His hair had already begun to recede; eventually it would probably all go. And if his appearance wasn't enough to turn women off, Henry's shyness usually was. If he were ever to capture a woman, she would have to be willing to be pursued, more than likely even work quite hard at it. So, at least for the present, Henry was doomed to remain pretty much a loner.

David, on the other hand, did not look or even act like the stereotype of a scientist. Despite his youth, he was generally credited with being the most brilliant physicist working at NORTECH. Yet he displayed a down-to-earth manner and genuine interest in people which allowed him to make friends effortlessly, even unconsciously. In fact, as David himself freely admitted, he was a social person who, if he did at times bury himself in his work, did so to offset a deep and only barely subconscious feeling of isolation. While Margaret Stetson's love for him had been deep and genuine, it had not been enough to compensate for the loss of both his parents. And while the various schools he attended gave him a splendid education, they were less successful at alleviating the isolation of a little boy growing up virtually alone. As a result, David acquired a need for people which ran counter to the prevailing mood of the "no commitment" generation of which he was technically a part.

Although David possessed a magnificent intellect, those close to him were often surprised to discover that he did not exhibit a great deal of ambition. Indeed, most of his earlier accomplishments could really be attributed to Mrs. Stetson's prodding, rather than his own initiative. Not that she had been cruel or even overly strict with him, but she was uncompromising where David was concerned. Even his interest in science was prompted first by Margaret, and it was she who encouraged him to pursue research, while David would have been just as content to spend his life as an undergraduate physics professor.

Margaret did harbor one concern about David. He had not displayed the degree of maturity she felt appropriate for his age. After some consideration, she determined that perhaps David still had some growing up to do. So, in her pragmatic fashion, Margaret Stetson had addressed the issue head-on. When David was awarded his doctorate, her graduation present to him had been twofold. First she used her influence to help him obtain a position at NORTECH. Then she effectively cut him off from any monetary support. Margaret explained to him her reason for doing so, assured him the restriction was temporary, and that she would be available in case of a real emergency. Although she tried to convince him that her decision was for his own good, David predictably became angry and stormed self-righteously out of the house, determined never to have anything more to do with Margaret Stetson. His resolve (along with his anger) lasted precisely one week, and within six months David had begun to enjoy his forced independence. Far from feeling any sense of resentment, he had been willing to admit that Mrs. Stetson was one smart, if tough, old lady.

As David and Henry continued their argument, even the two men's physical appearances presented discordant pictures. Henry, although only in his early thirties, appeared somewhat older, his age perhaps exaggerated by his tendency toward premature balding. His lanky appearance magnified by his six-foot-three frame, intensified his normally serious demeanor, so that most people felt distinctly uncomfortable around Dr. Henry Lindstrom, believing him to be somewhat conceited. In reality, what people often mistook for arrogance was no more than a tendency to become absorbed in the demands of his profession. Unfortunately, that remained a secret hidden from most of Henry's colleagues. As a result he had few friends, but in most cases seldom felt the loss.

By contrast, David was well liked by virtually everyone at NORTECH and was perceived by most of the women he worked with to be the most eligible bachelor within the organization. While not exactly projecting a movie star image, he was admittedly good looking, but more in the way women fantasized the boy next door should be. His sandy blonde hair and deep blue eyes had cast a spell on more than one woman at NORTECH. Yet, as handsome as David was, he projected a casual manner that caused most women to feel they had a chance at winning him. And David socialized enough to provide encouragement to a number of coworkers. Even so, he remained oblivious to the effect he created. While not adverse to marriage, he had convinced himself that his responsibilities just at this point in his career made it impractical to make the kind of commitment marriage would require. The truth was that although David knew a number of women he liked well enough, none of them had impressed him as offering the stability for which he was searching.

While David's and Henry's differing temperaments did result in clashes now and again, their arguments never seemed to interfere with their friendship. Being older, Henry naturally, if subconsciously, assumed the role of big brother, a relationship that David seemed to accept as well. Whatever the underlying reasons, David and Henry had become fast friends, and while their differences sometimes disrupted that relationship, they never seriously interfered with it.

Their particular argument this morning was not large enough to cause any real conflict, but it was significant nonetheless. Although neither man was aware of it at the time, the discussion was to become the focal point of their entire lives.

"Henry, you're beginning to sound more like an accountant than a scientist. Will you stop arguing for a minute and let me tell you about my discovery?"

"All right, I'll listen to you, but I still fail to see any relevance in what you've told me so far."

"Thanks," David answered. He needed to confide in someone, and he had a particular reason for wanting that someone to be Dr. Henry Lindstrom. "Actually, my research into the nature of light did come as a direct result of my current assignment. If you hadn't gotten on your soapbox, I would have told you that."

At this point Henry could not help noticing that David looked around quickly, as if checking to be sure no one else could hear, and his voice dropped to little more than a whisper.

"NASA is looking farther ahead then most people realize, and NORTECH intends to play an essential role in shaping that future. It stands to reason that the war in Vietnam can't last much longer, and once it's over, NASA can expect sizable increases in funding for space exploration. Henry, I'm violating confidentiality by telling you this, but if current research is successful, NASA will be sending astronauts beyond the moon into interstellar space sooner than anyone dreams, and NORTECH has been conducting secret research on a spacecraft designed to hold up to the demands of just such a mission."

"David, all of this sounds encouraging of course, but

what does it have to do with your work, and why are you so excited? You're acting like a kid who just made captain of the football team."

"Yes, I am excited," David agreed. "I hope after you've heard me out, you will be too, and not just about NASA's project. But let's get back to your original question. NORTECH's research has everything to do with our work. You're obviously familiar with the theory of relativity."

"Of course I'm aware of the basics of relativity. I probably haven't studied it in the same depth as you, because I never needed to apply it specifically to my work."

"Well, an understanding of relativity will not only be relevant, it's going to be absolutely essential to successful interplanetary flight. Just consider the problem for a moment. While a speed of 25,000 miles per hour is sufficient to escape the earth's gravitational pull and will certainly suffice for moon landings, for longer manned flights it just won't do. Oh, we might be able to make it to Mars, but at that speed, a round trip would take at least sixteen months. If we want to take the next step out to Jupiter, an astronaut would devote most of his active life to the trip. As for visits outside our solar system . . . Well, I think you can see the problem."

"Okay, David, so the distances are, if you'll pardon the pun, astronomical. I'm aware of that; so is everyone else involved in the space program. That's why we've always considered manned interstellar travel nothing more than a Buck Rogers fantasy. The general public may dream about it, but we know better."

David's voice dropped to a whisper, but the excitement in his eyes was undiminished. "That's where you're wrong. Some of us have been given special research assignments that aren't recorded in the general log sheets. Oh, we have a long way to go, and most of the research is being conducted in secret, but NORTECH is doing preliminary work on a spacecraft that will at least match the speed of light."

Henry gave an audible gasp, and his voice dropped noticeably. "Can you really be serious? Space travel at the speed of light? That's theoretically impossible. What kind of system will be used, and why is such an important project being kept secret?"

"One question at a time, Henry. Yes, believe me, this is all on the level. I don't know what kind of propulsion they're working on. It's not part of my assignment, and you're only given information about what you specifically need to know. As for why all the secrecy, you said it yourself. This level of space flight does sound like science fiction, and that's precisely how a congressional committee would respond. NASA doesn't want to ask for additional funds for this project, until research has progressed enough to convince even a tightfisted appropriations committee that this isn't just a pipe dream."

"So, you are serious, although what you've just told me is so fantastic, I'll admit I have difficulty accepting it. But you haven't answered my original question. What does all this have to do with your experiment?"

"Quite simply, Henry, my specific assignment has been aimed at trying to find some means of offsetting the effects of relativity on a spacecraft traveling at or near the speed of light. Otherwise an astronaut might travel to Alpha Centauri and back in nine or ten years, only to find on his return, several hundred years have elapsed on earth. That in a nutshell is the problem. But the really intriguing part that I . . ."

David paused, noticing for the first time another man standing in the doorway. He was a little past middle age with hair that had apparently just passed the halfway mark from black to gray. Despite the beginnings of a pouch around the stomach area, the man's immense physical strength was still apparent, his huge frame almost filling the doorway leading into Henry's office. Although he tried not to show it, David began to feel extremely uncomfortable as this man continued staring intently.

"Excuse me, Tom. I didn't see you standing there. Did you need to see Henry or me?"

"No, Dr. Evans, I was just passing by on my way to the Records Center."

David thought he detected something in the tone of voice that made him nervous, although even at his best, Thomas Creighton usually came across to most people as aloof, if not arrogant.

"May I ask what you and Dr. Lindstrom were discussing?"

"Just comparing notes. I need to get back to the lab anyway. We'll talk more later, Henry, when we have more time."

David tried his best to sound nonchalant, but he wasn't sure he succeeded. He then abruptly left Henry's office, intent on preventing further discussion. Later that afternoon be approached Henry in a side stairway.

"That was a close call. I'll admit I don't like Tom Creighton, but, more to the point, I don't trust him. I just hope he didn't overhear too much of our discussion, although I didn't get a chance to tell you the most exciting part. Can we get together tonight? I simply must let you in on where my research has been leading. I've been considering an idea that might present the opportunity of a lifetime, and I want you to be my partner."

For his part, Henry was disturbed by the events of the

day. He was trying to adjust to a side of David he wasn't used to seeing and didn't particularly like.

"I don't know. This all sounds awfully cloak and dagger to me. My first inclination is that I'd be better off staying out of it."

"Just hear me out; that's all I ask. After you've heard the whole story, if you still want to stay out of it, I'll respect your decision. Fair enough?"

Henry sighed and gave in. He knew how persistent David could be when he was obsessed with something, as he obviously was now. "Very well, I'll listen to what you have to say, but no promises. Understood?"

"Agreed. I'll see you tonight. Just don't tell anyone else about this. Technically, I shouldn't even have mentioned it to you, but I hope after tonight we'll both be part of something much bigger than even interplanetary flight. So long, Henry."

Chapter 3

More than anything else Ray Harris tried to blend in with his surroundings. On those occasions when he was able to succeed, he possessed only one characteristic that caused him to stand out, and even that could at times be used to his advantage. When people looked at him, they usually noticed his height first, or more precisely, his lack of it. At five-feet-four virtually everyone else dwarfed him, even most women. But it wasn't just vanity that caused him to expend so much effort to remain inconspicuous. His job required it. To compensate he had to become a master at disguise. Nothing too showy of course, because, to be effective, a disguise must allow a person to blend in without attracting attention. So in dress and mannerisms Harris attempted at all times to appear to be just like everyone else, wherever he might be. That required a wardrobe that varied from a conservative business suit to torn overalls and, on one occasion, a cowboy hat and leather boots.

Of course he had to be careful. The wrong disguise could destroy his cover, and the cowboy outfit had turned out to be his most disastrous example. A short man in a cowboy hat and boots looks like a little kid, and that's what happened to Harris. One slightly intoxicated accountant, who apparently thought of himself as a combination of Gene Autry and Tom Mix, began by making Harris the brunt of some crude jokes. But he didn't stop there. Once the attention was focused on Harris, somebody found out who he really was, and he barely got out with his skin intact. It all made for one big hassle, but that's the only way he could make it in his line of work.

Harris liked to think of himself as an investigative reporter, only too aware how grandiose the name would sound to the media in general. To most of them he would never be more than a two-bit hack for a second-rate scandal sheet.

"Arrogant bastards," he swore to himself. "Not real reporters. Just made up movie stars with their own half hour show. Bob Barker could do their jobs just as well. Don't know how tough it is digging up the skeletons. Big shots afraid to get their hands dirty. You need to have the guts to go after anybody, no matter how big they are, and the persistence to stick it out."

And whatever his faults might be, no one could deny that Ray Harris could sniff out scandal with the best of them. It had required unbelievable effort just to learn that David Evans was working for NORTECH. Somehow anything having to do with the Stetsons always seemed to be surrounded by secrecy. Still, it was just their tendency to protect themselves that convinced Harris there was a bigger story here than he had first thought. His hunch had turned into an obsessive drive to find out the Stetson secret, a search that so far had eluded him for twelve years.

This particular assignment had begun in 1954 with what was intended as merely a human interest article about Margaret Stetson, nothing more than a filler. Her life had proven to be a typical Horatio Alger story. She started out in this country as a young widow with virtually no resources. Almost from the beginning she made it big, chiefly through investments which nearly always turned to gold. Even the Depression had merely added to the Stetson fortune, which some people estimated to be worth over seventy-five million, although nobody knew for sure. The biggest difficulty was the almost complete vacuum of information about the family. Harris had been totally unsuccessful at filling in the gaps before Margaret Stetson's arrival in the United States. A brief article here and there in an old newspaper was all he was ever able to locate, and then often only by accident. It was almost as if someone had deliberately wiped out the family name up to the time she arrived in the States, like some of the Egyptian Pharaohs did to their predecessors.

Harris's problems started when he tried to meet with Margaret Stetson. His requests for a simple interview went unanswered, Mrs. Stetson curtly refusing to see him and offering no explanation. The real shock came one evening when he thought he had cornered her at the theater. He found out quickly, and unceremoniously, that Mrs. Stetson employed private bodyguards and made good use of them. Harris was never one to repeat a mistake, and he soon learned that she did indeed employ her own security and that they accompanied her and her son, Albert, everywhere they went. Harris also discovered they didn't hesitate to get rough if necessary.

That was when he began to suspect there was more to discover about the Stetsons than human interest. "When people go to that kind of trouble and expense to protect their privacy," he thought, "there has to be a skeleton somewhere."

He had spent the past twelve years, on and off, trying to dig up that skeleton. That was why he was here. If he couldn't get to the Stetsons, then Margaret's ward would have to do. The back door may take longer, but it still gets you into the house.

Harris had been waiting outside the parking lot at NORTECH for a little more than two hours, when he finally spotted the gold Ford Galaxie 500 he recognized as David's.

The ten dollar bribe to the clerk at DMV had paid off. He let the car pass by, making no attempt to hide his presence.

"That's just how the amateurs get caught," he said to himself. "Look like you're guilty and somebody's bound to notice. But play it cool, and you can go virtually anywhere and do almost anything without being stopped. It's only the rookies who act like they have something to hide that get spotted." And whatever else he was, Ray Harris was no rookie.

Once David's car had passed, Harris casually started the engine on his own car and leisurely pulled out into the street. "That's another dumb mistake that comes from watching too many TV shows. No point in getting creamed now. Just lose your chance."

He tried to keep a full block between his car and David's. Just close enough to keep him in view, no hurry, no sweat. After about fifteen minutes, Harris saw David pull into a duplex just off the main road.

"Can you figure it?" he mused. "His guardian is a multimillionaire, and this egghead drives a 62 Ford and rents an apartment in a dead part of town. Wonder if maybe they don't get along too well?" If that were the case, he would have another avenue he could pursue to get the information he was seeking.

Harris had already begun slowing down to find a place to park when he spotted the black sedan with the tinted windows parked on the opposite side of the street a few houses down.

"What the . . .? Even here?"

It was the antenna that gave it away. You can disguise a car, but an antenna like that has only one purpose — to call back to home base.

"Has this kid got the Secret Service with him?"

Harris asked the question aloud to no one in particular.

To his credit he recovered his former speed quickly without calling attention to himself. He continued down the street for three more blocks before pulling over to consider the situation.

"Wonder if the egghead even knows they're there? Wouldn't be surprised if he didn't," he concluded. "Damn kid with his nose in books all day."

But Harris could not help wondering why the Stetson family went to such lengths to protect themselves. To prevent a kidnapping? That would definitely be a possibility. The Stetsons were certainly wealthy enough to make ransom an attractive option for the right kind of crook. Even so, these measures seemed extreme, and they reinforced Harris's intuition. There was something more to the Stetsons, and now more than ever, he was determined to find out what it was.

As Ray Harris eased his car into the street to return to his motel room, he contemplated his next move. Okay, so he couldn't get to the kid either, at least not without some trouble. But there must be people who could, probably at NORTECH. And some of them had to be David Evans' enemies, or at least indifferent enough not to mind making a few bucks by supplying a little information. Intellectuals, punks, or politicians, they were all the same. Bottom line, everybody's out for number one, and that made his job a lot easier.

Chapter 4

Despite the fascination the space program held with the public, the salaries that went with the jobs did not always measure up to the image. Henry had a few years seniority at NORTECH, which translated into a slightly higher income, but David was still a newcomer, and his meager salary reflected his status. So, this evening dinner turned out to be the blue plate special at a local coffee shop. Sharing a typical reluctance among bachelors for the effort involved in preparing a meal, David and Henry often made do with one of the local restaurants which seemed to be springing up almost weekly, as the Mercury and then the Gemini programs required an ever increasing number of workers in and around Cape Kennedy.

Less than two minutes after David pulled into the parking lot, the same nondescript black sedan which had mystified Ray Harris only an hour before drove in, and two men dressed incongruously in blue jeans and western shirts appropriated a table across the room, but still within sight of David and Henry.

Harris had been mistaken about one of his judgments. David was only too aware that these men were private security guards supplied by Margaret Stetson (or more specifically by her son, Albert). He also knew they had begun accompanying him almost fifteen years before, when David was only eleven years old. When he became an adult, David tried to find out more about them, but he had never been able to discover why Margaret deemed them necessary. His attempts to determine the reason for their constant presence had met with the same firm resistance as his angry insistence that they be removed. Although he had tried more than once to break Margaret's resolve, he had found that in this issue, as in most matters, she remained altogether unyielding. In the end he simply made the best of the situation, and over the years had in a manner grown accustomed to the constant presence of his uninvited guests. They had been well trained, not only to be observant, but to remain inconspicuous as well. So, despite their constant surveillance, none of David's associates, not even Henry Lindstrom, suspected their presence.

After they had placed their order, Henry, not wishing to prolong the matter, began by reminding David of their previous conversation.

"I've had a couple of hours to think about our conversation this afternoon, and I must admit to some bad feelings about the whole subject. I hope you're not going off the deep end without considering the possible consequences. What you've described to me sounds very irregular, if not actually illegal. At least a Congressional committee might think so."

"But we're not working for the government," David reminded Henry. "NORTECH's a private corporation."

"You may be right, technically; however, considering the size of NORTECH's government contracts, we might just as well be a government agency. You're still feeling your way around here, and, believe me, it pays to be cautious. Becoming associated with something questionable could easily get you into hot water and might even ruin your career before it gets started. You have far too much potential to let yourself get nailed by a two-bit congressman who wouldn't know a proton from a poodle."

"Okay, Henry, just to ease your mind, let's clear up that objection first. Nothing we're doing is illegal. This research is still a minuscule part of NORTECH'S work, and these early stages are being financed entirely out of discretionary funds. Once it gets into full swing, NORTECH plans to lay out a complete proposal for NASA's approval, and Congress will be asked for some big bucks. The agency is gambling that once NASA gives the go ahead, nobody else will be in a position to bid against us, especially if we've already completed the preliminary research. But we need time to go a little further, at least until our testing produces concrete results. As a matter of fact, just last week I was making a report to the chairman of NORTECH, and during the conversation he revealed that he has already held substantive discussions with a key member of the House Committee on Science and Astronautics who is sympathetic to what we're trying to do. So, you see I have nothing to be concerned about on that score. Now, unless you have any other questions about that, I'm really anxious to tell you where my research has been leading."

"All right, assuming what you've told me is true, I do feel better about it. But before you continue, will you satisfy my suspicious nature about one other matter? If all this is really on the level, why were you so concerned about Tom Creighton's overhearing us?"

David sat back in his chair for a moment, considering just how to respond. Truthfully, he had wondered himself if he had overreacted when Creighton had interrupted their conversation that afternoon. Although he had to acknowledge that his suspicions were largely subjective, David was still convinced his concerns about Creighton were to some degree justified, even if he couldn't put his reasons into words. Almost unconsciously David glanced to both sides, as if to ensure that no one was eavesdropping and once again lowered his voice slightly as he had done earlier that day.

"You haven't had much interaction with Tom, have you?" David asked.

"Not really, but you know I don't socialize much, and our paths seldom cross at work. I have requested clarification on two or three of his research summaries that interested me, and his responses seemed professional enough."

"I don't doubt that. Tom's a topnotch scientist, or he wouldn't be at NORTECH. No, I'm more concerned with his temperament than his ability. Tell me, Henry, what do you know about Tom's personality?"

"Virtually nothing, but like I said, I just don't associate with the man. Why? What are you getting at?"

"Well, for one thing, I know that lately Tom's had a few really bitter quarrels with several colleagues. Seems like he's habitually questioning their work, making a real nuisance of himself."

"Creighton sounds like a particularly unpleasant fellow to work with certainly, but then I doubt that I'd be likely to win any personality awards either," Henry quipped.

"It's more than that," David replied, ignoring Henry's reference to himself. "About a month ago he actually got into a shouting match with one of the graduate assistants working here on an internship. I heard he almost struck the student before some of the others intervened."

"You're making me wonder if possibly the man's mentally unstable, although I find it hard to believe someone like that could pass NORTECH's psychological profile."

"Well, from what I hear, he didn't start acting strangely until about a year ago, apparently after his mother's death. Perhaps he's never been able to cope with that. But there's more to the problem than Tom's temper. He seems to view almost every issue in terms of absolutes. Not long ago he told me that he had even begun to question the morality of the space program itself. Wondered whether we were trying to do something God never intended us to do."

"That old line, again?" Henry laughed. "You know my feelings about that. If we weren't meant to travel in space, we wouldn't have been given the intelligence to master the technology. That same argument could have been used to impede every scientific advancement human beings have made, from the wheel to polio vaccine."

"I know, and I'm certainly not implying that I agree with Tom, but I am concerned about the direction he's heading. If he's disturbed about our trying to go to the moon, just imagine what he might think about a trip to another galaxy, never mind the ideas I've been kicking around. Everything considered, I had rather Dr. Creighton not be aware of my research right now."

"I understand, and I'm sorry for sidetracking you," Henry apologized. "The floor's yours now, and I promise no more unrelated interruptions."

"Thanks, but I'm still a little hesitant to tell you outright what I'm involved with. It all sounds bizarre, and I want a fair hearing. Let me begin by asking you a question which will probably sound silly to you. How many dimensions are there in our universe?"

For one of the rare times in his life, Henry Lindstrom found something funny, and he could not restrain a chuckle at what seemed such a ridiculously simple question.

"Well, if I remember my sixth grade general science, we live in three dimensions — length, width, and depth. But why do I suspect this is a trick question?"

"Yes, I suppose I did expect you to answer just as you have. You see, although most of us know the truth subconsciously, we instinctively fall into the popular misconception. Actually the universe has at least four dimensions. The one you neglected to name is time."

"Hold on now," Henry objected. "I don't see how you can possibly call time a dimension. You can make a three-dimensional model, of a cube for instance, or even represent one in a two-dimensional drawing. But how do you represent time in a model?"

"You don't represent it, because time isn't a visual dimension. It's so fundamental that none of the other three dimensions would have any real existence without it. And we don't normally perceive time as a separate entity for just that reason. Let me ask the question another way. If that cube you mentioned possessed length, width, and depth, but no duration, would it have any existence, at least any that we could perceive?"

"No, I suppose not in theory," Henry agreed. "But isn't that all we're talking about? You can't really believe that time is just like the other three dimensions. I can move about on that cube, assuming it's big enough. I can travel in any of the dimensions, but I cannot travel in time."

"Oh, but you can," David disagreed, "and you do. As a matter of fact, we all travel in time, or if you prefer, we are carried along by it at a fixed rate every instant of our lives. That's why we don't perceive the motion of time, anymore than we normally experience the movement of the earth that carries us along just as regularly and at a high rate of speed. If the movement of time were irregular, we would notice it quickly enough."

"Well, not that I'm accepting all this mind you, but I'll have to admit you present an intriguing argument. Does all this come from what we were talking about this afternoon, your research dealing with the effects of relativity on interstellar flight?"

"Yes, it has. But my research, as you rather vehemently pointed out today, has taken me in a different direction. It all began with my experiments dealing with the nature of light. Let me bait you once again with another question. Falling back to our normal perception of a three-dimensional world, can you tell me how you would expect a two-dimensional object to appear to us, say one that had length and width, but no depth?"

Henry leaned back in his chair for a moment, trying to visualize something his mind had no means of classifying. Just at this point their meals were delivered, so he was given another couple of minutes' reprieve to consider his answer. David thought that Henry's concentration was itself a good sign. At least now he was thinking about the subject, not just ridiculing it.

"Since I can't relate your question to anything I can actually picture, it's difficult to answer. Of course, you know that already. Discounting the fact that I've never even imagined, much less seen anything like you describe, I suppose if you looked at a two-dimensional object head on, you would see it just as clearly as we view three-dimensional subjects; however, if you saw it from the side, since it has no depth, you would see nothing. It would be just as if the object didn't exist."

David could not contain his enthusiasm and almost shouted in his excitement, resulting in some turned heads in the restaurant. Momentarily embarrassed at his outburst, David immediately dropped his voice to a whisper.

"Perfect!" David responded enthusiastically. "I knew you were the right person to get involved. That is exactly how a two-dimensional object would be expected to behave in a three-dimensional world. But you're wrong when you say we have nothing in the universe that exhibits these characteristics. There is one entity in our world that does behave just as you've described. Light, Henry! Light acts just like that two-dimensional object you described. Pass a beam of light through a vacuum, look at it head on, and you see the beam clearly; however, if you view it from the side, you see nothing. Light also possesses other characteristics that cause it to behave like a maverick component of our universe. Our need to construct both particle and wave theories to account for it (without completely doing so, by the way) show that, in some respects, light isn't at home in the universe in the same way other aspects of nature are. And up until now, the speed of light has always presented a boundary that nothing in the universe could ever exceed."

"Now slow down," Henry cautioned. "From a theoretical standpoint what you've said sounds plausible (and a big part of me can't believe I just admitted that), but have you been able to offer any proof? We're still scientists after all, and an unverified hypothesis is meaningless."

"No, I haven't. Now wait a minute," David continued, as Henry started to interrupt. "I haven't gotten any proof, because that hasn't been my purpose. I've been using my hypothesis merely as an axiom for my real research, and as a presupposition, it does seem to work well for me. What I wanted to demonstrate was the possibility that a two-dimensional and a three-dimensional world can not only coexist, but even interact in some areas, using the properties of light as my example of that premise. I've devoted the bulk of my research to an investigation of whether or not time itself could be manipulated in the same way we interact with the other dimensions in our universe."

"Just one moment," Henry burst out. "I know I promised not to interrupt, but I can't believe you mean what it sounds like you're saying. What precisely are you intending when you speak of 'manipulating time'?"

"I mean exactly what I said," David replied emphatically. "I believe with the proper equipment we can travel along the time dimension in the same way we do the other three. Here it is plain and simple. I believe that time travel is theoretically possible, and more than that, I have committed myself to making it a practical reality."

At this point Henry was staring at David with a look that seemed to suggest he was trying to decide whether or not to call for men in white coats.

"David, if anyone else had said to me what you just did, I would have strongly questioned either his intelligence or his sanity. You can take it as a compliment to our friendship and my respect for your ability as a scientist that I'm even listening to you. But can you really be serious — time travel?"

David was accustomed to Henry's bluntness, so he wasn't troubled by the intensity of his criticism, as some of Henry's other colleagues at times had been. Instead of jumping at the bait, he countered where he knew Henry Lindstrom's weakness lay, his devotion to science and the scientific method.

"You know, Henry, you sound just like the medieval prelates who branded Galileo a heretic, because he said the planets move. Is this the man who, more than anything else, is open to what science can teach, or do you feel we've already learned everything there is to know? Examine any advanced Physics textbook in use today. A large portion of what is taught would have sounded weird, even metaphysical, just a generation ago. The subatomic particles we're discovering now can't even be said to exist in the same way we think of most matter as existing. Henry, the universe is out there to be discovered, and we know now that reality doesn't fit the neat theories we learned in school. Don't fight that search; be part of the discovery. That's what you've always said to me. Now that's what I'm asking you to do. You're a scientist. Tell me where I'm wrong if you can, but do it as a scientist. If you can't, then don't close your mind, just because I'm asking you to consider something new, even radical."

Henry's mind was in turmoil. He started to answer and then lapsed into silence, staring intently at the plate in front of him, deliberately avoiding David's gaze. His emotions at that moment were a series of contradictions that he could not immediately sort out. On the one hand, what David was proposing seemed just short of lunacy. It sounded more like alchemy than science as he had always viewed it. Perhaps a deeper concern was Henry's recognition that what David was asking him to do would disrupt the comfortable and predictable career he had begun at NORTECH. But the bond between these two men was strong, and it exerted its own power over anything having to do with the two of them. Finally, there was David's accusation to consider. His charges had stung Henry more than anything else he might have said. Whatever he felt about David's research, Henry had to admit, grudgingly, that his response had been unworthy. He was a scientist. If he could not evaluate ideas objectively, he would have to question the entire direction of his life.

After two minutes, which seemed to both men more like two hours, Henry slowly raised his head to look David squarely in the eye. "I can't accept this right now. I'm sorry, but it's just too much all at once. But I will at least consider what you've said, as strange as it all sounds to me right now. You obviously have a plan. May I ask what you intend to do next?"

"Thanks, Henry," the relief obvious in David's voice. "I can appreciate how difficult this must seem to you. Take your time. We can talk more in a few days.

"As for my plans, that depends partly on you. I want you to be a partner in this undertaking, so I'm not going to do anything until I have your answer on that request. But I am just about ready to ask for help in implementing my project. Very soon I intend to meet with NORTECH officials to present my ideas to them and to request initial funding for developing a means for transporting into another time, first an inanimate object, and ultimately a human being. I have no illusions that NORTECH will be easily convinced. That's another reason I want you, Henry. I'm the newcomer here. Everybody respects your credentials and your commitment to the advancement of scientific knowledge. Having you on my side will make convincing NORTECH a lot easier."

"Well, you've certainly given me a lot to think about," Henry responded. "Let me take a night to sleep on it, and tomorrow you can go over the technical details. I don't think I'm up to hearing the specifics tonight. It's getting late, and I have to be in the lab early tomorrow."

"Go ahead. I'd like to stay a little longer. I'll see you tomorrow. And thanks for at least taking me seriously."

"I owe you at least that," Henry responded. "Although I'm not sure what I'll think tomorrow."

After Henry left the restaurant, David sat reflecting on the evening. Had he done the right thing? Had he presented his proposal effectively? No way to know. Without Henry's assistance he knew the heart of the research would be difficult, perhaps even impossible. "Nothing to do now but wait," he thought.

David paid the check and methodically went to his

car and drove away. About thirty seconds later, a long black sedan also pulled out and drove slowly down the same street.

Chapter 5

Creighton knew well enough what NORTECH officials would say about the propriety of the meeting he had just completed with Ray Harris. Company policy strictly forbade any employee from talking to the press without permission; however, Creighton understood that in this instance he could not afford to tell anyone about the call he had received the previous day, much less his response to it. Ordinarily he would have cut off any reporter asking for an interview, but this one had hit a nerve when he mentioned that the object of his inquiry was Dr. David Evans. Creighton had been observing David for the past two months, more than David himself realized, and he had come to suspect that he was involved in some type of research that was almost certainly immoral, if not actually dangerous.

That was happening more and more. The whole country had become obsessed with playing God, trying to reach heaven with a new Tower of Babel. Only recently had Thomas become aware that his coming to work for NORTECH had not been accidental. He had been placed here, because he alone recognized how blasphemous were these designs, and he had been chosen to be God's instrument in stopping it.

He had come to believe that the danger was even worse than he had earlier suspected. As evil as were NORTECH and all the other contemptible institutions that supported such monstrous goals, if he had correctly interpreted the work in which Evans was involved, it was an abomination more vile than even man's attempt to fly through the heavens as if he himself were a god. Creighton had come to suspect that Evans was not content with such blasphemy. Rather, he was actually trying to interfere with the order of the universe itself. Most likely he would never succeed, but if he did, the consequences could be disastrous. His voice had warned him of that.

Why couldn't Evans understand how evil his plans were? But what else could you expect? This whole generation seemed to be comprised of hippies and campus radicals, kids with no respect for God, their mothers, or anything else. How could they be expected to understand anything having to do with decency or divine order? No, it was up to him alone to protect the laws God had established for the universe, and if that meant providing some information to this reporter, he would have to supply it. Everyone thought Evans was so goody-goody, but evidently there was some dirt in his background. He didn't relish the thought of digging into someone's sordid past, but he knew he had to do whatever was required. After all, he was answering now to a Higher Power, and he must not fail. Whatever he had to do, his mission justified it. The voice had assured him of that.

Chapter 6

The deepening twilight cast long diagonal shadows across the street ahead. The evening had just reached that point when the failing sunlight makes it difficult to see, without being dark enough for the headlights to have any real effect in illuminating the road ahead.

As Henry Lindstrom drove the familiar maze of side streets to David's apartment, his stomach was in a knot, his mind still uncertain about the decision part of him knew he had already reached that morning. A little more than a week had passed. During that time David continually pressured Henry to join him in a project that he glowingly promised would likely be the most monumental undertaking of their career, while Henry, half wishing he had never become involved at all, searched almost hopefully for any defect in either David's logic or his research. He found to his dismay that every avenue he pursued, David had already investigated and was armed with ready and convincing answers.

Slowly, and contrary to his deepest prejudices, Henry felt compelled to accept the logic, if not yet the validity, of David's arguments. Only when he had allowed himself to admit even the possibility of time travel did Henry concern himself with the mechanics of the procedure, and it was in this area that he felt perhaps David's hypothesis might fail. It was one thing to discuss such matters as relativity and time travel abstractly. It would be quite another to devise a practical means for using one to make the other possible.

They had met alternately at their respective apartments every evening in order to be able to discuss the matter more freely. Both of them realized that this whole issue carried with it political ramifications for NORTECH, and, if the institute rejected it, could easily spell the end of their careers. At this stage secrecy was imperative.

By Thursday of the following week David had been able to weaken Henry's opposition, although Henry had not admitted as much even to himself. On Friday be found that he had no more scientific avenues of opposition to propose, and so it was with a degree of turmoil that he awaited their next meeting that night. As he sat down in David's study, and David began to explain some mathematical formulas he had been constructing, Henry suddenly stopped him and asked him to sit down for a moment. Slowly, hesitantly, he began what he knew might well be the most important conversation of his life.

"I've always been direct, and I'm not going to beat around the bush now, although, believe me, you cannot imagine how hard this conversation is for me. During the past week I've tried every tactic I could think of to disprove your theory, and I have to admit I've failed to do so. If I am to consider myself a scientist, I must reluctantly acknowledge that you have demonstrated that time travel is at least theoretically possible. I have one other major concern we need to discuss which might still invalidate the concept, but I am now willing to admit the accuracy of your research and the logic of your findings."

David's sigh was audible. "Thank you, Henry. You can't imagine how much it means to me to hear you say that. You were certainly a tough antagonist, and I will admit that your strong opposition was causing me to doubt my own conclusions. Your support now means more than you can know. Henry, we're both scientists and have looked at my theory from two different, although not unrelated, disciplines. Your agreement tonight convinces me more than ever that I'm on the right track. I'm glad we're a team again. But you mentioned another problem. Let's deal with it right now."

"All right then. It has to do with the mechanics of what you're trying to achieve. It's one thing to devise charts and mathematical formulas, but quite another to transform them into something tangible that works. I understand where you're coming from, but how on earth can you hope to put it into practice? Do you really have a workable plan for actually sending an object into another time?"

"You're right, Henry; the technical mechanism will be the crux of the whole experiment. Unless we can actually demonstrate that time travel is possible, all the theories and mathematics won't amount to anything. Fact is, I proposed the same question to myself over three months ago, and that's precisely where my research at NORTECH dealing with relativity comes in. It's also the area in which I most need your help. I think I could have conducted the research on my own, if I only had to worry about sending an object to another time, even though I'm convinced that's exactly what our first test should involve. But that would only be one more experiment. It wouldn't have any scientific validity, because we would have no way of proving that an inanimate object was transported to another time. No, eventually a human being must go and return if we intend to demonstrate scientifically that we aren't frauds. That's where your knowledge is crucial."

"How's that, David?"

"Although we don't have enough time to go into the details tonight, I've developed a theory that I think should work." At this point David showed that wisp of a childish grin Henry hated so much, because it seemed so undignified in a scientist. "Actually, it came as a direct result of the research we were so heatedly discussing last week. Remember, I was theorizing about the effects of relativity on interstellar space travel at the speed of light?"

"Yes, of course. But you said that program was still a few years away, and anyway, once you sent someone into space, only your descendants would know if it worked or not. From all you and I have discussed, I didn't understand you to mean that time travel would merely come from the normal effects of relativity on a spacecraft."

"No, you haven't misunderstood at all. I'm not proposing space travel. The time traveler would not move in space at all. But relativity is still the key to making the concept work. Imagine what might happen if a person could be placed in a confined area and had everything within that space, including the molecules of his own body, accelerated beyond the speed of light. Wouldn't relativity behave under those circumstances in precisely the same way as it would during space travel?"

Henry had that faraway stare he often developed while in deep concentration. Still looking as if he were focusing on the far wall, he answered deliberately.

"That would certainly seem to be a logical assumption, and of course you're the physicist, so if you say relativity will work under those conditions, I'm not about to argue with you. That brings to mind a more formidable problem, although right now it's more of a question. Do you have any idea what effect those kinds of forces might produce on a human body? The results might be hard even to conceive. In one sense it would be as if the body dematerialized in our time and materialized again in another. Could we even be sure the molecules of the body would travel in tandem? And what about clothes? One slight error and the time traveler might complete his journey, only to find the molecules of his suit intertwined with his body or something equally grotesque. Remember the 50s movie, *The Fly*?"

"We really are beginning to think alike," David responded excitedly. "Those are my exact concerns. That's why I need you as my partner. My research has required me to treat atoms and molecules abstractly, and I am as certain as I can be at this stage that the laws of physics will result in time travel under the circumstances I have outlined. I am convinced that, given enough time and money, I can indeed send an object into another time and retrieve it. I need your background to help me make this process work on a living human being, without destroying that person in the process. Are you with me, Henry? Just think of it — time travel! If we pull this off, it will mean the Nobel Prize for sure!"

"Yes, and if we don't (and right now my brain hasn't totally accepted successful time travel as a strong probability), we'll be labeled the Dr. Frankenstein's of the twentieth century.

"Let's be sure I understand this," Henry continued. "You intend to walk into NORTECH tomorrow and blithely tell them you want their support for a machine to travel through time."

David slapped Henry on the back and gave one of his distinctive laughs. "Henry, always the pessimist. Well, I don't believe I would have phrased it quite that way, but I guess that is just about what I have in mind. I hope it just sounds worse when you say it. What do you say? Do we go for it or not?"

Henry sighed and resigned himself to accepting what still seemed a fantastic notion, even though he had known he would when he arrived that evening. He knew then that the decision he had made would determine his future. He and David would either be hailed as the greatest scientists of their generation or be labeled as eccentrics, or worse. But David could in his own way be most persuasive, and once the decision had been made, Henry's scientific temperament took over. The reservations of a moment ago had not been altered, but he was now committed, so they occupied no further place in his thinking. The next step was to meet with NORTECH. As crucial as it was, that was one meeting neither of them anticipated with a great deal of optimism.

Chapter 7

Somehow the whole affair hadn't felt right almost from the beginning. Initially matters seemed to proceed smoothly. There had been no trouble scheduling the meeting. Although young and relatively new at NORTECH, David was still very much a respected member of the organization, and Henry's experience lent even more credibility to the team. So when David requested a meeting to discuss a possible new area of research, the chairman's secretary called back within hours to inform him that it had been arranged for the following Thursday.

The first hitch came on Tuesday when the meeting was postponed for the first time. "Just until Friday," the secretary had told David. Then on Friday the appointment was rescheduled for the following Wednesday, and now it was Friday again, more than a week after the meeting had first been scheduled.

David tried to convince himself there was no reason to be concerned. NORTECH officials were busy these days. Their schedules certainly required frequent changes. Besides, no one at NORTECH knew anything specific about the subject of the meeting, so why should there be any prejudice against it. Henry said nothing, but had difficulty hiding his concern. Something wasn't right, and deep down, both men knew it.

The arrangements for the discussion weren't designed to help alleviate their fears either. The meeting was held in one of NORTECH's conference rooms and was chaired, not by a fellow scientist as David had requested, but a midlevel staff member who could not possibly have understood the principles of time travel, whether he accepted them or not. Three other scientists were in attendance. As David had requested, one was a physicist, Dr. Jake MacKenzie, with whom David had worked on occasion and even had dinner with once. One other member of the committee worked with Henry in Nuclear Medicine. The third neither David nor Henry had expected, and David could barely contain himself, when he first went into the conference room and saw Dr. Thomas Creighton seated next to the chairman. What did hold him back was a firm grip from Henry's arm.

On the surface the conduct of the meeting was formal and proper, but after the first twenty minutes, there could be little doubt about the direction it was heading. Almost from the beginning Creighton virtually dominated the meeting. The chairman knew he was in over his head and was willing for anyone to take over his job. The other members were understandably reluctant to play devil's advocate with the kinds of questions NORTECH would reasonably be expected to pursue. That left only Creighton, and he appeared to be eager to take over the role.

He quickly discovered that David had conducted extensive research on his own and came well prepared to defend his understanding of relativity and how he expected to use it to transport a person into another time. Failing to make headway against David's theories, Creighton concentrated most of his assaults on Henry's explanation of how a human body could stand up to the forces exerted by the process of time travel. It had not taken long for him to realize that this was the weakest part of the proposal, if only because Henry had been involved in the project for such a short time and so had only the barest outline to present to the committee. At this point he wasn't absolutely certain himself whether or not his tentative conclusions were valid, and his cautious scientific temperament would not allow him to make claims which further research might not substantiate.

Near the end of the meeting Creighton's thinly disguised antagonism almost came out into the open. He had earlier tried and failed to discredit David's theory regarding the properties of time and its relation to the physical universe. Henry had followed with a brief explanation of how he anticipated a human body would respond to the effects of time travel. Creighton shrewdly perceived that this was the part of the proposal to attack. No sooner had Henry completed his presentation than he pounced.

"So, Dr. Lindstrom, it is your assertion that during the process of time travel the human body will be somehow suspended in a sort of never-never land, totally oblivious to the whole process. Is that a fair summary? I have to admit it has more of a ring of wishful thinking than scientific research. And you must admit you haven't presented the least bit of data to support your assertion."

"No, Dr. Creighton," Henry almost gritted his teeth, gripping the table to maintain his composure, while still trying to choose each word carefully, "that most assuredly is not a fair summary. My precise statement to the committee was that, as far as I have been able to determine, time travel will in effect suspend any perception of time for the time traveler. You see, the whole concept is so foreign to our experience that I find it difficult to describe without using what must of necessity be somewhat false imagery. What I am trying to convey, however, is that the process will quite literally have no duration, since time itself, relative to the time traveler, will have been arrested. Whatever an observer may perceive, for the subject the effect will most likely be instantaneous. There is no question of a person's being somehow conscious for an indefinite period, during which such life sustaining functions as circulation, respiration, and so on need to be maintained. They will no more have stopped, than one could say the lungs have ceased to function between breaths. And that is why I am reasonably certain that time travel should have no adverse physical effects on the human body."

"So many disclaimers," Creighton shook his head in protest. "'Reasonably certain . . . as far as I have been able to determine.' Why you even admit you employ, what did you call it, 'false imagery'? And you are asking this committee to recommend that NORTECH replace proven, well supported, and I might add quite profitable goals to fund research for a will-o'-the-wisp program that, by your own admission, you don't know will work, or even whether or not is safe."

"Dr. Creighton, your assessment is unworthy of a scientist," Henry virtually exploded. Almost immediately the startled looks of the committee made him regret the impropriety of his outburst.

"Forgive my abruptness, Dr. Creighton, but surely the purpose of this meeting cannot have escaped you. We are seeking funds to conduct research, not because research has been completed. Even though I have confidence in the validity of my position, my integrity as a scientist requires me to qualify my judgments regarding an, as yet untested hypothesis, until it can be verified by further research. Surely the committee can appreciate my position in such matters.

"As for safety, both Dr. Evans and I would naturally take every precaution to minimize any danger, either to ourselves or anyone else involved in the project. The initial tests would involve sending first an inanimate object, followed by plants, and finally research animals into another time, before any attempt would be made to transport a human being."

At this point, David, who had been silently cheering Henry on, rose to address the committee. While acknowledging Creighton and the chairman, he centered his attention on the two colleagues on whose support David and Henry were counting to get their request approved.

"Gentlemen, we have spent more than two hours evaluating the request Dr. Lindstrom and I have presented for your consideration, and frankly, I doubt that any benefit would be derived from further discussion. However, if I may, I wish to conclude this meeting by attempting to get to the heart of what I believe to be the real source of the reservations this committee has expressed toward our proposal.

"First of all, Dr. Lindstrom and I have pursued a legitimate request for a grant to conduct further research into the feasibility of developing a workable means to achieve some form of time travel. While I can appreciate how exotic, perhaps even fantastic, such a project may appear, that alone should not present a barrier to your approval of our request. Virtually all of the projects in which NORTECH is currently engaged would have seemed no less bizarre, even to the scientific community, only twenty-five years ago. Tomorrow's science all too often is derived from today's science fiction. If we haven't yet learned that lesson, we have had to ignore much of the technological progress of this century."

For the first time during the meeting, David could sense a degree of softening on the committee's part. Even the chairman was nodding in agreement. Only Thomas Creighton remained unresponsive, a slight frown masking his face. Yet, having begun, David was determined not to let his dream die without a fight. Allowing one more side glance at Creighton's piercing eyes, David exhaled slightly and continued.

"Despite the exotic nature of our request, we have presented a large amount of supporting data, outlining our theory of how time travel can be achieved, and not one of our conclusions has been successfully challenged from a scientific basis. The only argument given in opposition to our proposal is that our research is incomplete, a condition we readily acknowledge. Our work is deficient precisely because we do not have the funds either to pursue research or test the conclusions already derived from current experiments. That, after all, was supposed to have been the purpose of this very meeting. Simply stated, it seems contrary to any sense of logic to deny funding to pursue research, because that research has not already been conducted. Yet, such appears to be exactly what this committee has suggested to us."

"Dr. Evans," Creighton interrupted, "you have presented your case, and most eloquently, I might add. However, as you say, we have all the facts, and unless you have something pertinent to add, I suggest you allow this committee to deliberate your proposal, which I assure you will be given the consideration it deserves."

"Just two minutes more of the committee's time, Dr. Creighton, and I will have concluded.

"There has been one other concern during this meeting which has never been raised, at least not vocally, but which I believe lies at the heart of the matter. That issue, gentlemen, is fear. Fear of the unknown, perhaps fear of our technology progressing beyond our ability to control it. I can't say precisely what the present concerns are. But I do know that this same kind of irrational fear has been a specter that has haunted scientists ever since Galileo first had the courage to proclaim that planets do indeed move. The real question before this committee today is one that has been repeatedly addressed ever since the scientific method was first employed. Do we consider ourselves as protectors of the status quo, or are we willing to become seekers after truth, wherever that quest may lead us? Dr. Lindstrom and I have presented our proposal and what we are convinced is a workable program to transform that dream into a reality. Certainly the research we are pursuing is unusual, but our theories are based on accepted scientific principles, and we have shown the potential benefits to be derived from this research. The future of this program, gentlemen, is in your hands. I am confident you will reach the appropriate decision."

David knew he had made a favorable impression on the committee as a whole. Even the chairman seemed moved by his impassioned plea. Creighton, aware that his control appeared to be slipping, intervened abruptly. Nodding amiably to David and Henry, he made no direct reference to David's closing statement.

"Thank you, Dr. Evans — Dr. Lindstrom. This committee has one other related matter to consider. Once that is completed, we shall evaluate your proposal and inform you of our decision."

*　　*　　*　　*

Later that afternoon Henry walked slowly down the hall toward David's office, paused for a moment, and knocked softly. After waiting and getting no response, he finally opened the door and walked in.

"David, are you all right? I'm sorry to barge in, but when you didn't answer my knocking, I became worried."

"Sorry, Henry, I guess I didn't hear you. I've been sitting here, trying to figure out what went wrong. I don't know how I expected the committee to respond, but I did assume that scientists would have been more objective. I know the concept of time travel must certainly have seemed somewhat fanciful. Why, it took almost a full week of intense persuasion to convince you. I really must have been naïve to imagine I could sway NORTECH in just a few hours."

While sharing his disappointment, Henry had secretly felt all along that David had been too optimistic about the meeting. He decided that now was the time to express the feelings he had kept inside for the past week.

"David, you know I seldom mince words, and for your own good I'm not going to now. Frankly, I think you're being too hard on yourself and, for that matter, on NORTECH as well. Maybe the timing just isn't right. With the war in Vietnam consuming so much of the government's resources, NASA has to fight just to continue funding for the space program, and they wouldn't even get the budgets they do, if we weren't also in a race with the Soviets to land a man on the moon. That's the reality with which NORTECH has to contend. Once these priorities aren't so demanding, perhaps NORTECH can afford to look at more long-range programs, but at this time I don't think they have a choice. Believe me I've been here long enough to understand the political realities. None of us like it, but ultimately you learn to work within the system or you get out. I'm sorry to have to put it this way, but coming from a family as wealthy as yours, perhaps it's harder for you to accept."

David's anger had been pent up just below the level of his depression, and Henry's accusation was all it took to cause it to come spilling out.

"So I'm the spoiled rich kid, am I? If you only knew

how often I've had to deal with that stigma. But I really expected better from you, Henry. And all this time I thought we were friends."

"Now, hold on. I didn't mean . . ."

"Oh, but you did, and I'm beginning to understand why people talk about your being so dense. You've seen my apartment. You've driven my car. Is that the way a spoiled rich kid lives? You talk about my family, and that just shows how little you know. Henry, I grew up without a family. My parents were murdered. Did you know that? I thought not. You've met my guardian, Margaret Stetson, and, although I love her more than anyone else in the world, in no way has she tried to become what you blithely refer to as family. But she has attempted to instill her values in me. You know what she's like, no nonsense, British to the core. If there's one thing she's determined to teach me, it's self-reliance, and although it took awhile, I've become grateful to her for it. I've earned my own way, and I don't need friends who are shallow enough to accuse me of living off someone else."

"Now just a moment," Henry tried to defend himself. "I'm sorry if you feel I was out of line, but you know me better than that. Truth is, like it or not, we were sunk the moment we walked into that meeting. With Creighton bull-dogging the committee, what else could we reasonably expect?

"Look, this has been a tough day for both of us. Can't we forget what we just said to each other?"

David knew he had overreacted to Henry's criticism, and truthfully he did regret his part in their latest confrontation. Unable to attack the system that had frustrated his plans, he had instead, almost against his will, found himself lashing out at his best friend. At the moment he was exhausted and unable to sort out just what he felt or whether he was angry with Henry, NORTECH, or himself.

"I honestly don't know what I should do right now. My first inclination is to resign. I'm sick of everything and everybody connected with this place. I don't know if I can continue to work here after what happened today."

Not wishing to alienate David further, Henry ignored the implied affront in David's remarks. He decided to provide support rather than criticism.

"Look, you may be partly right. It probably is wise to get away for awhile. But to resign when you're upset would be foolish. You've got some vacation coming. Go off somewhere, and forget about this place for awhile. Once you've had a chance to think it over, I guarantee this situation will look different."

"The only thing I know for sure is that I don't want to think about it anymore today. I haven't had an evening alone in over a month. I'm going home now."

"Will you be in tomorrow?"

"I honestly don't know, Henry. Right now I have some things to think about."

"Okay, buddy. But will you promise to consider my suggestion?"

"I will," David answered. Henry sensed little conviction in his voice.

"Good night," David said perfunctorily as he left the office, not even bothering to close it.

"Tough break, kid," Henry said to himself. He had already experienced a few of the curves life unexpectedly throws, so he could feel a degree of empathy with what David was going through just now. He had turned out the lights and was in the process of locking up for David when his thoughts were interrupted by the harsh ringing of David's phone.

"Dr. Evans' office, Henry Lindstrom speaking," he

answered automatically.

"Henry," a pleasant, though slightly nervous voice responded. "I was trying to reach David, but I guess you'll do just as well. This is Jake MacKenzie. We never formally met before this morning, but I worked with David on his first project with NORTECH."

"I remember you from today's meeting, Dr. MacKenzie," Henry replied, making no attempt to suppress the chill from his tone.

"Look, I know you and David must be disappointed by the committee's decision, and that's what I want to speak with you about. I shouldn't even be talking to you, but the fact of the matter is, something was brought up in the meeting after you and David left that I think you ought to be aware of. Could we meet somewhere this evening and talk about it?"

"I don't suppose I have anything to lose," Henry responded, and then added with a touch of sarcasm, "You've already seen to that."

"I know how you must feel," MacKenzie responded sympathetically. "All I ask is that you hear me out."

"All right, your office or mine?"

"Oh! No! Please! Not here! I'll meet you for coffee at the Marian Café. Do you know it?"

"Yeah, I know where it is. Why all the secrecy?"

"I don't want it known I talked with you, Okay? I could get in trouble if it came out. But David didn't deserve what happened today, and I think both of you ought to be given the whole story. See you in thirty minutes?"

"Half an hour it is," Henry responded. "And, Dr. MacKenzie, sorry, about what I said earlier."

"Thirty minutes then. Goodbye, Dr. Lindstrom."

Chapter 8

David's apartment reflected an accurate picture of his meager lifestyle. Although a one bedroom cost twenty dollars more than an efficiency, David had indulged himself in that luxury, because he required the extra space to store his books, as well as a place to relax while reading them. Most of his graduate texts were kept in his office at NORTECH, but these were books he read for purely personal satisfaction and reflected an appreciation for a variety of literature — some classics, a number of best sellers, and a rather large collection of mystery stories. This passion for reading was one aspect of David's personality of which not many of his friends were aware and even fewer appreciated.

David's love of fiction, especially mysteries, had developed over a long period. It had begun during his childhood after he became a fanatical devotee of the *Hardy Boys*. Seven years earlier he had first discovered Sherlock Holmes in the form of a borrowed paperback copy of *The Hound of the Baskervilles*. From then on he was hooked and had over the years read virtually every case the fictional detective had taken on, intrigued almost as much by the Victorian setting as the stories themselves.

Tonight he had returned to the company of Mr. Holmes in an attempt to banish the events of this day from his mind. His hectic schedule rarely afforded the luxury of even a few hours in which to indulge his desire for reading. He decided that this would be the night, and the diversion had already provided good therapy for his unsettled nerves, that is until his concentration was abruptly shattered by the ringing of his telephone.

"What now?" he groaned to himself, aggravated at having the luxury of his privacy disturbed, while anticipating that the interruption might have some connection to the events of the day, just when he had been moderately successful at dismissing them from his consciousness. So it was with a degree of pleasure that he recognized the resonant voice of Mrs. Stetson.

"Margaret, what a pleasant surprise. I haven't heard from you in weeks."

"Well, David," she chided, "I'm not totally at fault, now am I? You never seem to be at home."

"I know," he replied languidly, suddenly reminded of all the events of the past few weeks. "I guess I've been putting more time into my work than I realized."

"David, is everything all right? You sound depressed."

He let out a soft chuckle. "I never could fool you, could I? You've always been able to read me like a book. I swear, sometimes I think you're psychic."

Mrs. Stetson ignored the suggestion, and instead pressed David for the cause of his depression.

"Oh, a lot of things, too much to discuss over the phone. Maybe I've just been working too hard. I had a problem at NORTECH, and I'm ashamed to say I overreacted. I even came close to alienating Henry Lindstrom."

"Isn't he that man I met when you first went to work at NORTECH? The two of you seemed to be such good friends."

"Yes we are. But today I almost destroyed our friendship. To Henry's credit, he took a lot of abuse from me.

He thinks I need a vacation. Maybe he's right."

"Well it would seem my calling now is fortuitous. You see, I received a cable from Albert today, asking me to visit him in London. He's arranged a meeting with a group of investors, and he thought it might be profitable for me to be present. I know you've never been to England, and I thought you might enjoy coming along. How about it?"

"I don't know. We're all really under pressure here, and I hadn't been thinking about anything as involved as a trip out of the country. Anyway, I'm not certain I could get off even if I wanted to."

"Oh, come now, you just finished telling me that you were advised to get away, and this is a perfect opportunity. I'm sure it can be worked out. I only plan to be gone a couple of weeks, and if it's the expense, perhaps you would let me help."

"No, it isn't the money. I have a little set aside. Besides, we've already discussed my financial situation. Although I didn't like it at first, I've come to relish my independence. So don't push the issue, or you may find that I'm learning to be just as stubborn as you."

"Indeed, I have begun to see changes in you, and I must admit I've always liked strong willed men, but I sometimes wish . . ."

"Wish what?"

"Oh, it's nothing. I'm just a silly old woman, and I should have seen how ridiculous it was to suppose you would want to go traipsing across the Atlantic with me."

"Nonsense, I'd love to go, if I just felt things would be all right here while I'm gone."

"Well, couldn't your friend, Dr. Lindstrom, look after your affairs for you?"

David started to remind Margaret that Henry wasn't

involved in the same research as he, when he suddenly realized that it wasn't his work at NORTECH that was holding him back. His real concern was still Creighton and a nagging feeling that he might not be satisfied with his victory today.

"I suppose I could arrange to have things at work taken care of, but even if I wanted to go, I couldn't just take off out of the blue."

"Of course not, David, and neither can I. Honestly, sometimes you forget that I have one or two responsibilities to attend to myself. I can't possibly leave before three weeks. Surely you can arrange to get off within that time. NASA has no launchings planned for the next two months, so you have nothing pressing other than your normal duties."

David laughed in spite of himself. It wasn't banana splits anymore, but Margaret Stetson still possessed a talent for cheering him up when he most needed it.

"I never did have a chance against you. You even checked launch schedules. No wonder you've made yourself rich."

Once again there was that remote tone in her voice as Margaret Stetson replied, "No David, my wealth isn't due to my own efforts. I have never forgotten the debt I owe . . . someone. But come now, are we agreed?"

David sighed, as he gave in to her once more.

"I suppose so. Get me the details, and I'll see if I can arrange things here. You know something?"

"What's that?"

"You're a pretty great lady. If I were a year or two older, I just might consider marrying you — if only for your money."

"Ah, go on with you. You just be ready to leave. Albert told me I'd better bring you with me. He's anxious to see you again too. Goodnight, David."

"Goodbye, Margaret."

Already feeling better about the situation, David turned his thoughts toward the trip itself. The more he considered the prospect, the better it sounded. He had never been outside the United States, much less overseas. England would be especially attractive, because he would be able to visit the area from which Margaret Stetson had emigrated so many years before. And he would enjoy seeing Albert again. It had been too many years already. David was deep in thought when he was interrupted once again, this time by the sound of his doorbell.

"After ten o'clock! Now who on earth could that be?" David mused, as he unlatched the lock and opened the front door.

"Henry," he exclaimed. "I certainly didn't expect you tonight, especially after the way I treated you earlier."

"Believe me, I had no intention of rehashing this day either, but something's come up that you need to know about. May I come in?"

"Of course. By the way, I've just about decided to go along with your suggestion about taking some time off, but I'll tell you about that in a moment. You look worse than I did this afternoon. What's happened?"

"I'll come right to the point. I've just concluded a meeting with Dr. MacKenzie."

"Jake? I wasn't aware that the two of you even knew each other."

"We didn't, at least not personally," Henry replied. "He called your office right after you left this afternoon, and since I answered, I guess he decided to confide in me."

"Confide in you? What's going on?"

"When we left the meeting today, do you remember

what Creighton's last comment was?"

"Why, just that the committee would consider our request and let us know, which they unfortunately did."

"No, that wasn't quite what he said. If you recall, he indicated there was another private matter that the committee needed to discuss first. Well, MacKenzie just filled me in on the substance of that 'private matter,' and I think you need to know about it. Does the name Ray Harris mean anything to you?"

"Harris? No, not that I recall. Why do you ask?"

"According to MacKenzie, Ray Harris is a reporter for one of those tabloid papers, and he has apparently contacted Creighton, asking for information about you, or maybe the Stetson family. MacKenzie wasn't too clear on that part."

David chuckled softly to himself.

"So you wonder if there's some dirty laundry I've been hiding. Is that it?"

Henry's expression remained unchanged, and his silence became noticeable.

"Hey you're serious, aren't you? Come on, what am I supposed to be — a spy — a drug pusher? Out with it."

"I wouldn't joke about this, David. And it has nothing to do with whether I believe anything about you or not, which, for the record, I don't. No one has made any specific charges, but they don't have to. You know NORTECH has an image to maintain. If even the hint of a scandal were to reach NASA, it might be enough to eliminate NORTECH from future contracts, and if what MacKenzie told me is true, that was the implied threat Creighton used to force the committee to kill our request. And you still aren't off the hook. Creighton has a weapon he can use against you now, and you may not be able to counter it, because, from what you tell me, you don't even know what it's all about. MacKenzie must be a good friend. He risked his own position with NORTECH to warn you how precarious yours is."

"Well, I hope both of you are making more of this incident than is warranted," David sighed, "but it really may not matter as much as you thought. You see I've decided to go to England for awhile as you suggested. After that, who knows?"

"I recommended a short vacation, not leaving the country, much less NORTECH."

"I know this decision sounds sudden, but the timing seems opportune. As it happens, Mrs. Stetson — you met her once last summer, remember? Anyway, she has to fly to England on business and has invited me to go with her, and I've decided to take her up on the offer. Getting four thousand miles away from Creighton might be the best thing for me to do just now."

"Well, I can't really argue that, but if I were you, I'd try to find out something more about this Harris fellow and what information he and Creighton may have. When were you planning to leave?"

"In two or three weeks, providing I can get the time and take care of a few loose ends. I don't foresee any problems. I'm overdue for some vacation, and nothing major is coming up for the next couple of months."

"Well, I'm glad you're in better spirits, anyway. You had me worried earlier. But please, I promised Dr. MacKenzie you wouldn't do anything to jeopardize his confidence."

"Of course not. I'll call Jake tomorrow just to reassure him. And thanks, Henry. I'm sorry about what I said earlier. I know my temper gets the best of me sometimes."

"Ah, forget it. Goodnight, David."

"Goodnight, Henry, and thanks again."

Immediately after Henry left, David glanced at his watch, considered the hour, then picked up the telephone and dialed.

"Hello, Margaret? Yes, sorry to call back so late, but I need to put a question to you. Have you ever heard of a reporter named Ray Harris?"

There was a meaningful pause, and when Mrs. Stetson answered, David thought he detected a troubling concern in her voice. "Why do you ask? You haven't told him anything, have you?"

"Not at all. As a matter-of-fact, I've never met the man, although apparently he's been talking to someone at work. He sounds rather unsavory. Who is he, and what's his interest in our family?"

Attempting not to sound too concerned, Margaret replied, "Oh, he's just a reporter from a scandal magazine who has become obsessed with snooping around our family secrets. I think it would be unwise to talk to him. You won't will you?"

"No, no, of course not. But what's he after? You don't have anything to hide, that I know of anyway. Is there something you're not telling me?"

"Come now," Margaret laughed wryly. "Surely, after all these years, you haven't become suspicious of me. You must remember that I am a very wealthy woman, and that makes me a target for certain types of people. I'm just concerned that if you talk to him at all, he might distort anything you say to make a story sound sensational."

"Is that why you have those bloodhounds tailing me, never giving me a moment's real privacy? Seems like quite a bit of trouble just to protect me from a two-bit reporter."

"Now, please don't let's start that argument again.

We've been over the subject many times, and I must insist that you indulge me in this. The guards are there for your own good, believe me, and if they keep men like Ray Harris from bothering you, then I'm glad we have them."

Despite a lingering feeling that there might just be a connection between the security guards and a certain reporter, David chose not to pursue the matter further. He had seldom been successful in challenging Mrs. Stetson's resolve. Besides, he had learned at least part of what he wanted to know. Harris wasn't totally bluffing. Margaret Stetson knew something about Harris, something she obviously had no intention of telling David. He would have to pursue the matter, but meantime at NORTECH his hands were tied. Until he knew what he was dealing with, he couldn't risk a confrontation with Creighton, who obviously had some kind of ace up his sleeve.

Considering all the events of this most unusual day, a week or so away from the conflict was beginning to look even more appealing. The damage that might be done by Creighton in his absence had to be weighed against the possibility of a confrontation with this Harris and a sticky mess for NORTECH. No, for right now a vacation to England was not only desirable, it just might turn out to be the most prudent course to follow.

Chapter 9

The night sky over London reflected a multitude of lights which blended together to form a shimmering mosaic as the Boeing 707 banked sharply, positioning itself for its final approach to Heathrow. The ten-hour flight had been tiring enough. Now jet lag was beginning to take its toll as well. Even as David pondered the sudden change in plans which had forced Margaret Stetson to postpone her own flight temporarily, he was still glad he had decided to make the trip, for at least two reasons.

The flight itself had already done much to relieve the stress which had been David's constant companion these past few weeks. In some respects he felt that he had left behind, not just the United States, but along with it all the nagging problems, disappointments, and questions that had recently beset his life.

He was also looking forward to seeing Margaret's son, Albert. David's relationship with Albert had begun shortly after his own parents' deaths. By then, Albert was already gown and intimately involved in administering the steadily increasing Stetson fortune. Since Albert rarely visited the Stetson estate for more than a few days at a time, and with David normally away at school, the two of them had not had any real opportunity to get to know one another.

Or did it just seem that way? On more than one occasion while he was growing up, David remembered that some of the time he spent with Albert Stetson seemed awkward for both of them. As a child he thought little of his association with Albert, but as he grew into adolescence and later as an adult, he could look back on a relationship that was in some respects self-conscious, and he was certain that, whatever the cause, there was more substance than imagination to his perception.

Despite the problems of those early years, more recently the two men seemed to have overcome most of the difficulties and found themselves corresponding with some regularity, even though David had not seen Albert for almost five years, ever since he left to head the London operation. David wondered if perhaps Albert too couldn't quite figure out what his role should be in relationship to David. Albert had inherited the same continental, almost Victorian, reserve that characterized Margaret Stetson, although in Margaret the sternness had been softened by her feminine nature. In Albert, however, this force completely dominated his personality. To most people Albert Stetson appeared immutable and implacable. While these qualities helped mold him into a successful businessman, they also prevented him from becoming closer to David at a time when he would most have benefitted from such a relationship. Now David was an adult, and Albert could simply accept him as an equal, a less awkward relationship. Having done so, he found he genuinely liked David, who for his part was equally glad of their friendship. Everything considered, David found himself looking forward to their time together with genuine anticipation.

The other reason David was glad to be making the trip was sitting in the seat next to him. Her name was Catherine Edmonds, and she was returning to her home in London after a vacation in the United States. David had been instantly attracted by her dark compelling beauty, accented by lustrous black hair and smooth olive skin which suggested a

Greek or perhaps Italian ancestry. Yet for all her aristocratic bearing, Cathy (as David had already begun calling her) was open and friendly without being forward. She was beginning what promised to become a successful career as an interior decorator, specializing in redecorating older office buildings in London, which always seemed to be in the process of renovation. Cathy seemed fascinated to meet someone directly involved in the American space program. To a European the whole concept of space flight, which only eight years earlier had seemed incredible, appeared fascinating, and Cathy flattered David with endless questions about his work at NORTECH and the times (usually just before launches) when he was actually present at Cape Kennedy. Saddled with his share of male ego, David responded to her questions enthusiastically, oblivious to Cathy's skillful use of what she knew to be a most effective technique for attracting a man, simply by letting him talk about himself.

In addition David was, perhaps unconsciously, particularly vulnerable just at this time. Although the weight of the depression he had experienced after the rejection of his program had lessened, an edge of bitterness remained, along with lingering doubts the rejection had produced. Now David suddenly found himself sitting beside a beautiful young woman who seemed content to listen to him talk continually about himself. Less than two hours into the flight David had already decided he had no intention of letting Cathy disappear when they arrived in London.

As he and Cathy exited the plane and searched the crowded, and for David unfamiliar backdrop of Heathrow Airport, he heard his name called excitedly in a familiar New England accent. Turning to his right, he saw a well proportioned man, who appeared to be in his fifties, waving to him. Albert Stetson presented the epitome of elegance. His overcoat was a smart camel color, which a closer examination would have shown to have been woven of the finest cashmere, and the precise fit suggested custom tailoring. His hair, for the most part rich silver, still retained strands of blonde here and there, which only imparted an added air of distinction. If judged only by appearance and bearing, Albert could easily pass for English nobility, presenting a marked contrast to David in his cheap blue blazer that looked even worse after being crushed for ten hours in an overhead compartment. Neither of the two men seemed to notice these peculiarities, however, as they greeted each other warmly.

"It's been far too long, David. I do hope British Airways took good care of you."

"No complaints, although I don't think I took Margaret's warnings about jetlag seriously enough. I hope after dragging me across the Atlantic, you intend to make this trip worth the effort. I fully expect to be wined and dined, you know. What I can't get out of your mother, I'm counting on from you."

"Never fear. What Mother doesn't know, we just won't tell. And I promise you'll see more of England than you ever wanted to. But before you do too much sightseeing, I want an opportunity to discuss your research with you. Mother said you were having difficulties of some sort."

"Oh, nothing that would be of any interest to you, I'm sure. I came here to get away from work, not to dredge it up."

"Don't be too quick to brush me off," Albert insisted. "I have more connections than you may be aware of, and anyway I've always been fascinated by your research. We'll talk more tomorrow.

"But I say, we're both forgetting our manners. You haven't introduced me to this lovely young lady."

"I'm sorry. Cathy, this as you've probably deduced already, is Albert Stetson. Albert, Miss Catherine Edmonds."

"It's a pleasure to meet you, Mr. Stetson. After hearing so much about you, I feel I know you already."

"Oh," Albert replied, glancing at David with a look that reflected something more than polite conversation. "Just how long have you two known each other? And please, do call me Albert."

"Very well, Albert. I didn't intend to leave the wrong impression. David and I just met on the plane, but it's obvious how close the two of you are."

Albert's face seemed to brighten slightly.

"How kind of you to say so. Will you be staying in London long?"

"Oh, Cathy lives here," David explained. "I took the liberty of offering her a ride home, if you don't mind?"

"I can make other arrangements, Mr. Stetson," Cathy replied. "I don't wish to put you to any inconvenience."

Albert responded courteously, but his face assumed the puzzled expression he had shown earlier.

"No trouble at all. I should be delighted to see you home."

"You're very kind to do this. I live on King's Row. It's in Chelsea."

"I'm certain my chauffeur will have no difficulty locating the area," Albert responded graciously. With a sweeping gesture he directed David and Cathy toward a long white limousine waiting beside the curb, and the driver assisted them into the car. A moment later it pulled out of the departure area and sped into the night.

*   *   *   *

David slept late the next morning, overcome, as he had predicted, by the effects of jetlag. When he woke a little after midmorning, he discovered a message from Albert waiting for him.

Good Morning David,

After you've had breakfast, I'd like for you to see my offices. My chauffeur will drive you whenever you're ready. I have a proposition I think you might find appealing.
It's good to have you here.

Albert

This was Albert's second intrusion into his private affairs, and David could not help but be puzzled by it. It appeared to him that Margaret had been talking to Albert, sensing David's dissatisfaction at NORTECH. His initial response was a slight annoyance at Albert's interference. David certainly didn't come four thousand miles for a job interview, and he hadn't even finalized in his own mind whether or not to leave NORTECH. That someone else should attempt to make the decision for him was a little irritating. However, a sumptuous, if rather belated, breakfast went a long way toward dispelling any negative feelings, and within a couple of hours David was sitting in Albert's private suite. The elegance of the offices, which had been the subject of a magazine layout two years before, was totally wasted on David, for whom luxuries meant very little. The two men had been engaged in the type of reminiscences that were customary, when at a break in the conversation, Albert abruptly changed the tone and addressed David directly.

"I understand you're not happy with your work at NORTECH."

For a moment David stared into Albert's eyes, trying to figure out if more was intended by the question than was apparent. Finally he responded.

"I can see your mother has been talking to you, and from what's being made of the situation, I regret even mentioning it to her. I did have a proposal refused that was important to me, but that's all there is to it. For all practical purposes the issue is closed. At least for the present I intend to continue with my previous research."

Albert smiled slightly, and answered David affectionately. "Please don't be angry with Mother or with me either. Although, if I may say so, I'm pleased to see you stand up to me. That's something you wouldn't have done when I last saw you. But allow me to get to the point. I have a particular reason for bringing up the matter just now. What would you say if I offered you the opportunity to continue the research you had wanted to pursue at NORTECH?"

"I would say that you were merely trying to be benevolent, especially since you could not possibly be aware of the nature of the research in which I was involved or the massive funding that would be required."

Even though they were alone and the door was closed, Albert leaned forward and lowered his voice.

"I'm not going to beat around the bush with you, David. I am perhaps more familiar with your project than you give me credit for. I haven't held on to the family businesses without developing quite sophisticated means of obtaining information. To be blunt about the matter, I am aware that you have been working on developing a means for transporting a person in time. As for your charge that I'm being benevolent, that's rubbish. I have already made preliminary inquiries with a defense contractor who has connections very high in the British government. Even though you're a scientist, surely you must be aware of the enormous implications of time travel, military as well as commercial. I have taken the liberty of making an appointment for dinner tonight. Do I cancel that meeting or not?"

David was, for the moment, absolutely speechless. He simply sat staring straight into Albert's inflexible gaze. Finally he spoke hesitantly.

"I truly don't know what to say. I think I'm most astounded that you were even able to find out anything about my project. But are you serious? Someone here really wants to fund time travel research?"

"It will be up to you to convince him, David. All I've done is set the stage for you. But, yes, there is genuine interest. Believe me, I'm not offering charity. I hope that one day you'll understand that. What do you say? Are you willing to — what's the expression — 'go for it'?"

"I hardly know how I should respond," David answered in amazement. "What about my work at NORTECH? I can't just leave it."

"Why not? Your work there is important, I know, but surely you're not indispensable. You do, however, appear to be the only person on earth who has treated the possibility of time travel as a subject for serious scientific pursuit. This is your dream, is it not? I am offering you what may be your only opportunity for achieving it. David, my success in business requires me to take risks. I'm asking you to do the same. Don't become discouraged just because you failed to convince one organization, whose priorities or prejudices might not have allowed them to give your work the consideration it deserves."

David's first inclination was to refuse, if only because he was fearful of raising his hopes just to see them crushed again; however, Albert's assessment had struck a nerve. Time travel had become his dream, and if there was even the remotest possibility of achieving it, he knew he must pursue that chance. So it was that David left Albert's offices to prepare for one more attempt to sell his ideas to another potential supporter.

By the end of the week two changes had occurred which were to influence David's future profoundly. He had secured the funding he required for his research to continue in England. With Albert's assistance, David cut through British red tape with a speed that astounded him, his new venture appearing to possess a momentum of its own. Before his return to the United States, David had overseen the formation of a corporation to provide a legal basis for the research. Funds for immediate expenses had already been deposited, and for the first time since he had conceived of the prospect of time travel, David Evans felt he just might actually make it happen. If he had not gotten caught up in the euphoria of seeing his project go from dream to reality, he would have recognized that obstacles were overcome far too easily, but for whatever reasons, he simply did not notice. Perhaps he chose not to.

The second change involved Cathy. Although not yet in love, David's attraction to her was deepening, and if he was not yet aware of the depth of his feeling for her, the signs were obvious to anyone who observed them together. Albert was very conscious of the direction their relationship was taking, and it gave him real concern. In his mind this European romance was not just inadvisable. It could threaten all his plans, and it needed to be stopped. He would consider just how to accomplish that purpose.

Chapter 10

The rain had begun during the night and so far showed no signs of letting up. It was a rare Saturday when Henry did not spend at least half a day in his office, but this morning he was enjoying the luxury of a late breakfast and a leisurely reading of a science fiction novel (a weakness he successfully hid from most of his colleagues at work), not bothering to try to get in an extra hour or two at NORTECH before leaving for the airport to meet David's returning flight. Since the weather was so miserable, Henry had been forced to remain cooped up inside his apartment. The time alone had given him a chance to consider the latest developments and to wonder once again if his decision to become a part of David's time travel project had been wise after all.

Henry was relieved that David would be returning today. He didn't like the turn events had taken at NORTECH while David had been gone. He was a scientist, and he preferred his life to be orderly and predictable, which it certainly had not been since David had persuaded him to become a somewhat reluctant partner in his project. The first jolt had been David's cryptic telegram, informing him that funding had been secured, seemingly out of nowhere. Henry had been involved in too many budget fights in this country to know how hard research money was to come by, and he had no reason to assume the British bureaucracy would be any easier to navigate.

The specific circumstances of this grant made him uneasy, but his apprehension came from more than that. Part of him was actually sorry the project had been resurrected. After David went to England, Henry had resumed his former research, with some disappointment to be sure, but somewhat relieved to find himself back in his familiar routine. David's telegram had destroyed that security, and Henry had to admit to a degree of disappointment that it should be so.

After finishing breakfast and, like a typical bachelor, absently piling the dishes in the kitchen sink, Henry read David's telegram one more time, hoping to discover some key to understanding what lay behind these new developments. Shaking his head in resignation, he glanced at his watch and decided it was time to drive to the airport. Before leaving, he used the telegram to mark his place in the book he had been reading. He then deposited the book in the center drawer of his desk which he locked out of habit. Then, with a doubtful look at the sky, he ran for his car. Somehow the day seemed to match his mood. He hoped it wasn't a premonition.

If Henry was somewhat depressed about the recent turn of events, David appeared to be elated. Once off the plane and through customs, he had begun talking excitedly about his plans for the project, and Henry sensed that any interruptions on his part would be pointless until David was finished. Finally, after fifteen minutes on the freeway, David paused and stopped to look at Henry for the first time.

"Say, is anything wrong? You're awfully quiet."

Letting out a small grunt, which for Henry Lindstrom passed for a laugh, he responded, trying to appear amiable.

"What else could I do? You've been going full speed for the past twenty minutes. No, nothing's exactly wrong, although there has been a ripple on this side of the Atlantic while you've been away. Perhaps I'd better begin with Tom Creighton."

"Creighton?" David frowned. "What's he got to do

with anything?"

"Nothing I've been able to pin down, but he's been asking a lot of questions about you, specifically the nature of your research. He's even been checking into your background. We both know who's behind that. He actually had the nerve to contact me. Can you believe that? Tried to convince me he was acting for your own good. I told him where to get off in no uncertain terms. Later I learned that he had questioned Dr. Wu in Chemistry and even tried to get information from Anita Larkins in Personnel."

"Anita! Why on earth would he go to her?"

"Come on, David, open your eyes. Not only does Anita have access to your personnel file, but everyone knows you dated her last year."

"Only for a short time, and anyway, what would make Creighton think Anita would help him?"

"I don't know. Possibly he thought if you two broke up, she might be holding a grudge. Maybe he was just fishing. That's not the point. The reality is that, whether or not he has discovered anything incriminating, Creighton has created a stink, just when neither of us needed it. I wouldn't be at all surprised if the director at NORTECH has been waiting for you to return to find out what this is all about."

David thought silently for a moment, and then let out a small sigh. "Strange," he said at last. "I wonder what can motivate someone to do things like that."

"Probably thinks of himself as the watchdog of the world or something. Whatever Creighton has in mind, we're going to have to deal with him, and we had better decide pretty quickly what our approach should be."

"Our approach? I thought our plans were settled. We're leaving NORTECH and going to England as soon as possible. That should resolve our problem and get Creighton out of our lives at the same time."

"You sound so confident." There was a barely perceptible pause. "I wish I could be that certain."

"What do you mean, Henry? You're not still having doubts about the theory are you?"

"No, not really, at least not concerning the scientific aspects of the project. It's the conflict this has caused. I'm used to people taking issue with my research, but that's the nature of science. There's something more to this, and I can't help it if I feel uneasy about it. Creighton's part of the problem to be sure, but there's something else besides that."

Henry paused and was silent for a moment. Seeing his obvious discomfort, David took the initiative.

"We are friends, after all. If you've got something on your mind, let's hear it. Better now than later as far as I'm concerned."

"Okay, but please don't get offended. I need to ask you one more time, and then I'll drop the subject forever. Does this reporter have anything on you?"

David laughed softly. "You want to know if I'm secretly a Mafia hit man, working under a false identity."

"You know that wasn't what I was thinking. But the man has obviously spent a great deal of effort to find out about you."

"You have my word on it. I cannot even imagine what it is he thinks he can find out, and I have no interest in pursuing the matter further. I hope you believe that, because it's the absolute truth."

"Of course, I believe whatever you tell me. I'm just trying to put everything that's occurred in some kind of perspective that makes sense. What about the Stetsons? I know they're very wealthy. Have they done anything out of the ordinary?"

David thought about the private guards who had been secretly surrounding him for over a decade and started to reply, but decided that was a subject best left alone.

"I'm not aware of any skeletons in Margaret's family either," David replied, dodging Henry's question with a half-truth. "Can we just leave it at that? I can't be held accountable for what some crackpot reporter thinks he might find out about me, no matter how bizarre his behavior might be."

"Okay, I guess I've given you enough third-degree, and I promise I won't bring up the subject again. But honestly the question has been preying on my mind, and I had to get it out in the open. I suppose you're right about the decision having been made. Even though I'm nervous about what we're about to do, believe me, I'm excited about the possibilities too. Look, we're coming to the turnoff to my apartment. Why don't you come back with me? I have some leftover lasagna in the refrigerator, and we can try to finalize our plans."

"Who could possibly turn down an offer like that?" David laughed. "Okay, Henry, you're on."

Within five minutes they were driving into the lot adjoining Henry's apartment building. Henry ran ahead through the rain that was still beating down in a steady stream to get the front door open, while David gathered some papers he wanted to go over later.

As soon as he opened the door, Henry noticed that the living room window was broken, and rain was blowing into the room through the opening. Apparently the damage had been there for some time, because the sofa under the window was thoroughly soaked, and Henry noticed a pool of water accumulating on the carpet around it. Thinking that a tree branch knocked loose by the storm must have blown through the window, he went toward the couch to inspect the damage.

Henry's next view was from the floor of the living room with David bending over him. His head felt like it was on fire.

"Are you all right?" David was asking excitedly. "What happened?"

For a moment Henry said nothing, as he tried to get both his eyes and his mind back in focus.

"I think that's supposed to be my question," Henry tried to make a joke, even as his head was throbbing. "I just came into the room, and I don't know what happened next. I guess I must have blacked out."

"You didn't faint, Henry. You were struck on the head. Be careful; you may have a concussion."

David helped him to a large recliner on the side of the living room nearest the kitchen, staying away from the sofa which was continuing to receive rain from the broken window.

"You rest while I call an ambulance and the police."

"Don't be too hasty," Henry objected. "I'm beginning to feel some better. I do have one terrific headache, but I really don't think I've been seriously hurt, and getting involved with the police is the last thing either of us needs right now. Let's try to figure out what's happened, before we decide what to do. Did you see anyone leaving the building?"

"No, I'm sorry I didn't, and I was only a minute behind you. Whoever it was must have left the same way he came, through that broken window. I must have just missed him."

"I suppose it was just a burglar. Probably nothing can be done about it now. I guess I do need to find out if anything's missing though."

"What you need to do is rest," David insisted. "First thing I'm going to do is get that window patched up and clean up this mess. If you won't let me call a doctor, at least lay down for an hour or so. Then, if you're feeling up to it, you can take a look around. And no arguments."

"You're probably right," Henry replied. "My head is beginning to throb again. I'll rest for just a few minutes."

"A few minutes" became two hours. By the time Henry awoke, his apartment had assumed a semblance of normalcy. David had patched the window with a large plastic drop cloth which wasn't as necessary as before, because the rain had since stopped, and the mid afternoon sun was sending a distorted beam through the translucent folds of the plastic. David had mopped up the floor. Although the sofa and carpet would probably have to be replaced, at least they no longer held standing water.

When Henry emerged from his bedroom, he found David working at the center drawer of his desk.

"Henry," David said, running his hand under the top of the desk, "I think this is where your burglar concentrated his efforts. The lock on your desk has been forced open. Can you tell if anything's missing?"

Henry walked over, and examined the contents of the drawers.

"I can't fathom it. Nothing seems to have been taken. Not that I kept anything of any real value in my desk, mainly tax files and other personal papers. A few of my research notes are in here, but nothing appears to have been disturbed."

"Somebody was looking for something. Are you positive nothing's missing?"

"No, I really don't . . . Wait a minute. Now if that doesn't beat all. There is one item missing. I'm sure I put a book in my desk just before I left to pick you up. I can't believe anyone would break into an apartment for one book."

"Neither can I. There must be something else. Think hard. Are you sure you put the book in there?"

"Of course I'm sure. I put your telegram in it to mark the place and . . ."

"Henry, that's what the thief took. He wasn't after the book. He wanted the telegram, or at least what was in it. Someone was searching your apartment for information about me or about our research."

"Creighton?"

"I would hate to believe that," David answered. "I know Tom has attacked my work, but I can't believe he would stoop this low."

"What about that reporter? What was his name again — Travis?"

"Harris — Ray Harris. Now that sounds more likely. He's a two-bit hack for sure. But this seems a bit much even for him. I doubt we can ever know for sure who did this."

"Maybe we ought to call the police anyway," Henry suggested.

"Now wait a minute, Henry. I thought you were the one who didn't want to get the police involved."

"I didn't, at first anyway, but this has turned kind of scary. Besides, what can it really hurt?"

"Involving the authorities now could seriously delay our plans. Suppose they should arrest either Harris or Creighton. We would probably have to answer all sorts of questions about our research, and an investigation could force delays or even cancellation of the grant I've arranged. I'm beginning to think we should leave well enough alone. After all, nothing of any real value was taken."

"I'm not sure that's wise, or even legal," Henry

countered. "We really don't know who did what here, or whether he'll be back."

"Look, if you don't feel safe, stay with me for the next couple of days, but I'm convinced more than ever that we ought to resign immediately and leave for England as quickly, and quietly, as possible. The break-in here is of little concern if we do that. But it should serve to convince us that things aren't likely to work out here anymore. All we have to do is submit our resignations on Monday, and, with a little luck, we can be on our way to England in two weeks."

"All right," Henry agreed. "I suppose now that the decision to go is definite, there's no reason to prolong it. But we'll have to tell NORTECH something. What reason should we give for leaving?"

"I don't see that we owe NORTECH any real explanation," David countered. "In fact, I suspect they'll be glad to see me gone. I've inadvertently made things difficult for the institute. All they need to be told is that we have accepted other positions. I would just as soon no one knew anything specific about our plans or even that we're leaving the country. Nothing good can come of it, and if we can get out without anyone knowing about it, all the better."

*   *   *   *

As far as David or Henry could know, everything went pretty much according to plan. The only element they had not anticipated was a delay in Henry's passport. As it turned out, almost a full month was required to straighten out the mix-up and obtain the passport. David had been so certain of the time element that he had already made reservations for the trip, and those had to be changed.

Except for that one complication, they would likely have succeeded in leaving without anyone knowing for certain where they had gone. But in one moment's lapse in judgment, David had made the call to the airline from his office at NORTECH and jotted down the flight number on his note pad. Copying the information in his appointment calendar, he threw the memo away without thinking. Shortly after David left his office, a large man in a white lab coat looked nervously around before entering. There in David's wastebasket, he retrieved the note he had carelessly dropped. It didn't contain much information — just enough.

Chapter 11

Hardly a moment was required for David to pick out Cathy waving to him excitedly at the gate. For reasons he had scarcely admitted to himself, David hadn't even told Albert exactly when he and Henry were arriving. Instead, he had phoned Cathy from Florida the day before they left. David could not help feeling guilty, but he hadn't wanted Albert to meet them at the airport. Now, as he saw Cathy, her smile eager, genuine, inviting, he admitted to himself for the first time that he must already have to some degree fallen in love with this beautiful woman, and he knew equally well that Albert would not approve, although precisely why he could not have said. This was a situation the human part of David would have to address, because it was one for which the scientist in him had no answer. Yet he knew it would have to be dealt with and soon. All of these thoughts pressed upon him, not one after the other, but in one chaotic jumble the moment Cathy came into view, and just as quickly they were all obliterated by the electric touch of her fingers stroking his hand and the eager warmth of her kiss. Yes, he would have to work all this out, but not now. For the moment it was enough to enjoy the present and let time stand still. Tomorrow would be soon enough.

David was so enraptured at seeing Cathy again that she was forced to introduce herself to Henry who had stood back, somewhat embarrassed by the reunion he had just witnessed. He knew about Cathy of course, but only what David had told him, and Henry immediately realized that

David had been less than candid about his feelings for her. He sensed the possibility of a wedding sometime in the future, and while he was delighted that David seemed so happy, the pragmatist within him could not help but contemplate the possible delays this complication might entail for their work. He had thought they were leaving their problems behind them. Now it appeared that nothing connected with this venture was going to be easy.

Most of these concerns were put aside the next day when David and Henry met with Albert for the first time. The most immediate task was to select a suitable location for the research laboratory, and resolving this problem became the sole topic of discussion that first day. Albert, who knew the surrounding area well, had already taken upon himself the initiative to investigate several properties which had seemed promising to him. David allowed him to go over the various locations in some detail before finally expressing his concerns.

"I don't want you to feel we're ungrateful for all the work you've done, and we shall certainly want to rely on your knowledge of the area, but I'm afraid none of the sites you have described to me would be suitable for our work."

"I don't understand," Albert replied, genuinely puzzled at David's insistence that none of the properties he had picked out would be acceptable. "All of the areas I have discussed with you have quite large buildings on the premises. Of course I understand that whatever site we choose will have to be remodeled, so if that's a concern, put your mind at ease."

David attempted to explain. "No, that's not the problem, and I have to admit to being partially responsible for leading you in the wrong direction. I simply hadn't thought through all the implications when I last talked to you about our research center. Aside from a large enough area of course, there are a number of concerns that must be addressed before we make any selection."

"Let's go over them then," Albert sighed. "Honestly, I had much rather deal with businessmen than scientists."

"I'm sorry," David laughed. "I know I seem somewhat arbitrary, but my objections are real. Let me take a moment to explain them to you."

"I wish you would," responded Albert, sounding quite perturbed.

"For one thing," David began, "we must be concerned about anonymity. We cannot afford any illusions about how our work would be perceived, certainly by the scientific community, but even more by the general public. Until our initial research is completed, absolute secrecy is essential. Disclosure of the real nature of our work would, at this stage, not just be a nuisance; it could conceivably sabotage the whole project.

"Another difficulty involves access to research facilities. Several of the locations you described to us are quite a distance from London, and I'm afraid we'll need to use the University's library on a fairly regular basis. So you see, Albert, we really do have some specific requirements to meet."

It was at this point that Henry, who had remained virtually silent throughout the entire meeting, spoke up.

"There's another limitation I've been considering, and it may be more important than the others you've mentioned, because it relates to the very nature of time travel. I've been doing some reading on my own, and if I'm correct, travel in time should not necessarily involve travel in space, so the nature and history of the location we select could be of great importance to the time traveler."

"I hadn't thought of that, but you're absolutely right," David agreed. "I don't know how I could have overlooked it."

"Gentlemen, please," Albert interrupted, "would you care to explain to an ignorant layman precisely what you are talking about?"

"Sorry, Mr. Stetson," Henry replied. "David and I have worked so closely together that we do seem to think alike sometimes. Would you rather explain it, David?"

"You brought it up, Henry. Go ahead."

"Well, without trying to get too complicated, the problem arises because, as I said, when a person travels in time, he won't be traveling in space. He will be in exactly the same location, just in a different time. H. G. Wells made good literary use of the concept."

"All right," Albert agreed. "I hadn't thought of that, but I still fail to see how this affects the location of the laboratory."

"If we travel into the future, it probably won't," Henry answered, "simply because, not possessing any knowledge of the future, we can't do anything to protect ourselves. And now that I think about it, I believe that we must travel to the past, at least for our initial trials. You see, Mr. Stetson, it will be imperative that we select a site that is, or has been, vacant until the recent past. Otherwise, the time traveler will be exposed to great risk. Imagine traveling in time, only to discover that the building you occupy has been remodeled in some way. You might find yourself materializing inside a wall for instance."

"But surely old blueprints can be consulted," Albert replied. "And couldn't the danger be eliminated by locating the center inside a large open space, a warehouse for instance?"

"Would you trust your life to the accuracy of an old blueprint?" Henry questioned. "Because that's precisely what the time traveler would be doing. Even a warehouse wouldn't be safe. What if large equipment had been stored there in the past? No, I'm afraid we really need to look for a recently vacant space if possible."

"A large vacant lot not too far from London. You don't ask for much," Albert laughed. "But at least I understand the conditions you require. Very well, I'll get to work on it, and this time, I want both of you involved in the selection from the beginning. I'll inform my people, and with any luck, I should have some prospective sites we can review tonight. We can go over them at dinner, and then, if any of them seem promising, we can look at the sites in the morning."

"Oh, I'm sorry," David apologized. "Could we possibly postpone it until tomorrow? I've already invited Cathy to dinner, and seeing her tonight is important to me."

Albert's face arched just slightly. The frown Henry saw there was unmistakable, although if David noticed any change, he gave no indication. Albert's response was rigid, making no attempt to disguise the irritation in his voice.

"All of your life you have taken your responsibilities most seriously, David. I know Mother tried her best to instill in you a proper sense of priorities, just as she did in me. I must admit all that seems to have changed recently, and I can only believe this young 'girl' is largely responsible for your somewhat cavalier attitude."

"Oh, come now, I think you're being unfair. Certainly I want to see Cathy. I don't feel the need to apologize for that, or for that matter, even answer to you or anyone else about our relationship. As for her age, I have no idea what you could be referring to. She's within a year of my own age.

What possible objection could you have to Cathy? You hardly know her. And if it comes down to that, precisely what business is it of yours anyway?”

David maintained his composure, but the defensive, even belligerent, undertone of his response took both Albert and Henry by surprise, because it was so unlike his normally amiable disposition.

“I apologize if I’ve offended you,” Albert replied, his voice noticeably softened. “I certainly intended no disrespect either to you or Miss Edmonds. I’m simply anxious, as we all are, to get this project underway.” He glanced at Henry, who, as the passive observer to this argument, looked most uncomfortable, and said reassuringly, “Of course we can go over the plans tomorrow. You and Miss Edmonds have a pleasant evening.”

*   *   *   *

The candles on the table cast soft shadows which served to isolate Cathy and David, while enhancing the romantic atmosphere. David had chosen a restaurant which was far more expensive than his limited means would normally allow, but he wanted to be extravagant tonight, partly he admitted because he wished to impress Cathy, but also because he wanted this night with her to be special. Even though he had been reluctant to use the word, everything in David’s mind and heart betrayed his intense love for her. While David had been involved in more than one romance before, nothing in his experience could compare with the depth of his feeling for Cathy.

He was sorry about the confrontation earlier with

Albert, and part of him knew that Albert had probably been right. There was an enormous workload just now that should not be put off. In a week or two, after the initial plans had been completed, there would be more time, but these early preparations were crucial. It was this knowledge and the subconscious guilt it produced that had caused David to flare up at Albert earlier. But even though he had been able to recognize the source of his feelings, he had been powerless to change them. Right now, having dinner with Cathy was more important than his work or even Albert's opinion of him. He was in fact enthralled with his newfound love, and just for the moment it was ruling him. Later on, he would be able to put his love for Cathy in perspective and allow it to be a part of his life, even if the most important part. Right now it was his life, and he could do nothing to alter its power over him. Actually, he had no desire to do so.

The deep blue of her eyes seemed to sparkle with a fiery brilliance of their own as they reflected the flickering candlelight. Tonight David felt that Cathy was the most beautiful woman he had ever known, and just being seen with such an exquisite creature filled him with pride and wonder. Yet he was just as captivated by Cathy's warmth and maturity, so different from the women he was accustomed to dating. Her own feelings for him were also genuine, and she made no attempt to hide them. That this successful young woman, who could have virtually any man she wanted, was willing to make herself vulnerable to David served to intensify his desire for her. She seemed everything he could ever hope to find, and for the first time in his life he allowed the thought of marriage to enter his mind without putting up any resistance.

Cathy was the first to break the silence. "I was afraid you wouldn't be able to keep our date tonight. I know you have a great deal of work to do, and I wouldn't want to interfere."

"Don't give it a second thought, darling," David murmured. "Tonight nothing is more important than our being together."

"I've attempted to be honest with you, as I believe you have with me. It's the way I am, and I couldn't change even if I wanted to."

"I know," David assured her, "and your openness is one of the qualities I most admire about you."

"Then I must tell you that I'm concerned that our relationship is going too fast for either of us. David, I do love you, and I have no qualms about admitting that. But, when you stop to think about it, we both know so very little about one other, do we?"

"No, I suppose not. But we have time, and I'm not rushing you am I? I certainly haven't meant to."

"No, of course you aren't," Cathy responded, her voice dropping slightly. "It's just that, well, to be perfectly honest with you, I'm not sure that I would be welcomed by your family."

"Why Cathy, what could possibly possess you to think such a thing? You've only met Albert and . . ." David paused slightly as he saw the look on Cathy's face.

"Cathy, you're not concerned about Albert, are you? I know he appears cold and stuffy at first, but he's really a fine man. He just hasn't gotten to know you as I have and once he does, I'm sure he'll love you too."

"I'm sorry, David. I have no doubt that everything you say about Mr. Stetson is true, and I really haven't been able to determine just what he dislikes about me, but I am certain he doesn't approve of me, or at least of us. He's always perfectly polite, but I can sense the coldness when I'm around him. You may think it's just a mannerism he's assumed after living here, but remember, I too am British, and I'm telling you that Mr. Stetson simply doesn't like me."

"Cathy, I really believe that all this is just your imagination, but even if you were right about Albert, it would make no difference."

David's look, as well as his voice, took on a wistful, almost nostalgic quality as he continued.

"You have made the same assumption other people have who don't know me well. While I am certainly closer to Albert and his mother than anyone else, they really aren't family. Margaret Stetson, his mother, was my legal guardian when I was growing up but not much more than that. I told you my parents were dead, but I guess I haven't been totally honest with you. Tomorrow I'll tell you the whole story. I'm not up to it tonight. But what you need to understand is that it really isn't for Albert to approve or disapprove. I love you, and that's all that matters."

"Oh David, if only it were as simple as that. I know that's the modern way of viewing relationships, but I'm afraid I'm not as modern as some other women. I truly believe that the Stetsons, even if not real family, mean far more to you than you are perhaps willing to admit, too much for you to endure a serious break. No, I couldn't be responsible for that. I'm truly sorry, David, but until this question gets resolved, I think it would be better if we didn't see one another."

For one moment Cathy looked as if she might break into tears. Quite suddenly as David started to respond she interrupted. "I don't believe I feel like dinner tonight. If you don't mind, I'd like to go home now."

David was just about to protest when he heard his name being called by the maitre d' who informed him that there was an emergency phone call for him at the desk. Turning to Cathy, he brushed her hair lightly with the tips of his fingers and, before going to take the call, extracted a promise from her not to leave until he returned.

While he was gone, Cathy tried to assess her own feelings. She loved David just as intensely as he obviously loved her and for many of the same reasons. Was she wrong about Albert Stetson? Could it be her dislike of him that made her feel as she did? She didn't think so. Cathy honestly didn't dislike Albert. She really had no strong feelings about him at all. He was refined and proper and displayed all the evidence of a most successful businessman. At the same time, she detected an undercurrent of something she could not quite identify. She was not necessarily sure that he even disliked her, but for whatever reason, she felt certain that Albert Stetson did not approve of her relationship with David, and whether he understood or not, she remained unwilling to continue seeing David under those circumstances.

Just at this point, David returned to the table, his eyes blank and his face deathly white.

"Cathy," he began, his voice straining to get out the words, "that was Albert. Margaret Stetson is dead. She had a heart attack in Boston just a couple of hours ago. Albert's arranging plane reservations. We'll be leaving tomorrow. I want you to come with me."

"Oh David, I'm so sorry, but I really don't think it would be appropriate for me to intrude."

"I've already spoken with Albert about it, and he wants you to come. Please do this for me."

Cathy could hardly bear the grief she saw in David's eyes, and as much as she dreaded going, she couldn't think of adding to his pain, not now anyway.

"Very well, if you want me to come, I will. After this

is over, we'll resolve our other problems."

In that one painful instant David had discovered that Cathy had been right after all. Margaret Stetson had meant more to him than he had realized, and her death was to prove to be a staggering loss. He also knew he must overcome Cathy's reservations about Albert, but right now, his sudden grief overshadowed everything else. Within a few minutes David and Cathy left the restaurant that had held so much promise earlier that evening. For both of them this had become the unhappiest night of their young lives.

Chapter 12

Fall had come early to New England. Autumn had always been David's favorite season, the sensuous part of his nature relishing in the brilliant display of color. Even the cold air brought by the first polar fronts seemed a welcome relief from the stifling summer heat, and the frigid air heightened his awareness, both of himself and the world around him.

Today, however, such thoughts were far from David's mind. As he stared blankly, only half seeing the richly ornamented casket as the brisk September wind endeavored repeatedly to dislodge the large spray of roses concealing the lid, he recognized the cold as merely one more enemy that must eventually conquer him.

His parents' deaths had occurred so long ago that, considering the brutal circumstances, his childish resiliency had been able to cope with the loss with surprisingly little trauma. Why was this funeral so different? Was it because Margaret had been the only one left? Not a mother figure, certainly, because she had been most careful to maintain a distance between the two of them. She had become for him, initially an authority figure, later a trusted friend, but never, at least consciously, more than that. Why then should her death have affected him so intensely?

In reality the grief David felt was not just for Margaret Stetson, but in a way for himself, especially for the awareness that it brought of his own mortality. Here, at this moment, the last bastion of childhood, the belief that we will live forever, had been shattered. The universe was now a more hostile place than it had been only a few days before. Only last week the world had been filled with beauty and promise, and David had been encouraged by new beginnings as he saw his dreams move toward reality. He felt confident of his future, a future that might even lead to his ability to control nature to a degree never before dreamed possible. Today, however, the world was full of enemies. Nature, his body, and most of all time itself, all unobtrusively conspired against the frail creatures that went about their affairs, deluded into believing that this existence was real. No, it was all illusion. The ultimate reality — the only reality — lay masked by a pitiful spray of red roses which could not even protect themselves, much less disguise the horror lying beneath.

As he would remember this day later, David would realize that, as far as he was concerned, the funeral might as well not have taken place. His mind sought to protect itself by flitting through a constantly swirling kaleidoscope of thoughts, feelings, and memories, as his unprepared emotions vacillated haltingly through successive stages of grief.

The effect of Margaret Stetson's death on David was profound. Although he would recover from it, some part of him would never be the same again. The casual observer might not have understood the intensity of David's feelings for this woman who had informally adopted him after the first crisis of his young life. Even her own son was scarcely as affected by his mother's death as was David. Of course Albert was by this time well into his fifties, and not only had he inherited his mother's stern temperament, he had also acquired that acceptance of the tragedies of existence which come to most of us simply by living long enough.

What no one, except perhaps Albert, could have suspected was that, despite their widely divergent ages and backgrounds, there existed between David and Margaret a kindred spirit. David was only barely conscious of it, but Margaret had understood that bond, perhaps to a greater degree than she would have wished. The one common factor which successfully bridged a gap of more than two generations was loneliness. For Margaret, like David, had known the pain of losing both her parents while still a child, and she too had tried to compensate for that loss by developing an open and giving nature which was not afraid of making commitments. In so doing, of course, she mirrored the Edwardian values of her generation far more than the Age of Aquarius under which David matured. Perhaps for that reason, she was even more driven than he to make the fulfillment she desired a reality.

David, however, had never been aware of these needs and aspirations that had motivated Margaret Stetson's life, primarily because her own past had remained virtually a closed off portion of her already private existence. Whenever David had tried to question her about it, she gently, but in a manner that permitted no refusal, set aside his questions and shifted his interest to other areas.

David knew that Mrs. Stetson had been widowed, apparently at an early age, although even this information he had first learned from Albert, who had once told David that he possessed no memory of his own father. In fact, when David was a teenager and his interest in learning about the family was sparked, he was surprised to find in his earliest conversations with Albert that he too had encountered the same reluctance in Mrs. Stetson to discuss anything specific connected with her past. Albert once told David that his father had come to seem almost mythological, because there existed virtually no external evidence that he had ever lived, no pictures, no documents, nothing to link him with this world. Now Margaret was no longer a part of it either. Was she at last with her long dead husband? All his childhood training and adult belief inclined him toward embracing that comforting thought, but the cold reality of death, assaulting him with its full vigor for the first time, produced a confusion that made it virtually impossible for David to pursue the question just now.

David was jolted to awareness by Albert's steel grip on his shoulder. Albert, as he would have expected, was handling his own grief well, and for that David was glad. He was, however, reluctant to accept the invitation Albert offered to return to the family home, not only because his own grief was so private, but also because he wasn't sure he wished to deal with the memories going back to that house might awaken. But Albert was persuasive as always, and when Cathy reluctantly agreed to accompany him, David acquiesced, lacking the energy even to protest any longer. It was easier for the moment simply to do what was asked, even if his whole being rebelled at the thought.

Chapter 13

The Stetson mansion had been constructed in the early 1930s. While the ravages of the Depression found much of corporate America struggling to survive, the Stetson fortune was just beginning to acquire the legend that time would only continue to enhance. It was to be a period during which Margaret's investments were so successful that some of her associates (as well as more than a few competitors) wondered if she possessed some kind of inside information. At one point there had even been a government investigation of one of her more profitable acquisitions, but nothing out of the ordinary had come to light. Still the talk continued, and over the years the legend actually enhanced Margaret's position, because, by reputation if not in reality, she entered any negotiations from the strongest of positions, the feeling of the other party that she came armed with knowledge and skills that she seldom possessed.

Margaret Stetson's personality could be felt as one approached the huge granite structure and was reinforced by even a cursory walk through the house. For all its size and elegance, the mansion displayed a New England practicality which managed to suggest a strict utility that was able partially to offset the decorations and furnishings which were elaborate, even opulent. Even so, form had been made sub-servient to function. Every room had been built with a purpose, and every corridor or hallway was designed for economy of movement.

Albert and David, who had both grown up under its

imposing protection, were accustomed to the trappings of wealth, but Cathy was astonished at finding such luxury in America. She was familiar with the castles and mansions of Europe of course, but she knew them only as a tourist. She was surprised to discover that she felt the same sense of being an outsider in David's childhood home.

Although Cathy easily pictured Albert amid the elegance of this house, she found it impossible to imagine David growing up here. Eventually she decided that this was indeed the Stetsons' home, but probably never David's to quite the same degree, and with good reason. She would later discover that David had spent relatively little of his childhood in the Stetson mansion. Because of his remarkably high intelligence, Margaret determined that the British custom of boarding school would be more beneficial to his upbringing. The experience helped shape David's priorities in ways that stood in sharp contrast with the Stetson image. When Cathy had occasion to discuss with David the time he actually lived in the Stetson mansion, she would find that, as with other areas of his life, he had for the most part disregarded his surroundings, virtually ignoring the wealth around him, because it held little meaning for him.

The first order of business was the obligatory meal custom seems to dictate must follow a funeral, even though the timing of the funeral necessitated that it be served late in the afternoon. Afterward, Albert had ushered David, Cathy, and Henry into what passed for a sitting room in the house. Almost immediately Cathy felt uncomfortable, although at the time she could not have given a reason. She would eventually conclude that the room was too imposing for a sitting room, dominated as it was by a huge fireplace capped with a massive oak mantle and accented by two large porcelain disks on either side. She was never able to imagine this actually serving as a sitting room. It seemed far too formidable for that.

The four of them remained there for perhaps two hours, when a call came from London. A problem had developed regarding some preliminary architectural plans which needed to be addressed immediately. Henry volunteered to meet with the contractor and hurriedly departed for the airport.

With only Albert, David, and Cathy remaining, the atmosphere in the room became somewhat more intimate. Albert began reminiscing, not of his mother, but of his own childhood. David was glad for the diversion, because just at that moment he didn't care to engage in conversation. As long as he could simply listen passively, he felt he could get through this day with a minimum of pain.

Of course, Albert had never known his own father, since he died while Albert was still an infant. That much David had been told many years earlier. He had never thought of it before, but today he was struck by the difficulty Margaret must have experienced, having twice in her life taken up the task of raising a child alone. For the first time he became conscious of the huge capacity of her love, followed by a fresh sense of grief that made him aware of how much he had taken her for granted.

David had gotten so involved in his own thoughts that for some time he had almost been in a world of his own and failed to hear Albert's voice directed toward him, until Albert's insistent call brought him out of his own thoughts.

"I say, David, are you all right?"

"What? Oh, I'm sorry. Forgive me. I guess I wasn't paying much attention."

"That's all right. Of course I understand. But there is something I wish to show you."

While David had been absorbed in his own thoughts, Albert had opened the family safe which was concealed behind one of the two large ornamental disks flanking the brickwork of the fireplace. Each of the disks had engraved on it the outline of a large sailing ship, a schooner of the type that had no doubt been a frequent sight in Boston harbor in the early nineteenth century. Albert had taken out a small wooden box which reflected a rich mahogany luster and appeared to be a number of years old. The box itself was not locked, but instead fastened with a simple latch. Albert opened it and removed an object covered in blue velvet of the type used to wrap gold or silver objects. He slowly, almost ceremonially, opened the cloth and drew out the small object which he handed to David.

David found himself holding a small silver pocket watch of the type that had been popular in the late 1800s. He could not help but admire the intricate outlines of a nineteenth century whaling schooner which had been delicately etched onto the case, apparently by hand. Suddenly a puzzled expression crossed his face. Albert answered his unspoken question.

"You are correct. The design of the ships on the fireplace was created to duplicate the one on this watch. You see, it belonged to my father. It is the only possession of his we have. Mother only made me aware of it about four years ago. Until then, as I had told you, I knew virtually nothing about my father. At any rate, Mother was adamant that you should have this."

For a moment David simply stared, unable to respond. Cathy was also examining the watch intently, and the question he saw reflected in her face gave the voice to his.

"But surely you can't mean it. This watch must now be yours. Your mother couldn't have meant to give it to me.

It was your father's, after all. I couldn't think of accepting it."

"Believe me," Albert insisted, "with all my heart I want you to keep this watch. Consider it a gift from me rather than Mother, if it will make you feel better about accepting it."

"I really don't know what to say. I would be thrilled to have it, if you're absolutely certain."

"I said it, and I meant it. You have accepted so little from Mother or me. It pleases me more than you know for you to have my father's watch."

"Very well, I shall consider it a gift. But for the present at least I want it to remain here. I have nowhere to secure it, and I would never forgive myself if anything should happen to it. After our project is completed and I return to the States, you can give the watch to me."

"If that is your wish," Albert agreed. "I shall return the watch to the safe until such time as you desire to claim it."

By this time Cathy had taken the watch from David. While admiring the intricacy of the engraving, she absent-mindedly turned it over and suddenly gave a little cry.

"David, look. There's an inscription on the back."

Albert, who had been standing all this time, suddenly went pale, and before anyone could respond, he quite literally snatched the watch from Cathy's half open hand and held it up to the light. Almost immediately the tension in his face lightened, and he handed the watch to David, who was wondering at Albert's obviously strange behavior.

"I apologize if I seemed abrupt, Miss Edmonds. Please forgive an eccentric old man. I had never noticed the inscription and was so overtaken by curiosity, I quite forgot myself. Here David, you read it to all of us."

David decided not to press the issue of Albert's

impulsive manner. Although he never quite got accustomed to it, he had experienced more than a few instances of what could only be classified as bizarre behavior in the Stetson household, and he had to a degree come to overlook it. He could tell that Cathy wasn't sure what to think. He would have to speak with her later, but now wasn't the time or the place for confrontation. Instead he took the watch Albert offered him, tilted it slightly so the light just rested on it, and with measured precision read out loud the words:

Time is the ship that propels our lives

After a moment Cathy broke the silence. "What a strange saying. Whatever can it mean?"

"I must say I'm as puzzled as you are," David answered. "Did Margaret ever tell you how your father got the watch?" he asked, handing it back to Albert.

Albert paused before answering, as if searching his memory. "All I can tell you," he responded deliberately, "is that my father had the watch when he first met Mother. That was almost sixty years ago," he added quietly. For a moment Albert stood silently, apparently for the moment losing himself in a world he had known as a child, a world long since past. There was an awkward silence as everyone in the room uncomfortably waited for Albert to speak again, assuming that Margaret Stetson's death was perhaps at last impressing itself on his normally controlled bearing. Finally, after a few moments which seemed much longer, Albert rather abruptly ended the discussion by responding that there was nothing more he could tell. He then suggested that since it had been such a trying day, perhaps they had best retire for the evening.

Seizing the opportunity to speak with Albert privately, David immediately said "goodnight" to Cathy, while offering the excuse that he was not yet ready to turn in. Under virtually any other circumstances Cathy would have felt slighted at being almost dismissed publicly, but she thought she sensed David's need to share his grief with Albert. Albert perceived David's motive more accurately. When Cathy had left, David remained for the moment uncertain just how to proceed. He decided to break the ice by bringing up a side matter first.

"Cathy and I will be returning to London tomorrow, and I failed to get a copy of the paper with Margaret's obituary. Could I impose on you to send me one?"

"Why certainly, I'll be happy to," Albert assented graciously. "But why leave so soon? Stay here and rest for a few days. It will give us a chance to spend some time together."

Here alone with Albert, David encountered an aspect of his nature that few others observed. True enough, the Stetsons exhibited the epitome of reserve, in their demeanor, if not to the same degree in their lifestyles. But their love for David and their acceptance of him from the day of his parents' deaths had been absolute and total.

While David had not shared to any great extent in the Stetson fortune, he believed his lifestyle had been appropriate for his particular situation. David understood his own nature, his struggle with a large measure of naiveté, an aspect of his personality that needed to be challenged by the realities of life. This was the reason Mrs. Stetson had somewhat arbitrarily forced David to fend for himself. Now with Margaret gone, David felt more than ever that her decision had been wise.

Despite the urging of his own reason, for the moment he was tempted to stay here in the Stetson mansion as Albert had suggested. The house provided comfort, security, and perhaps most of all, a sense of belonging. But it was this last feeling that jolted David back to the realities of the present and forced him to see that remaining in the Stetson home could only have an unhealthy effect. For him it would be like a haunted house, and David possessed the wisdom to realize his life lay elsewhere. He had to go back to England, to his work, and to Cathy, and the sooner the better.

"I'm sorry; I can't. I appreciate the offer, I really do, but it's impossible. Our research is just beginning, and Henry needs me in England right now. I hope you understand."

"I understand perhaps better than you think. Is it only your work calling you back to England?" Albert smiled slightly, his eyes making a quick glance toward the second floor.

David was embarrassed that Albert had not only comprehended the real reason he wished to talk with him, but that he had been the one to bring up the subject, even as David was still floundering for the best way to begin. He returned Albert's smile, trying as best he could to hide his embarrassment.

"You and Margaret always did seem to be able to read my mind. Did you know I never was able to feel I had any privacy in this house? You're right, of course, and I suspect you know very well I want to return with Cathy in the morning."

"Ah, Miss Edmonds," Albert responded as if the thought had only just occurred to him. "I perceive that the two of you have gotten quite serious about one another."

"Yes, we have. I see no reason to deny it. But I must tell you that Cathy feels you don't approve of her, and while, for the life of me, I can't imagine why you should object, I have to admit I do sense some measure of disapproval. Am I wrong?"

Albert, seeming to ignore David's question, stood up and walked over to the fireplace, picked up the poker propped against it, and began stoking the fire. Finally he turned around and looked David squarely in the eyes.

"Your observations have some validity, but please let me assure you that I have never really disapproved of Miss Edmonds. She seems a delightful young woman. In reality it is your own situation that gives me doubts. I would ask you to consider whether it is prudent for you to get emotionally involved with anyone just at this point in your work. Your research at this moment is crucial. Your whole future may be determined by the course of the next couple of years. Couldn't you put your personal plans on hold at least until your present work is completed?"

"But that is precisely what I have done my entire life," David protested, "and at your and Margaret's insistence, first during graduate school and even during my work at NORTECH. Just when do you feel I will have earned the right to a private life? Besides, I really fail to see why my relationship with Cathy should present any significant interruption. My work will continue. Actually, I believe I'll be even more effective because of Cathy. But I really don't know why I'm trying to defend my decision. Albert, I've always respected your analytical mind, but in this matter you're not being logical. I can't help but feel there's something more you're not telling me."

Albert colored slightly at David's accusation, but almost immediately regained his composure.

"Very well, David. From your perspective, I'm sure I must seem a stuffy old bachelor. And in reality," (Albert almost seemed to be talking to himself, instead of David) "I'm not at all certain that it matters now." Then turning more directly to David and taking the tone of a father figure, he continued. "You're absolutely right, my boy. Please convey to Miss Edmonds my profound apologies, if I have, by word or action, implied any negative response to her." And then more softly, directing his words to David, "And I mean that to you too, David. We only have ourselves now. Please, let's not the two of us quarrel. By all means, you and Miss Edmonds return to London tomorrow, and go with my blessing."

"Thank you," David beamed, grasping Albert's hand enthusiastically. "You don't know what a difference your approval will mean to Cathy and to me as well. I really am anxious to get back to my research, and with your reservations about Cathy resolved, I feel more optimistic than ever that we will be successful. Will you be returning soon?"

"Probably not for a few weeks," Albert replied. "There's the will to be probated, and a complete audit of all Mother's holdings will be required. But I will be keeping in touch."

"Okay. Well, it's getting late, and I have to finish packing. Don't forget that copy of Margaret's obituary."

"Oh, why certainly. I can bring it with me when I return to London. Goodnight, David."

After David left the room, Albert stood silently watching the flames dancing in the fireplace for a moment before extinguishing them. He realized for the first time that the responsibility for guiding David now fell to him alone. The obituary of course was out of the question. It could only raise issues which were best left alone. Now if he could only keep others from bringing its contents to David's attention, certainly an impossible task for most people. For once Albert was thankful for David's very private nature. It made his job easier. They were so close now. All the years of preparation were coming to an end. Albert for a moment felt a wave of guilt as he contemplated the task which lay before him, even though he knew (at least intellectually) that he was doing what David himself would want, if he could have been consulted. But that knowledge didn't make his job any easier.

Slowly turning away from the fire, Albert reached up to the safe and once again opened it, placing the watch safely within the box from which he had originally taken it. Even a casual observer would have noticed that the safe also contained what appeared to be another larger, rather ornate wooden box. Albert carefully locked the safe, stared at it momentarily, and then turned away.

"Mother," he said aloud softly, "I have always endeavored to follow your instructions even without fully understanding why, but until today I never appreciated how difficult it must have been for you all these years. I pray what I'm doing is right."

After a moment he methodically turned out the remaining lights and slowly mounted the steps. For the first time in his life Albert Stetson felt old, and the death of his mother had little to do with the feeling.

Chapter 14
London
1967

Almost eight months had passed since Margaret Stetson's death, and time, along with the insistent demands that life forces on the living, produced the desired effect upon David. He had in reality been fortunate that two simultaneous preoccupations, his work and Cathy, had forced him quickly back into the normal stream of his life, providing little opportunity for grief to take hold.

Final approval of a site for the laboratory had to be delayed until Albert could return to London, but David and Henry made good use of the time and had all but made their choice. When Albert arrived, all that was required was the formality of his approval to release the funds required to purchase the land. The property they selected met virtually all of David and Henry's requirements. During Albert's absence Henry had assumed the task of beginning the negotiations, and on his return Albert had been impressed that a scientist could find an ideal location, and at such a moderate cost. The property was located in an industrial area about twenty miles outside of London. It included a sufficiently large building which had only been built in 1962 which everyone agreed was recent enough not to present any danger. A review of the site plans disclosed that the land had been vacant before that for at least 150 years. This was as far back as records could be verified, but it seemed sufficient for the initial experiments. The building was a single story brick structure which had previously been used as a distribution warehouse. It had no internal walls or other barriers. Although it would require extensive renovation, very little structural alteration would be necessary.

Meanwhile, David and Cathy were obviously very much in love. Although no engagement had been announced, no one who knew either of them would have been surprised to see Cathy wearing a ring. Henry, knowing the deep grief David had experienced after Margaret Stetson's death, was happy to see the romance developing and was in fact actively encouraging it. Albert's feelings about the blossoming romance never seemed to surface. David knew him well enough to realize that his silence meant something, but Albert kept whatever reservations he may have had to himself, and he was forced to admit that David had been right in at least one respect. Far from impeding their work, his love for Cathy provided David a sense of security and belonging which he much needed, and as far as anyone could determine his research was totally unaffected.

David had agreed (although the idea originated with Albert) not to inform Cathy of the true nature of his work in London, at least not yet. Albert had been adamant from the beginning that the fewer people who were aware of the real purpose of their project the better. Although David felt badly about keeping secrets from Cathy, he understood the necessity for it and reluctantly acquiesced to Albert's wishes.

Albert's influence was invaluable in speeding up the architectural plans and building permits, and within six months the warehouse had been transformed into a skeleton of what would become a first-rate, although inconspicuous, research facility.

Before any equipment or supplies were delivered,

one part of the laboratory was sectioned off. This was designed to become the area from which the time traveler would begin the journey and to which he would return. In the interest of security all three men agreed that this portion of the laboratory should be completed before any other work was begun, so that it would appear (at least until near the completion of the research) to be nothing more than a small freestanding closet or storage area. Confidentiality was essential. Loose talk by curious workers had the potential for destroying the whole project. Another two months were required to install the equipment and obtain necessary supplies, so it was late May 1967, before serious work was begun. The bulk of the research was to take almost two-and-a-half years to complete, but before it was concluded the project would encounter two separate obstacles, both of which would threaten to terminate the experiment.

One was another conflict between David and Henry. While their disagreement proved to be short-lived and did not materially affect the work, it was perhaps most significant, because the subject of their argument would ultimately prove to be far more relevant than either of them could possibly have suspected.

The second would be a little longer in coming, but was to be even more threatening, and not just to the attempt at time travel. Before that threat ended, four people would be dead.

Chapter 15
March 1969

"Honestly, David, I don't believe you have any conception how exasperating your behavior can be. Here we are, two years into our research, having spent in excess of three million dollars, and you're threatening to stop the whole project because of some theoretical danger that likely exists only in your obviously overworked imagination."

David and Henry were at odds with one another again, only this time the stakes were higher than ever, and David had become a more formidable opponent than Henry was accustomed to dealing with. Recognizing Henry's outburst as nothing more than one more instance of his characteristic Texas temper, David chose to let him vent his frustration, knowing that any discussion would be pointless until Henry was willing to listen. After a moment of embarrassing silence on Henry's part, David continued.

"All right, I understand you're concerned about the future of our work. Believe me, Henry, so am I. You seem to be forgetting who originated this project in the first place. I, of all people, have no desire to sabotage what we've done, nor do I wish to stop our experiment. But I do have a real concern about what we're doing, and it could potentially affect not just our work, but the future or even the present existence of the entire world. You may call it imagination if you like, but that doesn't make the potential for disaster any less real. Don't forget that all scientific truth begins as speculation. Whether you agree with me or not, we are going to deal with this possibility, or I am prepared to end this whole project right now."

Henry wasn't used to this new confidence he saw in David, although he had seen it developing over the past two years. The first few months after Margaret Stetson's death had been trying for David, but they had also forced him to face some of the unpleasant realities of life from which his background had partially sheltered him. Then there was Cathy. If there could have been any doubt that David truly loved her, the effect she had on him had completely dispelled any reservations. Even Albert did not dare voice any opposition, at least in David's presence. The end result was that he had become far more forceful and self-assured than he had ever been before, and even though his assertiveness sometimes resulted in conflict, in his heart Henry was glad to see this new David.

Still apprehensive, but momentarily subdued by David's threat to withdraw from the experiment, Henry grudgingly acquiesced to David's demand.

"Very well, I'm willing to listen. But please, let's approach this problem like any other we are likely to encounter, without threats or coercion. No more talk of stopping our work. Okay?"

"That's better," David agreed. "At least now we can discuss the issue intelligently which, by the way, we never really have. Perhaps I was a bit hasty to suggest right away that our work might not continue. We never really got beyond that barrier, and I'll accept the responsibility for that. The question which both of us should have anticipated long before now only becomes a problem if we succeed."

"You do possess an annoying habit of speaking in riddles," Henry interrupted, his exasperation obvious. "Would you please explain to me how a successful experiment can present a problem?"

"In the same way that the Manhattan Project could have been 'successful,' but in the wrong place or at the wrong time. Without proper safeguards the whole Manhattan facility could have become a nuclear waste heap, along with the rest of New York. I'm concerned that if we aren't careful, the misdirected results of time travel could produce consequences potentially even more devastating."

"Will you get to the point?" Henry insisted, quite frustrated at what he felt to be David's stalling. "How could what we are doing possibly pose a threat to anyone, except I suppose the person who actually attempts time travel?"

David tried to respond calmly, hoping by doing so he could keep Henry's temper under control.

"The danger exists precisely because we have determined to go to the past rather than the future. Our whole body of research so far has been predicated on the assumption that our initial journeys in time will be to the past, and for sound reasons. Traveling back in time dramatically lessens the danger to the time traveler, just because the past is, within limits, a known commodity. And that's what frightens me about our project. Suppose we are successful, and we do transport someone back in time. Isn't it theoretically possible for that person to do something, either consciously or unconsciously, which might change the past as we know it? And if the past is altered, the future — our present — might also be endangered. The results could be catastrophic precisely because there are so many dominoes linking the past to the present. If someone inadvertently pulls one out in the past, who can predict how that action might affect the future?"

To his credit Henry had not interrupted David, and as he outlined his theory about the potential for danger, the scientist within him was able to suppress his fear of delaying the research, at least partially.

"Very well, I do understand your concern. But from where I stand, what you're suggesting sounds extremely hypothetical. Do you honestly believe the danger is that great? The probability of our doing anything to change the past seems rather remote. Besides, we both know enough about how the universe works to believe there are probably safeguards built in that make that kind of interference impossible."

"I tend to agree with you that the risk is probably fairly negligible," David answered. "But that's not the issue. However slight the danger, the results are potentially so devastating that right now I don't believe any degree of risk can be considered acceptable. In my opinion we either resolve this problem, or we have no choice but to discontinue our research."

"Stop suggesting that! It's almost like you're giving up before we've even tried to deal with the issue."

"Not at all," David insisted. "And I didn't mean to set you off again. I just want it understood that, theoretical or not, I believe the danger to be real, and I intend for us to address the issue seriously. I'm willing to drop the question for now, as long as you're willing to promise that no attempt will be made even to test our equipment until we have researched the problem in depth, and I'm satisfied that the danger has been eliminated. I know that the Time Portal is to be completed next week, and we really can't postpone that construction. But understand that this problem of possible interference with time has only been tabled. It must be resolved before any attempt at time travel is made. Agreed?"

"You have my word on that," Henry promised. "We've been friends too long to let something like this come between us, and I feel certain that, when the time comes, you'll agree that the procedure is as safe as it is humanly possible to make it."

"I'll accept that for now, especially since we do need to make preparations for the Time Portal. Where on earth did you come up with that name, anyway?"

"I don't really know," Henry answered. "Maybe some old sci-fi thriller from childhood. Like it?"

"I'm more concerned with whether or not it will perform as it's supposed to. How certain are you of that?"

At David's question Henry once again became the scientist, and the seriousness of his expression reflected the gravity with which he had approached this aspect of the project.

"Truthfully, not as certain as I would like to be. Of course the Time Portal was designed to serve two basic purposes. One function is to act as a shield, primarily to protect anyone or anything else in the room from whatever forces may be experienced in connection with time travel, effects we really cannot anticipate. I hope it will do just that, but how do we protect ourselves against something no one in all of history as ever experienced?"

"With the greatest of caution I would hope," David quipped. "And its other purpose?"

"The second and perhaps more important function of the Time Portal is to ensure that whoever is projected into another time is completely contained within a small restricted area. Every molecule of the time traveler's body will be revolving at a speed greater than the speed of light, and the only hope of a person's surviving that kind of experience alive is for those forces to be controlled — hence the Time Portal."

"And just how have you determined to accomplish

these seemingly insurmountable requirements? I know you've devoted the past three weeks to fine-tuning this concept. Have you made any changes from our original outline?"

"If you spent half the time with me as you do with Cathy," Henry laughed, "you would know as much about it as I do."

"Don't change the subject, Henry," David responded, obviously intent on doing just that himself. "Right now we're talking about the Time Portal."

"Well, in answer to your question, I haven't found that we need any really significant changes. The one problem I've been spending most of my time on is trying to determine what sort of shielding to use on the Time Portal. The solution I've decided on is nothing esoteric. The same procedure is used routinely to shield radioactive substances. I'm simply going to have the Time Portal completely encased in lead, two full inches of lead by the way. And there will be only one window, if you can call it that, four inches square made from clear acrylic six inches thick."

"That certainly sounds like overkill, but are you certain it will work?"

"Certain? Not at all. Now wait," Henry continued hurriedly, before David could voice his objection. "In one sense your portion of this project has been the easy part. All you have to be concerned with are the technical aspects, whether or not a certain procedure will in fact work. I, on the other hand, have been saddled with the problem of predicting how the human body will react when subjected to forces about which we know virtually nothing, forces that don't even exist yet except on paper. I'm not complaining, mind you, but I don't think you fully appreciate the theoretical nature of my part of the research. I simply cannot and never will be able to give you the same kinds of assurances about how time travel will affect a human body that you can predict about how a certain transistor will operate. There is going to be risk involved with our venture, David. You're just going to have to accept that."

"I do accept it, and I'm sorry if I appear to be demanding at times. It's just that I want — we both want — the danger kept to an absolute minimum. I'm sure you investigated using other materials."

"Of course I have, but lead still seems the obvious choice, and for precisely the same reason it's used to shield radioactive materials. The density of lead makes it the most likely element we know to contain whatever forces we encounter in the process of time travel. I think it will work. I am virtually positive that if it doesn't, no other substance currently available to us will, and I'm prepared to proceed on that basis."

"So am I," David agreed. "I'm not naïve. I expected there would be risks involved, and I'm prepared to accept those risks personally. I respect your persistence, and I'm sure you've done your homework, although we will need to go over your notes together. I just don't want to put others at risk, Henry. That's the part that I still feel uncomfortable about."

"Let me get the Time Portal installed. Then we will address your concerns, David. Somewhere there is a solution. There must be. We really have come a long way in a relatively short period of time. I know I thought you were out of your mind when you first proposed this whole idea, but I truly believe we're going to do it, and, barring any major interruptions, sooner than either of us dreamed."

"Well, I wouldn't be too optimistic," David cautioned. "It's been my experience that problems and interruptions are the excess baggage of research, and there's at least one that I know of that could cause a slight delay with us."

Henry didn't respond to David's assertion, because he thought he knew David's concern and didn't want to raise the issue once again. What he did not know was that David had an entirely different obstacle on his mind, one he hoped to address that very evening.

Chapter 16

The little pub lay nestled in a quiet hamlet on the west coast of England. From London one approached it along a country road, winding lazily through rural farmland almost completely divested of the accoutrements of civilization. Except for the road, the only signs of human habitation were an occasional stone cottage set off with a thatched roof, more often than not displaying a single trail of smoke lazily circling upward from the chimney.

David and Cathy had stumbled on "The Hungry Pelican" two months before on one of the rare weekends when David's schedule allowed him the luxury of a day's sightseeing. David, very much the sheltered American experiencing his first exposure to another culture, was attracted to the pub from the first moment he saw it. Once inside, the atmosphere of the inn fascinated him all the more. Its aging English Tudor construction, the heavy timbered roof with its weathered wooden shingles, and most of all, the rugged appearance it presented, sitting as it did on a small promontory which jutted bravely out into the Bristol Channel, provided a marked, yet ever so appealing contrast to the hectic urban bustle of the area around London where the laboratory was located. Only two visits were required for him to strike up a friendship with the owner, an amiable widow, whose late husband had been the most recent of the Sturbridge family to operate the pub, which had been handed down through a line of eldest sons ever since Cyril Sturbridge had first built it just three scant years after Washington defeated Cornwallis at Yorktown.

He had discovered immediately that part of him was drawn to this place, almost as if it had been built especially for him. Of course, experiencing the Dickinsonian atmosphere with Cathy enhanced his pleasure, but he soon discovered, with a measure of disappointment, that the pub would never evoke any response in Cathy that even remotely compared to the feelings David derived from it. It was in fact David's place, but not Cathy's in the same way or to the same degree, not because he shut her out, but because she was unable to share the appeal this particular spot had for him. It was one of those areas common to all lovers when they discover, usually with some degree of disillusionment, that there are aspects of the one they love which they cannot fully appreciate and which they will never be able to share.

They were sitting at a picture window, enjoying in silence the setting sun as its orange rays were reflected by the soothing motion of the waves crashing silently against the cliff on which the pub had been constructed. By now Mrs. Sturbridge had informally adopted the young couple and always made sure they were given an intimate table where they could be alone. Although she guaranteed that no one else disturbed the young lovers, she never felt their desire for privacy extended to her, so she did not hesitate to intrude her own presence at least for a few minutes.

"Aye, t'is a lovely evenin' t'is. Not a trace o' fog an' certain to be a full moon tonight. It makes me gladsome to see you young people here. We don't gets 'em so much anymore, leastways not since they put in the paved highway round the village."

David had taken an immediate liking to this living monument to a bygone era and responded fully to the genuineness of her affection for Cathy and him.

"I could eat here every day, Mrs. Sturbridge. But tell me, what about the young people in the village? Why don't they come here?"

"Oh, sir, after they's schoolin' they leaves here for jobs in the cities. Works in factories mostly. And it's not like it's their fault, now is it? They ain't much here for 'em, leastways na more they ain't. This were a seafaring village, it were. Me great uncle, and his father, and his father afore him were all whalers afore the mast. But them days be long gone now. Just a few fishin' boats, and soon them'll be na more too. I 'xpect I'll have to sell the pub in a y'ar er two. Gettin' too old to keep it up, I am. But I do hate to let it go, I do, 'specially seein' the pub leave the Sturbridge family after so many generations."

"Then you have no children?" David asked.

David had come to enjoy Mrs. Sturbridge's always pleasant disposition and her beaming smile which was not at all diminished by the sight of a number of gaps where teeth had once been. He regretted at once his question when he saw the pain it gave her.

"Me and me Alistair had one boy, we did, but he died in 44, at Normandy it wuz, sir."

"I'm truly sorry to have brought up such a painful subject, Mrs. Sturbridge," David apologized. "Please forgive me."

Almost immediately Mrs. Sturbridge brightened visibly. "Oh, sir, there be'nt nothin' fer ye to be 'pologizin fer. And besides, I got lots o' mem'ries tied up here, and most an 'em be good on's. Faces I can't quite forget, nor yet remember neither. I don't complain about me lot in life, ya see. Like I says, I got me mem'ries, I has, and that's more than lots o' folks these days."

"I suppose you've seen a lot in your time," David

suggested, and then suddenly reddened. "I'm sorry, I didn't mean to suggest . . ."

Mrs. Sturbridge released a shriek of laughter that was as total and genuine as it was coarse and uninhibited.

"Blimey, ya cain't be givin' no offence to nobody me age. I'm old enough, that's the truth, old enough to remember when neither the carriages nor the ships for the most part had anything to make 'em go 'xcept horses and wind. Lots o' old gaddies likes to talk 'bout how fine them days were, and they wuz in a way o' speakin', but hard — hard life wuz too. Make no mistake 'bout that. Ah, but I had me man, Alistair. An' the inn wuz a fine place in them days.

"But now look at me. You young 'uns oughtn' to be living in the past, 'specially the past o' a dried up ol' prune the likes o' me. But I sware I can see meself and me Alistair in the twa o' ya. In a way o' speakin' havin' you young folks here kinda brings Alistair back to me for awhile, if you doesn't mind me sayin' so."

"Not in the slightest," David replied. "I'm sure Mr. Sturbridge must have been a fine man."

"I'll be leavin' ya be now, and if ya be needin' anythin', yu'll be a lettin' me know."

Cathy could barely contain her laughter until Mrs. Sturbridge had left. "Isn't she hysterical? I've lived in England all my life, but I'll admit I've never found the likes of her, or this place. Whatever attracted you to it?"

"I'm not sure," David answered. "I suppose it's at least partially due to the very strangeness of the pub, and of course Mrs. Sturbridge is the most colorful person I've ever encountered. The ugly American gone slumming, I'm afraid. But this is my first time outside the United States, and I'm genuinely fascinated by the differences in culture. At least that's part of it."

"And the other part?"

"I feel like I belong here, almost like I've been here before. Does that sound odd?"

Cathy gave David a slightly amused look. "Well I should think it would sound odd, now wouldn't it? What could you possibly have in common with these kinds of people? Unless you're going to tell me you believe in reincarnation, and you were a whaling captain in a past life."

David turned a light crimson, embarrassed at Cathy's playful humor, even though he knew she was only teasing him.

"No, nothing as exciting as that, I'm afraid. But since you insist on knowing, I'll tell you. For all her ignorance, Mrs. Sturbridge reminds me of Margaret Stetson. Did you know that Margaret grew up in this area? All her wealth and even some of her education were acquired later in life. The truth is Margaret descended from the same stock that Mrs. Sturbridge reflects. Why, if she hadn't come to the United States, Margaret would have likely turned out just like her. And she did share some of the same values. How she treasured her memories, even though she seldom talked about them, with me or anyone else. I always knew that her past was important to her."

David paused for a moment. "I don't know. Perhaps it's my own past I miss, and I'm trying to find it in others."

Cathy gently stroked David's hand. "I suppose we've both lost out on our past, and for much the same reasons, haven't we? But David, what about the present? You talk about how tightlipped your guardian was, but can you honestly say you're any more open? I know virtually nothing about what you're doing here, and I don't believe it's entirely an oversight."

"What I'm doing is having dinner with the most

desirable woman I know, and for the life of me I can't think of anything else I'd rather be doing."

"You see, you're trying to change the subject again. Why can't you share your life with me? I feel like you're hiding your work, and sometimes it scares me. I know it sounds crazy, but I have wondered if you're involved in something undercover or illegal."

David smiled indulgently. "A spy or a drug pusher, eh. Well, you aren't the first person to consider just such possibilities. Even so, I'm not too flattered at your opinion of me."

"David, please."

"All right, I'm sorry. I suppose I do owe you some kind of explanation. Cathy, you know I love you, and despite what you're feeling, I trust you implicitly. If it were just me, I would share everything. But it isn't, you see. Henry and Albert are just as much a part of our project as I am. You're right. I have kept the precise nature of our research a secret; all of us have. It's been necessary, not because what we're doing is immoral or illegal, but because our research is so — unusual — that we don't want anyone to find out about it until we're ready. Can you understand that, Cathy?"

"I suppose so, at least partly. But darling, I'm not a scientist, and those things you're talking about don't matter to me. What's important is you — us — and what we have together. I don't like sharing you and especially with something that I can't even be told about. It may sound silly, but I almost feel like your work is a kind of mistress that you go to secretly to get the fulfillment you can't find with me."

"Cathy, I'm truly sorry if I have given you any reason to doubt my love for you. Yes, my work is important to me. I won't deny that. And right now it's also quite demanding. But darling, nothing can come between you and me.

"And you know what," David mused, looking around at the little pub, "I believe that's another reason I like this place so much. It seems so permanent, and that's what I've been looking for all my life, something — someone — whose love would endure. And I think I've found her."

While he was speaking, David had reached unobtrusively inside his coat pocket to bring out a small velvet covered box.

"I've had this for over a month. I've been waiting for the right moment, and partially because of something that happened at work today, I think that time has come. Cathy, you have expressed your concern that I haven't been willing to share my life fully with you. Tonight I want to do exactly that. Cathy, will you marry me?"

The dim lamp in a chandelier overhead served to focus the light reflected by the shimmering solitaire David held. For a moment time stood still for David as he searched Cathy's face for an answer, but what he seemed to detect most was confusion. No longer as confident and assertive, she continued to gaze unrelentingly at the ring David held out to her. After waiting five more seconds, that seemed an eternity, David forced the issue.

"Come now, darling. This can't have been a surprise. If anything, I should have asked you long ago."

At his words Cathy finally looked up squarely at David. The confusion was still there, but also a tinge of something else that seemed at least not to be rejection.

"David," she made an attempt at a laugh, although her words came out quite subdued, "you have a great deal to learn about women. A proposal of marriage is always something of a surprise, no matter how much a woman may have anticipated it, even longed for it. Can this really be happening?"

"I've made no secret of my love for you, and I believe you love me. Time won't alter that. Why put it off? Unless I've been wrong about your feelings for me."

"Oh, no! You know it isn't that. And you're right. There really is no reason to delay. Of course I'll marry you, darling."

Cathy leaned over for a lingering kiss that held promise of going on for some time, but after a moment Mrs. Sturbridge was at the table, a wide grin betraying her delight at what she had evidently observed.

"My, my, it don't take no eddicated person ta know whut's been a 'appn'in here tonight, it don't. This be a joyful occasion I'm a thinkin'."

"Indeed it is, Mrs. Sturbridge," David answered smiling. "I've been trying to soften this cold British heart for some time now, and I do believe that what finally did it was your steak and kidney pie."

"Pshaw, how you do go on, sir. Seems most o' you Yanks be charmin' 'nough ta get most anythin' ya want 'thout needin' no 'elp from the likes o' me."

Thoroughly enjoying Mrs. Sturbridge's provincial charm, David (after first giving Cathy a side glance to make sure she wasn't put out) decided to bait her some more. "So you're an expert on Yanks, eh? And how many Americans have you met, Mrs. Sturbridge?"

"Well, ya have got me there, sir, now ain't ya. True t'is, I don't be getting too many tursts, as ya might say comin' ta me pub. But I did now durin' the wars, both an 'em. I had me share o' troublesome on's, that's fer sartin. But mostly I liked 'em. They wuz like you, sir. Enjoyed their livin' they did, just like me an Alistair always done. Why ya know I hadn' thought on it for nigh fifty years now, but the very first Yank I remember come in me pub some years afore the war, the first 'on ya know. Me and Alistair had just been wedded a few months, an why I r'collect him so is that he wuz like you in some ways. Got hisself engaged to an English girl right here in me pub, he did. Cain't picture him, it bein' so long ago, ya see, but ya r'min me o' 'im sir, if yur no mindin' me sayin' so."

"Not in the least. I just hope Cathy and I can maintain our love for each other as well as you and your husband obviously did. But you ought to write down the things you remember sometime. You really have experienced so much you know."

"Oh, sir, I cain't write so well, and I do just 'nough cipherin' ta keep me tallies straight. But I do remember, an that's a fact. But if I may be so bold, it do pleasure me that me pub began with a weddin' and now it looks like it'll come close ta endin' with one."

After David and Cathy left, Mrs. Sturbridge kept thinking about the evening and her conversation with David. Such a nice young couple. But there was something about David she couldn't quite place, something that almost came up to her simple level of consciousness, but then sank down again into the recesses of her vast store of memories. But he certainly was a pleasant young man, she thought, so much like that first Yank she had met so many years before.

Chapter 17
June 1969

David was scheduled to return today, and from Henry's perspective it wasn't any too soon. The last two weeks had passed with agonizing slowness. Henry had methodically reported to the lab every day, not so much because there was any real work to do, but because he found it to be the best way of occupying his time. Henry was a loner by choice, but that didn't prevent him from being lonely. David's marriage would take some getting used to. Henry was genuinely happy for David and Cathy, but he was also relieved that they were due to return from their honeymoon today. Perhaps that was what made this time so lonely, the recognition that David's marriage forever altered the nature of their friendship. David was Henry's only real friend, and he had derived a particular pleasure from the way David had always looked up to him, much like an older brother. For one of the few times in his life Henry had felt needed, not just because of his work, but for himself. Now, although their friendship would remain, the relationship he had with David would likely never be the same.

The more Henry thought about the events of the past year, he doubted that David's marriage to Cathy was so much the cause as the result of the changes he had observed in David. A number of things could have contributed to it — his rejection by NORTECH, Margaret Stetson's death, or perhaps just an additional couple of years of experience with living. Whatever the reasons, when he saw David now, the differences were quite noticeable, and although Henry was certainly pleased with the changes, he still harbored a tinge of regret for what amounted to the loss of his only friend. And that made his work all the more critical. It had now become the most important part of his life, and it was the one real tie he still had with David that was uniquely his. Cathy couldn't touch it. That was why Henry had not been idle during the time David had been gone.

As usual, both men had almost immediately regretted the quarrel that had resulted from David's concerns about altering time. Their friendship was much too strong to allow a professional disagreement to affect their relationship for more than a day or so. But smoothing the ruffled feathers had not resolved the problem, and Henry understood David well enough to know that in his mind the concerns were still real and that his threat to shut down the experiment would be carried out unless somehow a solution could be found. So with little actual work to be done until David returned, Henry had decided to tackle the problem head-on, trying to view the question as David would in order to find a solution that would be acceptable to him.

Henry felt fortunate to be alone during most of this time, because he was forced to conduct a type of analysis that was completely foreign to anything he had ever attempted before. The privacy helped him concentrate. Unlike technical questions which can be solved by trial and error, the traditional methods of scientific research, the dilemma challenging him now was almost exclusively a puzzle for the mind. There were no measurements to take, no chemicals to mix and observe, not even any mathematical formulas to let you know whether or not you had found an answer.

Finding his mind to be a maze of whirling concepts that could never quite be pinned down, Henry immersed himself in all the literature he could find regarding time travel, most of it understandably eccentric if not utterly bizarre. In desperation he even read H. G. Wells, seeking in fiction the answer that the science on which he had always relied had failed to provide. As so often happens, a possible solution came to him early one morning after a restless night of sleepless frustration. His mind had been traveling in a direction that proved to be a dead end; however, it also gave him a path of reasoning that provided an answer that had so long eluded him. The question that remained was whether or not his solution would hold up to David's intense scrutiny? The clock registered the passing time with agonizing slowness. Henry was anxious to see David, but he was nervous too, aware that the results of this day might well determine the future of their experiment. Although he didn't like to admit it, the thing that galled him the most was his recognition that David held the upper hand.

The clock ticking silently on the laboratory wall had just passed the 10:30 mark when Henry finally heard conversation from the receptionist's area. David had at last returned. But almost immediately he became aware of a confusing babble that did not at all sound like a returning honeymoon couple. The receptionist at the front desk appeared to be agitated, and even though he could not understand the words, there was an excitement in her voice that indicated something other than David's arrival. Just as Henry was making his way to the front, the far door burst open.

Normally Henry resisted confrontation. This time he suspected that might be impossible. The man standing before him was large and imposing enough to suggest danger, but what sent a shiver tingling through Henry's body wasn't due to the man's physical strength. It was the eyes he noticed first. There was a glazed expression in them, and the way they seemed to focus not at Henry, but on a point somewhere behind him, gave the impression that this man was gazing straight through him. Henry was no psychiatrist, but even a moment's reflection told a horrifying story of disorientation and psychosis. The savage expression on the face of the man confronting him so contorted his features that for a moment Henry had been unable to recognize him. When he finally did, Henry's nervous anxiety was at least partially replaced by a deep sense of pity, even without knowing exactly what had transpired to produce the monstrous remnant of a human soul which stood before him. Forcing back the bitter lump in his throat, Henry decided that his best approach was to minimize the conflict in the situation. Burying the sense of desperation he was feeling, Henry offered his hand in greeting, trying his best to sound unconcerned.

"Good morning, Dr. Creighton," he said. "It's a pleasure to see you again."

Chapter 18

Despite his uncertainty about Creighton's mental state, Henry decided the best method of dealing with him lay in downplaying any anxiety or conflict he perceived. He forced a smile and tried to ease the situation.

"It's all right, Anne, Dr. Creighton and I are old friends. Tom, it's good to see you. Come, sit down."

Despite Henry's attempt to put Creighton at ease, he could sense that he remained extremely agitated. He glared at Henry, and his words conveyed an edge of marked hostility.

"I don't believe I would ever have characterized us as friends, Dr. Lindstrom. Your values, or perhaps I should say your lack of values, would have made any personal association between us quite impossible."

Ignoring the insult, Henry decided he should get Creighton out of the lab as soon as possible and the best way to accomplish that was to let him speak.

"Very well, Dr. Creighton, if that's the way you want it. You must have some reason for being here besides insulting me. Why don't you tell me why you've come all the way to England."

"I haven't just arrived here, Lindstrom. I've been in England almost as long as you and Evans have. When NORTECH refused to go along with your unholy scheme, you thought you could simply sneak out of the country and carry out your monstrous experiment elsewhere. Well, I stopped you there, and if I have to, I'll do the same here."

"So, it was you who spread that gossip about David at NORTECH. I honestly can't say I'm surprised, although I am disappointed that a fellow scientist could stoop that low."

Creighton's face turned a livid red, although whether from anger or a deeply buried sense of guilt, Henry could not determine. His response, however, was little below a hoarse shriek.

"You have the nerve to question my actions. I would have done even more if it had been necessary. I am involved in God's work, Lindstrom, and that's far more important than preserving your petty concept of professional ethics."

Once again Henry observed something in Creighton's features that sent a shiver through his body. It was a blank expression in the eyes, a sense that even as they were looking right at you, they were focusing somewhere else entirely. He had seen it once before four years earlier. It was the time he had requested personal leave and had never told anyone at NORTECH why he had asked for it. He had gone at the request of his sister to a VA hospital in Georgia to see his nephew who had just returned from Vietnam. He had been a platoon leader and had led his men into an ambush in which eighteen had been killed or wounded. His nephew had lost a leg as a result of the attack. But the damage to his mind had been far more devastating, and in some respects more crippling, than the injuries to his body. Henry still remembered the image of his nephew, staring vacantly from the hospital wheelchair, buried in a world of his own creation, because the world he knew had become too painful to endure. His eyes had possessed that same glassy stare when Henry had tried to talk to him that he now saw in Thomas Creighton. Henry felt certain that right now Creighton's sanity was tottering on the edge. He definitely needed to proceed with caution.

"Tom," he said quietly, adopting the soothing tone of a counselor, "why don't you tell me what it is about our work that seems so horrible to you."

"You thought you could just continue your abominable scheme here undisturbed, didn't you? Well, you're wrong. I know you haven't given up on your attempt to break out of the divinely imposed barrier of our own time. I remember the plans you outlined at NORTECH, and now that I see the machinery in this evil laboratory, I'm sure that's what you're attempting to do."

"Now hold on a minute," Henry interrupted. "I'm not saying you're right. But what if we are experimenting with time travel? Why does that seem so evil to you?"

"Just like so many of the materialistic scientists today, aren't you? Trying to play God, without even understanding what it is you're doing. But I'm onto you now, and I'm going to stop you."

Creighton had been slowly moving closer to Henry all the time he was speaking and now stood directly in front of him. Out of the corner of his eye Henry saw the glint of metal as Creighton jerked his hand upward. Imagining some kind of weapon, he instinctively reached out and grasped Creighton's hand, knocking a small camera to the floor, shattering the lens.

"You've broken my camera, you miserable . . ."

"And if you don't get out of here now, I may just have to break something else," Henry shouted. "I don't know what possessed you to think you could come in here and threaten our work like this, but I believe you've said quite enough. Now, are you going or do I call a bobby?"

Creighton hastily grabbed up the remains of his camera and glared at Henry. "I'm going all right — for now. But you haven't seen or heard the last of me. I'm doing God's work, and somehow He will show me how to stop you and that upstart Evans."

Henry moved closer to Creighton, edging him back toward the entrance. Still glowering madly, he reluctantly allowed himself to be forced out of the office.

Only when Creighton had gone did Henry notice the receptionist, standing like a frightened rabbit in one corner of the lobby. He smiled slightly and faked his best Texas drawl.

"Well, ma'am, have you had enough of wild and wooly Americans?" A bad joke certainly and an even poorer imitation, but it was enough to dissipate the tension. The receptionist laughed, and Henry broke into a wide grin, the incident put aside for the moment.

*　*　*　*

Later that afternoon Henry related his encounter with Creighton to Albert and to David, who barely had time to unpack before hearing of the incident and immediately heading to the lab.

"Creighton's intent on sabotaging our work," Henry insisted, "and I'm concerned that if he creates enough of a stink, he could do just that. Even if he weren't a personal threat, simply by calling attention to our work, he could easily undermine it. Somehow we have to stop him."

"I'm sure I can bring some influence to bear that should minimize the effectiveness of this man's opposition," Albert tried to sound reassuring. "I have very close ties to the people providing the funding for this project, and I'll have a talk with them, just as a precautionary measure you understand. Opposition anticipated loses much of its strength. One doesn't succeed in business without learning how to handle unsavory opponents, and this Dr. Creighton sounds as if he's quite inexperienced at the game. I shouldn't worry an inordinate amount if I were you."

"Perhaps you're right." Henry agreed. "And right now it's reassuring to have someone with your experience on our side, Mr. Stetson. Still, I'm not so sure that Creighton might not try something more direct, perhaps even violent."

"Oh, come now," David exclaimed. "I know Tom Creighton is self-righteous and thoroughly unpleasant, but surely you don't think he would resort to violence."

"That is precisely what I'm trying to make both of you understand. The man I encountered this morning had only one purpose on his mind, and I don't think he was particularly concerned about how he accomplished his goal."

David, however, remained unconvinced. "I just can't believe that Tom Creighton could hate me or you enough to resort to violence. After all, he is a respected scientist."

"Not anymore, he isn't," Henry countered. "I understand how hard this may be for you to accept, but I honestly do not believe I am exaggerating the danger. Creighton's convinced himself that the work we are engaged in is — well — evil. I guess he puts us in the same category as Dr. Frankenstein."

Henry let out a little chuckle, finding humor in his own analogy. "Now that I think about it, I brought up that good doctor's name myself when you were trying to convince me that time travel was possible."

"I understand that Tom has some strange ideas," David acknowledged. "We've discussed that before. But what sane man could possibly resort to violence over this?"

"That's precisely my point, David. I'm certainly no psychiatrist, but the only word I know that describes Tom's behavior today is psychotic. Believe me, his mind is close to the edge, if he hasn't lost his reason already. That's why I'm not overly concerned about anything as obvious as an attempt by Creighton to destroy our work simply by exposing it. That's just what the Tom Creighton we knew at NORTECH would have done, but the man I encountered today was operating on an entirely different and more primitive level."

During this last interchange, Albert Stetson had remained silent. Now he deliberately set down his pipe, stood up and spoke decisively.

"The two of you can go on arguing all night, but as I see the matter, the long and short of it is that Dr. Lindstrom feels the threat of danger to be real. As much as you may wish to argue about it, David, he is correct in pointing out that we were not in the laboratory. Under the circumstances we have no choice but to act on the supposition that his fears have substance, at least until they can be shown to be false. To do otherwise would be the same as inviting danger."

There was a momentary pause, and then David, obviously subdued by Albert's rebuff asked quietly, "What then do you suggest, Albert?"

"I should think the proper course would be obvious. A fulltime security guard at the center appears to be the first priority. We have accumulated too much irreplaceable equipment there to leave it unguarded anyway. I can easily arrange for a reliable — and discreet — service. We shall have to trust one of the guards at my own building for tonight. The other precaution is one I should never have neglected. I discontinued the private surveillance force when we arrived here in England. I see now that was a mistake."

"Private security guards?" Henry questioned. "What are you talking about?"

"I'll explain it all to you later," David answered, making little attempt to disguise his exasperation. "But please, Albert, must we bring them back? These past couple of years I've felt truly free for the first time in ages."

"I'm sorry, but I really must insist." Albert's authoritative tone reminded David momentarily of the time he had pursued the same conversation with Margaret Stetson. "Whether you appreciate it or not, I will resume their services. We may be thankful one day that Thomas Creighton tipped his hand prematurely. He made a bad mistake today. Let's make sure we don't."

Chapter 19

The voice spoke to Thomas more frequently now. The tone, at first demanding and accusing, had softened. Gradually the fear it had generated when he first heard it was being replaced by a feeling of satisfaction that he had been counted worthy of being chosen for the task which lay ahead. Literally for the first time in his life Thomas felt good about himself, and the more the forces of evil gathered to oppose him, the more he experienced the confidence that comes from knowing, really knowing, that he was part of a divine mission for which he was being given whispered instructions, first only in his dreams, but during the past months in waking hours also, and with increasing regularity.

Thomas Creighton's journey along the road to success in the physical world had obscured a tortured inward spiritual journey which almost no one else ever suspected. The reasons for his loss of faith were legion. As a child he had frequently found himself the victim of an abusive father, who habitually wore a thick leather belt with a large, heavy silver buckle, an instrument he sometimes used on Thomas as an outlet for his own despair. His father's sense of failure was underscored by simmering alcoholism that never allowed his family the escape abandonment would have provided, but just as effectively barred Thomas' father from any regular means of earning a living, so it was perhaps inevitable that Thomas became a convenient outlet for the rage and guilt his father experienced. Thomas' innate sense of survival had enabled him quite early to anticipate most of his father's rages, and since he felt nothing for him except hatred, the emotional damage had been less than might have been expected.

Consequently, his mother had become the sole recipient of Thomas' love, and therefore her influence on his life had been more intense — and perverse. Her existence had been, in its own manner, as pathetic as the struggles Thomas endured. She was a product of the destitution of her generation, a poverty of body, mind, and spirit which forbade her even the small luxury of questioning the lot fate had dealt her in creating her a woman, but which also encumbered her with the necessity of becoming the primary source of support for her family, removing even her capacity to dream of anything better.

Thomas' mother sought relief from her own unspeakable despair in the acceptance she found by burying herself in religion, aligning herself with a group whose intolerance was exceeded only by their fanaticism, hoping by mere association with such righteous people to purge the worthlessness that had come to characterize her life.

While she participated in virtually all the activities of her group, she defined herself principally by her service in tending the sick and dying. On those occasions when she took Thomas with her (partially to protect him from being left alone with his father), he was forced to sit alone, often for hours, forbidden to speak, or even to move in a way that drew attention to himself. So the earliest memories of childhood for Thomas did not include baseball and bicycles, but instead pathetic recollections of shadowy bedrooms, the muffled sound of strangled breathing, and most of all the hushed whispers (which only recently had he come to understand), as the silent watchers waited for one more Caller, whose coming provoked both dread and anticipation.

Yet, for all the terror these images conjured in his

tortured memory, Thomas possessed another secret, so dark and unspeakable he had kept it locked away, a memory he would have concealed even from himself, if it had been possible. It was a dream that came out of the half-nightmare, half-longing of his tortured adolescence. Thomas had just celebrated his thirteenth birthday and had gone to bed early, exhausted but happy, because his father had been out late, allowing his simple celebration with his mother to be a relatively pleasant experience. It was that time of the night when the day that has gone and the day that is yet to come are in even balance. In his dream Thomas was roused from a deep sleep by a soft rustling. His sleep laden mind struggled to wake up, already sensing the familiar fear that his father's presence aroused.

But the figure he saw standing at the door was not the bulky form of his father. In his dark nightmare Thomas observed his mother, treading ever so softly toward his bed, her eyes wide with anticipation as he tried to interpret the enigmatic smile on her lips, along with something else that didn't register at first. She was speaking to him soothingly, lovingly, with affection rarely given within the strained atmosphere of that tormented household. The lonely child within him longed to hold her, to bury himself in the arms she held out to him, but there was that indefinable something that caused him to hold back. And then through the murky landscape of his dream he realized that she wasn't wearing any clothes and that she was bending down over him, beckoning him ever closer.

The next morning Thomas was in agony, fearful that his parents might have somehow looked into his dark depraved mind and known what he had dreamed. But his father said nothing. He seldom did, and for once Thomas was grateful. His mother was smiling and cheerful. She had made

French toast, his favorite.

Thomas locked up his dream, seldom thinking of it consciously again, although he also bolted the door to his bedroom at night. He never had the dream again, but from that day on, a compelling awareness of guilt and despair took possession of his young spirit. Through all the years of his life this sense of utter worthlessness would remain an almost constant companion. Along with the rest of his fellow creatures, he had in his turn eaten of the forbidden tree. And it had fulfilled its dark promise.

The final process in Thomas' loss of faith occurred later in his life and in a more predictable environment. Despite the obstacles his miserable home life afforded, he possessed an inquiring mind which he recognized at an early age to be, not only his strongest asset, but most likely his only means of escaping the poverty in which he had been raised. With excellent grades, Thomas had found himself able to take his pick of several scholarship offers. As he progressed in his studies, he discovered an aspect of the universe more attractive to him precisely because it contrasted with the smothering cruelty of the mystical world in which he had been raised. By the end of his first year of graduate study, Thomas had in virtually all respects abandoned his belief in God, his loss of faith resulting, not from challenges encountered in his studies, but because exorcizing the supernatural offered the opportunity for a life that was clean and predictable. By denying God, Thomas was able to liberate himself from the chains that held him to his mother, from the dim bedside memories, and from the old dream which by now existed only at the edge of his consciousness.

But Thomas was eventually to discover that banishing God from his life had not destroyed the devil lurking within. The guilt from his childhood was still there, eating into his soul, but quieter now and no longer recognizable. It resurfaced after his mother's death when Thomas, standing helplessly by her bedside, was transformed once again into the little boy cowering in the corner. As he listened to her continuing struggle to capture one more breath, the whispered groans of pain as one part of her body demanded its own independence, regardless of the effect on the organism which was his mother, he too experienced the unbearable conflict of dreading the arrival of Death, even as part of him longed for its appearance.

By then Thomas had been working at NORTECH for more than four years. Although no one suspected, it was shortly after his mother's death that Thomas first heard the voice speaking to him. Initially it was unrecognizable, only a whisper that he could ignore if he chose. He heard it only twice the first year and perhaps three or four times the second; however, this was enough to cause him to abandon the skepticism which had characterized his adult life and revert to the strict supernaturalism of his youth. The voice had become audible and understandable. It comforted, it threatened; most of all it commanded. It was the voice of God, but the tone was one he recognized from earliest childhood.

For the first time he understood why his life had taken the direction it had. His childhood, his dream, even his studies in physics and the temporary loss of faith had been preordained. He had been chosen and guided for one purpose, one task, which would earn redemption and prove him worthy. The devil was using two men to attempt to destroy the order of the universe, and Thomas Creighton was the only one who could ensure that they failed. Today he had confronted one of the enemies and offered him the opportunity to abandon the fiendish scheme, but Lindstrom had refused, as Thomas had known he would. Now his way was clear. The only question was how best to accomplish his work. So far the voice was silent, so Thomas must wait. For how long he did not know — a week, a month, a year? No matter. When the time came, the voice would tell him what to do, and he would be ready. He was God's instrument, unfettered by law, convention, by any constraints of human justice or morality, and he would succeed whatever the cost.

Chapter 20

As far as anyone was able to determine Thomas Creighton had disappeared. The security guards put in place reported no activity even remotely suspicious, nor had Creighton made any further attempt to contact anyone connected with the project. Albert even hired a private detective in a futile attempt to locate Creighton, but he too came up empty. The only thing of which anyone could be certain was that Creighton was still in Britain somewhere. The detective checked international departures regularly, but Creighton had made no attempt to leave the country. Had he monitored international arrivals, he might have discovered the lead that could have averted tragedy.

*   *   *   *

After two weeks of searching, Albert gave up and decided to wait for Creighton to make another move, if he ever did, never suspecting that Creighton had buried himself in a cheap flat in the heart of London, after deciding to use the devil to fight the devil. That was when Creighton had sent a telegram to the United States. He didn't have to wait long.

Even with the excitement Creighton's interruption had created, David and Henry were anxious to get back to work. Progress was being made, but time had been lost because of David and Cathy's honeymoon. There remained the, as yet unresolved, obstacle that needed to be satisfied before David would agree to move forward, and Henry had determined that this was to be the day to attempt to put that problem to bed. He hoped he was ready, but he hadn't been this nervous since his and David's last meeting with NORTECH. He desperately wanted to avoid a similar ending. When David arrived that morning, Henry had already determined to confront the issue, but first he wanted to be certain David was in a receptive mood.

"Good morning, David." His tone sounded artificial, and he knew it. "With everything that's been happening, I didn't even get a chance to ask how you and Cathy enjoyed Scotland."

"It was absolutely breathtaking, Henry. Up until now London was practically all of Britain I had seen. I must admit I fell in love with the little villages and even the bleak landscapes of northern Scotland. We stayed in an inn that was a converted manor estate. It could have come right out of *Wuthering Heights*. Say, in all the excitement I don't think I ever showed you Cathy's wedding gift to me."

David reached inside his pocket and brought out a shiny metal object.

"What a beautiful pocket watch," Henry observed. "Silver by the looks of it. Very elegant, though not exactly today's style."

David just laughed. "It's not supposed to be. Don't you remember my telling you about the watch that belonged to Albert's father?"

"Oh, yes, that was after Mrs. Stetson's funeral. Did you ever bring that watch here?"

"No, it's still in the safe in the Stetson home, and that's where I intend keeping it. As far as I'm concerned, it really belongs to Albert. But take a look at this. Cathy found it on one of her shopping trips. Can you believe it? This watch is an exact duplicate of the one in Albert's safe. Look on the bottom."

In small letters, Henry could barely make out the phrase:

J. Stafford railroad watch — 1877

"You mean this watch is an exact replica of the watch you were given after the funeral? What a coincidence."

"Isn't it though? And just to make it more authentic, Cathy had the same phrase engraved on it." David turned the watch over so the wording on the back could be revealed.

Time is the ship that propels our lives

Just why Henry suddenly felt a slight sense of unease he could not have said. "Must be nervous about talking to David today," he thought to himself.

"Actually, there is one small difference between this watch and the one in Albert's safe," David said. "Look carefully on the back along the bottom."

Henry looked down at the bottom of the watch. "I see what appears to be writing, but it's so tiny, my eyes can't quite make it out."

David laughed. "It really wasn't designed to be read. It says, *'Reproduction 1968.'* Apparently, the manufacturer knew he was knocking off a legitimate style of antique watch, so he added that phrase to avoid legal problems. You're right about the size though. Even I can only read it with a magnifying glass."

"That's certainly a unique gift," Henry acknowledged. Then he abruptly changed the subject.

"David, I believe it's time we got back to work. While you've been away, I've been giving a lot of study to the question you brought up some time ago."

"The danger of altering time, you mean. I'm glad, because I'm still quite concerned about the potential for our interfering with time, and we really must deal with it."

"I hope maybe indirectly I've come up with a way to minimize (I won't say totally eliminate) the danger. Let me begin by using one of your favorite techniques and ask you a question. At an earlier time, we discussed the feasibility of avoiding that danger by traveling to the future, and that suggestion was rejected. Do you remember?"

"Of course I do. Surely you're not going to resurrect that idea. Certainly, it would eliminate the danger of altering the past, but we decided that the potential for danger to the time traveler was too great to risk traveling to the future."

"Yes, I remember that decision. Do you recall why we rejected that option?"

David thought for several seconds before replying. "I believe we discussed almost the identical concerns when we were selecting the site for our lab. To whatever degree the past remains relatively unknown, certainly the future must be considered an absolute blank. Since we have no possible way of knowing what will be on this site at any point in the future, we cannot risk transporting a person forward in time, at least not for our first attempts. Maybe if the technology is perfected, we could consider it, but that's just speculation. I simply don't believe the dangers inherent in traveling to an unknown future can be overcome at this stage in our research."

"And I agree," Henry responded. "But let me continue this line of reasoning a little longer, because I believe that very dilemma, and our response to it, may provide an answer to the more comprehensive concern. Tell me, why did you consider travel to the future as providing a solution to the problem we're discussing now?"

"Why I should think the answer to that question would be obvious," David replied. "We can't interfere with the future. We don't know the course of the future as we know the past, so anything we did there would only be one more part of the events that shape its course."

"Precisely, and I believe you have just stated what the real problem is. Merely being part of another time, past or future, does not within itself pose a danger. That only occurs if we consciously do something that alters history as we know it. In all the mundane affairs of the past of which we have no direct knowledge, we will have no more influence than we would in the future, or than we have in the present for that matter. Our actions this moment aren't changing the future, only helping to shape it. The same would be true of our actions in a previous time, unless we did something to alter the past as we know it."

"There's just one part of your theory I don't understand," David responded. "Granting that your thesis is correct, why on earth would we deliberately try to alter the past? Give me more credit than that."

"So, you think you wouldn't be tempted? Let me suggest a couple of possibilities. You go back just a few years to 1963. You know President Kennedy is going to be assassinated on November 22. Are you positive you wouldn't feel any inclination to try to prevent it? Or (and I regret using such a personal example), suppose you return to 1948. David, you might actually be able to prevent your own parents' deaths. But what would that do to your own past and even the very work in which we are now engaged? And we haven't even considered the danger of your coming in contact with yourself as a child. When you first brought up the potential for interfering with time, I'll admit I was skeptical, but the more I've had time to consider the danger, I've become convinced that your concerns have been valid all along.

"You see, David, I now understand that time is a cycle that must never be unraveled or interrupted. You must agree, because you were the one to perceive the problem in the first place. This principle is so elemental in allowing the universe to function, I really suspect that what we've been discussing isn't even possible. I believe the universe must have built-in safeguards to prevent that kind of tampering. Even so, I have also had a lot of time to think during these past few weeks, and whether the danger exists or not, I agree that we must act as if the potential for changing time is a reality. But I also believe that we can still travel to the past with relative safety, as long as we are prepared to adhere strictly to a non-intervention policy, no matter how great the temptation, or how insignificant the interference may appear at the time."

"Well, you've certainly done an about-face," David responded incredulously. "Naturally, I'm pleased that you concur with my feelings about the danger, but I'm more anxious to hear how you plan to avoid it. Care to elaborate on that?"

"That is precisely what I have been doing, although you may not have completely understood my logic. We both agree that nothing we did in the future would constitute interference, precisely because the future does not exist (relative to our experience) for us to change. My thesis is that the same can be said for the past. First of all, we don't really know the past, although we like to think we do. All we really have at our disposal are a few snips of history, at most an infinitesimal part of the trillions of individual events that happen at any given moment. The past is almost as unknown to us as the future. The odds against our finding ourselves in a circumstance to affect any of those events of which we do have knowledge must be so great as to constitute an insignificant factor. In the vast majority of our experiences with a previous time, we should be as free to act as we are in the present. Remember, just being in the past does not constitute any danger. That only happens if we consciously do something to change an event from what we know should occur."

"Let me be sure I understand you," David responded. "What you're saying is that the very knowledge that we possess the potential for altering time provides protection against our doing so. Is that right?"

"Not absolute protection, but it does provide a high degree of security. In the unlikely event we find ourselves in a situation in which our knowledge of the future might tempt us to change our actions, all that is required is the determination not to do so. We must in all circumstances act as if we had no inkling of the future. As long as we do so, our presence in the past should pose no real danger."

"I understand the basis for your proposal, but I wish I could feel as confident about it as you apparently do. You'll have to admit all this is rather theoretical."

"Well, yes, I suppose I have been talking basically about theory. But before you reject my reasoning, ask yourself what kind of evidence you would accept. Isn't most of what we have done so far been just as hypothetical? There is, after all, only one way of determining whether or not time travel is possible, and we're not very far from being able to make a trial of sorts."

"I'm not rejecting your idea, Henry, at least not yet. But I will admit that I would feel much more comfortable about continuing, if there were some concrete research or at least some known physical laws that support your hypothesis."

"So would I," Henry emphasized his agreement. "But, by the very nature of our research, that's probably impossible, not because the concepts aren't true, but simply because there is only one way to prove them. Wasn't that precisely the argument that was used against us at NORTECH? They wanted results before research, and we both know that science never works in that order."

"I can't argue with anything you've said," David sighed in resignation. "But this discussion can't simply be reduced to theory. I keep thinking of the terrible potential for unforeseen disaster if you're wrong."

"David, I've presented my case, and nothing more I could say would change it. I suggest you sleep on it, and see how you feel tomorrow. Let me add one more thing, and then we'll drop the subject for today. We can continue to go round and round about this whole matter, but ultimately we have only two options open to us. We can give up on our dream, abandon the research, and tell Albert that all the time and money have gone for nothing. Or we can continue, while accepting the restrictions time travel will impose on us. Since we are both in complete agreement as to the necessity of non-interference with the past, I feel the measure of risk is acceptably low. Most scientific advancements have been accompanied by dangers of one sort or another, and this one is more theoretical than most. At least we will have foreseen the possibility and prepared for it as best we could. That's all

I have to say about the subject for now.

"What I would like to do is move on to planning the next step, specifically our first actual experiment. First of all, when do you think we could have an actual trial?"

"Probably far sooner than you would have imagined," David responded. "Did you have a chance to go over my study regarding molecular stability at the speed of light?"

"Only in a cursory manner," Henry admitted. "I foresee no problems as long as we are concerned only with transporting an inanimate object. Actually, that experiment should go a long way toward proving or disproving your theory. Whether it applies equally well to a living subject is quite another matter."

"As long as the basic outline appears to be reliable, we should be all right," David agreed. "The first experiment will utilize a nonliving object, and since that one will be followed by a series of tests of increasingly complex plants and animals, we should have plenty of opportunity to test the theory before a human being attempts time travel. All the equipment was in place and had performed well during the preliminary testing before I left. The only incomplete part of the process is the Time Ship."

"Ah, yes, the real time machine, if we can be said to have one. Strange isn't it. Anyone taking a tour of our laboratory would naturally focus on the Time Portal, just because it occupies such a central location, even though the Time Portal is really no more than a booth intended to serve primarily as an enclosure for the Time Ship."

"More than an enclosure, I'd say," David emphasized. "The Time Portal is designed to serve two primary functions. First of all, the lead shielding should protect anyone in the room from any forces experienced during the process of time travel. We can't predict what we'll encounter, so we decided from the first to play it safe. Then the enclosure acts as a homing beacon for the Time Ship. By synchronizing the atomic clock built into the enclosure with the setting on the Time Ship, the time traveler should be able to return to the Time Portal at whatever date and time we preset simply by pressing a button on the Time Ship. And of course, the Time Ship also contains a timer which can be activated just prior to the time travel. After say five or ten minutes, or whatever interval the timer is set, the return is activated, and the Time Ship is back in the Time Portal at the time set on the atomic clock in the enclosure itself."

"Building in that timer turned out to be a stroke of genius," Henry acknowledged. "Since our first experiments will use inanimate objects, that timer will be our only means of knowing whether or not we are successful. Of course where human beings are concerned, the Time Ship will simply be operated manually.

"You know," Henry continued, "we really have covered a great deal of ground in a relatively short period of time. Does Albert know how far along we are?"

"No way," David laughed. "I know stodgy old Albert Stetson too well. If he had any inkling we were this near to a test, the wedding and honeymoon would have been postponed indefinitely.

"Besides," David was suddenly serious again, "I had to work through my concerns about altering time. I still do. What you've said today has merit, and ultimately I suspect I'll be forced to go along with you. But I need to be sure in my own mind. Plus there's one other thing I have to do, and I know you, and especially Albert, will object. I'm going to tell Cathy the real nature of our work."

"Now David, you know the need for security,

particularly after my confrontation with Creighton."

"Yes, I'm just as aware of the danger as you are. But after all, Cathy's not an enemy, and she is my wife now. It's not right to keep this from her any longer, particularly if I'm to be the first human guinea pig."

"Now hold on right there," Henry protested vigorously. "We never once discussed who would be the first to travel in time. I know this project was your idea, but there are other considerations. You just mentioned a big one yourself. You're a married man now; I'm not. So don't assume that you've got the job."

"Well, we won't have to decide that for some time yet. We have a number of other experiments to complete before we cross that one. But I'm still telling Cathy. And Henry, please don't let Albert know. I've never deceived him before, but I know that he never did really approve of my marriage, and additional conflict won't do any good. So not a word to Albert. Promise?"

"I promise, but I hope you know what you're doing."

"I do, believe me. Now, I'm taking the rest of the day off. By tomorrow I should have reached a final decision about the last phase of our work."

Chapter 21
October 1969

Ray Harris emerged from the lumbering subway car and quickly looked around. After spotting a "Way Out" sign, he methodically made his way among the multitude of homeward bound workers. Baker Street was one of the older stations in the London Underground system, and the station mirrored the rundown character of the neighborhood which it served. As Harris maneuvered his way through the maze of tile lined corridors and eventually up a steep wooden escalator that appeared to be old enough to have survived the Blitz, Harris began to wonder if perhaps he should think about giving it up and retiring. He had been considering that more this past year. Maybe it was time to hand his job over to one of the young kids who always seemed to be trying to upstage him. Were they really so much younger than he was when he began, or did it just seem that way? And why had he begun considering retirement all of a sudden? Was it really his age, or was it his obsession with this blasted case that seemed to go nowhere, but still kept sucking him in?

Now he had gotten himself tied up with this screwball, Creighton. He had learned to spot them early on, because in his business he met some real looney tunes. Most of them were harmless enough, but sometimes their fertile imaginations could provide the basis for a really good story and maybe even legal protection from slander. Occasionally though, you got one like Creighton. There was one thing about him that stood out, actually that really scared Harris.

With most of the people he encountered, all that was required was a pat on the back, maybe a cold beer, and you were completely in charge. Not with Creighton. His type was unpredictable, as Harris knew only too well. On at least two other occasions Harris had been forced to make a quick retreat, followed by an anonymous call to the funny farm. If he had Creighton pegged right, he was another candidate for the same institution. Not that Harris could let that stop him. Like it or not, Creighton had given him his first real lead on his pet story in two years, and no way was he about to let a case of cold feet allow this clue to escape.

It was a little after five in the evening, just the right time to get caught in the rush hour crunch. "Such a strange country," Harris mused to himself. He had lost count of the number of middle-aged men who got off the train with him, impeccably dressed in British tweeds, but obviously low level clerks, making their way to the cramped, dingy hotel rooms in which they passed an existence bordering on poverty. Already the evening sky had turned dark gray, and the temperature had continued to drop until the slow steady rain, which had been falling for most of the afternoon, hit the skin like ice pellets. If the temperature got much lower, ice or snow could become a distinct possibility even this early in the year. With any luck he could get this business over with and be back in his own hotel before the weather got any nastier.

The early darkness, coupled with freezing rain, discouraged any small talk or delay on the part of the crowds exiting the station, and after walking less than two blocks, Harris found himself on a street almost devoid of human companionship. He could detect only a few hardy souls, scurrying briskly for whatever protection their squalid surroundings might afford. He had located the street described by Creighton. In front of him were a long stretch of row houses which must have been built over two hundred years before and had at one time probably been elegant estates. However, at some point in the past they had been dissected and converted into a long series of ten to twenty room hotels serving the lower end of the bed and breakfast trade, along with a certain number of single men and women who rented by the month. The specified street number, along with a dilapidated sign, identified the hotel for which Harris was searching. Once inside, a cursory conversation with the attendant at the desk, who regained his memory only after Harris produced a five pound note, obtained the room number he desired. He made his way up two flights of stairs, somewhat more slowly than usual, because the cold and rain had triggered a painful flare up of arthritis in his knee. He eventually arrived at number fifteen and knocked briskly.

The door opened slightly. Only one small bulb glowed in the back, and since the hallway was even darker, it served to silhouette the face it outlined, effectively concealing, rather than illuminating its features.

"Dr. Creighton?" Harris inquired. "It's Ray Harris. I believe you've been expecting me."

After a pause that became uncomfortably drawn out, the door opened, and a perfunctory, "Yes, come in," sounded from just behind it. For some reason he did not immediately understand, Harris could not contain an involuntary shudder at the sound of Creighton's voice. Was it the disembodied tone, emphasized because the speaker had been rendered virtually invisible by the inadequate lighting? Or was Harris's reluctance to enter the room a measure of the remnants of his own humanity, traces of which remained, despite a lifetime of manipulation and compromise? As he would consider the matter later, what was most striking about Creighton's voice was that very contrast, its lack of humanity, not so much evil, as it was mechanical. Creighton had spoken only three words, yet they had been enough to impress even a cynic like Ray Harris that nothing he had ever done came close to placing him in the same category as the man with whom he was about to meet.

The room reminded Harris of some of the flop houses he had frequented in the States. One bare bulb of pitifully low wattage emitted all the light the room possessed. The effect was to merge objects and shadows into indistinct shapes. The furnishings were austere in the extreme, and a strong musty odor attested both to the age of the furniture and the general lack of anything more than minimal cleanliness. One twin bed stood in the right corner, covered by a cheap heavy quilt. At the end of the tiny room perched a small sink which also appeared to be in desperate need of a good cleaning. A freestanding closet stood next to the bed. The latch had disappeared, and one door stood ajar at a slight angle. Just this side of the sink was an ancient desk, covered with a mass of journals, books, and papers. Apparently Creighton had been working.

Harris could not help but ponder what combination of events could reduce a man, who only a little more than three years before had been a brilliant and respected scientist, to this condition. But, of course, that was none of his concern.

"Dr. Creighton," he said with practiced amiability, "it's a pleasure to see you again."

"Let's understand one another, Harris," Creighton cut him off abruptly. "Any meetings that occur between us are unlikely to be a pleasure to either one of us. I have not contacted you for a social call, and I have as little respect for you as undoubtedly you have for me. You are an evil man, Harris, in some respects as evil as Evans. But if I can use the devil to destroy the devil, so be it."

"You don't beat around the bush, do you? Okay, I like that. No conning each other. Cards on the table. I need your help to find out what the scoop is on Evans and his family, and I'm still convinced there's a story somewhere. But you must need me too, or you wouldn't have sent me that telegram. So what's it gonna be? You want to keep on insulting me, or do we get down to business?"

"Very well," Creighton replied. "As long as we understand one another. I believe we can help each other get what each of us wants."

"Great! Now, for starters, what's the story behind the Stetson fortune?"

"Stetson?" Creighton appeared genuinely puzzled. "I know nothing about any Stetsons. What does this have to do with Evans?"

"You weren't aware that Evans was raised by a Margaret Stetson? Have you met her son, Albert?"

"No to both questions, Harris. I neither know nor care about Evans' family. My one purpose in life now is to stop the evil plans they have concocted."

"So there's a mad scientist angle to this. Maybe I can do something with that. Why don't you tell me what Evans is up to?"

"I'm not sure I should tell you that. I want you to help me stop this unholy research, not plaster it all over the papers, at least not until I have proof of what they are doing."

"Look, if it's as bad as you say, maybe exposing it is the best way to stop it. Was this something he was working on at NORTECH?"

"No, certainly not. They tried to suck NORTECH into their foul scheme, but I prevented them. That's when they ran away and came here. Somehow they've gotten money, apparently quite a lot, and from all indications we haven't much time. Before long they will be ready to unleash their machine on the world, and the effects could be disastrous."

"Hold on now, one subject at a time. You keep saying, 'they.' Who's involved in this besides Evans?"

"Henry Lindstrom. He and Evans were working together at NORTECH, and they have both been involved in their diabolical project ever since."

"All right, this Lindstrom character may give us another angle to pursue. We'll see. Now, once again, Creighton, I must know what they're working on."

"Very well. I still don't trust you, but I suppose I don't really have a choice, do I? Evans and Lindstrom are trying to develop a machine to travel backward or forward in time."

Harris's boisterous laughter echoed through the small room. "Time travel!" he bellowed. "Are you trying to tell me that two respected scientists really believe they can press a few buttons, and presto, they show up for Lincoln's inauguration?"

"Whether you choose to take time travel seriously or not," Creighton snapped, obviously incensed at Harris's laughter, "I assure you that Evans and Lindstrom are in earnest, and evil though they are, their knowledge and ability are formidable. Given time and money, both of which they appear to possess, I have grave fears they will actually accomplish their unholy mission."

"So Evans and this Lindstrom are trying to build a time machine, and you want them stopped. What's your beef about all this, professional jealousy?"

"How dare you even suggest so base a motive? You obviously haven't been listening. I am doing God's work. I am His instrument to insure that this mission fails. What

Evans is attempting to do goes against the very fabric of the universe. It would pull down the boundaries that God in His wisdom has erected with effects that no one can predict. What they are creating is another Tower of Babel, but on a universal scale."

"Okay, so you're God's instrument. But tell me this, what's so dangerous about time travel? They're not using nuclear power or something are they?"

Creighton scowled in exasperation, stung by the unfairness that forced him to seek help from such a complete imbecile.

"You obviously do not understand. Indeed I doubt your feeble mind can even comprehend the danger involved. The threat time travel poses for the world is very real and far more formidable than the peril even of nuclear holocaust. The danger, understood by all rational people, is the possibility of altering time. If someone goes back in time, his every action contaminates the past, and the results for the future — our present — could potentially be catastrophic. Even you should be able to understand that we human beings were never meant to break out of our own time. Evans and Lindstrom are engaged in an unholy work that must surely destroy them in the end. My concern is that they not be allowed to annihilate the world at the same time."

"You know, this might turn out to be quite a story at that. Time travelers to destroy the world. And real scientists to boot. It isn't exactly what I've been looking for all these years, but it might turn out to be a good story. Okay, Creighton, we're partners. You must have had something in mind when you contacted me. Where do we go from here?"

"I need proof that Evans and Lindstrom really are attempting time travel. Once I have that, I can expose them and put an end to their project. But I can't do that alone. I confronted Lindstrom and saw enough to know I'm right, but I have no evidence. Going there was a mistake, because now their laboratory is too well guarded to get in. Besides, they know me. But they don't know you, and anyway this kind of investigation is your work. You're an expert at exposing such things. You get me the evidence, and you'll have exclusive rights to printing the story. Agreed?"

"I'm your man. Now, tell me everything you know about what's been happening since Evans came to England."

* * * *

As Harris left Creighton's hotel, he could hear the sound of Big Ben tolling faintly for the tenth time. He could use Creighton for his own purposes all right, but he recognized well enough the need for caution. Creighton was undoubtedly having similar thoughts right now. He could still be controlled, but if ever there was a fruitcake, Creighton was one. His mind appeared to contain a curious mixture of fanatical piety and cynicism, both kept in tenuous balance by a reason that seemed to be teetering on the brink and could collapse completely at any time. No doubt about it, Creighton was one dangerous man. Harris had never, in all his years as a reporter, carried a gun, but after tonight he thought he might keep one around — just in case.

And this whole Stetson mystery was getting more confusing all the time. How did it all fit together? For the past fifteen years he had been searching for some kind of story about the Stetson family, something that he was sure existed, but which the Stetsons were dedicated to preventing anyone from finding out. Now, if he could believe what Creighton had told him, this egghead Evans was spending his life trying out some mumbo jumbo about time travel. It all came down to loose ends that didn't fit anywhere.

The freezing rain was now mixed with snow, and the wind had picked up, occasionally emitting a soft groaning sound as it sent gusts through the narrow street, forcing Harris to bundle his overcoat tightly around him.

How to proceed? That was the question. At least he knew where to start looking again. The lab would be worth a try, but Harris knew he had to be careful. If what Creighton said about the security guards was true, there would be no point in trying to break in without careful planning. All he would accomplish would be to get himself caught, which would destroy his anonymity along with any hope of surprise. Albert Stetson presented another promising avenue, but he had tried to reach him before with no success. Then there was this woman Creighton said Evans had married. She might not know anything, but just because she wouldn't be suspicious, she might be persuaded to provide information Harris was seeking. Lots of possibilities after a couple of years of nothing. All in all, not a bad night.

By now Harris had reached the Underground, and as he stepped into a waiting train, he thought once more of Creighton. Apparently he had already screwed things up once. He needed to make sure Creighton stayed out of it from now on. All he needed was for that lunatic to try something else on his own.

Chapter 22
Wednesday
November 19, 1969

The clock on the nightstand read 4:43 a.m. Snow had begun to fall during the night, and the temperature, none too pleasant this time of year under the best of circumstances, had already dropped into single digits. Although David had turned up the antiquated furnace, he had done so only recently, so the apartment remained bitterly cold. Cathy had been awakened, first by the flick of the light switch in the adjoining bathroom, and then (after allowing herself to drift back to sleep) by the sound of the shower. She was roused again, and finally, by the aroma of coffee brewing in the kitchen. Cathy had acquired a taste for American coffee on her frequent trips to the United States, and she had discovered early in their relationship that David was virtually addicted to it.

Their flat was actually quite comfortable by English standards. Cathy, always the decorator, had wanted a more modern apartment, but David would have none of it. The same fascination with British culture that had drawn him to "The Hungry Pelican" had caused him to fall in love with the ancient building in which they now lived. Perhaps it was the two lions standing guard on the gate at the entrance. "Makes me feel like I'm living in a library," he had explained to Cathy. Maybe it was simply that the building was over 150 years old that attracted him to it. Eventually Cathy had given in, since the flat really was quite lovely and well-appointed.

With their combined income they could now afford a better place. Besides, Cathy reasoned that when David's research was completed, they would probably return to the United States to live, where 150-year-old homes were rare. Then she would get what she wanted. "Let David experience his culture for a while," she had decided. Her turn would come soon enough.

The only aspect of their flat neither of them had anticipated was the heating problem. The relatively small output of the radiant heaters that were standard British fare proved no match for sixteen foot ceilings and large rooms. Giving an involuntary shudder, more from anticipation than from the cold itself, Cathy threw aside the blankets and abandoned her body to the frigid air in the apartment. Quickly wrapping herself in the thick robe she kept beside the bed, she walked toward the light coming from the front of the apartment.

"Darling," she exclaimed. "Have you any concept of the time? It's the middle of the night. What on earth are you doing up?"

"I'm sorry, honey," David apologized. "I tried not to wake you. I've spent the past two hours tossing and turning anyway. Guess I'm just too excited to sleep. Such a monumental day, and almost no one in the world even knows it."

David beckoned Cathy to sit beside him on the sofa on which he had stretched out. She came to him with the eagerness common among young lovers and settled back into his arms, luxuriating in the warmth, both emotional and physical, she experienced there.

"This is so hard for me to believe, you know. Ever since you told me what your work was really about, I have to confess I've been quite unable to take it seriously until this week."

"Do you still doubt me, Cat?"

"Oh, no, darling; I've never doubted you. But, well — time travel. It's all so unreal when you stop and think about it, now isn't it?"

David sighed. How many times he had confronted that same disbelief, the illogical prejudice that assumes that what has not been done cannot be done. How could he expect Cathy to understand? Even Henry had been skeptical at first. Then there were the NORTECH officials. No, that wasn't true. It wasn't NORTECH, just Creighton and his own personal brand of fanaticism. Only Albert had accepted his plan without qualms or reservations of any kind. Perhaps that was why David felt so close to him. Albert had always believed in him, trusted his ability to do whatever he set his mind to, and seemed to understand when no one else did.

"Ha' penny for your thoughts," Cathy interrupted, noticing David's preoccupation.

"Sorry, Cat. I must have been daydreaming. Listen, darling, I know it's been hard for you, being kept in the dark and then having something as exotic as time travel sprung on you out of nowhere. If you can just trust me for a little while longer, I'm convinced the day will come when time travel will be as accepted as, well maybe not as commonplace as airplanes, but at least as conventional as space travel. And what we're doing today represents the first step."

"But surely you're not attempting time travel with a person today, are you?" Cathy's tone betrayed her sudden anxiety.

"Afraid I may go on a little trip without you? No, of course not. Today will only involve an inanimate object. But if all goes as planned, further experiments may follow rather quickly, and maybe within a month or two we'll be ready. All the same, today's experiment is still the culmination of my dream. By this evening I should have proof that time travel isn't just a pipe dream. Do you believe me, Cat?"

"I love you, darling, and whatever you do, I'm with you, forever."

Nestled deep in his arms, Cathy at that moment would have accepted anything David said. She gave him the support he needed and tried to sound as optimistic as possible. After all, she understood practically nothing of the principles involved, and David and Henry both seemed so sure of themselves. Then why did she have this recurring feeling of panic? She tried to convince herself that she was just being silly. Slowly she turned her face to David and kissed him, deeply and longingly, both of them blissfully unaware that it would be the last she ever gave him.

*　　*　　*　　*

The light, so intense, almost blinding! And cold, so cold! Sirens from hell, enticing, begging, threatening! No matter, he must continue.

"Don't listen to them. Hear only me."

White smoke, whirling, gyrating in a continual dance. No, only snow blowing around his face, hands, encompassing his body within its frigid embrace. And above everything, the shrill, demanding, uncompromising command. One task, only one. Nothing else matters, nothing, nothing and no one.

Onward, further toward the devil's lair. He can see it now, its entrance guarded by two demons, and hidden by the blowing snow.

"Enter from behind the demons."

Not easy to do, but finally he was inside.

"What now?

"The devil's book. Find it.

"Where? Where is it?

"The heart of the devil's lair. Up the staircase. Careful! Keep up your guard. Here, now. Search carefully. Not here. Over there perhaps. No. Somewhere. If only . . . Look out, danger!

"What should I do?

"Get out! Go — Now!

"There it is! The demon! Oh God! Help me! Help me

— Mo—

"Safe now, safe.

"No! Do not attempt it again. Go home. Wait."

Chapter 23

David thought he was getting to the lab early, but apparently he wasn't the only one unable to sleep. When he arrived, he found Henry already busily engaged in doing final checks on the equipment; however, as soon as he noticed David, he immediately abandoned his work and took him aside.

"Now, I don't want you to get upset, but I think I'd better warn you. Albert is on his way over, and he's demanding a meeting as soon as he arrives."

David's frustration was obvious. "Why is he choosing now, of all times, to interfere? Albert knows very well how crucial today's experiment is. We do not need any further delays."

"I can't answer that. I haven't even spoken to him directly. His secretary just called with the message. But I thought I'd better prepare you for it."

"Never mind. We'll attend to Albert when he gets here. Meanwhile, how are the final checks coming on the Time Portal, particularly the temperature and humidity controls?"

"We were lucky. The faulty reading we got yesterday turned out to be just that, a defective gauge. It's already been replaced, and we're getting normal readings again. Unless something else unexpected comes up, my part should be completed in about thirty minutes. Then we'll be ready to proceed."

"Thank goodness for that at least," David sighed.

"With a little luck we might still pull off this test today. That is, if Albert doesn't try to interfere."

"Now don't start getting worked up." Henry tried to soothe David's frustration. His nervousness was all too apparent. "You know how your temper can be, especially when you're under stress, and right now you're like a coiled spring ready to let loose."

David started to respond, stopped himself, and then let out a small chuckle. "You're right I suppose. I guess we both have reason to be on edge today. Looks like you couldn't sleep either. But think of it. Today is the first real test, the dream of a lifetime."

"Yes, I do understand," Henry responded reassuringly. "And just maybe inside I'm more nervous than I care to show. But today, more than ever, steady nerves may be critical. And remember this is only a test. The odds are very strong it won't go perfectly, if it works at all, and we'll have to go back and correct some problems. That's what we're trying to learn today. Even if we're lucky, and the equipment should perform exactly as it's supposed to, we're still a long way from our ultimate goal — sending a human being back in time."

"I know! I know! But it's still the first time, and whatever we accomplish later, I don't believe anything can exceed the anticipation I'm feeling right now."

"Well, hold onto that feeling, because I just heard a car pull up, and I think we both know who it's likely to be."

A moment later Albert Stetson was past the security guard outside the building and making his way rapidly toward the heart of the laboratory where David and Henry were waiting to receive him.

"Good morning, gentlemen. All ready for today's experiment?"

"Not quite," David answered. "We still have some tests to complete. Henry has already corrected one potential problem, which thankfully wasn't difficult to fix, but if there should be any further delays, we may need all the time we have to complete the experiment today."

"Dr. Lindstrom, let it never be said David can't be a diplomat when he wants to. What you are trying to tell me is that you wish I would butt out and let you get on with your work."

Somewhat flustered at being found out, David tried to cover his feelings. "Now, Albert, I didn't quite mean that exactly."

"Oh, but you did. And don't concern yourself about it. I quite understand. However, you must realize that I too have a large stake in this venture, financially and in other ways. I have no intention of interfering with the scientific aspects of your work, believe me. But I do feel it to be essential, before we begin the actual experiment, to take a moment and plan out exactly what we hope to accomplish, so we can be certain that the experiment today will enable us to do that. You learn very quickly in business that investing five or ten minutes up front can prevent costly mistakes and a great deal of wasted effort and money. So, like it or not, I'm afraid I'm going to have to insist on a short meeting, just to ensure that we are all in agreement about what's going to happen today. I'll pull rank if I have to."

"You know that won't be necessary," David acquiesced. "But I did mean what I said earlier about potential problems. I intend to hold you to your promise about keeping the meeting short."

"Ten minutes, fifteen at the most. And just to keep us from getting bogged down, we won't even go to the conference room. If you don't mind, I'd like to go over the plan in the laboratory itself. I haven't even seen the lab since it was finished. I would be most interested in that."

"Why don't I continue my final checks?" Henry suggested. "That way, you can show Albert around, but we should still be able to keep to our original schedule."

"Excellent idea," David answered before Albert could object. "Henry is doing the final testing on what we have euphemistically labeled the Time Ship. The Time Portal, as you know, is in the back of the laboratory. Will you follow me please?"

"Of course," Albert replied. "But didn't you do most of the actual work on the Time Ship? Why did you decide to have Dr. Lindstrom test it?"

"Just an added precaution. Technically speaking, Henry isn't testing the Time Ship. I've already done that. He's actually verifying my results. If something goes wrong, it's not going to be due to a mechanical or computation error."

"Well, you do seem to have thought of everything. Ah, here we are."

David and Albert had reached what appeared to be a solid block of lead. It contained only one tiny window, and the door was only slightly bigger than a large person would require to squeeze through.

"Well," Albert laughed. "I can see that you have no plans to allow me to travel in time. I would barely fit through such a small door."

David ignored the insinuation. "We made the door as small as possible for two reasons," he explained. "First, even using hydraulic pressure, that lead door is difficult enough to open or close, so the smaller the better. Also, not knowing for certain what kinds of forces we might encounter, we wanted to keep any breaks in the lead shielding to an absolute minimum. Whatever else anyone may say about our work, no one's going to be able to accuse us of failing to take every possible safety precaution."

"But there's only one window, and it seems far too small to get a good view. Will no one be able to observe the process of time travel as it occurs?"

"Not directly," David answered. "We have mounted a closed-circuit TV camera to view the interior of the Time Portal. We'll be able to watch through this monitor, or at least Henry will. I'll be at the controls, at least for the first part of the experiment."

"Afraid you might have a Medusa on your hands?"

"In some respects, yes, we are concerned about the unknown. The forces we encounter are likely to be unpredictable. We decided we simply couldn't risk a larger observation area. I just hope the lead walls are enough."

"Now as I understand it, whoever or whatever is to travel in time simply goes into what you call the Time Portal and is propelled into the past or future from there."

"Not exactly, Albert. Remember, the Time Portal is little more than a transport area, a warehouse if you will."

"A rather costly warehouse may I remind you."

"So it is. But the real time machine, if you insist on calling it that, is the Time Ship. The Time Portal does act as home base and serves as a kind of beacon for the Time Ship, but it's the Time Ship that really creates the field for time travel."

"And just what sort of field is that? I'm sorry, David. I know you've explained all this before, but I'm afraid I don't have the aptitude for it."

"Quite understandable. Actually what happens is that the Time Ship generates a force that results in accelerating everything inside the Time Portal beyond the speed of light, including the molecules of the Time Ship itself, along with anything — or anyone — connected to it. Then Relativity determines what happens. The reality of the process is far more complicated than that, of course, but that's as simple as I can put it without spouting a lot of mathematical formulas that would be meaningless to you anyway."

"Don't bother about that," Albert replied. "You have told me what I need to know. Now about today's experiment. Just what precisely do you plan to achieve?"

David continued answering Albert's questions, trying to be as accommodating as possible. "As you know, this will be our first real attempt at time travel. We have already explained the necessity for going to the past, not the future, so I hope you have no questions in that regard. Today we want to accomplish two goals. The first is to demonstrate that the equipment functions as it's supposed to. That much you already knew. What we have not discussed with you is a proposal Henry made earlier this week. He was wondering if there was some way of proving, or at least indicating, that we were successful at achieving actual time travel when an inanimate object is being sent to the past."

"And you feel you can accomplish that?"

"Yes, we do," David replied. "When we made our original plans, it was irrelevant what sort of object we transported back in time. All we expected to observe was the object disappear and, at the appropriate time, reappear within the Time Portal. What we now intend to do today is to send a watch, actually the reproduction of your father's watch Cathy gave me."

"You had best hope your equipment does work properly," Albert chuckled. "Lose that watch, and you may have greater problems to deal with at home. But seriously, how can transporting that watch be used to verify that time travel really took place?"

"It won't prove it in any strict sense; however, it should give us a strong indication that we have succeeded. You see, what we are now proposing is to send the watch into the past with the timer of the Time Ship set to return it after remaining in the past for one minute; however, it will be set to return to the Time Portal after five minutes have elapsed in the present."

"I see," Albert nodded. "If the experiment works as planned, the clock here should read five minutes faster than the time on the watch when it returns."

"Only four minutes faster, Albert. Remember, one minute will have elapsed in the past also."

"Oh, of course. But David, wouldn't an atomic clock measure the results more accurately, as well as providing evidence as to whether or not time is actually suspended during the process of time travel?"

"Perhaps you should have been a scientist instead of a businessman, Albert. You're right, an atomic clock would be more accurate, and we actually discussed that possibility, but eventually we rejected the idea. First of all, it's expensive and bulky. We could possibly transport it, but not without difficulty. But more importantly we or, perhaps more precisely, I was reluctant to risk stranding such an advanced scientific instrument in the past. In case the return mechanism doesn't work properly, sending a watch that at least appears to be an antique style is far safer than some unsuspecting bumpkin from the past stumbling on an atomic clock."

"But isn't the Time Ship itself just such an advanced scientific instrument?"

"Yes, it is, Albert, and I regret that we must use it; however, we have no choice. My justification is that it can be made harmless by our shutting off power at the Time Portal.

The Time Ship would then become a time machine with nowhere to go. It would be, for all practical purposes, quite useless."

"You two just about finished?" Henry drawled.

"Dr. Lindstrom, I didn't hear you join us."

"Just came up. I've finished the final checks, and all the equipment appears to be okay. Gentlemen, we're ready to proceed whenever you are."

"That's great news!" David's face lit up at Henry's announcement. "Why don't you stay for the test, Albert?"

"You couldn't make me leave now. Where shall I stand? I don't wish to be in the way."

"Just to the side of the Time Portal will be fine until we're actually ready to begin. It will only take a few moments for us to prepare. Henry, what time is the clock on the Time Portal showing? I want to synchronize my watch to the second."

"Just a moment. When I give the signal, it will be precisely 10:18. Are you ready to mark?"

After a few moments David nodded.

"All right, just a few more seconds. Six — five — four — three — two — one — Mark!"

"Got it," David acknowledged. "You left the system powered up, didn't you?"

"Yes, and I set the Time Portal to project the Time Ship to what I think should be around thirty years in the past. Of course we don't know exactly, and at least for this experiment, there's no way of ever finding out precisely what year we hit."

"Never mind about that," David replied. "Thirty years should be a safe number in any case. Where's the Time Ship?"

"I've already set it inside the Time Portal," Henry

responded. "All you have to do is place the watch inside it and set the return timer."

David almost reverently removed the watch he had developed a habit of carrying since Cathy had given it to him. He looked at it momentarily before placing it in a small compartment built into the Time Ship. "What time should I set the return for? We must be exact for this experiment to mean anything."

"I know," Henry agreed. "Let's think it through. It's now 10:24. Five minutes should be enough for verifying all the settings on the Time Portal, but to be safe let's allow eleven. That means the Time Ship will be launched at exactly 10:35. If we set the return mechanism for twelve minutes, no it's now only eleven minutes from now, that should allow the Time Ship and your watch to remain in the past for exactly one minute. Meantime, we set the return time on the Time Portal for 10:40. If everything works right, at 10:40 the Time Ship and your watch will return to us, and your watch should register 10:36. Agreed?"

"Sounds right to me. Let's do it."

Verifying the maze of dials visually one last time took a little more than four minutes. The massive lead door was closed hydraulically and so presented no great difficulty, although it took almost thirty seconds to shut completely. At 10:31, at a signal from David, Henry set the latch on the door.

"What now?" Albert asked breathlessly, breaking his silence for the first time during all the last minute preparations.

"Now, we wait," Henry answered. "David will control the operation from this center over here just outside the fenced in area around the Time Portal. Actually, the process has already begun. We had to reach full power, which we did some time ago. Now one lever will do it. We just have to wait for 10:35."

For the next four minutes the quiet within the room became almost overpowering, but no one dared break the silence. At two minutes before the designated time, David moved into position.

At this point Henry called out to Albert. "Mr. Stetson, we have no way of knowing what to expect now. May I suggest you sit further away, just in case there are any unforeseen reactions?"

"Not on your life," Albert protested. "I have a front row seat for this." To prevent any further dispute, Albert Stetson promptly seated himself beside the TV monitor.

"Have it your way. There's no time to argue about it anyway. One minute to go, David. Everything ready there?"

"All set. Give me a countdown, will you?"

"You got it. We'll begin at thirty seconds — now! Mr. Stetson, if you insist on staying here, you're on your own. Just be ready for whatever happens when David pulls the lever. Fifteen seconds, David."

"Don't concern yourself with me," Albert replied. "Just concentrate on what you need to be doing."

"All right everyone, this is it. Ten — nine — eight — seven — six — five — four — three — two — one — Now!"

The next moment the three men were assaulted by a variety of chaotic forces that they perceived in different ways.

Henry and Albert, staring intently at the monitor, saw the Time Ship with the watch inside become a ghostly, translucent object, just before disappearing. This they had hoped for. The whole process took less than a second. But they had no opportunity to express their elation, because immediately after David pressed the button to transport the watch to the past the laboratory itself was engulfed by massive forces that sent all three men reeling, grasping frantically for some solid object for support, only to find that everything they touched was similarly affected by some form of turbulent energy assaulting the laboratory. Within the instant it took for the watch to disappear, the laboratory returned to normal. Henry and Albert had both been hurled unceremoniously to the floor, while David had maintained his seat only by holding desperately to a large steel beam on the Time Portal.

There was a long interval of silence as each of the men cautiously stood up, after first insuring they had sustained no injuries. They had not known what to expect, but clearly the forces generated by time travel went far beyond anything they had ever experienced. Finally, Albert broke the silence. "That was some experience," he quipped. "What was it, an earthquake?"

"It felt more like movement to me," Henry suggested. "Like being caught in a hurricane, although, no hurricane was ever that strong. Why the wind must have been two hundred miles an hour or more. David, are you all right?"

When David responded, he was uncharacteristically subdued. His voice was little more than a whisper. "It wasn't a wind or even a force of any kind that we have ever encountered before. I think our brains just registered what happened as movement, because that's the closest experience we have that we can relate it to. But nothing really happened in the lab. Look around you. All the equipment's in place, furniture in order, even the papers on top of your desk are undisturbed, Henry."

"Why, you're right." Henry seemed genuinely puzzled. "But something knocked me to the floor. You can't argue that away."

"You threw yourself on the floor, nothing else. You perceived a force you had not experienced before. Your brain interpreted its power as movement, and your body responded; that's all."

"Hold on," Albert interrupted. "Even a layman such as I will argue with that. Something did happen. Why should we all experience the same hallucination? Why you yourself felt it. I saw you."

"I never said it was a hallucination," David replied. His subdued manner reflected his awe at what he alone understood had just transpired. "But I am telling you that the force we experienced was not anything new or unusual. It is with us at all times, even now. What we felt was the flow of time — which we interrupted. We should have anticipated it."

"Oh, come now," Albert asked incredulously. "Are you implying that the same force we all felt in this laboratory is around us all the time? If that's so, why don't we feel it now?"

"Because now we're moving in sync with it," David answered patiently. "Think for a moment, Albert. The earth is spinning on its axis at a tremendous speed. At the same time, it's hurtling through space. Yet we experience neither movement, because we are moving with it at precisely the same speed. Time carries us along in the same way, and because we are propelled with it, we are not conscious of its movement. But a moment ago, we interrupted its natural course. For one split second we stood outside the normal flow of time. We are the first people ever to experience the force of time as it really exists."

"We can continue this discussion later, gentlemen," Henry interrupted. "In the meantime, in less than two minutes, if everything goes as planned, David's watch should return. We're likely to have a repetition of our earlier experience, so I suggest we prepare for it. David, you had better brace yourself at the console. I have to watch the monitor, but Mr. Stetson, I suggest you close your eyes. That should lessen, and if David's theory is correct, maybe even eliminate the sensation."

"I appreciate everyone's concern for my welfare; however, I wish you would cease trying to prevent me from being a full participant in this experiment. I haven't been this excited in years, and I have no intention of missing any part of whatever occurs today."

"Suit yourself. Places everyone. It's almost time."

Once again silence descended on the laboratory, as every man present stared intently at the clock mounted outside the Time Portal. Just before the second hand registered precisely 10:40, David turned his gaze on the instruments in front of him, and Henry looked intently at the TV monitor.

Anticipating what was to happen made it only a little less frightening. The sickening rush of movement returned, and almost instantly ceased, and there inside the Time Portal was the Time Ship with no damage, or at least none that could be observed through the monitor.

"Inside quickly," Henry shouted. "We must verify the time shown on the watch."

David instantly pressed the button that both unlocked and opened the door to the Time Portal. Even as the door was still swinging open, he fairly leaped inside and grabbed the watch. "10:36 and 38 seconds," David exclaimed excitedly. "We've done it, Henry! We have actually created an opening to the time barrier!"

"Well done, David!" Albert beamed. "I knew my confidence in you wasn't misplaced."

"We must make plans for further experiments as soon as possible," David said excitedly. "Now that we know the system works, we can . . ."

He was interrupted in mid-sentence by the jangling of the telephone.

"What timing. Now who can that possibly be?" David exclaimed, barely concealing his exasperation as he picked up the phone. He said nothing, but after a few seconds his face contorted almost as if in physical pain, and he turned pale.

"Are you positive?" he asked after a moment, his voice unusually quiet. "Couldn't there be some mistake? I see. Yes, I'll come right away."

"What is it?" Henry asked. "Who was that?

David could barely speak, as he choked out the words. "That was the police. Cathy's had some sort of accident. She's dead, Henry!"

Chapter 24
Monday
January 5, 1970

This was the second time Harris had met with Creighton, and if he thought he had trouble before, now he was certain of it. Just trying to hold a coherent conversation with Creighton was becoming difficult, and he had a hunch the situation wasn't likely to get any better. For the first time in over fifteen years, Harris seriously considered giving up his search and turning Creighton over to the police, or at least a shrink. But he had invested too much of his time and energy to turn back now. He decided to plunge ahead, a decision he would come to regret before very long. In the meantime, he had to try to determine just what Creighton had been up to since their last meeting.

"Dr. Creighton, you simply must get hold of yourself and answer me. Do you know anything about Mrs. Evans' death?"

It was obvious that something had happened to Creighton. At this moment he was no longer the arrogant, self-righteous crusader he had been earlier. His response came across as hesitant and defensive.

"I've never even met the woman. Why are you so convinced I had something to do with it? The paper said it was an accident."

"Reporters and cops are often wrong, believe me. That newspaper report means nothing. But what sounds fishy to me is your saying you can't remember anything you did the day Mrs. Evans died. If a cop ever heard that, you'd find yourself in an interrogation room in short order."

"But it's the truth, so help me. I don't even remember going to bed the night before, although I must have, because I woke up after noon, and the papers said Mrs. Evans died around midmorning. I've been under a lot of stress, and I simply overslept. Hasn't that ever happened to you?"

"Yeah, but none of my enemies ever got murdered when I couldn't remember where I was or what I was doing. Now you listen to me and listen good. I don't know anything about what happened to Mrs. Evans, but whether you had anything to do with it or not, I want it agreed that you aren't to do anything unless I know about it. I'm going to be casing their lab for any chinks in security. Like it or not, we're going to have to find some way to get in there, and as much as I wish I could do it alone, I'm going to need your help later. But right now I want you to lay low and leave everything to me for awhile. Do you understand?"

"Yes, I understand," Creighton replied abjectly. "But how long will it be before I hear from you?"

"I don't know. That's not your concern. I will be contacting you, and that's all you need to know. For now, just stay out of sight. I think you're okay. If the cops had anything even remotely linking you to Mrs. Evans, you'd have heard from them by now. Just lay low — that's all."

Once more Harris tuned out the small internal voice, telling him that with Creighton he was in over his head. He really had no choice. He had put in too much of his life to back down, and like it or not, he still needed Creighton. Right now he wasn't the arrogant fanatic Harris had confronted earlier. Creighton was a frightened puppy, and as long as he stayed that way, he could be controlled.

As long as he stayed that way.

* * * *

The police could find no evidence of foul play; nothing taken and no signs of forced entry. From the evidence it appeared that Cathy had somehow lost her footing on the stairs and fallen, breaking her neck instantly. There was the matter of the expression on her face when they found the body, but it wasn't enough by itself to warrant further investigation. The coroner's report gave the cause of death as a broken neck due to an accident, and as far as anyone knew, that ended the matter.

Henry had wondered more than once how the three of them had gotten through the past two months. Albert had been more surprised than he at the depth of David's grief. Of course, Albert had always remained somewhat on the outside as far as Cathy was concerned. Although he had outwardly approved of their marriage, part of him had never fully accepted Cathy's relationship with David. For that reason they had tended to share more of their lives with Henry than with Albert. Henry remembered his concern just after the wedding that his friendship with David might be weakened, but it hadn't worked out that way. If anything, the two of them had grown closer, with Albert playing less a part in David's life. So it was that Albert never really understood (or at least never accepted) the depth of David and Cathy's love for each other. For Henry, who could at least sympathize, if not actually feel what David was going through, the agony of the funeral and its aftermath had, in its own way, been trying on him as well.

He was especially concerned when David's grief took the form of lethargic sullenness. Henry had called and received no answer enough times to know that David was simply ignoring his phone, and from all indications, he seldom left his apartment. He had not heard from David in over a week, although Albert had managed to see him the day before, and the report he gave was appalling enough to frighten Henry into action. He decided he had to intervene before David's life spiraled further into a pattern from which he might never recover.

After the third ring of the doorbell went unanswered (even though Henry had seen a light glowing conspicuously from an outside window of David's apartment), he determined to force David to respond. This time he pressed the doorbell and held it down. After about forty-five seconds, a surly voice, which Henry only barely recognized as David's, growled angrily through the still closed door.

"Go away and leave me alone." The words were slurred and not easily intelligible.

"David, it's Henry. Let me in."

Silence.

"Please, David."

More silence.

"I'm not leaving until I see you, so you might as well open the door."

"I don't want to see anyone right now," the voice behind the door answered.

"I'm not going to accept that. You might as well let me in, because I am going to see you tonight, whether you like it or not."

After another moment's pause, Henry heard the scraping of a latch, and the front door swung open. David was only partially visible in the half-light reflected from inside the apartment, but what Henry saw astounded him. The wreck of a man that stood before him bore almost no resemblance to the amiable, brilliant young scientist he had come to love as a brother. David was wearing a bathrobe, which if Henry could judge by its appearance had been his only dress for the day, if not longer. He was unshaven, his hair matted and in need of washing, and there was a marked sallowness in his expression which Henry attributed to the strong aroma of whiskey that came, not just from David, but actually emanated from the apartment itself.

"My God," Henry exclaimed in astonishment. "Albert said you were bad off, but I never dreamed you could let this happen."

"If you came to give me a lecture, you can consider it done and leave me alone. I told you I don't want to talk now."

"David, you must snap out of this. I won't pretend that I understand how devastating Cathy's death must have been for you, because I'm sure I don't. But other men have faced the same loss and gotten through it and so can you. You have to go on with your life. In your heart, you must know that Cathy herself would be horrified at what's become of you."

"What does that matter, anyway?" David was sobbing now, unable to control the fresh wave of grief that poured over him. "What does anything matter anymore?"

"You matter, David — to Albert and to me. Do you think I enjoy standing here talking to you like this? But you must consider where your life was going before this terrible tragedy. Stop for a moment and consider what we accomplished the very day . . ."

"That's what you're really concerned about, isn't it? For you it's the fame, and to Albert it's the money."

"I'll not even dignify that remark with a response,"

Henry said softly, "because I know it's just your grief talking. There's no need to deny what, in your heart, you know to be untrue. I came here to say one thing and to deliver something. Then I'm going to leave. What you do with your life after that will be up to you."

Henry searched David's eyes for some sign he was listening, that he would hear the words he wasn't even sure he knew to say. He saw nothing to provide encouragement, but realizing that this might be his only opportunity, he determined to say what he had prepared to say, not at all certain what the effect might be.

"David, you're very young, and in your life you've experienced your share of suffering — maybe more. Whether I, or Albert, or anyone else for that matter, understands the depth of your grief is irrelevant, because ultimately you stand on your own feet or you don't stand at all. Life forces all of us to grow in different ways, but I've seldom seen it happen without tragedy or disappointment of some kind. I'm not much of a religious man, not nearly as much as you are, or at least as you were, but it's always seemed illogical to me to accept all the good things in life without a word and then ask why we deserve the bad. I don't pretend to understand why the universe operates as it does, but I've lived long enough to know that fairness has little to do with it. The important thing is to live life and learn from it. But enough lecturing; I have something to give you."

While he was speaking, Henry reached inside his coat pocket and took out a small envelope. He stretched out his hand, and when David made no move to take the envelope, Henry grabbed his right arm, stretched out David's limp hand, and placed the envelope forcefully into it.

"Albert asked me to give you this. I don't know what it contains, but he thinks it may help. In the meantime, I'm going to be in the lab tomorrow at the regular time. I hope, for your sake, that you're there too. Goodnight, David."

After Henry left, David tossed the letter aside, and as he did so, it turned over so that he could see his name written in a thin elegant script even his drugged mind instantly recognized. His despair momentarily forgotten, he eagerly picked up the envelope, tore it open, and extracted three pieces of stationary, containing a letter written in the same hand as the envelope. As he read the contents, the ravages of grief that had marked his face were replaced by a look, first of shock, and then wonder. As he finished reading, he slowly ran his hand almost lovingly across the name inscribed at the bottom of the last page and then buried his head in his hands as he gave himself over to another wave of grief that came from somewhere deep within his soul.

Chapter 25
Tuesday
January 6, 1970

Henry didn't arrive at the lab until almost 9:00. Ordinarily he did his best work in the morning and could often be found already absorbed in his research by 6:30; however, after his meeting the night before, Henry had been in his own way almost as depressed as David. David had been his only real friend, the one part of his life that had so far prevented the obsessive scientist within him from completely dominating his personality. In many ways their friendship had exerted a healthy influence on both men. Henry's calm, logical approach to difficulties (a product of intensive, and by now almost habitual, use of the scientific method) had more than once been instrumental in keeping David's temperamental outbursts in check.

At the same time, Henry had been included, sometimes unwillingly, in a number of social settings with David and so had broadened his own spectrum of friends, as well as his social skills, in a manner which his withdrawn nature would never have permitted him to accomplish on his own. In addition, the role of older brother, which he had assumed with David, had been immensely satisfying. So he viewed David's current depression with a dismay that reflected his own sense of loss and the helplessness he felt at being unable to alleviate the pain David was experiencing.

Even though their first actual experiment with time

travel had, as far as could be determined, been completely successful, Cathy's death and David's retreat into grief had effectively shut down the project. Theoretically Henry, with perhaps some minor assistance from Albert, could have continued on with more sophisticated experiments on his own, but no such steps had been taken. Despite David's biting accusation of his and Albert's motives, neither he nor Albert felt inclined to continue until David could be persuaded to participate. In fact, Henry had at one time actually made just that suggestion to Albert, because of the mounting costs which continued to accrue, even though no real work was going on. He had been surprised at the vehemence of Albert's insistence that no experiments be conducted without David being present. At the time Henry had been somewhat embarrassed at being made to feel insensitive to David, but as he considered the confrontation later on, Albert's outburst had seemed extreme. Ultimately he characterized the episode as one more example of the enigmatic character of Albert Stetson.

It was already well after noon, and Henry would normally have gone to lunch, but he had gotten so completely absorbed in his work that be failed to hear the door to the lab open. Only when he heard his name called, did he turn to see David standing before him.

"Do you still want a partner?" he asked, not shyly as Henry might have expected, but matter-of-factly.

Henry understood David perhaps better than any other living person, and he could tell immediately that somehow David had come through his battle a winner. It wasn't really the old David standing before him. As Henry would soon discover, that man had in some sense died with Cathy. The process of molding the new David that had begun with the death of Margaret Stetson had somehow been completed by the further tragedy of Cathy's death, and by it David had gained the strength he was to need, even though none of them knew it yet. The change was, Henry felt, decidedly unnerving.

"David!" Henry exclaimed, ignoring the question and the implied apology contained within it. "You don't know how glad I am to see you. I'll admit when I left last night, I didn't feel like I had gotten through to you. And you're looking well too."

"Thanks for being tactful, Henry. A shower and shave do help, and not just my appearance, but I know I still look awful. For one thing I've been doing far more drinking than eating lately. Why don't we get some lunch? I'm starved."

"Great idea. Something with plenty of calories and little nutrition," Henry suggested enthusiastically.

"I have a better idea, Henry. I called Albert, and he's on his way over. Why don't we let him treat us to the kind of place only he can afford. I need to talk to both of you anyway."

Even though it meant effectively closing the lab for the day, Albert had insisted on taking David and Henry to the Dorchester located in the fashionable Mayfair section of London. Immediately recognizing Albert as a frequent patron, the maitre d' promptly escorted the three men to a table somewhat isolated from the crowd where they could talk in relative privacy. After they had ordered, there was an awkward silence as Henry and Albert, as if by tacit agreement, waited for David to begin. His first words confirmed Henry's initial impression.

"First of all, I owe both of you an apology, as well as my gratitude, for waiting me out. I know I've put a real test on our friendship, and I'm sorry for it."

"Look, David, you don't have to explain anything."

"No, Henry, I need both of you to understand something of what I've been going through the past couple of months. You see, it wasn't just my love for Cathy. She had brought out a part of me that I had never allowed to surface. Henry, you're a scientist because you love science. I'm a scientist because I love the protective solitude the work provides."

"I don't understand," Henry seemed genuinely puzzled. "Ever since I've known you, you were one of the most social men at NORTECH."

"Social? Yes, I suppose I was, but only in a superficial way. I went to parties and had a number of friends, but except for you, none of my friendships had any depth. I lacked any real commitment, because I was afraid of it. That's supposed to be my generation's hang-up, isn't it?"

"And Miss Ed — Cathy changed that?" Albert asked softly.

"Yes, she did. Albert, you grew up without a father. Even though you had everything you needed, didn't that create a vacuum in your life, or at least have some effect?"

"More than you can possibly know." Albert's response was remarkably sober, especially for him. "Of course you had grown up without either of your parents."

"Yes, I did, and when Margaret died, I felt more alone than ever. Thank goodness I had already determined to marry Cathy when that happened, or I would have wondered if I was using our relationship to try to make up for that loss. But I know now that I wasn't. My love for Cathy was real, and it freed me from my constant quest for security. Then when she died, for awhile anyway, my life just tumbled in. I didn't like what I had become. I just couldn't find the strength to change it."

"What finally brought you out of your grief?" Henry asked. "Did it have anything to do with the envelope Albert had asked me to give you?"

David's expression didn't change at Henry's question, but there was something, perhaps the slightest shifting of the eyes that made Henry feel David's mind was rehearsing his answer, that there was more than he was prepared to tell.

"Perhaps it's too simple to put it all down to the letter. I think I would have come out of my depression eventually, but Margaret's letter forced me to take an honest look at myself. I did that last night."

"What was in that letter, anyway," Henry turned to ask Albert, "and when was it written?"

"Strangely enough, I do not know the answers to either of your questions," Albert responded. "Sometime before Mother died, she gave me the letter with instructions to give it to David at any time he seemed in need of help or advice. That's all I can tell you. However, if Mother's letter somehow was able to reach you, David, that's all that's important."

"Thank you, Albert, and if you don't mind, Henry, the letter was private. I wish to keep it that way."

"Now, as Henry told me last night, I need to get on with my life, and I believe the best way to do that is for us to continue our work. Have you conducted any more trips into the past?"

"No, we haven't," Henry responded. "We considered another experiment, but Albert isn't really qualified to assist, and time travel is a two man job. Besides, this whole project was yours from its inception. Neither Albert nor I felt it was right to proceed without you."

David, remembering his accusation from the night

before, colored slightly. "Well, I'm back now, and we've lost enough time. We need to accelerate our program to make up for the delays. How soon do you think we could make another experiment?"

"I've made sure that the equipment has been maintained properly, but a complete check of the entire system will still be required," Henry answered.

"Before we begin the system check," David continued, "I suggest we outline a schedule for the next experiments. Now that we have fairly well established that time travel is possible, I believe we need a clearly defined program, culminating of course in sending a person back in time."

"You have changed, David," Henry laughed. "I thought you were the one who didn't have time to plan."

"We all have room to grow, and I've come to appreciate how valuable your advice has been." David's words were simple and sincere, but the tone in his voice underscored how much pain had been required to mold him into the person he had now become.

"Gentlemen," Albert interrupted jovially, as if determined to change the subject and perhaps the somber mood the conversation had taken, "you've wasted another day, not to mention hitting me up for quite an expensive meal, but I believe we're on track again. And, best of all, David is back with us. Now when do you think you will conduct your next experiment?"

"Let me think for a minute," David replied. "We should be able to work out the details of the various time travel experiments fairly easily. What do you think, Henry? Allow one day for that?"

Henry nodded his approval.

"That just leaves a complete test of the equipment

which can be done in two more days."

"That's only if we encounter no problems that need correcting," Henry cautioned. "Remember our equipment is complex, sensitive, and highly experimental. For all of it to check out in perfect order would be little short of miraculous. Realistically, we'd better allow three days for testing and correcting any problems."

"You're probably right," David agreed. "Albert, let's plan on four days from now. If we're able to get ready earlier, we'll let you know."

Albert became enthusiastic again. "That certainly sounds encouraging. Today is the 6th, so four days from now would put the next trial at January 10, a Saturday. Would you prefer to skip the weekend, and plan for the following Monday?"

"No way," Henry objected. "Once the testing is complete, we must go right away, or we have to conduct the tests all over again. Besides, I think we're all anxious to get on with this project. I can almost taste a Nobel Prize next year."

"Very well, gentlemen, Saturday, January 10, will be the day." Raising his glass, Albert offered a toast. "Here's to sending a person back in time very soon."

His words were to become prophetic earlier than any of them could have imagined.

Chapter 26
Thursday
January 8, 1970

Harris had been careful to remain out of sight of the guards that provided security for the facility. His intense scrutiny, however, had allowed him to observe enough to know almost immediately when work resumed. Determined that his years in and out of the Stetson case were finally going to pay off, he was willing now to take whatever risks might become necessary. The whole affair had developed into an obsession that had its grip on Harris's will, just as certainly as latent insanity had corroded the steadily deteriorating mind of Dr. Thomas Creighton. The combination possessed all the potential for disaster.

Creighton had to be considered the wild card in this whole affair. Harris knew the true nature of David and Henry's research but could not prove it. He didn't even understand enough to know exactly what type of evidence he could photograph or steal to incriminate them and hopefully allow him to negotiate some sort of deal. What he really wanted was a tradeoff; the skeleton in the Stetson closet (whatever that might turn out to be) in exchange for his silence regarding their research. But to get his hands on something to use as leverage, he needed Creighton. Stable or not, he was the one tool Harris had at his disposal to obtain what he wanted. Once he got it, he would think of some way to get rid of Creighton, but the problem right now was to get something with which to blackmail David, and his plan for overcoming that little difficulty was risky indeed.

It was now almost 7:45 p.m. The sun had long since set, and darkness had brought along with it one of the coldest nights England had experienced that year. Outside, billowing snow had made driving extremely hazardous. Before long it might become impossible. Harris was attempting to warm his aging frame, while simultaneously fortify his courage at a pub a few blocks from the laboratory.

Creighton was already fifteen minutes late. Normally Harris wouldn't have been concerned, but lately anything having to do with Creighton made him nervous. When they had made their plans the night before, Harris had been forced to rehearse the strategy over and over before he felt confident that Creighton understood the role he was to play in the events of this night. Creighton was still basically coherent, but his attention span was getting shorter, and his consciousness could suddenly shift from reality into a murky world that Harris had no desire to try to comprehend. Although he wasn't willing to admit it to himself, for one of the few times in his life he was afraid. He had never been above a little blackmail or petty larceny, and breaking and entering was his stock in trade. But he had survived over the years by always knowing where to draw the line, and Creighton had all the potential for causing the kind of trouble of which Harris had no desire to be a part. Every element of common sense that had guided Harris all his life screamed out to him to leave now and call the authorities to pick up Creighton. He forced the thought deep into the recesses of his subconscious and continued to wait with growing impatience. When a few minutes later a hand tapped him lightly on the shoulder, he almost jumped out of his chair.

"Don't ever do that again," he hissed. "Want to give

me a heart attack?"

"Sorry, Harris. You're not having second thoughts, are you?"

"Don't concern yourself about me. You just concentrate on doing your job. Now, let's go through this one more time. We can't afford any slipups."

"I think I know what I have to do."

"You can't 'think' you know. You have to be sure. More to the point, I have to be sure you're sure. Now, did you rent the car, like I asked you to?"

"Yes, and I used Lindstrom's name like you told me. But I still don't understand why I couldn't have just made up a name."

"Call it my own little joke if you want, but I do have a more practical reason. I want any edge I can get, and Lindstrom's name on the ticket just might distract the cops long enough for me to get on a plane if that should become necessary.

"Now, about tonight. When we leave here, you're to walk to the laboratory and wait across the street from the front entrance. I'll stay here for a few minutes before following to give you enough time to get in position. Then I'll take the car, and just outside the lab, I'm going to plow the car conveniently into a telephone pole that's located within sight of the front office. In this weather that shouldn't strike anybody as unusual. If necessary, I can get the horn blowing, and it'll look like it's from the accident. That's your signal. Now, do you know what you're supposed to do then?"

"I'm to break into the side window."

"No, you are not to break into it!" Harris seethed with frustration. "Break that window, and the guards are sure to hear you. The alarm's been disabled, and the window should be unlocked. I've arranged it."

"You mean you've bribed one of the guards?" Creighton asked. "Suppose he should tell?"

"I didn't exactly bribe him," Harris countered. "I kind of made a trade with him. My silence for a little favor. So don't worry. He won't talk, not unless he wants to spend the next five years in prison."

"So once I'm in the lab, I'm to look for concrete evidence that Evans and Lindstrom are attempting time travel and bring it back with me, or at least photograph it. Is that right?"

"Now you're with me. Are you sure you know what to look for?"

"I think I've already seen it. There's a big closed off area that looks like it's where they intend time travel to originate from. If I can get in there and get a picture or two of the instrument panel, that should do it. If I'm lucky, I may even be able to get some of their notes."

"Don't count on it. Evans and Lindstrom may be dodos', but since Stetson's involved too, you can bet security's going to be just as tight inside as out. That's why I'm nervous about this whole business. We're taking an awful chance, but I don't know any other way to do it."

Harris paused for a moment, noticing that Creighton's expression had changed. He was staring with the blank expression Harris had seen before. The fearful puppy of a moment before had been replaced by the Creighton he didn't like. Harris couldn't be sure if he really saw him or not.

"There's no reason to fear," Creighton intoned. "We will succeed, because we must. The hand of God is with me, and I cannot fail."

Harris was not reassured.

*   *   *

The cold itself would have been miserable enough, but when Harris and Creighton left the pub, they discovered that the wind had picked up noticeably, and it caught up the falling snow, buffeting their exposed faces in gusting swirls.

"No doubt about it," Harris mused to himself, "this is definitely going to be my last case." He had accumulated enough over the years to live in mild comfort, and this night had convinced him the time had come.

"Maybe buy a little place in South America," he reflected, somewhere he could live quietly, without worrying about his past catching up to him. "Yep," he thought, "the time has finally come."

Harris slowly but unobtrusively circled the laboratory. He had cased it enough to recognize the security station dimly lit just inside the entrance. He wanted to check the parking lot just to be sure everyone had gone home, but decided the danger of being spotted made it too risky. "Besides," he thought, "nobody's going to be crazy enough to stay this late on a night like this."

After checking to be sure no other cars were in sight, Harris pulled over and turned to Creighton. "Okay, this is it. You're two blocks away. I'll give you five minutes. That should be more than enough time. Then I'm going to cause that little accident we talked about. As soon as you hear the horn start blaring, you get in and get out quick. Those guards won't be distracted for long. Got it?"

"I've already told you I'm ready. Let's get this over with."

Creighton let himself out of the car, and as Harris watched him walk deliberately toward the laboratory, he wondered how this night would end. He waited a moment to be sure Creighton was on his way then slowly pulled out into the still deserted street.

*   *   *   *

Five minutes and fifteen seconds had gone by when Creighton heard the shrill honking of a horn. He had concealed himself outside a warehouse across from the laboratory behind an assorted collection of junked industrial equipment that exhibited various stages of cannibalization. As soon as he heard the horn blaring from around the corner, he immediately leaped across the street, not even pausing to notice whether or not he was being observed. He found the window unlocked just as Harris had promised. One strong upwards push and it was open. A moment later he found himself in a small conference room in the back of the laboratory. Fortunately the room was dark. In fact the only light he could see came from somewhere toward the front of the building. Creighton assumed it emanated from the guard station.

He was wrong.

Even with the infusion of an extra surge of adrenaline, induced by the excitement of his clandestine mission, Creighton found that his middle-aged body was already exhausted from the exertion. He waited for perhaps two minutes to catch his breath, as well as gather his courage, before opening the office door and slipping surreptitiously into the main part of the laboratory.

Almost immediately his heart sank, and Creighton crouched down, uncertain how to proceed. The light he had seen when he first entered the building, the one he thought was given off by the guard station, actually came from the middle of the laboratory, and in the split second it took Creighton to see it, he also observed David bent over a mass of papers. His intense concentration had prevented him from observing Creighton's movements.

Knowing that the guards outside might return at any moment, a rational person would most likely have given up the attempt. Creighton, however, had not been completely rational for some time, and unexpectedly seeing David, far from dissuading him, actually provided the catalyst his unsteady psyche required. In a moment's time Creighton completely lost the precarious mental balance that had been steadily deteriorating, and his consciousness became something less than fully human. Not knowing how to respond to this unanticipated turn of affairs, Creighton did what he had been doing more and more during the past few months. He retreated to the security of his voice, which was always eager to provide, not just advice, but urgent demands, commands Creighton felt powerless to disobey.

Even his visual perception altered to reflect what his tortured mind told him he was observing. The image of David, working unobtrusively at his desk, alternated with a distorted parody of demonic concentration, as frightening to the eye as it was chilling to the soul. Even though Creighton's fevered vision reflected only his own tormented view of himself, he became convinced that he had come face-to-face with ultimate demonic reality, just as his mind had done when it had been unexpectedly confronted by Cathy at the top of the stairs. His mission had now been completely transformed into a compulsive obsession, and his association with Harris was becoming a fading memory, still partially present somewhere on the borders of his consciousness, but reflecting only a part of his newly defined purpose. Faced with the disintegration of his very humanity, Creighton's brain responded in the only manner left to it. He became little more than a stereotype of his primitive ancestors, a half-conscious savage, whose motivation had been stripped to one naked goal, and whose intellect remained only to serve that purpose, a whispered order transmitted to his tortured mind in the form of a single command.

"Kill!"

Without a moment's question or hesitation, Creighton moved to obey the insistent voice, uttered in the shrill tones of his dead mother. A large wrench, carelessly laid aside, replaced the war club of the Stone Age savage. It would do.

Had it not been for one, otherwise trivial, irrelevant event, Creighton might have carried out his purpose. Just as he approached David, the thick glasses his strongly myopic vision required reflected the headlights of a passing car. The light was infinitesimal, just enough to distract David's concentration and cause him to look up and in a split second recognize his assailant, even as the blow came crashing down, glancing off the side of his skull, and propelling him into unconsciousness.

Standing over David's body, Creighton contemplated his next action. One strong blow to the head and David would be dead and his mission accomplished. But with the perceived danger eliminated, Creighton returned to almost full control of his consciousness. His mind clear once again, Creighton observed the laboratory. He immediately realized that David's death would not eliminate the threat posed by the project. The research had already been done and construction of the facility completed. Lindstrom could easily carry on alone. Killing David now would not halt the implementation of time travel or protect the world from its devastating effects. As he pondered his next move, suddenly his voice gave him the answer he sought, and as he realized what he must do, a smile of satisfaction spread across Creighton's face. Yes, he would use the devil's own instrument to kill the devil himself. He dropped the wrench he held and turned away from David's comatose body. He knew what he must do.

*　　*　　*　　*

David's return to consciousness was slow and attended by a throbbing pain in his head such as he had never before experienced. As his eyes finally became focused, aiding in his efforts to regain a measure of consciousness, his first sight was a security guard bending down, frantically intoning "Dr. Evans! Dr. Evans!" Suddenly his memory returned, and he bolted upright with a force that startled the guard attending him.

"Where's Creighton?" he mumbled excitedly.

"Who? There's no one else 'ere, Dr. Evans. When we 'eard the equipment start up, we came back inside right away. But we've searched the building top to bottom. It's empty. You can be sure o' that."

"Equipment running, you say?"

"Yes, it was. Andrew and me, we both 'eard it. Sounded like a motor running. We 'eard it even from outside, but by the time we got in, it had stopped. Only thing though,

Andrew and me, we both got real dizzy for just a second. Then we was fine. We ain't been drinkin' though. You 'ave me word."

The guard's remark had instantly cleared David's grogginess and replaced it with a gnawing concern which he attempted to hide. Before he could find out what had really happened, he had to get rid of the guards.

"Neville, are you certain no one's still in the building?"

"I don't think so sir. Andrew searched the place top to bottom, while I was tryin' to revive you. 'E's checkin' outside now, but it appears whoever it was has got clean away. But that don't seem possible sir, now does it? What do you suppose 'e was after?"

"It was probably just a burglar. Listen, Neville, have you called the police yet?"

"No, we ain't. We was so concerned about you sir, and making sure no one was still 'ere, you see. But we'll get right to it."

"No, don't call them."

"But sir, what if the burglar comes back? And what if 'e's stolen anythin'?"

"I don't think he'll come back, at least not tonight. And I'll determine whether anything's missing. But Neville, our research is at a critical point, and I had rather not deal with a police investigation right now."

David knew his excuse sounded thin, but he had no choice. The police simply could not become involved, not if his fears proved justified.

"I'll tell you what to do. I want you to call Dr. Lindstrom and Mr. Stetson. Tell them what's happened, and have them get over here as quickly as possible. Meanwhile, I'm going to check the laboratory for any signs of theft or damage. Then we'll decide what to do."

"Whatever you say sir. You sure you're all right? 'Adn't we at least ought to 'ave a doctor look at that cut on your 'ead?"

"No thank you, Neville. I expect I'm going to have a terrific headache, but I was lucky I guess. I'm sure there's nothing to be concerned about."

David fervently hoped he was right, but just now his concern was causing him more distress than his head. If his fears were correct, their problems had now become far worse than he wished to contemplate.

Chapter 27

With the security guard gone for the moment, David lost no time checking out the Time Portal. Little more than a glance was required to confirm his fears. He had left the power on while testing some of the instruments, but there was one difference now. The time setting should have been at zero. Instead, it had been moved slightly to the left. What had been a vague feeling of anxiety suddenly crystallized into chilling certainty.

As David comprehended the significance of what had evidently transpired while he was unconscious, he tried desperately to determine what his next action should be. As he was pondering the situation, the returning guard forced him to put that particular dilemma aside and attend to a more immediate one.

"Dr. Evans, I found this character snoopin' 'round outside. I think it's the same person what 'ad the accident in front of the lab just before you was attacked. 'E seemed okay at the time and insisted on our not callin' the police, but I just caught 'im hidin' outside the window what leads into the conference room. 'E must be the one what attacked you. I guess we better call the police now and 'ave him taken away."

"Not just yet, Neville." The voice came from the front of the laboratory and bore the unmistakable authority of Albert Stetson. "And just where may I ask is Andrew? I have seen no sign of him anywhere."

"I know, Mr. Stetson. That really is peculiar, now

ain't it? 'E was 'ere just before the attack on Dr. Evans, but since then I ain't seen 'im nowhere. Surely, sir you don't think . . ."

"Precisely, Neville. I don't intend to 'think' I know what occurred here tonight. I'm going to find out. For now, don't call anyone. Just go back and do your job."

"Will someone please tell me, what's been happening here tonight?" Henry had just walked in the door, and from his disheveled appearance, he must have gone to bed early that night.

"Just one minute, Lindstrom. Neville, I want you patrolling outside, just in case anyone else is involved in this. If you find Andrew, I want to see him immediately. Otherwise, stay outside until you're called. Do you understand?"

"Right you are, sir." Neville had only seen Albert Stetson in this mood twice before, but he had learned quickly enough not to contradict him at those times. "But what should I do with this 'ere bloke?"

"Don't worry about him. I'll take care of this person myself. I need you on your rounds and quickly. This building has been left unguarded far too long already."

"Yes sir, Mr. Stetson. Just as you say, I'm sure."

As the guard left, Henry turned toward David.

"Are you all right, David? Neville said you were attacked."

"It was a clumsy job. I'll have a headache for awhile, but otherwise I'm fine."

"That's good news," Henry said, his relief apparent. Then he turned, directing his next question to Albert.

"Why didn't you want the police called? Obviously, we have the assailant right here. Shouldn't we have him arrested?"

"Now, wait just a minute," Harris broke his silence for the first time. "I haven't attacked anybody. You're not going to pin that rap on me."

"Henry," David interrupted, "he's telling the truth. I have no idea who this man is, but I did manage to get a look at the person that hit me, and I'm sure it was Thomas Creighton."

"Creighton," Henry gasped. "You mean it's come to this? He actually attacked you?"

"I can't be certain, but I think his mind may have gone. He looked so wild that I almost didn't recognize him. But I am sure that this man wasn't involved."

"Don't be too hasty about that," Albert interrupted. He turned toward David, while still keeping a firm grip on his prisoner. "You may not know who this is, but rest assured he knows you. Isn't that right, Mr. Harris?"

"How did . . . ? Now look, I don't want any trouble. This was all Creighton's idea, you know."

"Perhaps I know more than you wish I knew." Albert's gaze was itself enough to frighten Harris, who knew he had gotten in far beyond what he was prepared to deal with. "And I can make a pretty good guess about the rest."

"Okay, so you know who I am. That doesn't mean anything, and you can't prove it anyway." Harris was talking tough, but Albert could see the apprehension that registered on his face. He felt certain Harris was bluffing, simply because he couldn't think of anything else to do.

"Oh, we could start with trespassing, if you like. But that's just the beginning, and I have a feeling that, if we really get down to it, this business with Creighton may expose a lot of other details you might not relish having to explain."

"If that's the way you feel, why don't you call the cops? Don't want to, do you? I know what's going on here, and I don't think you're ready for it to become public knowledge. Am I right?"

"Now look Harris." Henry couldn't take it any longer. "If you think you can blackmail us, you're quite mistaken."

"Please, Dr. Lindstrom. Let me handle this," Albert insisted. "I'm used to dealing with his kind.

"You're right, Harris. We are not particularly anxious for the authorities to become involved in this. Now the question is, which of us has more to lose by bringing in the police? For us involving the police may be slightly embarrassing and could conceivably delay our research by a few months. Regrettable certainly, but merely a slight setback. On the other hand, I can't believe that you really want the authorities investigating your past too carefully."

"I've done nothing illegal here," Harris asserted, trying once again to defend himself. "Evans himself said that it was Creighton who attacked him, not me."

"And you think we'll have any trouble proving you were involved? Besides, I know why you were so quick to act on Creighton's request for you to come to England. Once the police find out about that little matter in Charleston last year, I think extradition might come rather quickly. Wouldn't you?"

"How did you know about that?" Harris asked incredulously.

"A man in my position has to anticipate problems," Albert replied with satisfaction, seeing by Harris's expression that his threat had hit home. "After all these years, I would have thought you had learned that. But enough of this. I think we can come to some agreement without involving the police in this. Are you willing to cooperate or not?"

Harris knew when he was beaten. He had never dealt

with anyone as commanding as Albert Stetson, but neither had he ever directly confronted his mother either.

"All right," he sighed. "You seem to be holding all the cards. What have you got in mind?"

"For right now, I am going to escort you to our security office, where you will wait quietly while we conduct some business among ourselves. And if there is any attempt to escape or to cause trouble of any kind, you know what to expect. Now, shall we go?"

As soon as Albert and Ray Harris had left the lab, David turned to Henry anxiously. "I didn't want to say anything in front of anyone else, but we have a much larger problem on our hands than even Albert is aware of. It's about Creighton. I think I know what happened to him."

"I just assumed he escaped," Henry said. "What are you suggesting?"

"Look at the Time Portal. Do you see the time setting?"

Henry gasped in astonishment. "You don't think that Creighton used it?"

"I hope to heaven I'm wrong. But all the evidence points to Creighton's having transported himself to some point in the not too distant past. The Time Ship that is always stored in the Time Portal is missing too. Everything fits."

"Why would he do something as crazy as that, especially since he believed time travel to be evil?"

"Who can say? We've both observed before that his sanity seems precarious at best. I doubt that logic can be used to understand any of Creighton's actions from now on. His attack on me indicates that. Perhaps it was even an accident. Creighton may have been looking for evidence to incriminate us and transported himself inadvertently. But none of that really matters at this point. The question now is what do we do about it?”

“What can we do?” Henry shrugged with resignation. “We don’t even know for sure that your theory is right. Creighton may have simply escaped and taken the Time Ship with him.”

“Yes,” David agreed, “but we can’t afford to assume that, nor do we have to. What we can do is bring him back. All that’s required is to put the time setting back to the present and activate the return mechanism. If Creighton has simply stolen the Time Ship, nothing should happen because it’s still in the present, but if he has been transported to the past, we ought to be able to return him to the Time Portal. At any rate, we have to try.”

“Of course you’re right,” Henry agreed. “I’ll begin preparations, while you get Albert. He’s involved in this too and deserves to be here when we make the attempt.”

“Make what attempt?”

Albert had returned just in time to hear Henry speaking. David explained their concern to him, while Henry realigned the settings on the Time Portal. Within a few minutes, the equipment was ready. Henry closed the door to the Time Portal, more out of habit than necessity, since their previous experiences indicated that it provided only limited protection from the forces generated during time travel. A nod to David at the console and the switch was pressed. Instead of the sickening sensation of movement they had come to associate with time travel, all that transpired was an alarm bell and an error reading on the console.

“What happened?” Albert asked, the uncertainty apparent in his voice. “Does this mean Creighton did steal the Time Ship?”

“I wish the explanation were that simple,” David replied bitterly. “If that had been the case, there would have been nothing, no response at all. You explain it to him, Henry."

"You see, Mr. Stetson, while the Time Ship can ordinarily be operated from here, we also built in a switch to control the operation from the Time Ship itself. Creighton must have figured out how the Time Ship functions and locked us out. He's set it to manual operation, effectively preventing us from forcing him back to the present."

"You mean he's gone somewhere in the past, and there's nothing we can do to stop him?" Albert asked incredulously.

"We could go after him," David suggested. "We have a spare Time Ship, and although we can't pinpoint exactly the time period to which he transported himself, we know the approximate setting. But even with that, we could easily arrive a year or two later than Creighton."

"Or earlier, for that matter," Henry added. "Pursuing Creighton into the past involves terrible risks, David. Surely there must be some other way."

"Then think of one — either of you. But if you can't, then I don't believe we have any choice but . . ."

David was suddenly cut short by the activation warning on the Time Portal, which had been left running ever since the original attempt to force Creighton back to the present. A moment later the three men were taken off guard and thrown to the ground by the now familiar forces associated with time travel, forces which this time they were neither expecting nor prepared for. David was the first to stand up. Believing that Creighton must have returned to the present, he pressed the button opening the door to the Time Portal and prepared to defend himself, not knowing what sort of weapons he might face. When No one emerged from the Time Portal, David cautiously approached and looked inside.

Chapter 28

Henry, standing off to the side of the Time Portal, could see nothing of the interior, but the expression on David's face was enough to convince him that the adventures of this night were far from over. There was no way either Henry or Albert could appreciate David's feelings at that moment. His first response to what he saw within the Time Portal had predictably been one of shock, but after a moment this emotion had been replaced by a gradually increasing comprehension, as his mind resurrected memories that had been buried for twenty-two years.

It was Albert who finally rushed to David's side to offer assistance, as well as to see for himself whether or not Creighton had returned from the past. "Dr. Lindstrom, I think you had better come here and see this." His tone was firm and commanding, but filled with apprehension nonetheless.

As Henry peered inside the Time Portal, he confirmed that Creighton had indeed returned to the present. He was difficult to see clearly at first, because the Time Portal was never designed for someone with his massive frame. His body almost completely filled the space. And the Thomas Creighton in the Time Portal was not exactly the same man who had broken into the laboratory earlier that evening.

One of the changes was not immediately obvious, but once observed was undeniable. For some reason Creighton appeared to have aged, not dramatically, but showing perhaps a little more gray in his hair along with the beginnings of wrinkles in his forehead and around his sunken cheekbones. He also possessed a full beard which he never had in all the time David and Henry had known him, not even when he had accosted Henry in the laboratory some months earlier.

Only after several minutes had passed, however, did Albert first comment on any of this, for the one overriding image that immediately presented itself was the knife buried deep in his chest, along with the glaring expression of malice that still transfixed the unseeing eyes of the body that had once been Dr. Thomas Creighton.

"Are you all right, David?"

The words came from Albert, who had finally turned his gaze from the grotesque corpse inside the Time Portal to notice that David had continued to stare at it intently, almost as if in a trance. David was in fact remembering the trauma which had lain dormant in a hidden portion of his memory since that day in 1948. The key that unlocked his subconscious was his recognition of the knife that had been used to kill Creighton. As a boy he had occasion to see it often. He had even been allowed to use it a few times, whenever his father had taken him hunting.

Albert's repeated question accompanied by a firm grip to the shoulders finally got David's attention.

"It was Creighton. He was the one who killed my parents. But why? I don't understand any of this."

"We shall probably never know for certain," Albert responded. "I suspect he was really trying to kill you all along. Your parents unfortunately merely got in his way."

"But why go back in time to kill me? If he wanted to do that, Creighton had the perfect opportunity tonight."

"I believe I can answer that," Henry responded. "Killing you tonight would not have achieved his purpose. His ultimate goal after all has been to stop the time travel experiment, and your death would not have accomplished that, because our work is too far along. Creighton would have realized that from observing the state of our equipment. But if he killed David Evans as a child, he would destroy your work as well, because you would never live to conceive of time travel in the first place."

"That theory certainly makes sense," Albert agreed. "But how do you explain the fact that Creighton seems to have aged? Is that an effect of time travel?"

"I don't know. The aging process is baffling to me as well," Henry agreed.

"I believe I may have the answer to that question," David replied. "Although certainly it's possible the aging is some unanticipated effect of time travel, and one we may have to take into account, I'm inclined to accept a more commonplace explanation. Creighton may have been in the past for five years or more. He killed my parents in 1948. My guess is that he was transported to a date sometime during World War II, effectively trapping him in England until the war ended, and he was free to travel to the United States to continue his search for me. Even then, some time would have been required to locate me. He would have had no clear idea of where to look, and Evans is a fairly common name. No, I suspect Creighton is simply about five years older than he was when he broke into the lab earlier tonight. That would explain the beard also. Even though I only saw Creighton for a second tonight, I'm virtually positive he did not have a beard then. He must have grown it in the past, and that necessitates enough time to do so."

"I'm still puzzled about the Time Ship," Henry said. "Why would Creighton even have it with him? Surely he would know that if he succeeded in killing you, our whole project would simply never have occurred. He couldn't return to the present, because the equipment would never have existed."

"The problem could have become even worse than that," David answered. "If Creighton had succeeded in killing me, theoretically be couldn't have traveled into the past to do it, because the project would never have begun in the first place. It's called a paradox."

"Yes," Henry replied, "and that's why, from a scientific standpoint, I still believe it is impossible to alter time. It would contradict the very nature of the universe as we know it to be."

"Or one can just as plausibly argue that this is precisely the danger involved in attempting time travel at all," David countered. "The events tonight demonstrate just how frightening that danger could be."

"I don't wish to bring up that issue again," Henry responded, "but I have one further question. We tried to bring Creighton back earlier without success. Then a little later, the Time Ship and Creighton mysteriously materialized on their own. How do you explain that?"

"I'll admit that part disturbs me," David answered. "I can only think of one possible explanation. Someone must have pressed the return button on the Time Ship. It may have occurred accidentally, or Creighton may have done so as he lay dying. I don't have the answer, but certainly it isn't comforting to think someone from the past may possess knowledge about the workings of time travel."

"This is all most interesting, gentlemen," Albert interrupted, "but we must deal with more urgent matters. While I can appreciate your concern about what has already happened, don't forget that right now we are standing here with the corpse of a man who has obviously been murdered, and at the same time we are holding his accomplice in this building. We must come to some agreement as to how to proceed, and we must do so quickly."

Just at that moment, a threatening voice, punctuated by a scream of obscenities, could be heard coming from the front of the building.

"It would appear that Mr. Harris may be getting restless again," Albert sighed. "Once he figures out that we really have no right to hold him, we may be faced with the additional complication of having him run away or even go to the police. I have an idea that may get him out of our hair once and for all. I'll attend to him, while the two of you check the equipment, and see if you can come up with some means of resolving this mess."

Without waiting for a reply, Albert purposefully walked away, leaving David and Henry to deal with the problem at hand.

Chapter 29

Perhaps thirty minutes had passed before Albert returned. Thursday evening had now become Friday morning, and the events of this most unusual night were beginning to tell on Albert's features, or at least that was what David attributed the strain to. He looked more tired than David could ever remember seeing him before.

"Are you all right, Albert? You really don't look well."

"Don't I? Just tired I suppose. This has been some evening, you'll have to admit."

David wasn't convinced, but decided to let the matter drop. "The next question we have to deal with is how we should proceed after all that's occurred tonight. I suppose we ought to report all this to the police."

"Do that and you can kiss our entire work goodbye," Henry reminded him.

"I understand that, and it's regrettable to be sure, but what else can we do? Creighton's disappearance has to be reported and explained, and Ray Harris probably knows a lot more of the story. We can't just pretend that nothing happened tonight."

"Yes, we can," Albert replied forcefully. Hearing David suggest bringing in the police roused him somewhat from his lethargy. "That is precisely what we must do. Now wait just a moment," he continued over David's attempted objection. "Let's think our situation through. Just what do you suggest telling the authorities? A former respected scientist follows you to England, goes insane, attacks you out of the blue, 'accidentally' transports himself to the past, and is brought back with your father's knife buried in his heart. And, by-the-by, we haven't one shred of tangible evidence that time travel really occurred. Is that what you propose telling the police?"

"When you put it like that, the idea certainly sounds ludicrous," David admitted. "But don't forget we do have Harris, who presumably knows about Creighton and most likely about our time travel project. There's nothing to prevent his telling the whole story, whether we like it or not."

"Oh, you think so, do you?" Albert sniffed. "I shouldn't put too much stock in anything Mr. Harris relates to anyone. First of all, whatever he may surmise, he can't really know any more about the research going on here than Creighton was able to tell him. Also, it is highly unlikely he has any concrete evidence. Otherwise, there would have been no need for the attempted break-in. Since both he and Neville have been secluded in the security shack in the front of the building, neither one of them has any inkling of the more bizarre events of the night, so we have no cause for concern from them. As far as Creighton's disappearance is concerned, you may rest assured there was certainly no love lost between Harris and him. In order for Harris to push for any kind of investigation into Creighton's disappearance, he will have to implicate himself in this whole shoddy affair. Now you tell me, if we offer him a choice between simply walking out of here and never being seen or heard from again, or face being charged in an illegal break-in, assault, and possibly implicated in a murder, what do you think he will do?"

"I don't know," David replied. "You're probably right, but it gives me chills just listening to you. You sound so cold, so calculating."

"So practical, you mean. I'm sorry, David. I didn't intend for my words to come across quite as callous as they obviously did. Truly, I regret Creighton's horrible death quite as much as you do. But we must face reality. We all know what really happened, and we all agree that we have virtually no chance of convincing the authorities of the truth. At best, your work will come to a halt, probably forever. More likely, all of us will be facing a murder charge, for which we have no plausible defense. I may indeed sound calculating, but what would you have us do?"

"I don't quite know. If we weren't so close to proving everything we've worked for. Perhaps if we could demonstrate that time travel is possible, we might be able to tell the truth and make people believe us."

"And just how would you propose accomplishing that?" Henry asked.

"Well, we know the equipment's working. It was used successfully at least twice last night. Since we have already proven that, what if we skipped the preliminary experiments, and went for the big one right now?"

"You mean," Henry gasped incredulously, "send one of us back in time right now, after the disasters we've just experienced? You can't be serious!"

"Look, I don't relish the idea of sending someone back in time right now anymore than you do, but as much as I hate to admit it, Albert is right. We must adjust to the realities of the situation. This night has been a disaster of major proportions, but abandoning our dream of a lifetime won't make any of it better, and it won't prevent us from winding up in a lot of trouble. At least if we go on with our experiment, we have a reasonable chance of proving the truth to a skeptical world, and the risk involved does seem to be acceptably minimal. You said yourself the equipment appears to be working properly."

"The operative word there is 'appears,'" Henry emphasized. "A complete check would take at least two full days."

"Two days we don't have," David emphasized. "This arguing back and forth is senseless. Do you have a better suggestion?"

Henry started to answer, then fell silent.

"Then it's decided."

The impatience on Albert's face was obvious as he listened to the two scientists weigh what, for him, had already been determined by the circumstances. "While you and Dr. Lindstrom are working out these details, I'm going to send Neville home and have a talk with Mr. Harris. I think I can safely promise that after tonight we'll have nothing to trouble ourselves about as far as he is concerned."

"You may be right," Henry responded, "but I can't help wondering just what Harris is going to do when the news about Creighton hits the papers."

"As long as we're set on burning our bridges," Albert replied, "I might have a suggestion in that regard also. David, isn't it true that your machine can transport an object to the future as well as the past?"

"Yes, that's so. But I don't see what that capability has to do with this situation."

"I believe I understand," Henry said. "You're talking about Creighton, aren't you?"

"Precisely, Dr. Lindstrom. All we have to do is transport Creighton's body into the future, and that problem is gone forever."

David continued to be amazed at how events were working themselves out. "You know, Albert, if this conversation had taken place just yesterday, I would have doubted your sanity, and maybe I would have been right. But now, I don't know, I guess I have to admit your idea sounds logical. What do you think, Henry?"

"I share some of the same concerns as you. Who would have imagined our dream a few years ago could possibly lead to this situation? But it has, and we must deal with the reality with which we are confronted. With some reservations, I am forced to concede that Mr. Stetson's plan is a good one."

"Then it's settled," Albert decreed. "Both of you know what needs to be done, and you don't require my presence. Let me have that little chat with Harris, while you do what you have to." Without waiting for a reply, Albert turned about and walked out of the laboratory.

Since Creighton's body had never been moved from the Time Portal, little preparation was required. The dial on the Time Portal was set as far to the right as it would go, indicating a time setting in the far distant future. Before the body was transported, however, Henry took one last precaution. Hastily constructing a shallow tray from thin plywood, he secured it to the top of the Time Ship. Filling the tray with sulfuric acid, Henry feverishly closed the door and immediately transported Creighton before the acid had time to eat through the already smoking wood and onto the Time Ship.

"There," he said. "That should prevent someone in the future from using the Time Ship. When it materializes, all that anyone should find is a corroded heap of metal. I believe we just might be safe."

Chapter 30
Friday
January 9, 1970

With Albert gone and the decision now made for the first controlled attempt of a human being to engage in time travel, David and Henry were confronted with a question they had repeatedly preferred not to deal with over the preceding four years. Who was to be the first time traveler? Both men had started to bring up the subject countless times, but some other more pressing concern always seemed to force the issue aside so that it was momentarily forgotten. The real reason for putting off the question, however, was more connected with the egos of the two men, and it revealed one of the bonds which had over the years cemented their friendship, a relationship which was at times difficult for an outsider to comprehend.

With the first Apollo landing on the moon not quite six months earlier, the U. S. space program had reached its peak, both in accomplishments and in the popularity it enjoyed, not only in the United States but around the world. In the years since they left NORTECH, David and Henry had watched some of the astronauts whom they had known projected to a level of fame normally reserved for movie stars and sports heroes. Now, in these early morning hours, these two men, who had been working under the tightest secrecy feasible for a private undertaking, were presented with the opportunity to break out of that anonymity and actually upstage all of them. But just as with the moon landing, there could be only one first time traveler. Who was it to be — David Evans or Henry Lindstrom?

Each of the men presented what seemed compelling reasons as to why he should be the first to journey through time, arguments which the other summarily rejected. To those who had known David and Henry for any length of time, this final disagreement, though more important, differed little from the multitude of disputes that had often threatened, but never shaken their friendship.

In the end the argument was resolved, as so often happens in this unpredictable world in which we live, by a means so bizarre, given the immense importance of the project, that even to this day the half dozen individuals who know of the experiment discount the account as only a legend. In the end it wasn't to be arguments, logic, scientific qualifications, or even persuasive emotions which decided the issue, but an often used arbiter of lesser disputes. Henry tossed, David called, and in such an inauspicious fashion fate selected David Evans to experience what must surely turn out to be the most significant journey any person had heretofore undertaken.

By the time the preliminary testing of the equipment had been completed, the sun was just beginning to lighten the morning sky, giving off a brilliant reflection from the layer of snow that had accumulated during the previous night. Albert had returned and reported confidently that Harris would never again trouble any of them. He also suggested that too much had already transpired to attempt the experiment without all of them getting some rest. David did not agree and questioned the wisdom of delaying. He argued that since Albert had allowed Harris to leave, they were risking his bringing in the police before they could complete the experiment which might provide the evidence for their only defense. Henry broke the tie by siding with Albert. His decision was based partially on Albert's assurance that any interference by Harris was all but nonexistent. Henry's primary concern, however, was David's condition after the assault, as well as the danger of an error resulting from fatigue. The three men agreed to rest until three o'clock that afternoon and then meet once again in the laboratory. Extremely doubtful that sleep would be possible, David settled into his apartment and was proven wrong within minutes. Albert, however, made no attempt to rest. He knew that, as far as he was concerned, it was out of the question. He both dreaded the coming day and yet wished it to be over. For him time passed slowly indeed.

*　*　*　*

Shortly before three that afternoon, one by one, the three men assembled once again in the laboratory. The biting cold which had lingered from the day before was accentuated by a blowing wind that stirred up gusts of the remaining snow and whipped it viciously against the body. Not surprisingly, there was little sign of activity on the street as Henry literally bolted from his car into the warmth of the lab. He was immediately struck by two circumstances which seemed odd. One was the absence of any security guards. Even the front door was unlocked, and Henry simply walked in to find Albert in the front office. Then there was the atmosphere of the place. Or was it just Albert? Henry had never known him to be so quiet, so unassuming. Albert Stetson had always presented the epitome of a "take charge" person, invariably exuding confidence and drive. This afternoon, he was merely

233

going through the motions, quite thoroughly and correctly to be sure, but in a manner that dampened the mood for what Henry anticipated to be the experience of a lifetime. He determined that it would be prudent to address only the first of the questions that were on his mind that morning.

"Mr. Stetson, were you aware that Neville isn't here, or for that matter, anyone? The lab has no security whatsoever."

"Yes," Albert's voice was slow, almost laborious. "I have dismissed all of our security force, since I believe after today their services should no longer be required. As it has turned out, the two threats to the project have already been eliminated, so I believe we have nothing to fear. Besides, we don't want any observers for this part of our experiment. Wouldn't you agree?"

"I suppose so." Henry tried to make light of the issue. "It's just that I've kind of gotten used to them by now. Body guards just seem to be a natural part of your life. But you're right, I suppose. We really don't want any interruptions today."

"By the way, has David arrived?" Henry asked, still unsettled by Albert's demeanor, although trying not to show his concern.

"Yes, he has," Albert replied. "He and I have been going over the plans for today's experiment. He's in the laboratory now."

Henry knew that this was his last opportunity, and he took it. "Mr. Stetson, David must have told you that we had determined that he was to make today's journey back in time, but I wish you would help me convince him to allow me to go instead. I assure you I'm not asking for purely selfish reasons. David has always worked the controls and has demonstrated his proficiency each time. I know the procedure of course, but

I've never actually done it except in test situations. I don't think my first time at the controls should come when David is involved. It's not safe. Besides, David was put through quite a lot last night, not to mention his wife's death, which we all know now was possibly not accidental. He's under tremendous stress, and I don't believe he ought to be attempting this right now."

"Excuse me," Albert responded, his voice guarded, if not actually accusing, "but precisely what is it you would like for me to do?"

"Why I should think that would be obvious. You have great influence over David. Surely, you don't want to see him endangered unnecessarily, and if you back me up, he might be persuaded to let me go in his place."

"Dr. Lindstrom, if I had not known you for the length of time we have worked together on this project, I would have to assume you were trying to snatch David's dream of a lifetime from him. However, I have come to respect your integrity and your friendship with David, so I am willing to give you the benefit of the doubt. But you are quite mistaken if you think to persuade me to use my influence to talk David out of his role in today's experiment. This day promises to be the culmination of all David has worked for. I am not prepared to take that from him. Furthermore, as you yourself indicated, the two of you have settled the matter among yourselves. I have made a deliberate effort to limit my role in this project to providing organizational and financial backing. I have never deluded myself that I was competent to contribute to any of the operational decisions you have made. I do not intend to begin today. I suggest we drop the matter, Dr. Lindstrom."

Henry was struck, not only by the force of Albert's rebuke, but by his unaccountable insistence that David should be the one to make the trip. However, recognizing that he was definitely outvoted, he said nothing in reply, perplexed once again by the strange quirks of the Stetson family.

As if to mollify the force of his rebuke, Albert turned the discussion to the procedures outlined for the day, speaking in a tone that betrayed nothing of their previous conversation.

"Now as I understand it, Dr. Lindstrom, the plan today calls for David to be transported to a time period about fifty years in the past. Am I correct?"

"Yes, if we are successful, David should be sent to around the year 1920. You see, we cannot calibrate the Time Portal accurately until we can verify at least two different settings, preferably three. That's what we have always intended for the first few journeys to accomplish. David is to stay in the past only long enough to verify the exact date and then return to the present. Once we have two or three settings on the Time Portal identified, we should be able to make subsequent trips to the past with some degree of precision. Right now, I'm afraid there's a good deal of guesswork involved."

"That certainly seems logical," Albert replied. "Was there any reason for trying to make the first trip fifty years in the past, or was that merely an arbitrary figure?"

"Not at all arbitrary," Henry answered, happy for the moment to have the conversation back on professional matters. "That decision is just one more instance of our concern for safety. Since we really don't know precisely how far in the past a particular setting will achieve, David and I determined to allow for a possible error ratio of one hundred percent in either direction. So, if we plan to go to the year 1920, we need to anticipate that David may arrive anywhere between 1870 to the near past, although I am inclined to believe that we are more likely to go farther back in time rather than nearer the present. If you recall, this was our original concern when selecting this site. The present building was built only eight years ago, four of which we have been here; so, we know its recent history. Before that the site was vacant for 150 years, so we should have little to worry about in that regard. Also, although I didn't mention it at the time, David did some checking on his own. Even though this immediate area was rural fifty years ago, the highway that runs north half a mile from here had already been constructed and led straight into London. That means it should be quite unlikely that anyone would observe David should he materialize in the past, yet he will be able to find his way easily."

The two men had been walking slowly and deliberately toward the laboratory, and by now they were approaching the conference room where Creighton had broken in the night before and where David was now engrossed in last minute calculations.

"Ah, Henry, you've finally arrived."

"Yes, I'm here, but are you really certain you want to proceed? We can still put this off, you know."

"And risk having all our work go for nothing? No thanks. There really is no reason for delay. The equipment's functioning perfectly and I'm ready. Besides, now that the day's finally come, I feel light as a feather. Any other objections?"

Henry could think of a few, but a sidelong glance at Albert Stetson convinced him that further opposition would prove pointless. He gave up with an audible sigh.

"As long as you're certain, you know you have my support."

"Good. Now, can you think of any further matters

that need to be addressed?"

"There is one aspect of being in the past that I am not sure either of you men have anticipated," Albert responded. "Even a short visit to the past will almost certainly involve contact with other people, and both of you have been so adamant that you not influence the past, I wonder that you never considered how your clothing will cause you to stand out. Even the polyester in your shirt could raise questions, David."

"Why of course, you're right!" David exclaimed. "But I don't know what we can do at this point. I just got through arguing against any further delay, and I'm not sure we can afford to."

"Fortunately for you gentlemen, I foresaw the problem some time ago and have made provision for it. Look in that locker, David."

When he had opened one of several metal lockers lining one wall, David found a zippered garment bag which he took out and placed on the conference table.

"Go ahead, open it," Albert said. "Consider it a bon voyage present if you like."

Opening the bag, David found a dark gray tweed suit, all wool by the feel of it, shoes with eyelets rather than laces, and a derby hat that looked positively ridiculous.

"Certainly not fashionable by today's standards," Albert joked. "But these clothes should ensure that you don't stand out too much. I've taken care to have all the labels removed, so there will be no evidence that these are modern imitations I acquired from a costume shop. Go ahead and try them on. They should fit quite well I should think."

"But if you bought these several months ago, how did you know David would be making the first attempt?" Henry asked. "We hadn't even decided ourselves."

Albert did not respond for a moment, and then replied, somewhat deliberately Henry thought. "I knew David well enough that I was fairly certain that he would be the first one going. And as it happens, I was right, now wasn't I?"

"Over my repeated objections," Henry thought to himself, but once again did not respond.

David had already begun changing into his old-fashioned clothing, and within a few moments the transformation was complete.

At the sight of David made up in such antiquated attire, Henry shook his head with amusement, making little attempt to control his laughter. "I'm sorry, but I do wish you could see yourself," he smirked with satisfaction. "Let's just hope you don't have to convince anyone that you're a scientist in that getup."

"That's quite all right," David replied good-naturedly. "You can have your little joke. But very shortly I may be all too glad to be wearing this 'getup' as you call it.

"But seriously, Henry, I do wish you would take care of this for me." David's voice suddenly became reflective as he took the watch Cathy had given him and pressed it into Henry's hand.

"But you're never without this," Henry protested. "Besides, it's enough in character to pass with your costume."

"Yes, it is almost, but you're forgetting the word 'reproduction' and the date on the back. I know the lettering is tiny, but I don't feel we should take any unnecessary risks. Having anything that links me to what will be the future would be foolish. I had my reservations, even when we transported the watch itself to the past for only one minute, and the more I thought about it later, the more I became convinced that we were unwise to have used it at all.

"Hey, don't look so gloomy, both of you. I'll get it

back in a few minutes — by your time anyway."

"I'm sure you're quite right, my boy," Albert responded. "Now, there is one final matter we need to consider. We really have no way of knowing just how long you may need to remain in the past, so you are likely to need some money, and I've taken the liberty of procuring a little sum for you."

David took the envelope which Albert offered to him. Opening it, he exclaimed in surprise, "Albert, there must be the equivalent of a thousand dollars."

"Precisely five hundred pounds, my boy, and not a single note printed after 1870. I should think that amount will be adequate to cover your needs, as well as protect you from any questions that might arise."

"Surely I don't need even a tenth of this. I'm certainly not going to remain in the past that long."

"I don't know quite how to say this," Albert replied. He appeared to be measuring his words. It seemed to Henry that the depression he had sensed in Albert Stetson when he first came to the lab that morning had returned. "I have the utmost confidence in both of you, and I would not interfere with your dream for anything. Yet we must face realistically the possibility, however unpleasant it is to consider, that something might go astray. I want to be certain you have the means to sustain yourself in the event your return should be — delayed."

"What you really mean is, if the Time Ship should malfunction, and I became stranded in the past. You don't have to be afraid to say it. Yes, Henry and I both know that's a risk, even though a small one. And you're also right about this being my dream. Right now, even if I knew that I would be unable to return, I would still go. Consider how far we've come in the four years since Henry and I began work on this project. A lot has transpired during those years, and I have grown closer to both you and Henry. But maybe the most important change has occurred within me. I've discovered a strength I never knew I possessed. I suspect tragedy has a way of either making or breaking a person, and I can't for the life of me figure out how it can force a young character like me to face up to the world, yet at the same time quite literally destroy a poor devil like Creighton. But now I'm ready, truly ready, for whatever lies ahead."

"I know you are." Albert, for the first time David could remember, was literally choked with emotion. "I have watched you develop into a fine young man. Mother would have been immensely proud of you."

"Hey, you two," Henry interjected. "It sounds like you're saying goodbye to each other. Why, in less than an hour David should be relating the most fantastic story in the history of mankind."

"I have no doubt you're right," David answered, "and I see no reason to prolong this. We're ready. Let's do it."

Chapter 31

Although Henry put on a cheerful front, he could not restrain a gnawing anxiety now that the moment had finally arrived. Part of the reason for his concern he attributed to Albert. He generally appeared distant and aloof, actually arrogant was the word that came to mind. None of these terms described Albert today. Henry had searched all day for an explanation for Albert's disposition, but ultimately he had to admit he was baffled. He was sullen, even depressed, and his despondency was infecting Henry. David was so elated at the coming experiment he didn't pick up on Albert's mood. Remembering the stinging rebuke he received just a short while before, Henry let pass his final opportunity to dissuade David from making the attempt. Over the years it would be a decision he would come to regret, providing many sleepless nights, wondering if events might have turned out differently had he been more adamant.

Before allowing David to enter the Time Portal, Henry insisted on verifying the settings, the power levels, and even David's blood pressure and pulse. The equipment and David all checked out perfectly, and a part of Henry felt a sense of disappointment that it should be so.

Could it be that Albert was right after all? Did he envy David this opportunity? In the few seconds Henry allowed himself to consider the question, he was forced to admit that Albert's accusation was at least partially justified. Yes, he was jealous of David, even though the whole project had been David's initially, and his original skepticism had been no less than even Creighton's. But this was to be a day for the history books. In five years who would remember anyone on that first Apollo mission to the moon except Neil Armstrong? Next year, it might well be Evans and Lindstrom. But the year after, would it be just Evans? Henry abhorred these feelings, but honesty compelled him to acknowledge their existence. Yes, he did wish he were going instead of David.

Nevertheless, that admission wasn't the sole reason for Henry's anxiety. David was his colleague, and at this moment, as much as he detested the feeling, he had to some degree become his rival. Despite any competition between the two men, however, their friendship ultimately outweighed any other relationship. And as David's friend, Henry knew there was another reason he wished he could take his place. He was afraid. Had they checked the equipment properly? What really would happen to a human being? After all, the only person who had attempted time travel was dead. And there was an aura of something that seemed a foreboding of disaster. Even Albert sensed it, and Henry knew he felt it, although neither said anything, allowing the game to continue toward an uncertain conclusion.

"Henry, are you listening to me?"

Henry realized that he had heard nothing David had been trying to say to him. "I'm sorry. I guess I let my mind wander for a moment."

"Well, get with the program, will you? This certainly isn't the time to become distracted. Ready to set the Time Portal?"

"I suppose so. You're the one making the trip. What settings do you prefer?"

"Let me think a minute. It's almost 3:50 now. The equipment has been thoroughly tested and brought up to full power. I see no reason to delay any longer than necessary. That would only increase the chances of a mechanical failure. Set the automatic timer on the Time Portal for 3:55. That should provide ample time for me to strap on the Time Ship and for you to get the door sealed."

"And the return time?"

"Five minutes should be sufficient. That would have me and the Time Ship back here at 4:00 p.m."

"But surely," Albert interrupted, "five minutes could not possibly allow you enough time to verify that you have returned to the past, much less identify the exact date."

David could not contain a glint of amusement. "Albert, you still don't quite understand. Once I am in the past, I can stay as long as I like, five minutes — or five years for that matter. I won't return until I press the switch on the Time Ship. The return setting on the Time Portal merely determines that whenever I do press that switch, I will return to this spot and at 4:00 p.m. on this date. Do you understand now?"

"I suppose so," Albert sighed. "At least as much as my brain was meant to comprehend anything as nebulous as time travel."

"Don't concern yourself with it. In less than fifteen minutes, by your time, I expect to have even more marvels to relate to both of you."

Nothing more remained to be said, and as the reality of the moment forced itself on the three men, an awkward silence ensued, broken finally by David.

"No point in delaying. Henry, I want to make all the necessary adjustments inside the Time Portal. I know you feel uncomfortable about activating the Time Ship, so I've decided to relieve you of that responsibility as well. I'm going to use the automatic timer. That way, should anything go wrong — well, at least you won't blame yourself."

"That's really not necessary. If you want me at the controls, I'm willing to handle them."

"No, that's just the point," David insisted. "I don't want either you or Albert directly involved in what happens today. All you need to do is observe from the monitor. That's the way it's going to be. No arguments. Okay?"

"If that's the way you want it," Henry agreed. "It's 3:52 now. Better get ready."

David took the half dozen steps required to bring him to the Time Portal. As he stepped inside, for the first time the Time Portal seemed to Henry to take on an uncanny resemblance to an execution chamber. He wondered if it struck the others the same way. He didn't ask.

Henry assisted David in strapping on the Time Ship. If he looked foolish before in his Victorian era clothing, the addition of the Time Ship made him appear especially ludicrous, more like a character out of a Jules Verne novel than a twentieth century scientist. Henry could not help but think that under other circumstances he would laugh at the spectacle. He would say something about it on David's return. At this moment, however, he could not muster anything cheerful, much less humorous to say.

Just over thirty seconds were required to set the dials for the journey and return times.

"Less than two minutes to go. Are you sure, David? We can still postpone this."

"We have to go sometime, and I honestly cannot see that anything would be gained by waiting. Be sure the door to the Time Portal is closed. Don't worry. In a few minutes, at least by your reckoning, I'll be reporting a most fantastic adventure to you. Trust me."

"Goodbye, my boy." Albert offered his final farewell.

His face had become absolutely pallid and his voice choked with emotion. He positively astounded Henry, who had never seen him express the slightest sign of affection, by grasping David's arm tightly, and almost, but not quite, embracing him.

"Thank you again, Albert. We wouldn't be here if not for your help."

"Less than a minute," Henry cautioned.

"Right you are," David answered, breaking free from Albert's grip. "Close the door."

Henry pressed the button, activating the huge hydraulic arm that controlled the entrance to the Time Portal. Half a minute was required to seal David inside.

"Twenty-two seconds," he called out to Albert. "Get ready."

Both men braced themselves for the forces which by now they had come to anticipate. Henry, seated at the monitor, grasped the desk tightly. Albert could lessen the unpleasant sensation by closing his eyes, but Henry's attention was required at the screen. As the only scientist in attendance, he had to observe the procedure in order to record the results in the log.

"Ten seconds," he called out. "This is it."

Just as the second hand on the clock marked 3:55, the now familiar sensation that so strongly mimicked movement once again turned the laboratory into a whirling maze of violent, although silent forces. Because of the previous experiences with time travel, this one, for all its emotional intensity, was from Henry's perspective somewhat anticlimactic. The monitor provided such an incomplete view of the Time Portal that he was unable to see David's expression clearly. Also, since Henry had never viewed the process from this vantage before, he was surprised at how quickly it went.

Almost before Henry could blink David disappeared.

With David gone the laboratory suddenly seemed cold and empty. Henry and Albert who, except for their common bond to David, would never have been friends, suddenly found themselves alone. The silence that pervaded the room was almost palpable, neither of the men making any attempt to force a conversation they knew would only be contrived. Instead they both watched as the clock on the laboratory wall marked the seconds and eventually the minutes. The ensuing five minutes seemed to Henry to be the longest of his life.

Finally, just seconds before the 4:00 p.m. deadline when David was to return, Henry for the first time broke the stillness that had marked the past minutes by warning Albert to prepare for David's return. Unblinking, he stared intently at the monitor and breathed a sigh of relieved exhilaration, as the forces associated with the movement of time engulfed the laboratory once again.

"He's back," Henry proclaimed exuberantly. But his elation was to be short-lived.

"It can't be," he cried out suddenly.

"What is it?" Albert called out. "What's happened?"

"I don't know yet," Henry answered excitedly. "There was a momentary boost in the power level, and it appears the initial settings may have altered. I have to get in there fast."

Even as he was speaking, Henry had already pressed the button to open the door to the Time Portal. Immediately leaping from his chair, he bolted to the still opening door, pausing only long enough for the aperture to widen sufficiently for his lanky frame to squeeze through. What he discovered sent a sickening feeling welling up in his stomach and generated a sense of despair that he had never known before. The Time Ship had indeed returned home. It lay on the floor, looking like a hiker's backpack that had been accidentally abandoned. David, however, was nowhere to be seen.

Chapter 32

"He isn't there, is he?" Albert's voice reflected a tone more of resignation than actual inquiry, his voice uncharacteristically low, even somber.

"No — no, he's not."

Henry's response bordered on desperation. He was attempting not to give way to the fear that was rapidly welling up inside, his voice barely audible, his gaze still fixed on the chamber, as if perhaps David might somehow still be concealed in its tiny area, even though it barely allowed room for a large person to stand in.

"Can anything be done?" Albert asked. "Surely you can bring him back."

"Don't you understand?" Henry replied, making no attempt to hide the frustration he was feeling. "It's the Time Ship that comes back. David is now trapped somewhere in the past without it. But you're right about one thing. I have no intention of leaving him. There's only one thing to be done. I must try to go back and rescue David myself."

"What do you mean?" Albert seemed genuinely bewildered. "You just said he was trapped without the Time Ship."

"Not now," Henry answered abruptly. "I must check something. I'll answer your question in a moment."

Henry had run back to the monitor to retrieve the experiment log he had filled out before David left. His eyes darted quickly from the log, to the Time Ship, then to the dials on the Time Portal. Albert must have watched him make this same visual calculation at least five times before finally letting out a sigh that expressed the depth of his frustration without words.

"Something's been changed. I don't understand how it could have happened, but somehow the settings on the Time Portal have been altered, and on the Time Ship too."

"I have tried to be patient," Albert blurted out, "but I must insist that you tell me what has happened. I do have a right to know." Both men were clearly on edge and beginning to take out their helplessness on one another.

Henry looked up at Albert, his excited motions of the past few minutes gone, replaced by a weariness borne of despair. "You're right, of course, and I wish I had a better answer for you, but I don't."

"Why, Henry? What's happened?"

"It's the settings. They've been altered. I can't tell precisely what they should read or how they've been changed. Unless I can duplicate those settings exactly, I can't find David. Even a fraction of an inch could put my return off by several years, and David will be trapped in the past forever."

Albert said nothing in response. His face took on the look of stony indifference that Henry had always felt was Albert's method of hiding from his feelings, or at least his way of concealing them from other people. He turned and slowly walked softly to the Time Portal, paused at the entrance and looked inside, although Henry could not tell whether he was really looking or just thinking. After a moment, he just as deliberately stepped inside, his massive frame virtually filling the chamber, and ran his hand over the Time Ship. Almost casually he turned it over.

Henry had just begun to caution him not to touch anything, when Albert suddenly called out excitedly, "Dr.

Lindstrom, come here at once!"

As Albert stepped deliberately out of the confines of the Time Portal, Henry observed that he had picked up the Time Ship and had turned it over to expose the straps which only a few minutes before David had used to connect himself to the instrument.

"Come here! Look at this!"

An envelope had been taped securely to the bottom of the Time Ship. The mere sight of it increased the anxiety Henry was already experiencing. He had over the past few years been forced to deal with David's unpredictable nature more than once. The difference in their two personalities was the single most frequent source of conflict the two men experienced, Henry's scientific logic butting into the opposition that seemed so often to erupt from David's impulsive temperament. Henry said nothing in reply to Albert's excited outcry, but instead resolutely took the Time Ship from his outstretched hands, peeled away the tape which secured the envelope to it, and methodically turned it over. The envelope was completely blank.

"From David?" Albert asked hopefully.

"Almost certainly." Henry's response did not sound nearly as optimistic. "Perhaps you should open this." Henry held the envelope out to Albert. "You're the nearest thing to family David has."

"The envelope isn't addressed, so I believe we can safely assume it is intended for both of us. Please, go ahead."

Henry deftly tore the edge of the envelope, releasing a letter written in a hand all too familiar to both men. Once again he looked at Albert Stetson hesitantly.

"Go on, Dr. Lindstrom, please."

Henry momentarily scanned the heading and then began reading. With mounting excitement, he first read aloud the date on the letter — *September 3, 1910*, as Albert cried out in delight, "Good Lord, he's done it!" Henry started reading again, trying to contain the agitation he was feeling.

I recognize that what I have done must come as a shock to both of you. I'm truly sorry for the situation I have put you in. All I ask is for you to hear me out before you make any judgments concerning my actions.

First of all, let me divest myself of my scientific obligations by confirming what you must already have surmised. I am in what for you is the past. The actual experience of time travel was incredible, although not especially pleasant. The equipment performed perfectly, exceeding our most optimistic expectations. Should you desire to continue the experiments, Henry, I am confident that you will be successful.

Now a few words about the actual experience of time travel, although I am all too aware of my inability to describe the sensation adequately. To the extent that my experience can be used as evidence, it would appear that our theory of almost instantaneous transport was correct. I deliberately tried to observe the process in the smallest detail, but everything occurred so rapidly that I feel fortunate that my optic nerve was not destroyed in the process. You see, it was not a matter of images of the present being replaced by images of the past in any kind of sequential order, although when we observed the process from the laboratory that is precisely what we would have anticipated. Instead, my view was duplicated, like a double image on film. I saw the present, and I saw the past, both at the same time. To say the sensation was unpleasant cannot begin to describe it. The experience was absolutely horrifying. My mind could not quite latch onto reality. *My eyes tried to focus, but the dual images would not permit them to. In any future experiments I strongly urge you to make certain the subject is blindfolded to minimize this aspect of time travel.*

Strangely enough, the chaotic experience we felt in the lab does not hold for the person traveling in time, at least not during the process. I must now describe something that will appear to contradict what I just related. For the instant involved, while my body struggled to cope with the process, something else within me felt completely at rest. No, it was even more than that, and I know that what I am about to relate must sound rather metaphysical. I felt as if I was truly at peace for the only time in my life, and just for that moment, in the presence of something really remarkable. And I experienced a sense of disappointment that it had to end. I understand perfectly well that what I have just related contradicts the frightening aspects of the double images of time travel. However, inexplicable as it may seem, both aspects of time travel occurred just as I have described them. I have thought a lot about it, as you may well imagine, and I have a theory. It seems to me that the disorientation and fear I experienced as I perceived two time periods simultaneously was, even though a unique event, one that was completely within the framework of the universe and natural law. That other impression, the sense of calm that I have attempted to describe to you, I am virtually certain originated from some source outside the universe, at least the universe as we know it. If all this sounds mysterious, I am sorry, but you were not there. As a scientist, I can only relate what happened and my response to it.

The truly frightening aspect of time travel came when the process was completed, and I arrived in the past. I attribute the sensation to the result of being thrust back into the flow of time, and it was remarkably like the feeling we experienced in the lab, but magnified beyond comprehension. There was an added feeling of being thrust into the past, much like jumping off a rapidly moving train, except that experience seems tame by comparison. It quite literally knocked the breath out of me, and I cannot emphasize too much my conviction that time travel should not be attempted by anyone in less than perfect health. The assault on the senses, both mentally and physically, results in a strain on the system that could conceivably be dangerous.

Having the foresight to check out the old maps proved to be of great benefit. The street in front of the laboratory was still there, but of course it was only dirt with a little gravel sprinkled on it. But the road gave me orientation and a direction to travel. An hour's walk brought me to a small village. My clothing helped me not appear anachronistic, although I was quite overdressed compared to the farmers who seem to comprise the main portion of the population.

Before the first day was out, I rented a furnished room and purchased more appropriate clothing. A half hour at the local pub, along with a glance at the local newspaper, was sufficient to determine that I had returned to Thursday, June 11, 1908. I can say that now without flinching, but as much as that information must be affecting both of you as you read this, I do not believe it is possible for you to conceive how I felt. The exhilaration, the feeling of accomplishment, was almost overpowering. I could hardly contain myself.

Fortunately, the local townspeople's only conception of Americans comes from penny novels about Buffalo Bill and wild Indians. Come to think of it, for this period, they are not too far wrong. Anyway, they expected an American to behave strangely, and I am certain I did not disappoint them. But I learned my lessons quickly.

I eventually took up residence in a village near the west coast of England, and the people here are so simple and trusting that before long I could blend in reasonably well. Not that I really share their camaraderie, but at least they have come to tolerate my presence without constant whispering. Occasionally, one or two of them will even stop and share a short conversation with me. It will take time with these people, but they have already ceased viewing me with suspicion, and I am confident that eventually they will come to accept me.

So much for the scientific report. Now I must attempt to explain a situation you are going to find difficult to understand or accept. As you have probably guessed by now, I have determined to live the remainder of my life in the past. Believe me, this is not a decision I have reached lightly. I have struggled with it for quite some time. You need to understand that while presumably only five minutes have transpired for the two of you, I have been in the past for a little over two years. During that time I have established myself as a rather successful inventor. I do enjoy some rather unique advantages over my competition wouldn't you agree? Of course I'm careful not to make use of any really new technology. I just take what they already have and improve on it. The life I have settled on has brought me a contentment that the hectic pace of my own generation never provided. Of course, living in the past requires giving up a number of technological conveniences that your time considers to be necessities. Without romanticizing the hardships, let me just say that I am content with the tradeoff. Whether or not either of you would be is, I hope you will agree, quite beside the point.

I would, however, invoke a word of caution. I'm sure

you remember our dispute concerning the danger of altering the past. More than ever, that possibility looms before me. The danger needs to be taken quite seriously, so seriously in fact that in my judgment, the dangers inherent in time travel may be so great that it would be best to allow our technology to remain a secret and make no further attempts.

Specifically, I want it clearly understood that no heroic endeavors to "rescue" me from the past are to be attempted. As you will come to understand, I neither need nor desire any interference with the life I have determined for myself. If the alterations I made to the Time Ship operated as I hope, they have caused the settings on the Time Portal to be changed as well. Sorry, Henry, but I simply could not take the risk that you would attempt something foolish.

Since explaining all of this to outsiders would be awkward for you to say the least, I suggest that, should any questions arise, you simply claim ignorance of my whereabouts. I have no other family to be concerned with, but Creighton's disappearance could still cause the police to become involved. In that case my "disappearance" could actually serve a beneficial purpose by deflecting suspicion from either of you without endangering me.

There is one final matter that needs to be discussed, and I'll address this to you, Henry, because I can almost hear you asking if my decision to remain in the past isn't contradicting my own strong concerns about the dangers of allowing my knowledge of the past to alter it and therefore change the future? I have not changed my views regarding that subject in any way. I am still just as convinced as ever that I must never allow my knowledge to interfere with events in even the smallest way. However, I have already experienced some evidence that perhaps there may be controls built into the universe that make such alterations far less likely than I at first envisioned. Even so, I still perceive the threat of interference to be real and have resolutely determined to act under that assumption. Nevertheless, I am also convinced that my staying in the past does not in itself pose a threat. In any case, the decision has been made and cannot be reversed. I could say more about the subject, but I do not believe it would be prudent to comment any more than I have.

It's hard to close, knowing that this will be the last contact I shall ever have with either of you.

Henry, you have been a true friend, more than any brother could have been. At least we fought like brothers on more than one occasion. Should you decide to publish our accomplishments, you are welcome to all the credit, but I hope you will consider carefully my caution about time travel. I know you can't prevent someone else from discovering the process, but perhaps you can delay it until human beings are better able to cope with the technology. I'm already able to observe how here in the past advances are coming faster than our ability to control them. Unfortunately, I can foresee some of the disasters that are coming, but I cannot permit myself to do anything to prevent them. But you can, Henry. Think about that, will you?

And now, Albert. How can I express how much you have done in a most difficult position? You and Margaret have been such an important part of my life, and only recently have I come to understand how much I owe both of you, more even than you know. Thank you seems so empty, but the words are sincere.

Goodbye to both of you. Whatever you think of my decision, try not to judge me too harshly.

David

"That's all there is," Henry said quietly, handing the letter to Albert.

"You want to try to go back in time after him, don't you?"

"Of course I do." Henry's reply was adamant. "Surely you wouldn't consider letting David remain stranded in the past?"

"Hardly stranded I should think. Certainly I have no wish to be separated from David for the rest of my life, but to impose my own will seems rather selfish, don't you think? Besides, David indicated that it might be difficult to go back to the same time. Was he correct in his evaluation or not?"

The look on Henry's face revealed his frustration without the need for words. "We always knew David was brilliant. I don't even know how he did it, but he has succeeded in altering the setting on the Time Portal. I know the approximate setting, but even the smallest difference may represent years. Trying to find him will be going against tremendous odds; I admit that. Still, we have to make an attempt."

"And just why?" Albert asked. "Certainly I'm sympathetic, but you read his letter yourself. Didn't he sound more content than he has been in years? Try, just for a moment, to look at this situation from David's perspective. He has already attained his goal in life. The accomplishment is his. The honors are all that remain, and we both know that David's satisfaction always came from achievements, not accolades. In addition, he has experienced more than his share of tragedy here. Can you honestly say you could blame him for wanting to get away from this place, even this time? If David has discovered a life that has brought him the happiness that he failed to achieve in our own time, then I am not prepared to deny him that happiness. You claim to be his friend, Henry. If you are, then prove it. Let David live the life he has chosen for himself."

"You should have been a lawyer, Mr. Stetson," Henry's voice now contained more than a tinge of sarcasm. "While you were speaking, I kept trying to picture David in that world. Frankly I can't, and I believe that over time David would come to realize the mistake he made. Well, I'm not prepared to give up and let him go, just because of one letter that David probably came to regret he ever sent. Besides, I feel partially responsible for this whole situation. David was in no condition to make this experiment today. I should have insisted that I go in his place."

"In no way must you consider yourself to blame for what has occurred," Albert pleaded. "Nor do I believe it proper for either of us to second-guess David's wishes. I know he always was impulsive to some degree, but I think you will agree that, however dreadful the tragedies David has endured, they have strengthened him and made him a wiser man. David was no longer the brash young scientist you knew. Today he was a strong, determined, and quite courageous young man. Henry, you must let him go, just as much as I."

While Albert was making his impassioned argument, Henry appeared to be only partially listening. He had turned once again to the dials on the Time Portal and was intently making comparisons with what he observed there and David's copy of the research log. He had been acknowledging Albert's presence with only the barest sounds that were noncommittal at best. Henry finally walked back out of the Time Portal, stepped over to the monitor, and with one push of a button turned off the power that controlled the process of time travel. Only then did he turn to face Albert, a look of resignation on his face.

"There's nothing more I can do right now. Fortunately, from David's standpoint I have all the time in the world. With or without your help, beginning tomorrow, I will find a way to reach David and convince him to return with me."

"Dr. Lindstrom," Albert's tone for the first time became menacing, "I should think that through most carefully if I were you. I had hoped to convince you to drop this foolish attempt to find David; however, if necessary, I have other means at my disposal. You seem to be forgetting whose equipment all this is and the source of the money even for your salary."

Henry did not respond well to threats, so Albert's warning merely served to heighten his resolve, as well as bring his Texas temper out into the open. Most people who knew Henry never would have believed him capable of raising his voice, but on those few occasions when Henry lost his composure, he always left an impression on the object of his anger. This was one of those times.

"Don't try to intimidate me, Stetson. I'm not one of your 'gophers.' You may have a lot of influence, but I'm not so sure the agency providing the funding for this project will see it in the same light. The British government might be interested as well."

"There never has been any source of funding for this project other than directly from my own finances," Albert replied triumphantly. "Nor has the government any knowledge or interest in it. It has been, from start to finish, a strictly private affair."

For one moment Henry found himself unable to respond. He could tell that Albert Stetson wasn't lying. He knew it by the look of confidence in his face. It was the expression of a man who has just laid down four aces. He also believed Albert was telling the truth, because that had always been the one aspect of the whole project that never made sense. He knew (or should have known) that multimillion dollar grants aren't secured in a week's time, but four years ago he had chosen to ignore that inconsistency, because it was convenient to do so. Now his earlier indifference was coming back to haunt him.

"I don't care," he finally lashed out. "I'll go public with this. My colleagues will help me, once they see what David and I were able to accomplish."

"And just what proof will you show them?" Albert asked passively. "Your notes perhaps? Anyone could create those. David's letter? Do you really want that letter to be exposed to the likes of Ray Harris, and, by the by, that brings up another difficulty. I've gotten rid of Harris, but I doubt he'll stay away, if he reads the kind of story I think you'll create. There is also Creighton to be concerned about. If Harris gets involved, it's only a matter of time before his association with Creighton comes out. Then we'll have not one, but two disappearances to explain, and while I shall most certainly have some questions to answer, I have no motive to do away with either man. You, on the other hand, had ample reason to hate Creighton after he sabotaged your request with NORTECH. And as far as David is concerned, it wouldn't be the first time professional jealousy has turned one partner against another, now would it? Why I could testify in all honesty that you attempted to persuade me to influence David to let you take his place."

"I can't believe you would stoop that low," Henry sneered. "Just tell me one thing. Why are you doing all this? You and I have never been that close I know, but we've always respected one another. And David, what can you possibly have against David?"

"Dr. Lindstrom — Henry," Albert's reply softened, and for just a moment Henry thought he sounded almost apologetic, "believe me, I harbor no ill will toward you and certainly none toward David. I have spent my life looking after David's interests, and whether or not you can appreciate my actions, that is precisely what I am doing now. I truly regret having this situation come between us as it has, but I am determined to honor David's request. Come now, it's getting late. Go home and get some rest. There's really no necessity for us to quarrel like this. I feel certain that once you've had an opportunity to consider the matter, you'll agree with me."

"I really doubt that," Henry made no attempt to conceal his disgust. But, even though he would not admit it to himself, he knew that if Albert Stetson made good on his threats, Henry would be no match for him. Realizing that further argument would be futile, Henry abruptly turned away and stormed out of the laboratory.

Albert watched as Henry deliberately traversed the distance from the inner laboratory to the outer door of the building. He could not help but muse over one other time he had been left alone and compare the similarities, as well as the differences, between those two occasions. Although he felt no satisfaction over what had happened today, at least he had accomplished the assignment he had been given so many years before, an obligation he had accepted on trust, because his mother had steadfastly refused to confide her motivations to him. Everything had gone just as it should — as it must.

"I have completed the task you left me, Mother, and I hope to God I have done the right thing."

Albert walked toward the front of the building, his footsteps echoing through what had suddenly been transformed into a large, cold, lonely place. When he reached the door at the entrance, he paused for a moment to gaze outside. The intermittent snow, which had alternately advanced and retreated over the past few days, was once again coming down in large flakes, which the gusting wind took up and blew in chilling swirls.

As he peered out into the cold, Albert attempted to picture David in the world he had chosen, a world, he could not help acknowledging, no longer existed. To some degree, he felt a strong need to seek forgiveness from some source for what he had done. At the same time, another part of him cried out in protest that he was the party most injured. Just where did guilt lie in this confusing world? Only one aspect of the universe seemed constant — it was neither fair nor compassionate. In one sense he was forced to admit that Creighton had been right. The world is inexorable, unrelenting in its demands on the puny human beings who daily live out their short lives under the delusion that they have control over them. He had always believed in God, and he supposed he still did, but at the moment that faith brought little comfort. Albert Stetson buttoned the richly tailored cashmere overcoat he liked so much, turned out the lights to the building, and stepped out into the cold evening air.

*　　*　　*　　*

Henry slept that night, although he never understood how. Even so, his rest was fitful at best, disturbed by a dream that he felt certain was repeated again and again, a dream he was never able to remember, but which he sensed was particularly unpleasant.

The next morning he remembered the watch David

had entrusted to him before the disastrous experiment. He woke to discover that at 2:20 in the morning the watch, which had always kept perfect time, had ceased to run. Henry determined to have it repaired, but as it turned out, other events delayed that resolve.

At first Henry had determined to stay in London and fight Albert Stetson's decision to close down the project, even though common sense told him it was a battle he was almost certain to lose. An impromptu visit by a policeman later that day caused him to reconsider. It was really only an inquiry into the rented car that had crashed into the pole in front of the laboratory. The only thing suspicious about it was that the car was rented in Henry's name. By the end of the day Henry was cleared, since it was obvious that the signature on the rental agreement was forged. Anyway, the clerk remembered that the person renting the car as a large individual, looking nothing like the tall, lanky Texan. Questions remained unanswered, but nothing was found that implicated Henry in any illegal activities. Apparently Ray Harris had kept his word, and no one appeared to have reported Creighton's disappearance.

The complications were enough to cause Henry to yield to what he perceived to be inevitable. Within three days, he was on a plane bound for the United States. In later years he would have occasion to relive these days and would berate himself for the ease with which Albert Stetson enforced his will on him, even though at the time he felt he had little choice.

Later Henry did take David's watch to a jeweler, and then another, and another. None of them could find any mechanical defect which should prevent it from keeping time; however, all were equally unsuccessful at getting the watch to run. One shrugged it off, saying that rust and corrosion appeared to be the result of water damage. Eventually Henry kept it as the only remaining physical link with his colleague and best friend. Over the following years friends would occasionally inquire as to why he should carry a watch that didn't keep time. Finally they quit asking.

Chapter 33
April 1991
Northern Georgia

Gazing out the single window in his office, Henry Lindstrom was presented with a pleasingly tranquil view of the college quadrangle, complete with flagpole, a small but decorative fountain, and a crisscross of narrow sidewalks, designed to prevent the student population from creating their own less aesthetic paths across the manicured lawn. At this time of year the area was even more brilliant as the randomly interspersed pink and white dogwoods were just coming to their peak.

Henry's office was dominated by a massive oak desk, a minor extravagance, but one of the few privileges that fell to a department head of a small, but financially struggling institution. However, it was the bank of filing cabinets that made the office look smaller than it actually was. His wife occasionally teased Henry about being a packrat, especially as far as his work was concerned. The cabinets contained years of notes, tests, research papers, as well as articles he had written for scholarly journals going back to his years in graduate school. It represented his life, and he was never able to find the resolve to throw out any of it.

He had tried to mask his uneasiness from his secretary, but he knew that, although she said nothing, she was aware that Dr. Lindstrom appeared troubled today. Whether or not she had connected his manner with this morning's appointment he could not guess.

Outwardly the years had been kind to Henry Lindstrom. He kept the hair that still attached itself to the sides long so he could at least attempt to brush it over the top. What there was of it had turned a rich gray that might change to white in a few years, and his face was beginning to show a few wrinkles. In his case none of this really mattered. Since Henry had never possessed a physique or appearance that could even remotely be described as sexy, these effects of aging, far from detracting from his appearance, actually tended to make him look distinguished. Succumbing to the fitness craze that had transformed the country, Henry had taken up running three years earlier, and this sport more than anything else had allowed him to maintain a trim figure, although something about his bearing had virtually eliminated the lanky profile of his younger days.

Everything considered, he exhibited the demeanor of a distinguished college professor, an image made all the more authentic precisely because Henry made no attempt to cultivate it, anymore than he had ever concerned himself with the impression he made on others. Outwardly his life had become predictable and tranquil, and for the most part appearance reflected reality. Only in one aspect did Dr. Henry Lindstrom conceal himself from his family and colleagues.

Twenty-one years had passed, years which, everything considered, had been happy ones. Albert Stetson, whatever his faults may have been (and Henry had in the past years dwelt on them all), had actually been a benefactor of sorts. He had used his considerable influence to smooth over what seemed to Henry to be insurmountable difficulties and allow him to leave England for the United States within three days of that unfortunate afternoon when David had disappeared forever. He had even assisted Henry in obtaining a research and teaching position at MIT, a post Henry had maintained for six years before resigning to become a department chairman at a small college located in the north Georgia mountains.

None of his colleagues had understood what could motivate a Henry Lindstrom to give up the prestige and promise afforded by his position at MIT. Sometimes Henry himself wondered if he had been fair to the wife and three children he had acquired during this period. His family life had, in an age of deteriorating relationships, remained relatively serene, and his oldest girl would be ready for college next fall. His salary didn't allow for many extras, but with his wife's income from a small craft shop, he anticipated that they should be able to swing college, although not without some hardship. If Henry had one disappointment, it came from his inability to produce a son. The name he had picked out he never explained to his wife, although she had agreed, since Henry seemed so insistent. Eventually Henry reconciled himself to the reality that he would never possess the opportunity to make use of the name, because after the third daughter, the Lindstroms concluded they had acquired all the family they needed.

Henry had never been able to confide even to his wife the real reason he had sacrificed his career for the anonymity of a small college town. She was aware that he had been engaged in some type of research over the years, but since he had virtually no money except what he could save on his own, his work took on more the form of a hobby than serious experimentation. At least that was what his wife and the few associates that knew of Henry's work tended to assume.

In reality Henry was not the sort of person to give up, and in his heart he had never abandoned his plan to rescue

David from the past. His decision to accept Albert Stetson's assistance was pragmatic, determined by Henry's logical analysis of the situation. First of all, at the time he lacked the technical expertise to bring David back. Furthermore, he had enough experience in dealing with Albert Stetson to realize that should he choose to oppose him in any manner, there could be absolutely no doubt of the outcome. So he had left England and taken up his life again in the United States. Far from surrendering his dream, however, Henry had decided to invest his own life if necessary to accomplish what he had failed to do that bleak day in 1970. He comforted himself with the knowledge that if he could perfect the process, he could actually bring David back from the past to which he had been transported, or even transport himself back to a period before the disastrous experiment in order to explain the necessity of calling off the research. Henry took some comfort in realizing that he need not be concerned about the passing of time, his only limitation being the span of his own life.

Recognizing the demands of a full teaching and research career, Henry had determined to make a personal sacrifice and take a less taxing position, which would still allow him time to invest in the research which was his life's real goal. Unfortunately, time was rapidly becoming his real enemy. At fifty-six, Henry had accomplished much over the intervening years. The speed and accuracy of computers had overcome the major hurdle the three men had faced in 1970, and Henry felt he was now able in theory to pinpoint a particular time period and transport a person to that precise time. What he lacked was funding to rebuild the hardware, and for that dilemma he had so far been unable to find a solution. Henry's private nature had not changed over the years, so not even his wife or children perceived the growing frustration that he felt at possessing the solution to his life's pursuit, but having no means to implement it.

The buzzing of his intercom broke the chain of thought that had absorbed Henry for the past few minutes. "Mr. Hardison is here to see you," the voice coming through the intercom said cheerfully.

"Show him in, please — and, Nancy, hold my calls."

"Certainly, Dr. Lindstrom."

Henry seated himself at his desk, hoping it would endow him with an air of authority. If he didn't feel confident, maybe he could at least give the appearance of self-assurance. A moment later the door opened, and a distinguished looking man stepped inside. As Henry rose to greet him, the man smiled deferentially and took Henry's outstretched hand.

"Dr. Lindstrom," he said in a voice possessing a decidedly New England accent, "so good of you to see me on such short notice."

"A pleasure, Mr. — Hardison, is it? Well, you certainly knew how to pique my interest."

While he was speaking, Henry was mentally trying to assess this man who had so abruptly brought the past back into his life. Hardison presented a decidedly dignified, even a cultivated appearance. He was some years older than Henry, mid to late sixties he would guess. His hair was bright silver and exquisitely cut. The dark gray pinstriped suit he wore appeared to be of the finest cut. "Probably hand tailored," Henry thought.

But the one aspect of this man that Henry noticed more than any other was the way his eyes stared directly at him, as if he could read his very thoughts, a disturbing characteristic to say the least.

"If ever the label 'legal eagle' fit anyone," Henry

mused, "this man deserves it."

"Mr. Hardison, you indicated on the phone that you are here representing Mr. Albert Stetson. To be specific, you are his attorney. Is that right?"

"Yes, that is correct, but I am also Albert's friend, and that friendship has a lot to do with my coming to see you."

"Let's be honest with one another, shall we?" Henry declared. "Obviously if Albert Stetson sent you here, he must have filled you in on when and under what circumstances he knew me."

"Quite the contrary, Dr. Lindstrom. Truthfully, Albert has told me nothing specifically about you or his association with you. Since you seem inclined to 'clear the air' so to speak, I will admit to you that he cautioned me that you might be predisposed to think of him as your enemy, and me as well merely by association."

"'Enemy' is perhaps a strong word, Mr. Hardison, although, at an earlier time, I might have thought the term appropriate. I am not unaware of or ungrateful for the help Mr. Stetson put forth on my behalf some twenty years ago, yet even that assistance was not given without having some strings attached to it. Shall we conclude the subject, which appears as distasteful to you as it is to me, by my saying that Mr. Stetson and I had a rather severe quarrel, that I have always suspected that he possessed a somewhat manipulative nature, and quite frankly I don't believe he can be totally trusted. I hope what I've said hasn't offended you."

"Not in the slightest," Hardison replied. If he felt any emotion at Henry's sharp criticism of Albert Stetson, Henry could detect no sign of it. "Indeed, I appreciate your candor. It will make my job easier knowing your feelings. I have admitted that I am Albert's friend. May I speak a moment as his friend?"

"Please continue, but I do have a class in thirty-five minutes."

"Then I shall be brief, if it is within the province of an attorney to accomplish that." The attempt at humor did little to dissipate the tension Hardison felt emanating from Henry.

"As I said, your words do not surprise me. Albert had already led me to expect just such a response, and in all fairness, I can understand how Albert impresses people in the manner you have suggested. He is, after all, a most successful businessman, and an ability to conceal one's feelings and sometimes one's purposes can be as important in business as I have found it to be in the practice of law. Perhaps, Dr. Lindstrom, what you perceive as cunning derives more from your unfamiliarity with the nature of the business world than with any conscious deception on Albert's part.

"In addition, Albert is admittedly a very private individual. He does not lightly reveal himself even to his closest friends. If I may be so bold, I have heard you described in virtually the same manner. Yet this characteristic I have always attributed to his upbringing. Did you, by any chance, ever meet his mother?"

"Just once," Henry answered. "And then only briefly."

"A most cultured and charming lady, and, by the way, perhaps the wisest woman I ever had the good fortune to meet. Her influence on Albert was profound and I believe contributed much to what you perceive as his secretive personality. But I have promised to be brief. Much more could be said, but it would most likely be to no purpose. Instead I wish to tell you why I have come. Then you may judge for yourself."

Henry said nothing, but he noticed Mr. Hardison take just the slightest indrawn breath before continuing.

"I must tell you, Dr. Lindstrom, that Albert is dying, and he feels it imperative that he see you one last time. The purpose of my visit today is to persuade you to agree to such a meeting."

Henry forced himself to maintain an emotionless composure, unwilling to reveal his feelings to this stranger whom he still felt to be in some sense an adversary.

"Frankly," Henry responded, "I am completely mystified that Mr. Stetson should make such a request. He and I have had no communication since I returned to the United States over twenty years ago. I regret Mr. Stetson's condition, and I certainly do not wish to appear callous. However, as apparently even he recognizes, our relationship ended under somewhat strained circumstances, and I cannot see that anything could be gained by renewing it."

"Believe me, I understand your feelings. Indeed, I anticipated you would respond just as you have; however, I do beg you to reconsider."

"But you haven't provided me with any reason to do so," Henry protested. "If Albert Stetson wants this meeting so much, surely you can tell me what it is he wishes to discuss. And couldn't it be handled just as well through an intermediary such as you?"

"Nothing would give me greater pleasure than to put an end to your suspicion by providing the answers you seek," Hardison responded, "But honestly I do not know why Albert feels this meeting to be so crucial. I do wish to emphasize, however, that in his mind it is essential."

"I do not wish to appear discourteous, but it seems we are simply talking in circles. I can understand that Albert Stetson is used to getting what he wants, but in this instance I am prepared to be just as unyielding as I have known him to be. You have given me absolutely no reason why I should meet with Mr. Stetson, and without that I am not inclined to agree to your request."

Hardison said nothing for a moment, but his piercing eyes continued to stare at Henry, making him distinctly uncomfortable. After a moment, he heaved a sigh of resignation.

"You can be a formidable adversary, Dr. Lindstrom, and it appears you leave me no choice. You have asked for a reason to meet with Albert. Very well, I shall provide you with one. There is one other purpose for requesting this meeting, although Albert had wanted to tell you this himself. The information I am now going to relate is not the reason he wishes to see you, but perhaps it will convince you of the importance of his request. Anticipating your reluctance, he has instructed me that, should I deem it necessary, I am authorized to inform you that, since Albert has no surviving family, his will designates you as his principle heir. Within a few weeks, perhaps even a few days, you may expect to find yourself wealthy beyond your wildest imaginings."

Hardison's smile betrayed the satisfaction he derived from the effect his pronouncement had on Henry, and he decided to make the most of the tactical advantage he enjoyed. Rising quickly, he extended his hand to Henry, who took it mechanically.

"I don't understand," Henry finally found his voice. "Why should Albert Stetson favor me of all people? What you have said simply doesn't make any sense."

"Then may I suggest you raise that very question with Albert. Perhaps then you will receive the answer you seek. At any rate I have provided you with all the information I have. The next move, as they say, is now up to you."

Hardison started to leave, then turned abruptly and suddenly pulled an envelope from the inside of his coat pocket.

"By the way, Albert felt this might ease the burden of making the trip," he said, handing the envelope to Henry before finally taking his leave.

Henry had been quite put off guard by what he had just heard, and for a moment he stared at the envelope as if uncertain what to do next. After a few moments he opened it to discover two items which appeared so typical of Albert Stetson that for the first time he allowed himself to consider the possibility that what he had heard just might be true. One was a round trip ticket to Boston — first class. The other was a bundle of one hundred dollar bills, ten of them.

Chapter 34

Henry had not passed beyond the arrival gate at Logan terminal before being approached by one of the airport attendants.

"Dr. Lindstrom, will you come with me please?" Although Henry had never seen the man before, he obviously knew enough to recognize Henry by sight.

The attendant demonstrated his efficiency, as he personally assisted Henry with obtaining his luggage and having it carried to the door. At a slight hand signal, a white stretch limousine pulled up to the curb and halted. A uniformed chauffeur popped the trunk, jumped out, and efficiently deposited Henry's luggage. Henry could not help observing that in that setting his suitcases looked rather shabby.

After seeing that Henry was seated comfortably inside, the chauffeur spoke for the first time. "Reservations have been made for you, sir. Here is your confirmation."

The chauffeur was every bit the professional, as he handed Henry a small slip of paper bearing the logo of one of the most luxurious hotels in Boston. After everything else that had happened, Henry wasn't surprised.

"My instructions are to drive you directly to the hospital. Mr. Hardison will meet you there."

"I see," Henry replied. "Are you employed by Mr. Hardison or Mr. Stetson?"

"I have been Mr. Stetson's driver for the past twelve years, sir."

"Then perhaps you can tell me, is Mr. Stetson's condition as serious as Mr. Hardison led me to believe?"

For just a moment the stoic professionalism of the chauffeur was marred by a suggestion of what appeared to be genuine sadness. Could it really be that Albert Stetson's impending death was a cause for sorrow? "Mr. Hardison will have to fill you in on that, sir."

"I'm sorry if I appear bold, but I am curious. Does your hesitancy come from loyalty or reluctance to speak about your employer?" Henry asked, testing his earlier impression.

"Reluctance, you say? Not when we're speaking of Mr. Stetson, if that's what you mean. And if you'll not think it impertinent of me to say, they just don't come any better than Mr. Stetson, and I've been employed by him long enough to know. I've seen him in all kinds of situations, business and pleasure. You won't ever deal with a more honorable man than Mr. Stetson. But I'm speaking out of turn, sir."

"Not at all," Henry responded. "I'm sure Mr. Stetson appreciates having such a devoted employee."

Sensing that the chauffeur had no desire for further conversation, Henry lapsed into reflective silence, trying to put all the pieces together both from the past and the present. If this was some sort of scheme, Stetson was certainly playing it to the hilt. Although he didn't like to admit it, the seemingly transparent loyalty of the chauffeur made Henry feel decidedly uncomfortable about his own evaluation of Albert Stetson. Of course people are seldom simply good or bad. Nevertheless, here was a man who had a ringside seat in Albert Stetson's life, and his evaluation of the man's character was far different from what Henry's impression had been for so many years. Why should that be?

Henry's thoughts were interrupted as the limousine pulled up to a curb at a side door of what he assumed must be their destination.

"This isn't the hospital entrance, is it?" Henry asked, puzzled by the chauffeur's actions.

"This is the entrance to the wing where Mr. Stetson is a patient," he answered. "You will be met inside."

"What about my luggage?"

"It will be in your room at the hotel, sir."

A little reluctantly Henry acceded to the chauffeur's instructions. As puzzling as the whole situation was, like so many other elements, it had Albert Stetson's touch.

Immediately inside the door Henry encountered a desk so large that there was little doubt that at least part of its purpose was to block the hallway, barely allowing room for one person to pass. Behind the desk sat a security guard who smiled pleasantly, but whose massive bulk was enough to deter anyone from questioning his authority.

"May I be of assistance sir?" The man seemed friendly enough, but Henry doubted that assistance was the only responsibility for which this man was hired.

"My name is Henry Lindstrom, and I'm here to see Albert Stetson."

"One moment please," the guard responded mechanically, his eyes immediately turning to a paper in front of him, apparently a list of some sort. "Ah, yes, Dr. Lindstrom is it? But I don't recognize you as a doctor at this hospital."

"I'm a college professor, not a physician. I'm only here as a visitor."

"Very well, Dr. Lindstrom. I will need to see some form of identification, please. Just a formality, you understand."

Handing the guard his driver's license, Henry

observed, "No, quite frankly I don't understand. I've never been to a hospital with security such as this."

"Thank you, Dr. Lindstrom," the guard responded, returning Henry's license. "It's only this wing of the hospital that's controlled. The patients here are usually celebrities, political figures, or the like; people in the public eye. Certain restrictions are necessary, that's all. Now, if you will proceed to the bank of elevators to my left, and get out at the fifth floor, you will be met."

Henry knew of course that hospitals sometimes included VIP suites, but he still felt awkward at the privacy (or was it isolation) that the rich and famous sought to preserve even at the end. He had little time to consider the matter before the elevator opened, and Henry found Mr. Hardison waiting to greet him. Obviously the guard downstairs had called to inform him of Henry's arrival. The efficiency was a little unsettling.

"I'm delighted you agreed to come," Hardison beamed. To Henry his smile suggested not just cordiality, but also satisfaction at having succeeded in accomplishing his mission. "Albert was most pleased when I told him you had agreed to see him."

He escorted Henry past the nurse's station, through two massive double doors, and finally into the hospital wing itself. Henry could never have imagined a hospital looking like this. The walls were covered with rich mahogany paneling and decorated with original paintings, exquisitely framed. The floor was covered with plush carpeting. Huge chandeliers trimmed in gold provided lighting. The effect was to present the illusion of being in a five star hotel. All aspects of the appointments combined to suggest an aura of opulence that the vast majority of the patients or visitors to that hospital would never have dreamed existed.

"Mr. Hardison, I hope Mr. Stetson understands that all I've agreed to do is see him, and I still have reservations even about that decision."

"I dare say Albert understands your feelings better than I do," Hardison acknowledged. "Your kindness will mean a great deal to him, especially now."

"How is Mr. Stetson doing?"

"Not well, I'm afraid. Fortunately today has been one of his better days, at least so far. There's really nothing the staff can do for him, except provide medication for pain, and when that becomes too great, sedate him. He has begun to experience lapses in consciousness, and the doctors now say death will come very soon, perhaps even the next day or so, certainly within the week. But this morning he was coherent and able to converse fairly well. Ah, here we are."

They stood outside a large door. Hardison gave two quick raps, and the door was opened by a man in civilian clothes, who Henry surmised primarily by his physique, was nonetheless a part of Albert Stetson's private security. Apparently recognizing Hardison, he ushered both of the men in without saying anything.

Henry found himself in a small suite of rooms, richly furnished as he had come to expect. Once again there was the illusion of a grand hotel suite. The sitting room maintained a European atmosphere, actually a distinctly Victorian look. A door to the left opened up into another room through which Henry could just see the foot of what appeared to be a massive canopied bed. "Probably intended for the family to use," he thought to himself. Another door on the right remained closed.

"Has Doctor Tischler been here this afternoon?" Hardison asked the man who had admitted them.

"Not yet. He left word that he would be delayed, but

he expects to be here around 6:00. Is there a message?"

"Just tell him I'll call at his home tonight, if I haven't heard from him. How is Albert holding up?"

"Not much change. He's weak, but coherent, and although he doesn't complain, I think the pain is getting pretty bad. He has refused any medication today, because he knows it makes him sleep. Is this Dr. Lindstrom?"

"I'm Henry Lindstrom," Henry interrupted, feeling distinctly uncomfortable at being talked about in the third person.

"Mr. Stetson gave specific instructions that he wanted to see you the moment you arrived, but if you need to freshen up, there are facilities in this suite."

"No, I'll see him now."

"Come this way, then."

Henry was escorted through the door to the right, which the guard held open for him. Hardison started to go in, but immediately the guard gently, but firmly, extended his left arm, effectively blocking his entrance.

"Sorry, Mr. Hardison, Mr. Stetson was emphatic that he wished to see Dr. Lindstrom alone."

Hardison stepped aside, at the same time giving Henry a glance that he had difficulty interpreting. Henry felt that no matter what happened, he and Hardison could probably never become friends; business associates, perhaps, but little more. He stepped through the doorway with the guard following.

For the first time Henry felt as if he really was inside a hospital after all. The room was fully as spacious and well appointed as the rest of the suite, but furniture and art work, no matter how bright and luxurious, could not mask the chilling technology of the medical profession. The bed was occupied, although at a distance the person lying on it could scarcely be seen, connected as he was to a proliferation of what is euphemistically termed "life support" equipment.

As Henry, with some reluctance, approached the stark hospital bed which had been raised at the top just enough to keep the head at a slightly vertical angle, he could not restrain a momentary urge to shrink back from the grotesque figure that only his reason identified as Albert Stetson. He had of course aged, just as Henry had over the past twenty-one years. Mentally calculating Albert's age as being somewhere around eighty, Henry wasn't at all surprised at the deep silver hair, still superbly styled. "It must have been brushed just now for me," Henry thought to himself.

But it was the body on the bed that caused Henry to hesitate, not wanting to take those last two steps that would bring him to the bedside. Through the years, whatever else Henry had envisioned about Albert Stetson, he had always respected his bearing, the way he commanded obedience and (Henry now had to admit) respect from virtually everyone around him. The person stretched out on the bed was so unlike the Albert Stetson he had known that Henry could hardly believe him to be the same man. The hands, protruding motionless from the sheet, were shriveled and the fingers pointed till they almost resembled claws. The face appeared shrunken and skull-like, with eyes peering out of sockets so deep that it was impossible to determine whether or not they could actually see. In one moment the resentment Henry had held onto for more than twenty years changed to a feeling that the Albert Stetson he had known before would have tolerated less than pure hatred. Henry simply pitied him.

"Charles?"

The rasping voice brought Henry back to the reality of the room and its contents.

"Yes, Mr. Stetson?"

"Is that Dr. Lindstrom with you?"

"Yes sir; he's here."

"You may leave us, Charles."

Henry had no idea how much, if anything, this man knew about his relationship with Albert Stetson, but he suspected that anyone Albert Stetson selected to head his security staff would be competent enough to have developed a fairly complete file. At any rate, for a moment he remained motionless, except to turn and give Henry a look that conveyed his suspicion without words.

Perceiving the guard's hesitation, Albert repeated his request, only this time it became a command. "Leave us, Charles — now!" And then more softly, "Really, Dr. Lindstrom presents no danger to me, and at this point it wouldn't matter much anyhow, now would it? But before you go, help me up. I wish to converse with my guest like a man at least."

Still maintaining his stony wall of silence, Charles, as Albert had identified him, grasped Albert firmly under the shoulders and, with one seemingly effortless motion, lifted his almost skeletal frame slightly forward, allowing him the illusion of sitting up in bed. Utilizing four pillows which lay at the foot of the bed, Charles placed them securely on either side of Albert to prevent him from slipping down. Then, still maintaining the silence that seemed the man's dominant characteristic, he followed the instructions he had received and left the room. Henry barely heard the click of the latch as the door was pulled to.

"Well, Dr. Lindstrom," the voice that came from Albert was labored and rasping. "We meet again, one last time. We have some unfinished business to conduct, you and I, and not much time in which to conclude it. Shall we begin?"

Chapter 35

"Before I tell you why I have sent for you, would you mind pressing that switch?" Albert asked, one bony finger indicating a red button on a small lamp table beside the bed. Henry obliged, and within seconds the door swung open to reveal not only Charles, but two other men who had been in the sitting room.

"No cause for alarm, gentlemen," Albert's voice was subdued but reassuring. "Would you please ask Edward to step in here? I find that I need him after all."

"I'm right here, Albert." The voice was that of the attorney, Hardison. It suddenly occurred to Henry that Hardison had never offered, nor had Henry inquired, as to his first name.

"Excellent. Do you have the item I requested with you?"

"Yes, I do, Albert. I personally removed this box from your private safe this morning as you instructed."

"Thank you. Please bring it in and give it to Dr. Lindstrom. Then leave us alone again."

"Albert, you have been my friend far longer than my client, and I have no desire to challenge you unnecessarily, but do consider carefully. I have no idea what this box contains. Won't you please just allow me go over the contents, not just as your attorney, but as a friend?"

"Edward, you of all people know how I dislike having my instructions questioned. Indeed, you are one of the very few from whom I would even tolerate it. Nevertheless, let me assure you that in this instance your concerns truly are groundless. The contents of the box are of a purely personal nature and do not have any bearing on my business or financial affairs. Whether you approve or not, as of this moment they belong to Dr. Lindstrom. Please bring them at once."

"As you say," Hardison replied with a tone that suggested resignation rather than agreement. He left the room and returned a moment later, cradling a rather large wooden box which, with some hesitation, he placed in Henry's hands.

"Edward," Albert's labored voice was faint, yet still as commanding as ever, "I suggest you learn to accept Henry Lindstrom, because, like it or not, you will soon be dealing directly with him. Now, may we please have some privacy? I'm getting rather tired, and I have an urgent matter to discuss."

"Very well," Hardison responded. "But please don't exert yourself too much."

Albert waited until he once again heard the click of the door latch, before turning his head slightly to face Henry as directly as his position on the bed permitted.

"I must ask you to forgive what you must perceive as rudeness on the part of my staff. It derives, not so much from distrust of you, as loyalty to me. Over the years we have all found that a little suspicion has served us in good stead on more than one occasion, as I suspect even you would agree. Do you recall the time when you tried to convince David that Thomas Creighton posed a threat, and he was unwilling to believe you? It was my support that placed the guards back in the laboratory."

"Not that they did much good," Henry blurted out, and immediately regretted the tastelessness of his remark. "I'm sorry. I didn't mean to say that."

"But you are quite correct," Albert replied. "I have never flattered myself that all my decisions have been the right ones, but I do regret more than you can know your own feelings toward me." Henry started to reply, but Albert waved him off, his gaunt arm raised with obvious difficulty.

"Please don't attempt to deny it. We really don't have the time for such polite duplicities, or at least one of us doesn't. I know that you are suspicious of me. I suspect even hatred isn't too strong a word to describe your feelings. That is why I wanted to see you this last time, to try to make things right between us."

"Whatever my feelings may be, I cannot believe that you feel it necessary to repay me with an inheritance," Henry responded. "Such monumental extravagance makes no sense whatever."

"No, it doesn't, Henry, not as restitution anyway. Believe me, your place in my will has nothing to do with repaying any debt, nor is it an attempt to soothe my conscience. Please, do not misunderstand. What I have done I would do again. I would not take back any of my actions, but I do regret that they, of necessity, created such a negative impression of me.

"Enough of this," Albert changed his tone abruptly. "We're talking in circles. Let me tell you why I asked to see you. By this evening I trust you will understand more clearly.

"I expect you will have difficulty accepting what I am about to tell you, and that's why I asked Edward to procure the items you are holding now. They have been in the possession of the Stetson family for almost eighty years and have not been opened since my Mother sealed them almost that long ago. The seal is still intact, is it not?"

"Yes, it is," Henry answered, noticing for the first time the quaint and ornate design of the box. The edges came together at the top which had been bound with heavy tape and secured with some type of wax on which the initials *MS* had been delicately inscribed, apparently by hand. He also observed that whatever color the wax had been originally, it was now a dark brown, and the box itself emitted a somewhat musty odor.

"Within that box," Albert spoke, more slowly and deliberately than before, "I expect you will find proof that what I am about to tell you is true. Indeed, I suspect you will come to know much more than I about this matter, because, you see, even I have never opened it, as the seal proves. After you have examined the contents, I would like to see you again. What you do then is entirely your affair."

"You know, Albert," Henry replied (the switch to first names completed without comment on the part of both men), his eyes examining the ornate raised design on the box he was holding, "you always had a talent for melodrama. I certainly hope the mystery contained here is worth the secrecy that seems to have surrounded you all your life. At least you make life interesting."

Henry paused, and when there was no response, he raised his eyes. At first glance Albert appeared to have fallen asleep, but some indefinable abnormality about the body's position raised an alarm in Henry's mind. Without hesitation he raced to the door and called out to the men waiting outside. The man Albert had identified as Charles, along with what must have been another member of the security staff marched briskly into the room, while Edward Hardison ran quickly to the nurse's station. In less than half a minute, a nurse came in, followed moments later by a man who appeared to be one of the residents. They swiftly ushered everyone out and closed the door to Albert Stetson's room.

Everything had happened so quickly that there had

been little opportunity to say much of anything, but waiting now in the sitting room, Henry approached Hardison.

Sensing Henry's thoughts, Hardison attempted to put him at ease. "Don't worry, Dr. Lindstrom, no one suspects you of harming Albert. We've seen this before. I'm afraid he may have had a stroke. He's had a number of minor ones over the past few weeks, and there is really nothing that can be done except make him comfortable. The doctors have warned us that he probably could not withstand either a major stroke or many more of the small ones. We have just been waiting, you see.

"Sometime, after everything settles down, I hope that we can get to know one another better. While you were inside with Albert, his reproach caused me to reflect on what he said to me, and I believe his criticism was justified. You see, Dr. Lindstrom, I have handled Albert's affairs ever since he returned to the United States — more than twenty years. In that time I have come to know him well and to respect his character and resolve. I am forced to acknowledge that Albert was correct when he implied that my loyalty to him has resulted in a degree of unwarranted suspicion. I should have learned by now to trust Albert's instincts about anyone. I suppose what I'm trying to say is simply that I'm sorry if you have felt under suspicion or used in any manner."

"Well, I appreciate your sincerity, and right now I certainly could use a friendly face. But as for what Albert and I discussed, I'm afraid we were just getting around to the subject when he lost consciousness. He did, however, tell me that the box you gave me would provide proof of what he was about to tell me. With your permission, I'd like to take it with me. Assuming it contains nothing of a confidential nature, I'll be more than happy to share its contents with you once I've had an opportunity to examine it."

"I have no basis for denying your request. Technically, my approval isn't even required. I appreciate your asking though. Look, there's really no reason for you to stay. Why don't you go to your hotel? I'll call you if there is any change."

After Henry left, Hardison could not help but wonder just what connection a man such as Albert Stetson could conceivably have with a Henry Lindstrom, especially to leave him such a vast fortune. At first he had suspected blackmail, but quickly dismissed it. Albert Stetson would never have given in to blackmail. Anyway, under the present circumstances, Albert should have been immune to any threats, no matter what the nature of the secret. No, he was certain his suspicions of Henry Lindstrom had been unfounded. Hardison made his living by being able to see through the masks people use to hide their true identities, and although Henry most likely had his own secrets, Hardison was certain that they did not affect his dealings with Albert. In that regard the very openness of Henry's distrust convinced him that there was nothing sinister about Henry Lindstrom. That only left Albert and the strange box he had almost ceremoniously given to Henry. He had thought he knew almost everything about Albert. They had developed a friendship that had endured for so many years. But apparently the Stetson family had managed to preserve at least one secret. Now the box and whatever it contained was in the hands of Dr. Henry Lindstrom, and as much as he wished to protect at least Albert's reputation, there was absolutely nothing he could do. Hardison was not accustomed to this feeling of helplessness. He didn't like it.

Chapter 36

By the time Henry had checked into the hotel and settled into his room, afternoon had turned to evening. The sky had taken on a purplish cast, while a few high wispy clouds still retained a distinctly pinkish tinge, reflected from a setting sun that had all but completed its circuit for the day.

He felt tired. Not that he was surprised by that. More and more frequently Henry's body had a way of reminding him that he was no longer a young man, and when he looked in a mirror now, he could see that reality reinforced by the gray that dominated the hair remaining to him and some wrinkles that hadn't been there the year before.

There was another, perhaps greater reason for Henry's fatigue just now. This afternoon he had seen his own mortality reflected in the shriveled features of Albert Stetson. The recognition that the natural processes of time would eventually conspire to place him where Albert Stetson had been today, along with his acceptance of that most basic human link he shared with him, had done much to wipe away the years of resentment. Whatever Albert's responsibility for the past had been, the future had exacted its own inexorable payment.

Why had Henry allowed the past to be resurrected? Was it greed after all, or was it something else? He was finding his motivations difficult to assess. Henry had always been a man of simple tastes. His obsession had been science, and as long as he had enough money to allow him time for research, he was truly happy. He could not shake a nagging suspicion that, far from enhancing that singularly important segment of his life, immense wealth might make its own demands and in the process destroy the tranquility and contentment that had, for the most part, characterized his life.

Had he come then for his family? Now there was a real need that money could in fact alleviate. Not that he was poor by any objective standard, but he could not deny how agreeable a change it might be not to have to worry about stretching his family's income just a little further. Simple things, such as buying a new washing machine, instead of repairing their old model one more time. And he contemplated his daughters' educations, an expense he could no longer postpone. For the first time he might be able to consider the best schools, even without scholarships.

But Henry had to admit that these concerns had not been uppermost in his thoughts on the way to the hotel this evening. What most often came to mind were memories of the old research, buried for twenty years, images of David. He thought again of the halfhearted attempts at duplicating the experiment, of trying somehow to undo the past.

The choices cancelled out one another. Continue his research at MIT, and have money to invest in his private project, but no time in which to do it. Or abandon his research, teach full time, and have no resources with which to implement the knowledge he had gained. He had chosen the latter, but the failure was obvious. Could he have arranged his life differently? Henry wondered.

Now everything was possible once again. No, Henry wasn't a young man anymore, but he and David had done it all in only four years, and he still possessed all the logs, reports, and experiments. Working fulltime with unlimited finances he could still accomplish his dream. And in that one instant Henry knew precisely why he had accepted Edward

Hardison's bait. The impossible was now possible again. Even after twenty years David could still be saved from making a disastrous mistake.

The harsh ring of the telephone interrupted Henry's thoughts. He assumed it must be his wife, momentarily forgetting that she had no way of knowing where he would be staying, and he mentally berated himself for not having called her earlier. He had elected not to tell her about either Hardison or the real reason for his trip. "No use raising false hopes," he had rationalized. She had said nothing when he left, though she had always been able to tell when Henry was less than open.

Mechanically he reached for the receiver. The voice that answered wasn't the one he expected, and the somber tone of the speaker hinted at the message.

"Dr. Lindstrom, this is Edward Hardison. I deeply regret having to inform you that Albert died about fifteen minutes ago. The doctor said he simply didn't have the strength to fight anymore."

"Well, I don't know if you will believe me or not," Henry responded, "but I am truly sorry. I know how close you and Albert were."

"Of course, he knew how little time he had left, and I believe he was as ready as anyone can be. But I do regret that he was unable to complete his conversation with you this afternoon. It seemed to be so important to him."

"Yes it did," Henry agreed. An awkward silence followed as neither man knew quite what should come next.

"Have you by any chance examined the box Albert gave you?" Hardison finally asked.

"No, I haven't, Mr. Hardison."

"Please, my name is Edward. After all, we are going to have to deal with one another at least for a little while."

"Very well, first names it is. I only just got back to the hotel and haven't had a chance to open the box yet."

"Should you wish to safeguard it overnight, I would be only too happy to keep it in my private safe."

"Thanks for the offer, Edward, but in light of everything that's happened, I think the expedient thing for me to do is examine the contents tonight or at least as much of it as I can. Besides, my curiosity has been aroused now. I doubt I could sleep anyway."

"As you wish. With your permission, I would like to make the arrangements for Albert's funeral. He left rather specific instructions, and they are somewhat lavish. Since the cost will come from the estate, if you wish to review the arrangements, I can go over them with you."

"Certainly not. Whatever wishes Albert expressed should be adhered to precisely."

"Thank you. I'll let you know the details. After the funeral we can meet for the formal reading of the will; however, as I already told you, other than some relatively small bequests to his staff, you are the only heir. From this moment on, you are quite a wealthy man. I truly hope you derive much pleasure from that knowledge."

"To tell you the truth," Henry admitted, "I'm not really sure what I feel just now. All this has happened so quickly. I need to sort it all out, and I have a feeling this box is going to help. Call me tomorrow. Edward, could I prevail on you to make arrangements for my wife to fly here? I think we should both attend Albert's funeral."

"Consider it done. I will call you tomorrow morning with the flight information. Good night, Henry."

Henry had told Hardison he wasn't sure of his feelings, and he meant it. A man he had known and about whom he still nurtured strong, if ambivalent feelings, had just died and in the process transformed him into a multimillionaire. But right now, none of that seemed real. Sleep was out of the question. His first action was to call his wife and tell her about what had happened. The effort involved in convincing her helped Henry to believe it himself. By the time he hung up the phone, he decided the next priority was to examine a box that had been waiting almost eighty years to reveal its contents.

Chapter 37

Henry first took the precaution of assuring that the door was securely locked and the windows covered. He knew there was no reason for concern, not a rational one anyway. Still he did it. He wondered if he was becoming as secretive as Albert and whether this was a foreshadowing of what his life was going to be like from now on.

The box lay on top of the dressing table where Henry had placed it when he first came in. He had looked at it before, but now he examined it more closely. It was old to be sure, and although Henry was certainly no judge, he suspected that it might be quite valuable as well. It was a substantial piece of workmanship, constructed of what appeared to be dark mahogany, which time had transformed into rich ebony. The outside had been magnificently carved, apparently by hand, the surface displaying a design consisting of real and mythological creatures in a pastoral setting.

"Extremely gaudy and characteristically Victorian," Henry thought to himself. Surprisingly the box contained no lock whatsoever. Rather it closed by means of one ornate clasp made of brass.

Henry placed the box once again on the dresser, removed the tape surrounding it, carefully unhooked what remained of the clasp, and attempted to lift the hinge. The lid would not budge. The wax seal had hardened so completely that it served to protect the box almost as effectively as any lock might have done. Henry reached into his pocket and drew out the pocketknife he carried out of a habit formed from years working in a laboratory. Although several attempts were required to cut through the hardened wax, eventually the knife did its work, and Henry carefully raised the lid.

The interior had been covered with a royal blue satin fabric and was not nearly as deep as the exterior of the box would have suggested. But it did not need to be, since it only contained one item. Henry reached in and pulled out the small package that lay inside, noting that it had been covered with white tissue paper which the years had turned a dark sepia color. Tearing away the wrapping, he discovered what appeared to be a small notebook, but it bore none of the exquisite trappings he would have expected of anything belonging to the Stetson family. Instead the little volume appeared to be quite cheaply made, and the cloth covering was badly deteriorated, as were many of the pages. The book was apparently designed to allow it to be adapted to serve a variety of purposes, depending on the needs of the purchaser. The title page and apparently a significant section at the beginning must have become lost or been destroyed before the book was deposited in the box; however, a cursory glance at the first surviving page of the volume left no doubt as to its function. The book had obviously served as a diary. Sensing that at least a portion of the information Albert wished to reveal to Henry before his death lay in this little book, Henry settled into the richly padded recliner he supposed was standard fare in hotels such as this and began to decipher the handwriting in the diary. It was written in a cursive script that was both precise and delicate, almost a form of calligraphy. Henry suspected it was written by a woman.

The first several pages contained nothing extraordinary, nor did they reveal the identity of the writer. Henry was able to discern that the year being described was 1908 and that the writer appeared to be a young girl, unmarried, possibly in her late teens, caught up in the anxieties and discoveries of adolescence. She worked in a textile mill and, judging from her diary, seemed to have been as preoccupied with young men as was the oldest of his daughters. Despite her obviously lower class status, the young diarist must have received some education, as her writing was remarkably good for someone in her station in life, although it was reserved and formal in the style of the day. Her most noticeable peculiarities were her rather sparing use of punctuation and a penchant for dropping final consonants even in writing, undoubtedly a reflection of her actual manner of speaking.

Putting all the pieces together wasn't too difficult, and Henry very quickly felt that he knew whose diary it was he had before him. Intrigued by the sense that some mystery might be contained within the pages of the musty volume, yet still feeling somewhat a voyeur for reading a young girl's diary, Henry nevertheless settled back to discover whatever secrets might be revealed in the diary before him. Deciphering the document was at first a slow and tedious procedure, made even more difficult by missing or partially destroyed pages, faded ink due to a large number of water stains, and the quaint spelling and phraseology characteristic of someone semi-educated in the Victorian style. Nevertheless, as Henry's eyes grew accustomed to the style of writing and the peculiar forms of the letters, he became less conscious of the writing itself and found himself increasingly able to concentrate on the story being unfolded. At first the relatively uneventful life of this simple working girl from so long ago was almost putting Henry to sleep with its monotony, when suddenly he began reading an entry that made him alert and intent once again.

26 June 1908

Received a half day holiday today due to the owners birthday. Sarah and I decided to sneak over to the new pub what Molly Sturbridge and her husband Alistair just took over on the coast, The Hungry Pelican they calls it. I know it was quite the naughty thing to do, and I should likely be canned if my employer was to discover that I had gone to such a place, but that was part o the fun o it. Beside, hadnt Molly Wexford been one of my best friends at the mill before gettin herself married last year?

O and we did have such a fine time. So many fishermen, tellin o their ships and catches. Why bein right there at the sea you could just almost smell the salt even as they was talkin about it. Sarah got a pint o ale, but I was too scared and just had some tea. I did take a taste o hers though but didnt like it. It was foul tastin and I almost gagged just tryin to get it down.

But the really excitin part was that I met a yank there and what a wonderful strange man he was. I never did quite find out what an American was doin here in England and such a fine cultured man he was too. Why the man spent all the time askin me and Sarah questions, just like our lives was somethin important to talk about. And he was a handsome man, he was. But alas I never even learned his name nor gave him mine it not bein quite fittin since we wasnt really introduced proper.

Sarah wants to go back to the pub next Saturday after work, but Im afraid o gettin caught. And yet it would be ever so grand to see the American gentleman again. He told us he was boardin right there in the pub in one o the rooms up above that gets rented out. I know that I oughtn to go. But he sure was a handsome man.

Two or three pages of the diary had apparently become lost, because when the narrative continued, four days had passed, and the top of the page merely related some incidents at the mill, some kind of tiff between the writer (who Henry was now convinced was Margaret Stetson) and a coworker. Too much had happened this day, and he suddenly became aware of how extremely tired he was. As much as Henry wanted to continue, he found himself nodding and unable to concentrate. Carefully returning the diary to the box that had been its protector for so many years, Henry retired for the night.

He couldn't exactly remember his dreams the next morning, but he knew that David had been part of them as had Margaret Stetson. He was also certain that they had not been particularly pleasant, but had been in some indefinable way curiously familiar.

Chapter 38

For two days the diary Henry had begun reading lay untouched in his hotel room, not from lack of interest, but because of the insistent demands occasioned by Albert's death. The mountains of paperwork Edward Hardison kept thrusting at him left virtually no time to pursue the matter. He hoped Edward really could be trusted, because he had been overwhelmed by the sheer number of documents he had signed, having to do, not only with the Stetson estate, but also the vast holdings and numerous business ventures with which the family was connected to varying degrees. Today, however, Henry had been given a reprieve of sorts. Albert's funeral was the only activity formally scheduled.

Henry and his wife, who had joined him the day before, were being driven to the cemetery where the body of Albert Stetson was to be laid to rest. Carolyn Lindstrom was almost six years younger than Henry, whom she had met while working as a lab technician at MIT where Henry was teaching at the time. From the beginning, their temperaments and expectations led them naturally, almost predictably, toward one another. Carol was in no sense unattractive, but she would never have been described as glamorous, simply because makeup and clothing were not the highest of her priorities. First her obsessive interest in her work and later the incessant demands of motherhood made their claims on her time and in so doing charted her life. Carol Lindstrom never did stand out socially, although she attended and occasionally hosted the expected staff functions, at which she conducted herself correctly and, of course, predictably. Friends of the Lindstroms sometimes had difficulty imagining these two introverted people even possessing anything like a passionate nature, despite the evidence of three children. For their part, Carol and Henry never cared for glamour or excitement, finding contentment instead simply in one another and their family. And it was this simple, uncomplicated lifestyle that Henry most feared might be disrupted by the present turn of events.

Henry had maintained only one secret from his wife during all the years of their marriage. He had never found a way to tell her about the time travel experiment except in the broadest terms, and he had always described it in such a manner that she would never suspect the project ever advanced beyond theory. Henry at times felt a degree of guilt for not being open with his wife. His reluctance to share with her came, not from a desire to deceive Carol, but because that part of his past evoked unpleasant memories upon which he preferred not to dwell. Now the very possibilities opened up by his inheritance from Albert Stetson had turned that wealth into a two-edged sword, forcing Henry to face squarely the dilemma of what to do with those experiments, and how to tell Carol the full story after so many years. Becoming instantly rich was complicating his life in ways he would never have anticipated.

Although Henry had some idea of the dimensions of the Stetson fortune, the implications of immense wealth continued to surprise him. The various officials who attended Albert's funeral comprised a veritable "Who's Who" of the economic and political community. Massachusetts Governor Weld was there, along with one of the editors of the Boston *Globe*. Even the *Wall Street Journal* sent a reporter to cover the event. Henry forced himself to face the reality that, like it or not, he was destined to walk in different circles in the future, a situation he viewed with some degree of reluctance, while acutely aware that his family considered the prospect exhilarating.

As the chauffeur pulled the limousine to the side of the road behind others that had formed a caravan from the funeral home, Henry felt a vague, but disquieting sense of déjà vu. Only when he reached the newly dug grave did he recognize the basis for his feeling, which came with the realization that he had been at this very spot before. There, beside the opening, freshly dug to receive the remains of Albert Stetson, was the marker bearing the name of Margaret. Of course, Albert had never married, and it would only be natural that he be buried beside his mother. But the scene brought back memories of that other time when he had come here with David, and the intrusion of those recollections only served to magnify the sadness normally associated with funerals.

Henry had always nurtured an intense dislike for funerals anyway. They made him uncomfortable because they kindled emotions, and Henry was not a person given to an open display of his feelings. Even after his brother's death years before, he had dealt with his grief privately in his own way. This one was worse, because he had no strong feelings for Albert Stetson, and for the most part those he did have had not been favorable, although he had to admit the events of the past week had managed to muddle his thinking in that regard. The first shovel of earth thrown into the open grave brought his mind back to the present, and just as he turned, he saw Edward Hardison approaching.

"You must be Mrs. Lindstrom," he smiled broadly, for the moment ignoring Henry, while firmly accepting Carol Lindstrom's outstretched hand. "So good of you to come."

"Carol, this is Edward Hardison, Albert Stetson's attorney — and friend."

"A pleasure, Mr. Hardison," she responded. "Henry has told me about you, of course."

"I hope he hasn't painted too negative a portrait of me. Regrettably, circumstances forced both of us to begin our association somewhat as adversaries. I hope we're past that now. How long had you planned to remain here in Boston?" Hardison asked, turning his gaze toward Henry.

"To tell you the truth," Henry answered, "I haven't quite decided. Despite everything that's happened, I have no immediate plans to quit teaching. I enjoy it too much. Although I have been involved in some private research I just might wish to pursue more seriously."

"I quite understand," Hardison replied, "and I didn't mean to pry; however, there are a number of formalities to attend to which may require a little time. I have attempted to prioritize the elements of Albert's estate that require immediate attention, and most of the more pressing matters can be completed within a matter of a few days, a week at most. This would allow you access to at least some of the Stetson funds for your own use. Could you see your way to remaining that long?"

Giving Carol a sidelong glance that possessed all the elements of a longtime marital signal, Henry responded, "I see no problem staying that long. My classes are covered for awhile."

"Fine, and after tonight you should find your stay far more pleasant. Tomorrow you will be able to check out of the hotel and begin living at the Stetson mansion. It took some doing, and of course final transfer of ownership will take a little more time, but, for all practical purposes, you may consider the home your own."

"Oh, Henry," Carol said excitedly, "how marvelous. Your description of the house makes it sound quite grand."

"It certainly is," Henry agreed. "I was there once before a number of years ago, but I remember thinking I had seen nothing that could compare with it, at least not in America."

"Is that so?" Hardison asked. "When were you at the mansion? I don't believe Albert ever mentioned it to me."

"He would have had little reason to do so. Ironically, I was attending his mother's funeral at this very spot."

"Strange, I didn't realize that your association with Albert went so far back."

"Actually I knew Albert only superficially. I was at the time working on a research project with David Evans."

Henry found himself feeling decidedly uncomfortable at the direction the discussion was taking and was endeavoring to respond to Hardison's question without encouraging a lengthy conversation.

"Oh, yes, I've heard bits and pieces of that story. I always sensed that Albert never liked to talk much about it. Apparently David just disappeared without a trace, and no one was ever able to locate him."

"Yes, well it was a long time ago. Now, if you'll excuse us, we really need to be getting back to the hotel."

"Very well," Hardison replied. "Come by tomorrow morning, and I'll have the keys to the Stetson estate. It was a pleasure meeting you, Mrs. Lindstrom."

"Thank you for all you've done for us, Mr. Hardison," Carol replied graciously.

Henry quickly led Carol to the limousine and hurried her inside. He was silent during the drive to the hotel. Carol noticed it, and years of living together enabled her to sense Henry's need for privacy, so she said nothing.

Later that evening, Henry was once more alone in their hotel room, having encouraged Carol to take advantage of the visit to do some shopping. Actually Edward Hardison's questioning had again aroused his curiosity. He took out the ebony chest which he had placed on the top shelf of the closet, and once again removed the diary, which he felt certain described the life of the young Margaret Stetson. Settling back in the recliner, Henry searched until he found the entry he was looking for and began reading.

4 July 1908

I cant say if it was right or wrong, but I went back to The Hungry Pelican this afternoon, and sure enough the American gentleman was there. I know his name now. Its David, and I do think hes grand. Is it really possible to fall in love so soon after meetin a man? And how could I ever hope to think he could give a second thought to an ignorant girl like me.

When I told him me name, he looked at me so strange, like he was lookin at me, but seein somebody else. I declare I dont know quite what to make o it all. But hes so mannerly and anyone could see how well bred he is. I feel like a real bumpkin around him I do. But Ive decided to do somethin about it. Startin tomorrow, Im goin back to me old teacher from school. He always said I was smart if I had just applied meself. Well, Im goin to do it, and before ya know it I wont be half so embarrassed to talk right up to David. Just wait and see if I dont.

Henry stared in amazement that his initial opinion

had been so dramatically confirmed. Now he knew at least a little of what had happened to David when he went back in time, but there was obviously far more to this increasingly complex story. Hearing his wife's knock at the door, he placed the book inside the chest, depositing it quickly back onto the shelf. Tomorrow, by one means or another, he meant to get to the bottom of this mystery.

Chapter 39

"Can all this really be ours?" Carol asked, as she gazed in wonder at the elegance of the Stetson home.

"Well, technically it isn't, not yet anyway," Henry cautioned. "But Hardison assures me that it's just a matter of a little time and my signature on some papers. So, I suppose we can treat this house as our own."

"Oh, but Henry," Carol sobered suddenly. "I'll never be able to keep up a house like this. And the yard! However will we be able to maintain it?"

Henry could not suppress a smile at his wife's failure to comprehend the magnitude of the changes in their lives.

"Honey, whoever lives in this house will require the services of at least a maid and a gardener. I'm afraid you're not just a housewife anymore. From now on you're going to have to manage the staff."

"Oh, but that's so expensive."

"We can easily afford it — and so much more. My dear you might as well get used to a life of leisure, because that's the lot we've drawn."

"Oh, darling, I do love you so!"

"Me or my money?" Henry quipped.

"What do you think?" she asked, her voice dropping to a whisper, as she rested her head against Henry's chest.

Henry reached out with one hand and slightly raised her head, firmly pressing his mouth to her upturned lips. "Have I told you recently how much I love you, Mrs. Lindstrom?"

"I think so," she sighed, "but it doesn't hurt to tell me again.

"Henry," Carol rose up suddenly, "is all this going to change us? I mean, we're not used to this kind of life, and you hear so much about how it destroys some people."

"Well, I'll tell you, Mrs. Lindstrom," Henry began speaking in his most exaggerated Texas drawl, "it just so happens I've spent some time thinking about the same possibility."

"Oh," Carol responded playfully, "and have you come to any monumental conclusions?"

As Henry looked at Carol, he suddenly felt he truly was the luckiest man on earth. The lighthearted smile on his face was replaced by a more serious expression.

"You know what I think, honey? Money doesn't change people, not unless they let it. And we're just not going to let it.

"Besides," Henry resumed his previous playful demeanor, "can you really imagine me getting into the tuxedo and dinner party routine?"

"I suppose not, dear," Carol agreed. "It's just that all this is so overwhelming. I honestly don't know where to begin."

By now Henry and Carol had made their way into the sitting room, the same room Henry could not help recalling, where he, David, Cathy, and Albert had gathered after Margaret Stetson's funeral.

Suddenly an idea came to Carol. Flush with excitement, she turned toward Henry. "Darling," she began breathlessly, one sentence tripping immediately upon another. "I just thought of something we could do with a little of the money. Could we do some traveling? We've never been able to afford a real vacation, not since our honeymoon, and I've always longed to see Europe, and you really don't have to teach anymore. You've been to Europe, but I never have. Oh, could we go, please?"

"Well, if you'd stop long enough to take a breath and give me a chance, I might answer you."

"I'm sorry," Carol laughed. "I guess I did get carried away, didn't I?"

"Just a little," Henry laughed, although his humor seemed a trifle forced and Henry suddenly appeared a bit nervous.

"Carol, sit down beside me a minute." Henry motioned her to a large sofa, the same one, he recalled sitting on the afternoon after Margaret Stetson's funeral. He took her hand and gently caressed it with his thumb, looking intently at her face, as if searching for something. After a significant pause, in which the gaiety of the previous moment was completely dissipated by his sudden seriousness, Henry determined that now was the time to share the one secret he had kept from his wife.

"I'm thrilled that finally I will be able to do all the things for you I've always wanted to do. I love you so much, even though I've never been particularly romantic. I hope you've always known that."

"Darling, what does all this have to do with going to Europe, and why so serious all of a sudden?"

"Carol," Henry began hesitantly, "I would love more than anything in this world to go with you to Europe — or Timbuktu for that matter, and I promise you some day we will do all that and more. But just now I've been thinking a great deal about this money and how it could provide a real opportunity for a project I've wanted to complete for a long time. Would you object if I did quit teaching and got involved in research fulltime for awhile?"

"Are you referring to your time travel experiment, dear?" Carol asked matter-of-factly.

"How could you possibly know I was still involved in that?" Henry asked in amazement. "I've felt guilty for so long not confiding in you as it is."

"Darling, we've been married for almost eighteen years. Give me a little credit. I knew when the time was right you would tell me all about it. Can I assume that time has come?"

"Almost," Henry countered, wondering just how much Carol did know. "This whole project is tied up with the Stetsons, and in some respects with their fortune. I've recently come across some documents that I must examine before I can decide how to proceed."

"What you're trying to tell me is that you need some time to yourself. Am I right?"

"Just a little dear. By tonight, I should be finished, and then I'll tell you all about it."

"Well, a trip to Europe would be lovely, but you know it can wait, if your research needs to come first. Meantime, I really need to get back to the children. All this excitement has been difficult for them too. Why don't I fly back and provide them with some moral support and give you some time alone."

"You won't mind leaving this house?"

"We'll have the rest of our lives here, if that's what we want. You get your work done and give me a call when you're ready."

Quite suddenly Henry reached out and gathered Carol into his arms for a long, lingering kiss. A little out of breath, Carol finally pulled herself free. "Dr. Lindstrom, what was that about?"

"That was my way of saying thanks for being so

understanding, and to let you know your stodgy old husband hasn't completely forgotten how."

After Carol left him to pack, Henry contemplated once again how lucky he was. To others, his and Carol's life together might have seemed monotonous. As far as he was concerned, he was content and happy, which was more than a lot of people he knew got out of life. As for the future, he would wait and see. Right now he was anxious to get to a task he had put off far too long. First get Carol to the airport and then back to that diary.

*   *   *   *

It was early evening before Henry finished the diary, and the story it related had truly been astounding. He had always maintained a healthy respect (even if sometimes grudgingly given) for the single-mindedness which seemed to constitute an almost inherited trait of the Stetson family. Albert had certainly possessed a dogged determinism, which had stood him well in his business dealings. After tonight, he was convinced Albert must have learned it from Margaret. As he read further into her diary, he was amazed at how completely she had followed through on her resolve. Within two months, the grammar in her diary improved perceptibly. In less than a year, her diction and spelling were absolutely polished, even while maintaining the formality characteristic of the period. Although still a poor textile worker, Margaret Stetson had already begun the transformation into the compelling woman she was to become.

Margaret's commitment to improving her image was one sphere of her life which commanded Henry's respect.

There were two others.

The first was the depth of her love for and trust in David, which allowed her to accept the truth when he revealed it to her. As he read the final entry in her diary, Henry felt he could empathize with Margaret's struggle to accept what must be true, even when all her beliefs and preconceptions must have resisted that truth. In some respects her own conflict seemed one small example of her whole civilization's agonizing journey into the modern world, a voyage made erratically and fitfully, and occasioned by wars and convulsions the world had never before experienced and hopefully might never see again. Her words, echoing from so long ago, reminded Henry of his own confrontation with David, and he read her account with a degree of empathy he would have never thought he could feel for her.

The other characteristic manifested itself most strikingly in her courtship of David. In an age when most women were taught from childhood not to aspire beyond their appointed station in life, Margaret possessed the ability to see what she wanted and the drive to make it happen. Had she been a woman in today's world, her actions would not have seemed that unusual, but for a turn-of-the-century mill worker, such resolve was indeed remarkable.

Henry's assessment had been based on the last entry in Margaret's diary.

14 September 1909

Who would have thought of such a day as this has been? I should be happy, for I have succeeded in becoming engaged to the man I love, but my head is nearly spinning with what I must now believe to be true. My David comes from a time I don't share. He grew up in a world I cannot even begin to dream of. Can it be real, or am I losing my mind?

It all started out so fine. We met again at "The Hungry Pelican." David says it has a special meaning for him, but I could tell he didn't want to talk about it. I think it has something to do with his life before, or should I say his life after. I'm so confused I hardly know what to think anymore. I suppose I shall have to get used to a lot of secrets from my husband, and I don't like having to do that, but I do trust him and I love him so, and I know he loves me too. I think I shall have to learn to be content with that.

Anyway, it was there in the pub he proposed to me. Not that I wasn't expecting it. We've been seeing one another for over a year, and we've both known for more than two months now that we loved one another. I suppose David needed time to work out how to tell me about how he came to be here. Not that he did it at once. He proposed first. Of course I said, "Yes," right away. Then he got a real serious look on his face and told me that before we could be wed, he had something very important to tell me about himself, and could we go somewhere we could be alone and talk? There was a bit of a chill in the air, but I had my shawl with me, so it was not so bad that we could not take a stroll along the coast. It must have been near high tide, for the waves were crashing against the cliffs something fierce and the sky so clear you could see every star God ever made, shining as bright as those new electric lights that were just put in the hotel in town.

David took my hand softly. He is so gentle, not at all like the rowdies that most of the boys around here tend to be. We walked for several minutes, and I think he must have been trying to think out how to tell me. Finally David bent down and kissed me, long and hard, but somehow gentle too.

We came to a stone bench built along the side of the path for people to rest on, and he asked me to sit down there, and then right out of the blue, he tells me that he has come from the future, that he will not truly be born for another thirty years. Well, I thought he was joking with me, and I was a little put out that he should make light at such a solemn time, but before long I could tell he meant it. Then it was I got a little frightened. I'm ashamed to confess I wondered if David had escaped from an asylum somewhere. But what finally convinced me was when he took a coin from his pocket that had the year 1969 on it. David acted strange about it. He said he brought it with him by accident and only discovered it later. He only kept it to show it to me, and after tonight he said he was going to destroy it. David seemed so forceful about it that it almost frightened me in a way. The figure on the coin was unusual looking. He said it was an American president, that it was Mr. Roosevelt of all people. Yet, for certain it didn't look anything like Teddy, and I told David so. He said it was a relative of his, and in time I would come to know who it was.

And that was that. The fact is I believe him. If a girl can't believe in the man she is to marry, then she oughtn't to be doing it, I say. And I know that, whatever else may be false in this world, my love for David and his for me is true. If I can have that, I will gladly take whatever else' life may have in store for me. Neither of us has any family to consult, so we're just going to be married, and in only two weeks I shall be Mrs. David Evans. My but it does sound grand.

With Margaret's jubilant hopes for the future, the narrative came to an end. Henry carefully replaced the diary in the tissue that had protected it for so many years. He now knew part of the story. Indeed, he had already learned enough to question the security he had always found in the predictability of science. But the diary had only revealed a portion of what happened to David. If only Albert Stetson had lived a little longer, he might have explained it all. Now, more than likely, Henry would never learn the rest. But the more he considered the matter, he began to think that maybe that was for the best. Perhaps it was even a hopeful sign. The final chapter of the story wasn't revealed by Margaret Stetson, because perhaps David's life wasn't finished yet. That was all the encouragement Henry needed to finalize his resolve to resurrect the experiment that he had been waiting more than twenty years to complete.

Chapter 40

Henry had just finished wrapping Margaret's diary when the ringing of the door bell caused him to jump involuntarily. The house was so massive and silent, especially with Carol gone, that any noise tended to echo through the empty halls, clattering like a mischievous poltergeist searching for some unsuspecting mortal to torment.

"Good afternoon, Henry. I just dropped by to see if you and Carol had settled in yet."

Henry wasn't completely sure that Edward Hardison was giving his real reason for coming, but he appreciated the courtesy and was not as prone to perceive an ulterior motive as he might have been a few days earlier. At this point, he was inclined to give Edward the benefit of the doubt and attribute the visit to curiosity.

"There's still a great deal more to be done before either of us will really feel at home here," Henry replied. "Carol has gone back to Georgia. We've been away from the children for some time now, and if you leave three teenagers alone for too long, you can never be certain what you'll find when you return."

"Fortunately, those days are past for me. Well, since you're alone, why not have dinner with me? As it happens, my wife has a civic club meeting this evening, so I am also on my own tonight. Albert told me once that this house became positively gloomy if you stayed in it alone, and I have no doubt that's true. What do you say?"

Henry had spent enough time with ghosts that day, so

his decision came easily. "Very well; it's kind of you to ask, and I would enjoy the company."

"I know an excellent Italian restaurant, if that suits you."

"I'm in the mood for anything. I really just want to get out for awhile."

"Fine. Shall we say eight o'clock? I'll pick you up."

"Eight it is," Henry agreed.

After Hardison left, Henry felt once again how accurate his assessment of the house had been. The ghosts seemed to return immediately. He wondered if they would ever leave.

*　*　*　*

Later that evening Henry sat in his bedroom, alone once again. He knew that sleep was out of the question, as he found himself at the mercy of conflicting emotions. That seemed to be happening a great deal since his first meeting with Hardison in his office. Could it really have been only two weeks ago?

At this moment he regretted not having returned with Carol to the familiarity and security of his own family. The house that seemed massive before had become ominous with the onset of night.

"I've got to get hold of myself," Henry thought, disgusted at his own feelings. "I'm acting like a scared child afraid of the dark. Most people would be thrilled to live in a house like this."

He tried to imagine what it must have been like for David here. Did the house have ghosts then? Or was it

David's ghost whose presence he felt most? Did it really even come from the house, or from somewhere within himself?

"Questions without answers," he thought. "At least perhaps better left unanswered." Even so, this was one evening Henry had no intention of leaving questions unanswered, especially in light of what he had learned, seemingly accidentally, from Edward earlier that evening.

The dinner with Edward had proven to be profitable in two respects. Edward had given Henry the combination to the family safe in which presumably the box had been kept through the years. What else might that safe hold? Now Henry could find out.

But the part of the conversation that sent Henry's mind reeling came while Edward seemed to be probing him for information. He had been most curious about the contents of the box Albert had entrusted to Henry the day he died. Henry wasn't surprised by that, and he had made up his mind beforehand that he wasn't quite ready to reveal what Margaret Stetson obviously had intended be kept secret, at least not until he could decide how he should proceed. With every passing minute he became more and more confident that he could fulfill what he considered his ultimate responsibility to David, and instinctively Henry felt certain that Edward Hardison would not have approved.

Even though Henry had been unwilling to talk about the mysterious box, Edward had discussed it quite freely, perhaps using his own limited knowledge to entice Henry to reveal what he had learned about the contents. Hardison described the one instance when Albert had shown the box to him, explaining that it contained valuable information about his family, although even Albert himself had never violated his sacred promise to his mother never to open the box, but to pass it on whenever he felt circumstances required it.

Henry had been listening to Edward's reminiscences about Margaret, Albert, and this strange box which the family had felt such a strong need to protect, when Hardison had mentioned casually that Albert had told him Margaret had once said the box had been constructed with a false bottom. Immediately Henry recalled his first impression on opening the box, that the inside seemed so much smaller than the outside would have indicated. If there was a second compartment in the box, might it contain another, perhaps final piece to the puzzle? Henry knew he could not rest until he found out the truth, whatever that might be.

Not having the combination to the safe before this evening, Henry had merely placed the box inside an antique roll top desk that stood in one corner of the sitting room. "Not particularly secure," he had thought even at the time. Not that he had been overly concerned. Instinctively Henry felt the time for safeguarding the contents had ended.

Once again he took out the box and raised the lid. Removing the diary and laying it aside, he felt carefully all along the sides and bottom for any sign that might confirm his suspicions, but found none. The bottom and the sides all appeared completely smooth, uniformly covered with blue fabric glued to the surface and further secured by two brass rivets in opposite corners of the box.

Suddenly it struck Henry as odd that there should be two rivets rather than four, one in each corner. On an impulse, he pushed lightly against one of the rivets and felt it give. He pressed it harder. Certainly it was moving, perhaps on a spring, but nothing else happened. He tried the other rivet and obtained the same result. There must be a key here, but what was it? Maddened with frustration, Henry pressed hard on both rivets simultaneously, and suddenly the bottom of the box had come free in his hands. Smiling in triumph, he lifted it aside and reached in.

Within the newly revealed compartment, Henry found another item wrapped in the same tissue that had been used for Margaret Stetson's diary. Its shape betrayed its contents even covered as it was. It was a rather large envelope. As Henry gently tore aside the wrapping, he gave an involuntary shudder, the smile of the moment before replaced by a look of foreboding. He felt that here was the end of the story for which he had been searching. He was not at all certain he would like what it might reveal. The envelope contained only one word:

Henry

As if this were not enough to send a shiver throughout his body, Henry's gaze was drawn to the handwriting which was unmistakable — and all too familiar. His feelings of apprehension were reinforced just by picking up the envelope. It must originally have been creamy white and had obviously been manufactured of the finest quality paper. But that must have been long ago, as the paper was now brittle with age and streaked with varying shades of brown. With a sinking spirit, he began reading what his intuition told him would be David's last letter to him.

Dear Henry,

So much to say, and so little time in which to do it. But I suppose that's largely my fault. Time — that's what all of this has been about, hasn't it, and I always thought mine was unlimited. Well, too late I've learned my lesson, but fate, or God perhaps, seems to be working things out in spite of me and my meddling. I suppose there is some comfort in that, although even now I am still struggling to summon the courage to fulfill the promise I made to you and to myself when we first began this business. In the laboratory it all sounded so theoretical and even more so at the time I resolved to stay in the past. Now all of that is over. I know what I must do and am resolved to carry out my responsibility. But knowing that I must die tonight doesn't make it any easier to accept.

As he read those words, Henry took an involuntary breath and felt his stomach tighten. After a moment his mind cleared, and he forced himself to continue reading.

I've been rambling, I know, and I have so much to do and so little time remaining. Let's begin.

I determined to remain in the past after I had met Margaret and fallen in love. I wouldn't blame you if that relationship seems strange, but it really isn't. The young girl I've fallen in love with here is nothing like Margaret as I knew her. They really are two different people as far as I'm concerned, and I'm certain Margaret herself is largely responsible for that. You see, here she has only known me as I am now, her husband. For her the future is just as blank as anyone's. She knows nothing of Creighton, my parents, even her responsibility for raising me after their deaths.

I can only imagine what it will be like for her. How does a person come to grips with seeing her husband as a child, even taking on the responsibility of raising him? I suspect the only way she could cope was to send me away to boarding school and keep her distance. Some people accused

Margaret of being cold and unfeeling toward me, never understanding just how much love motivated her through all those years alone.

What was I thinking to become so deeply involved in the past and bring all this about? Well you may ask. I've pondered the same question over and over, and honestly I don't know whether I had any real choice. You know how I painted a horrifying scenario about the risk of altering time. Now that I'm faced squarely with the possibility of doing it, I don't believe I overplayed that danger at all. The effects of such tampering could indeed be devastating, so monstrous in fact that I pray with every fiber of my being that perhaps it isn't possible. Someone or Something in the universe surely must intervene to protect human beings from themselves. Not that we can't affect circumstances, sometimes tragically. But the way I have seen events unfold here strengthens my belief in a God wiser than any of us, and that trust gives me some consolation.

I must get back to the story at hand. I suspect you know by now that Margaret and I met, fell in love, and married. Henry, that wasn't an accident, nor was it interfering with the natural order. It was simply the way things had to work out. The one task remaining to me today is to explain this whole bizarre situation to Maggie and prepare her for the task that lies ahead. First of all, I must convince her that she must find my parents and be there for me to raise me. All of that must happen to complete this whole strange cycle of events.

I have also determined to explain to her something of what is to happen in the future. That's not meddling, because we already know that she is to become wealthy in a fairly short period of time. She can only do that by understanding something of the future and how to take advantage of it.

Maggie is a strong woman. We both know that. At least I have the advantage of having seen the end of the story and knowing she will succeed.

I wonder if by now you have guessed the rest. It's Albert, although Albert is really his middle name. Maggie suggested it as his first name, but I insisted on naming him after you. He's only a year old, you see, and his future is the main reason I must follow through with my plan tonight. Is it so hard to understand that I must sacrifice myself, so my wife and son may live? Anyway, that's what I have decided to do. I am determined that Albert must never know the truth. I must make Maggie understand, because I have no doubt he would never agree if he knew. We all know the role he will play in these events, but he will merely be following his mother's instructions out of love for and loyalty to her, never suspecting that he is helping his own father. But you must not fault him for that, nor attribute selfish motives where there were none.

Do not misunderstand. In spite of everything, I do not regret my determination to remain in the past. The last four years of my life have been gloriously happy. Even had I known what the end would be, I don't believe my decision would have been any different. Anyway, as I have already indicated, fate seems to have woven its web around us. Ultimately, I doubt that anything could change the course of events now.

Goodbye, Henry. Remember me with affection, and

At this point the letter ended, the bottom of the page missing. Henry would never know David's final words, but clearly he had said all he intended to say. With a heavy heart Henry laid aside David's letter to ponder the irony of an ancient tragedy involving his young friend, a disaster that he still could not fully comprehend. Then, with a vague sense of unease, he noticed for the first time the date of the letter, written in the European style which David had by then adopted, 14 April 1912, and almost as quickly the lettering on the stationery told the rest of the story. The name engraved at the top of the paper read R.M.S. *Titanic*.

For several minutes Henry sat motionless, stunned by the reality of a disaster made even more terrible, because David knew it must happen, but which he could do nothing to prevent. One last piece of paper enclosed with David's letter told the rest of the story. It was from the travel agency which had booked passage for David and his family to come to the United States. It was written in the artificially condescending fashion that typified business correspondence still under the edicts of Edwardian etiquette.

Mr. David Evans, Esq.

I regret to inform you that your previous booking has been cancelled. As you must be aware, the current coal strike has forced many such cancellations, and I am sorry that your ship is among those whose sailings have been terminated.

I do, however, have most happy news. It took a great deal of doing, but I have been able to book second class passage for you, your wife, and infant son on the maiden voyage of the new White Star liner, Titanic and at no additional cost to you. Although it departs on 10 April, which is later than your originally scheduled sailing, it is well within the time period you had indicated you wished to leave.

I hardly need tell you that second class on the Titanic will be equivalent to first class on any other liner now engaged in the transatlantic trade.

  Trusting that these new arrangements will be satisfactory, I remain,

Your obed. serv't,

Josiah Maitland

Chapter 41

At first what Henry had read made no sense. Why had David allowed himself to board that doomed ship? Suddenly it became obvious. The only reason David could have for refusing to sail on the *Titanic* was his knowledge of what was to happen to her, and that was the one promise they had made. Under no circumstances could the time traveler allow his knowledge of the future to have any impact on what he did in the past, no matter how strong the temptation.

So David had accepted the hand fate had dealt him, without telling Margaret until it was too late for her to change his mind, if that had been possible. Henry knew that if he told the story to any of his friends, not one of them would believe it. But they hadn't known David. His decision was so like him — conscientious, stubborn even, with the idealism that had characterized the 60s.

Now, as Henry finally did reach the bottom of the box which had held the answers to so many mysteries, he found one more document, a column cut out of the Boston *Globe* dated April 20, 1912, detailing some of the passengers who had been aboard the *Titanic* when she went down. Included was a notice that the American inventor, David Evans, who was bringing his English bride and infant son to America to resettle in the city, had been among those lost when the mighty ship went to her grave. The article confirmed the irony of the change of ships and indicated that, although the tragedy had made future plans uncertain, for the present at least, his young wife, the former Margaret Stetson and her one-year-old son, Henry A. Evans, who had both found places with some of the other women and children in one of the lifeboats, would remain in Boston since they had no living relatives in England.

The paper even included a photograph of the couple taken at their wedding two years earlier. Margaret had been strikingly beautiful with long dark hair that presented an uncanny resemblance to Cathy. Most of all, David looked happy, happier than Henry ever remembered seeing him.

*　*　*　*

It was now almost midnight. Henry found himself extremely tired, and not just from fatigue. At the same time, he was full of nervous energy that he needed to use in some way. He walked downstairs, noticing how his footsteps echoed throughout the empty house. Could he and his family really live in it?

Eventually, Henry found himself drawn once again to the setting room where so much of this story had played itself out. As he sat by the fireplace, attempting to make sense out of all he had discovered, his hand unconsciously reached into his pocket for the watch that had been his constant companion over the last twenty years. Henry had wondered at how the silver had corroded, for over the years the watch had become old and tarnished, although it still showed the outlines of a whaling vessel on the front and on the back the inscription which Cathy had engraved when she had purchased it as a wedding gift for David.

Time is the ship that propels our lives

The hands had remained rusted and still for more than twenty years now. Again he thought of the tragic irony the watch itself symbolized, for it had been acquired to replace the one that Albert had given to David, the one he said had belonged to his father. And tragically so it had.

Suddenly it occurred to Henry that the original must still be in the safe from which Albert Stetson had taken it the evening after Margaret's funeral. Curiosity drove him to find out.

As he walked toward the wall where the safe had been concealed, something occurred that was to alter forever his complacent faith in an orderly and predictable universe. The watch in his hand began to glow. At first Henry thought it was only his imagination, but as he moved toward the safe, Henry actually felt a tingling in his hand. At the same time the watch began to vibrate, and Henry had difficulty holding onto it. Or was that just his hand trembling?

Whatever the cause, the watch slipped from his outstretched hand and fell to the floor. Instinctively Henry kicked it across the room and stared in astonishment as the glow almost immediately faded away. Approaching the watch cautiously, Henry stooped down to study it more carefully. It was exactly as before — old, tarnished, and rusted. He hesitated for a full minute before finally summoning the courage to touch it cautiously. The watch was slightly warm, but otherwise it was exactly as it had been before he approached the safe with it.

More determined than ever to understand what he had just experienced, Henry reached into his pocket for the combination Edward Hardison had given him that evening. As a precaution, he first picked up the watch and placed it on an end table in a far corner of the room, but still within clear view. Walking up to the fireplace, Henry removed the large porcelain disk which concealed the safe. He dialed the combination Hardison had given him, and the safe opened effortlessly.

Inside he found a jumble of papers, undoubtedly important, but of no concern to him at that moment. Far toward the back he discovered a small wooden box which closed with a simple latch. Inside the box, wrapped in velvet, was the watch for which he was searching. Yes, surely this was the one Albert had given to David after Margaret Stetson's funeral, the same one David had returned to Albert for safekeeping. At first glance it looked identical to the one he had left sitting on the table. Even the discolored streaks seemed remarkably similar to those on the other watch. Perhaps more extraordinary was the fact that this watch too recorded the same fateful hour — 2:20. Only later would Henry discover this to be the exact time the *Titanic* plunged to the bottom of the Atlantic Ocean.

Still scrutinizing the watch he had removed from the safe, Henry absentmindedly walked back toward the table, the better to compare both watches in the light. As he came within three feet of the table, the watch in his hand seemed to take on the eerie glow he had only moments before experienced from the watch now sitting on the table. He stepped backward, and almost immediately the glow was extinguished.

An idea crystallized in Henry's mind, and his scientific temperament determined on an experiment to test his theory. Walking to the fireplace, he grasped the brass shovel used for cleaning ashes from the fireplace. Placing the watch from the safe on the shovel, he slowly took a step in the direction of the table on which his own watch lay. Nothing happened, so he took another hesitant step, and then another. There it was; the watch was indeed radiating light.

Another step and his outstretched hand could feel a slight warmth emanating from it. At this point Henry paused to stare at his own watch lying on the table not three feet away. It too was glowing, appearing to mimic what was happening to its twin.

Oblivious of the possible consequences, Henry took two more steps forward. Initially he observed the body of both watches change from tarnished silver to take on a different color, a color which Henry was never able to describe, because, he said, it had no counterpart in any combinations found in the visible spectrum of light.

This was not to be the worst of the experience, however. As Henry would relate this portion of the events in later years, he always emphasized that this was just one more phenomenon he could never describe accurately, because no words existed to portray something that no other human being had witnessed. Perhaps their previous experience with time travel came closest to mimicking what occurred that moment, but for Henry it remained far more frightening than even the forces accompanying time travel. The room, the very house itself, began to alter in ways the mind could hardly comprehend. Part of the house was there, but parts of it were changed. Different rooms appeared to merge partially with the structure of the house as he knew it, almost as if another reality was trying to intrude itself into our world. He tried looking beyond the house at what lay outside, but the entire landscape swirled and shimmered as if none of it was totally real. Henry always shuddered at that memory when he talked about it as he did once with Carol, and then only three other times in his life. Carol knew Henry well enough to read his body language, and she always felt there was more to the story than he was willing to share. Nevertheless, she never pressured him for more information. She had learned enough to recognize how painful the subject was for him to recall.

Henry quickly backed away, and within moments no evidence remained of the phenomenon he had just observed. Everything was back to normal. He picked up the watch he had taken from the safe, confident now of what he would discover. He turned it up so that the bottom was visible, and there in tiny letters, faint, yet still legible was the inscription:

J. Stafford railroad watch — 1877

With every fiber of his being Henry resisted taking what he knew must be his next action, but now there could be no turning back. Slowly, carefully, he turned the watch over. On the back was the inscription, just as David had described it.

Time is the ship that propels our lives

But that was not the writing for which he was searching. Henry had to find a magnifying glass to read the tiny letters, but there they were at the bottom.

Reproduction 1968

So Henry's theory had proven to be correct. David had, after all, been right, as strangely enough, in his own twisted fashion, had been Creighton. And the irony lay in the knowledge that the only time David did in fact alter the processes of time was the very instance he consciously attempted to avoid doing so, when he failed to take his watch with him into the past — where it belonged.

The past had now come full circle with the present. He knew what he must do, and he could not rest until the task was concluded.

*   *   *   *

Henry had worked throughout the night. It was now midmorning, but the excess adrenaline coursing through his body hid his own fatigue from him.

His first action had been to place both watches inside glass containers, taking every precaution to keep them well apart. The next step was to place a call to a former colleague at MIT. Henry knew the man must have thought his request at such an hour quite peculiar, but out of friendship he had agreed to allow Henry to secure what he needed from his laboratory.

Taking the watch he had removed from the safe, Henry poured in enough of the sulfuric acid he had obtained that evening to destroy it completely. After the watch had been completely dissolved, he evaporated the liquid, leaving only a small residue of metallic powder. Only then did he inspect the other watch that had been kept isolated on the table in the sitting room, confined in a glass beaker for added protection. It too had been reduced to powder, just as Henry expected it would be — because it was the same watch — although even Henry's scientific mind could barely accept that truth. Carefully separating each of the two mounds into three tiny piles, Henry then sealed them in plastic, cautiously labeling each one to prevent accidentally confusing them. Confident of his next step, he then addressed four envelopes in which he placed all but two of the samples, taking care to keep the envelopes far apart.

Early the following morning Henry conducted what must surely qualify as one of the most unusual calls ever made. He engaged in a conference call with four other people, who shared only one quality — Henry Lindstrom trusted each one implicitly. One was a woman, a former student, now a systems analyst in Silicon Valley. The next was a high school principal in Wisconsin, who had been Henry's roommate in college. Then there was the minister of the church he and Carol normally attended — well, that Carol attended anyway. Finally, he got in touch with one of his former colleagues at NORTECH, who had some years before become an astronaut and was currently involved in training candidates for the Space Shuttle.

Three hours were required for Henry to tell them his story, to answer their questions, overcome their skepticism — and convince them he was not mad. Finally each one agreed to play his or her part, which simply involved burying the envelope Henry sent them, to prevent any possibility that the contents from one might ever come in contact with any of its counterpart. Henry would himself dispose of one of the samples. The sixth he determined to keep safely locked away. Was it from scientific curiosity or as a reminder of science's limitations? Henry could not have said himself.

Later, all his preparations completed, Henry sat alone once more in the Stetson mansion. Now that he had a moment to consider the events of the past few days, he was amazed at how dramatically his future had literally been wrested from him, and its course changed, by a past he had never even suspected.

Images, painful images of David, resurfaced from somewhere deep inside where Henry had buried them so long ago. Again he thought of his work of the last twenty years, of his plan to return to the past to prevent this very tragedy that had just been revealed to him. He already possessed the technology, and now he had the money. He knew he could do it. Didn't he owe it to his friend at least to make the attempt?

Again he pondered the nature of man, and time, and the implacable universe that we occupy, but cannot hope to master. Maybe he ought to have a talk with that minister.

He thought again of David's final confidence (or was it just hope) that nature somehow protected itself against the interference caused by an arrogant humanity, struggling to understand the world in which we live. As he stared at a small envelope of powder, Henry could not help but wonder if perhaps even in his madness, Creighton had understood something about the universe that two arrogant scientists, still too young to accept their limitations, were unwilling to accept.

Somehow it seemed appropriate that David had chosen to live in a time when such was the prevailing philosophy; before two world wars, climaxed by the horrors of Auschwitz and the mushrooming cloud over Hiroshima, eliminated forever even the possibility of such cocky self-assurance; before a burgeoning population and a poisoned environment threatened the continued existence of life on earth.

Yet, the very disaster that had taken David's life had in many people's minds represented the beginning of it all, or at least had been prophetic of an uncertain future. The *Titanic* had been the epitome of man's confidence in his ability to control nature — the unsinkable ship. After she was lost, could anyone really feel safe in this world again?

A grandfather clock tolled somewhere in a far corner of the house. It was noon. Henry realized there was one more ghost remaining to be exorcised, and now, finally, he thought he knew how it could be done. Walking over to the telephone, he dialed long distance. After five rings, Henry's spirits were lifted by the sound of Carol's cheerful "Hello."

Something in his voice must have made her suspicious. "Henry, are you all right?" she inquired. "You sound tired."

"I am tired, more tired than you can imagine. I'm going to pack a few things and catch the first flight out. I want to come home."

"Are you sure you're okay? Something's happened, hasn't it?"

"Yes, but everything's all right now. I'll explain when I get home. At least I'll try.

"Carol — I love you."

"We love you too, darling. Hurry home."

"There's just one more thing."

"What's that, Henry?"

A smile spread across Henry's face. "You remember how you suggested we might do some traveling. How would you like to spend this spring in Paris?"

Chapter 42
Friday
February 4, 2011

Carol could not help but consider how ironic it was that next week she would celebrate her seventieth birthday. Celebrate? Hardly. Despite every attempt to shut out the memories, everything seemed to remind Carol of something. It isn't just possessions you accumulate during nearly forty years of marriage. More than anything, it's the memories that stick with you. And Henry and Carol certainly had their share of those.

As Carol thought back especially on the past twenty years, she had to acknowledge that, for the most part, they had been contented ones. Yes, the wealth had made their lives easier, but in the end her happiness wasn't due to the opulence of the house, the parties they gave and attended, or even the occasional celebrity they bumped into, all results of the inheritance Henry had received from Albert Stetson. No, what came to mind this day were the recollections of the quiet and private times she and Henry had spent together.

Exactly two weeks had passed since Henry's funeral. His death had been swift and relatively painless, his failing heart finally unable to continue to struggle. Carol's grief after Henry's death had been deeper than she would have anticipated, the anguish that can only come from those who have experienced both deep love, as well as shared struggle. Quite simply, Henry and Carol had lived and enjoyed a good life together in ways that, for the most part, had little to do with their wealth.

Snow had accumulated overnight, but the snow plows serving the greater Boston area had done their work, so driving was not especially difficult. Carol had finally decided she had regained the emotional strength to perform one of the necessary rituals that accompany death. She and Morgan, her thirteen-year-old granddaughter, were going through Henry's various possessions, the painful ritual of sorting through the remnants of a life, deciding what was important and what was not, what to dispose of and what to keep. Within days of Henry's death, Carol had decided to sell what had been the Stetson mansion, although she could not adequately explain even to herself, much less anyone else, why she felt the need to leave it.

Her memories of life in this home had been for the most part pleasant, even though after their three girls left, it became far too large for just the two of them. Even so, the old house had seen fun and laughter, especially in later years when grandchildren came to visit or when Henry and Carol entertained. Yes, life in this stuffy old house had been good. Why then did she feel compelled to leave it? Partially, Carol decided, she needed to leave the mansion precisely because of those memories. She felt certain that, given enough time, the happy memories would return, but just now even the best of those memories came with too sharp an edge, which they would retain until worn down by the healing power of time.

There was another, perhaps more powerful motivation that led Carol to determine to sell the house. Henry could have explained it to her, as could Albert, and perhaps even Margaret herself. Despite all the good times they had experienced in this house, Carol understood (although perhaps not consciously) that the house only responded positively when it was shared by people whose lives were not dominated by it. Since Henry's death, Carol had felt as if the house were actually haunted, never realizing that Henry, and before him Albert, had both used that same word to describe what it was like to be alone in the house.

"How silly to believe in a haunted house," Carol thought to herself. She would have been ashamed to vocalize her thoughts in front of her granddaughter, "especially," she thought, "a house where we accumulated so many good memories."

Even so, Carol also had to acknowledge that not all the memories of this house had been pleasant. The feelings invariably seemed to surface when she had been alone in the mansion, not every time, but often enough to leave an impression. It took the form of a persistent feeling that she really wasn't alone. Carol had never been superstitious, so she rationalized her response by reminding herself that the house was old, large, and difficult to heat. On and on the explanations went, and they satisfied her as long as Henry and the girls were living with her. Now Henry was gone, and in less than a week Carol had decided she could not live the rest of her life alone in this house. Not that it was threatening. There had been no banging closets or creaking stairs, no poltergeists levitating furniture. It was just a feeling, a sense of something intruding itself into her life, a presence that was more than she cared to live with.

The morning had been spent going through closets, sorting out Henry's clothes and other items, the collection of personal belongings that each of us accrues over a lifetime, reminders of special parts of our lives that come to mean so much to each of us, but which others may never appreciate. While the experience had been painful, she found she was able to get through it. "Carol was a trooper," Henry had always said. It had taken all morning and into the afternoon, but finally that portion had been finished.

The next item to tackle Carol had deliberately postponed, because she knew the experience would be more painful. She had to go through Henry's desk. Much of what she found she could not understand. Once again she found herself confronted by Henry, the packrat. It had become a joke between the two of them, one of the areas in which she treasured even the conflict, because it reminded her of how truly happy their lives had been together. As much as it pained her, most of it would have to be tossed, the remnants of a lifetime of labor that in its time made a difference, but no longer had significance.

The last item she wanted to examine this evening was the family safe. Carol had never been through its contents, not because Henry was secretive (he had given her the combination), but because she never felt the need. She never consciously thought of it, but at this moment it reminded her of the special degree of trust the two of them shared. Tonight the necessity had forced itself upon her, so Carol approached the fireplace where she knew the safe to be hidden behind a porcelain disk. She tried to move the disk which hid the safe from view, but it was heavier than she expected. While she felt she should be able to lift it, she decided to enlist help.

"Morgan," she called out to her granddaughter, "would you please help me move this?"

With the two of them working together, the disk moved relatively easily, and they laid it aside, exposing the safe. Carol dialed the combination, and the door to the safe slid open, in the process emitting a strident squeal, undoubtedly generated by the friction of hinges that had not been oiled for many years. Even though the reason for the sound was obvious, both Carol and her granddaughter jumped suddenly at the noise. "Just one more reason to leave this house," Carol thought to herself. At the same time, she turned to Morgan and laughed, relieving at least some of the tension.

Reaching into the safe, she discovered the same items Henry had encountered twenty years earlier, when he had first been given the mansion — Margaret's diary, David's letter to Henry, and a yellowing article from the Boston *Globe*, all carefully preserved.

Carol had no way of fully comprehending the significance of these items. Henry had confided in her the basic account of the research into time travel, sharing with her the success at transporting David into the past, and even the terrifying experience with David's watch. At the same time, Carol had always felt there were parts of the story he kept to himself. Her trust allowed her to be content with what Henry chose to relate to her. Understanding his very private nature, she never pressured him to reveal more, recognizing that the subject was painful for him.

Now she was faced with the details of events she had been told about only in the most general terms. Seeing the items all at once, rather than sequentially as they had been presented to Henry, her initial response was merely confusion. Once again, the Stetson mystery presented itself and would have to be decoded. Carol said nothing to Morgan, but she knew that she would have to delve into a part of Henry's life he had never felt comfortable sharing with her. Despite her desire to finish, she decided that she did not possess the strength to pursue that task tonight. Besides, it was dark now. This was a job that needed to be tackled in the daylight.

Chapter 43
Sunday
February 6, 2011

Carol had spent a good deal of Saturday trying to understand the items she had removed from the safe. She had slept little the previous night. She tried to blame it on being alone in the mansion, but she knew that wasn't the whole reason. What she had read overwhelmed her and made her wonder how much she had failed to understand about the man to whom she had been married for so many years. If it had been anyone else, she would never have believed what she had read. But Carol knew Henry, and that was enough for her to accept what she had discovered, even though every fiber of her being cried out against it. She could not help but believe that her loyalty was one trait she shared with Margaret Stetson, whom she had previously known only from the little Henry had told her. Reading Margaret's diary had transformed her into a real person, one whom Carol could not help but admire.

Morgan had again wanted to help. Her mother, still struggling to come to terms with the reality of her father's death, had dropped Morgan off, and now she and her grandmother were going through Henry's desk, looking for anything they might have missed, when the doorbell interrupted their work. Carol opened the door, surprised, yet pleased, to see Edward Hardison waiting outside. He looked pale and thin, merely a shadow of the imposing attorney

Henry had first met. Contrary to Henry's earlier prediction, Edward had become a valued advisor, helping Carol and Henry navigate the changes brought about by their inheritance of the Stetson estate. Over the years, the suspicion and mistrust which both men had initially felt had vanished, and their relationship had deepened until Edward was now a very dear and trusted friend. He had retired a number of years before and was now in his late eighties. Even though age and illness had weakened his body, he retained his sharp insight and cultured demeanor that had first impressed Henry so many years before.

"Good morning, Carol," Edward began. "I hope you will pardon this intrusion."

"Not at all, Edward; please come in." After ushering him into the parlor, Carol attempted to put all of them at ease.

"It's good to see you again. We were all so pleased that you felt well enough to attend Henry's funeral. I know it was a real effort for you to get out at all."

"Carol, nothing could have prevented me from paying my respects, and from offering my deepest condolences. I have been considering how our relationship began with such a rocky start, yet eventually developed into a deep friendship. I feel in some respects as if I have lost my own brother."

"Thank you, Edward. I know that Henry felt the same way about you. We spoke of you so often, and Henry expressed the same amazement that we all became such good friends."

Carol noticed a slight change in Edward's demeanor, as if he was almost embarrassed. It was an expression she could not recall ever seeing in Edward Hardison.

"Carol," Edward looked down slightly, almost apologetically, "I have something to give you, something

Henry asked me to keep for him, I believe it was twelve years ago. I do not know the significance of any of it, but Henry indicated that it was something he wanted protected. Knowing that I had ample space, he asked me if I would hold it for him. All he would tell me was that it was something he did not want in this house."

With that, he handed Carol a manila envelope of the kind that closed by a simple string on the back.

"Edward," Carol sounded puzzled, "this is most strange. Henry never spoke to me about giving you anything to keep for him. Does it involve any investments or something related to the estate?"

"No, Carol," Hardison assured her. "I feel certain this does not involve financial matters at all. I feel badly that it might affect your opinion of Henry, but let me assure you that I am convinced he was not trying to hide anything from you. On the contrary, I got the distinct impression he was attempting to protect you, although from what I cannot say."

"You mean to tell me," Carol asked, with just a hint of disbelief, if not sarcasm, "in all these years you have never opened this envelope or even asked Henry what it contained?"

"Carol, I understand your skepticism. Indeed, I dreaded coming to you this morning precisely for that reason. You must understand that my profession was above all built on trust. Henry trusted me, and I in turn reciprocated that trust. I never found reason to question him further, and my dear, it pains me to think that anything I have said might cause you to think ill of Henry in any way."

"I'm sorry, Edward," Carol replied, subdued and somewhat embarrassed at her previous accusation. "I'm afraid my emotions sometime still get the best of me. I know in my heart that if Henry kept anything from me, it was because he felt it was for the best. Did he leave instructions for you to give this to me?"

"No indeed, Carol," Edward assured her. "In all honesty, I believe Henry may have put it out of his mind, perhaps deliberately at first. Over the years, I suspect he actually forgot about it. You see, there were some dealings that Albert Stetson had with Henry. Neither man ever confided in me about the matter, but I know, as I am sure you do as well, that it was not an entirely pleasant relationship. I suspect that somehow the contents of this envelope were preventing Henry from going on with his life. He needed to have it removed, but could not perhaps bring himself to destroy it. At the same time, this is not my property, and I have no right to keep it. I came to you this morning, because it would no longer be prudent for me to keep it."

Carol reached out and gently placed her hand on Edward's arm, neither of them willing to say out loud what they both knew to be true. Also, she felt guilty about her earlier suspicions, of Edward certainly, but even more her doubts regarding Henry. Carol's instinct was to have Edward destroy whatever was in that envelope. Why look again into what must have been a painful portion of Henry's life? Would it perhaps be better to "let the dead bury the dead?"

If this revelation had been made two days earlier, that is precisely what Carol would have done. Now that was impossible. She had examined Margaret Stetson's diary. She had also read David's letter to Henry. Obviously, there was more to this story than she knew. Carol had thought the house haunted before. Now it felt absolutely possessed. Could anything free her from the ghosts? Carol wasn't sure, but she knew of only one possibility, and she determined to take it.

"Edward," she answered warmly, "I appreciate more than you know the way you have served Henry and me over the years. You safeguarded our investments. More than that, you watched over a secret for many years without ever questioning why. Now that responsibility falls to me. Thank you again for being a trusted friend for so long."

"Carol, I have always held great affection for you as well as Henry," Edward replied as he rose, steadying himself with his cane, and handing the envelope to her. "Goodbye, my dear," he said finally, once again expressing a familiarity so contrary to his normal bearing.

"Goodbye, Edward," Carol replied, unable to contain a note of sadness in her voice, their very silence acknowledging what neither of them possessed the courage to say aloud. The cancer was advanced. Edward had perhaps a few weeks remaining. Carol most likely would never see him again. Although she knew it embarrassed him, she reached out and hugged Edward tightly. Still maintaining his almost regal bearing, Edward nodded slightly and stepped out into the cold where his driver waited.

Chapter 44
Monday
February 7, 2011

It was all over now, or at least she hoped it was. Carol was in the sitting room once again. She had built up a fire in the fireplace to help take the chill out of the air, although truthfully she could not have said for certain just why she felt so cold right now. Did Henry feel as she did when he first discovered the truth? She knew the answer, because she still remembered the weariness in his voice when he had called her from this very room so many years before, a fatigue resulting not just from lack of sleep, but from dealing with mysteries that perhaps no human being was meant to fathom.

The envelope from Edward Hardison had contained three items. She would never have understood the first, except it was part of the story Henry had related to her and which she had at times considered so bizarre she had difficulty accepting it. After all, it was nothing more than a tiny plastic envelope containing a small amount of metallic powder, and if he had opened it, Edward might have laughed that Henry would consider such an insignificant item worthy of such secrecy.

Now Carol understood. More than that, now she believed. Here was proof, well not proof exactly, but at least evidence that everything she had read, everything Henry had told her, was true. Seeing that tiny bit of dust made the whole story real as words never could, and Carol seemed to feel her heart actually skip a beat when she first saw it. She knew it would never persuade anyone, but it didn't have to. It convinced her, and part of her regretted knowing all she had learned during the previous twenty-four hours.

For some reason she was reminded of the story of Eve in the Garden, and she felt that perhaps for the first time she understood what that story was trying to say to an arrogant humanity, obsessed with its own importance. Henry had dedicated himself to science, to the advancement of knowledge, a noble endeavor certainly. Then why did looking at that small plastic envelope make her feel like she had eaten from a tree she had no business touching? Edward never comprehended why Henry had given it to him. Today Carol felt she did understand, and she was glad Henry had shielded her from it as long as he had.

The second item in the envelope was even more profound, and it made Carol marvel that Henry's heart had been able to hold up as long as it had, considering the weight he had carried for more than nineteen years. In addition to the small packet of metallic dust, the remnants of a watch that by rights ought not even exist, Carol found the missing portion of the letter David Evans had written Henry just before he knew he was to die when the *Titanic* sank. Again she read the words.

please try to understand. Even in the present, events sometimes control us. How much more has this proven to be true in the past.

Maggie's coming back now. Sorry to leave you this way, but I must attend to a far more difficult task

Affectionately,

David

Actually, this was not the end of the letter. At the bottom was a postscript, scrawled hurriedly in a frantic hand.

Henry, there is less than an hour left before the ship sinks. I think I understand now. I believe all of this can still be avoided. When you find this, do not attempt to go back for me. I want you to send the watch back to this time. I don't even need to find the watch. It just needs to be in the past where it belongs. I think if you do that, my future may change as well. Please, Henry, I'm relying on you.

For a moment Carol stared uncomprehendingly at what she had just read. How had Henry retained his sanity after discovering this final piece of the puzzle? There remained, however, one last document, left specifically for Carol, a final message from her beloved Henry, and what it contained caused her to admire his courage even more. She had read it alone yesterday, marveling at how like a Greek tragedy this story had unfolded.

March 20, 1994

My Darling,

If I know Edward, I can write this with the assurance

that he will never attempt to violate my confidence by looking inside this envelope. I also suspect that you have never looked inside the safe in the sitting room. If you had, I would not have to write this letter. Once I am gone, I know you will be forced to examine the contents of the safe, and I feel compelled to try to explain what you will find there.

Of course, you knew about our time travel experiment, but I could not bring myself to share all of it with you. The documents in the safe will explain part of it. For a little over a year after I discovered them, I was convinced they told the whole story. Would that they had!

On the basis of the documents which hopefully you have now read, I made up my mind to give up the attempt to bring David back, feeling that this was what he wanted. How naïve I was.

Twice in my life I overlooked the obvious, because it was convenient to do so. The first time I let my emotions overrule my reason was after funding was obtained for our project by Albert Stetson in such a short period of time. I know I told you that story. You would think I would have learned from that, but you know how hardheaded I can be.

Carol could not suppress a silent laugh, still painful because it was accompanied by a fresh wave of grief. Hardheaded? She had often teased Henry by telling him that if someone hit him on the head with a rock, the rock would break. It was one of his qualities that softened the analytical scientist within. Would she ever stop missing him? She continued reading.

Now I must tell you about the other time I chose to

ignore what should have been obvious. I discovered the truth about eighteen months after we had moved into this house. I know you remember that time, because it was the only time in our marriage that either of us considered divorce. It was so much worse for you, because I found myself unable to share with you what precipitated my behavior. With all my heart I ask your forgiveness. Fortunately, we got through those struggles. I suspect it's more accurate to say that your love got us through it, and it was during this time that I learned what a truly remarkable woman you are. Now the time has come for me to explain what caused me almost to lose you and everything I love.

About a year after we had moved into the Stetson mansion (strange how we still call it that) I discovered the end of David's letter to me. Never mind how I found it. We both know this house has too many secrets. I remember thinking at the time I first read the letter that the ending must have gotten torn by some unaccountable accident, perhaps even ripped away while Margaret struggled with her one-year-old Albert, as they tossed in the ocean, waiting for rescue. What was I thinking? Look at the letter yourself. It wasn't ripped. It was cut cleanly at the end of a line. It was never lost or torn. The ending was purposely removed. Even the envelope is a different paper from the letter. How could a scientist be duped so easily? My only defense is the confession that I wanted to be deceived. It was easier to deal with, and I wanted the mystery to end. Now it must. This story has haunted too many people for almost a hundred years. It's time to end it.

David always admired Margaret Stetson's courage and tenacity. How little even he knew. I am convinced it was Margaret who removed David's last appeal to me. She knew that if I ever read it, I would move heaven and earth to get that watch back to the past, because we both know that is where it belonged. She was right, because when I first found David's plea for help, I wanted to start it all up again, rebuild the equipment, and send that watch back where it belonged. Of course I couldn't, because it no longer existed. I was almost mad with guilt. That's why I became so difficult to live with. I know I should have told you everything, but it all seemed so insane I didn't know how. Finally, after a couple of weeks, I remembered what had happened that awful night when I first read David's letter to me and discovered two watches which in reality (if that's even the right word) was one watch. I am sure I told you the story, how as the two watches came closer to merging together, I experienced the beginnings of an alternate reality, a blending of the present as I knew it as well as another present, one that might have been. I know now that sending the watch back, perhaps even bringing those two watches together, would have altered the present.

What I have never revealed to you, or to anyone, was that the experience wasn't just visual. I heard voices of people and saw shadows moving in the house. Most disturbing of all, I heard one voice that I am convinced was David's. Carol, I am certain I could have done it. No, I could not have brought him back, but I could have changed the past enough, so that he would have survived. Maybe that was the way things were supposed to turn out. Immediately after I discovered the end of David's letter, that is exactly what I thought should have been done. Then why had Margaret, of all people, removed David's frantic plea for help so I could never find it?

I believe at last I know the answer. Margaret was right. No wonder David loved her so much. She was wiser and more courageous than any of us. She knew what two egotistical scientists could never admit. Some things are best left alone.

At the same time, I must admit that it appears obvious that David was supposed to take the watch with him into the past. That must have happened, because there is no other way it could have gotten into the safe years ago. But that did not happen in our perception of reality. We changed the past, and the only time it occurred was when David deliberately tried to avoid changing it, by leaving the watch here. If that doesn't give all of us a degree of humility, I don't know what will.

None of this changes our world as it is now. I don't know if our present is what it should have been, or how that may affect the future. I only know that the present is what it is, and it's time we stop trying to correct it. David was right to be concerned from the beginning. Even Thomas Creighton in his mad ravings knew that some things should never be attempted.

Goodbye, my darling, Carol. If anything does survive time itself, it will be my love for you. If there is a lesson from all this, it's not to live in the past. I did that for too long. Please, don't make the same mistake.

With all my love,

Henry

While Carol was reading, her granddaughter had crept softly into the room. Carol started suddenly when she saw Morgan idly begin to read Margaret Stetson's diary.

"What are these, Grandma?" she asked innocently.

"Nothing important, dear." Carol tried not to show her apprehension. "It's just some old papers we no longer need to keep. I'm going to burn them." Carol knew that decision must include Henry's last letter to her. As much as she wanted to preserve it, she was convinced that all of it had to end, and the only way to be certain of that was to eliminate anything that had to do with the horrifying events of the past. Carol took everything, the diary, David's and Henry's letters, even the packet of metal powder, and threw all of it into the fire that already burned brightly in the fireplace.

"Fire is supposed to purify," she thought hopefully. "Let's pray that it really does." Carol never took her eyes off the fire, watching in silence as it enveloped all traces of what had come to embody a terrible tragedy. Eventually only ashes remained. Carol carefully stirred the ashes, extinguished the fire, and then turned to her granddaughter.

"Morgan, I've decided to leave this house right now. Somehow, I can't bear living one more night in it alone. I want to stay with you and your parents for a little while, until I can find another place to live. Would you like that?"

"Oh, Grandma, that would be wonderful," Morgan burst out excitedly.

Suddenly, a combination of grief and confusion, coupled with a sense of final release brought out the tears she could no longer hold back.

Morgan enveloped Carol in her arms as tightly as she could. "Grandma, I miss Grandpa too, but everything will be all right."

"I'm sure it will, honey." Carol dried her eyes. She even managed a smile.

Carol prayed that the promise she had made to Morgan would prove to be true. At least she felt a degree of confidence, knowing that everything relating to the events of the past would be destroyed. Perhaps even this old house was free now to enjoy better times. Surely once she left, the ghosts would be banished forever.

Carol turned out the lights, stepped outside with Morgan, and locked the front door. The twilight had almost completely turned to darkness, and, contrary to the forecast, snow had begun falling again. A strong wind picked up the snow and collected it into small swirls that brushed against her face, even as the frigid air penetrated her body. She and Morgan got into her car, and Carol drove slowly into the gathering darkness. She did not look back.

Epilogue

Today another family occupies the Stetson mansion, a happy family, judging from the laughter that can sometimes be heard echoing throughout its many rooms. No one has complained of ghosts or strange events emanating from the mansion.

As is so often the case with old houses, there always seem to be areas in need of repair. Before long the flooring in the former sitting room will have to be replaced. Perhaps a workman or a member of the family living in the house will discover the large box hidden beneath a section of the floorboards.

Carol had understood Henry perhaps better than even she realized. He was indeed a packrat where his work was concerned. Despite the misgivings he must have felt, Henry was never able to bring himself to destroy the logs that detailed his and David's research. Everything is waiting there. All the information necessary for making time travel a reality.

Made in the USA
Monee, IL
07 July 2026

56552161R00203